I0657972

Other books in this Series by Julia Caesar
(arima Publishing)

THE TAPESTRY OF TTEN

BOOK 5. SWORD OF SANCTUARY

JULIA CÆSAR

Published 2014 by arima publishing

www.arimapublishing.com

ISBN 978-1-84549-632-6

© Julia Caesar 2014
Book Jacket artwork and design Chris Howard of Blondesign.
Blondesign@gmail.com

Printed and bound in the United Kingdom

Typeset in Garamond 11pt

Swirl is an imprint of arima publishing.

arima publishing
ASK House, Northgate Avenue
Bury St Edmunds, Suffolk IP32 6BB
t: (+44) 01284 700321

www.arimapublishing.com

For my readers, family and friends
In Particular,
Terry Brady
For his relentless pursuit of punctuation.
John Mercer – for all things scientific
Jay Bartlet – who inspired most things
poisonous or horrific.
Jenn and Jacqueline – who provide trails
for my characters.
Carol Leather – proof-reading;
Pete Turner –.IT services.
My husband Ken
Who stops me giving up
(and makes the tea).
For my fearless family of critics,
Jez Caesar, Lindsay Munro, and lastly,
My wonderful Mother

TERI CAESAR

On whom I modelled Ikella te Syrene.

And who recently passed
"Through that door into a different Sand".

CONTENTS

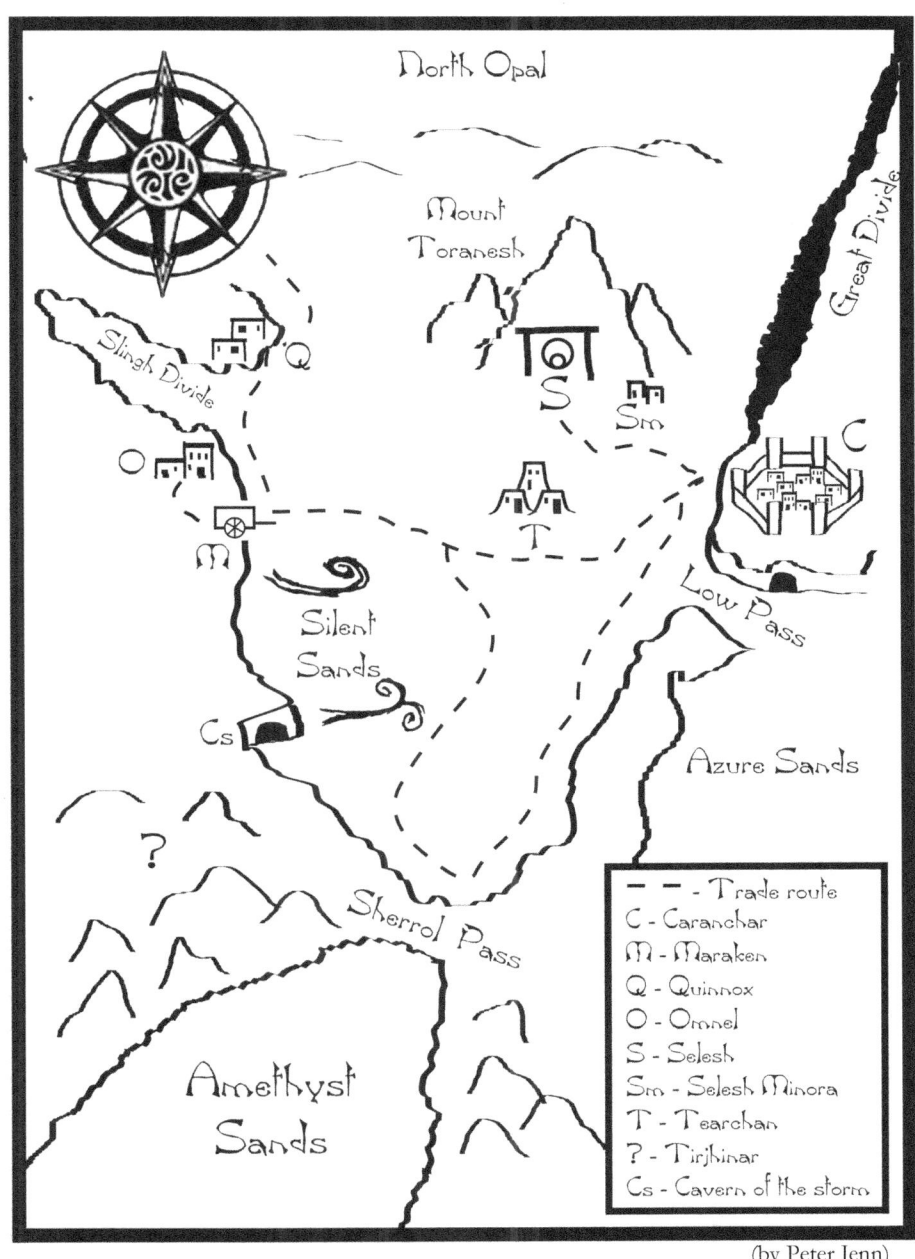

North Opal

Mount
Toranesh

Slingh Divide

Great Divide

Q

O

M

Silent
Sands

Cs

S

Sm

T

Low Pass

Azure Sands

C

?

Sherrol Pass

Amethyst
Sands

- - - - Trade route
C - Caranchar
M - Maraken
Q - Quinnox
O - Omnel
S - Selesh
Sm - Selesh Minora
T - Tearchan
? - Tirjhinar
Cs - Cavern of the storm

(by Peter Jenn)

Found in the Effects of the Master Spy Olneth –
Trail Map of the Western Fringes Opal

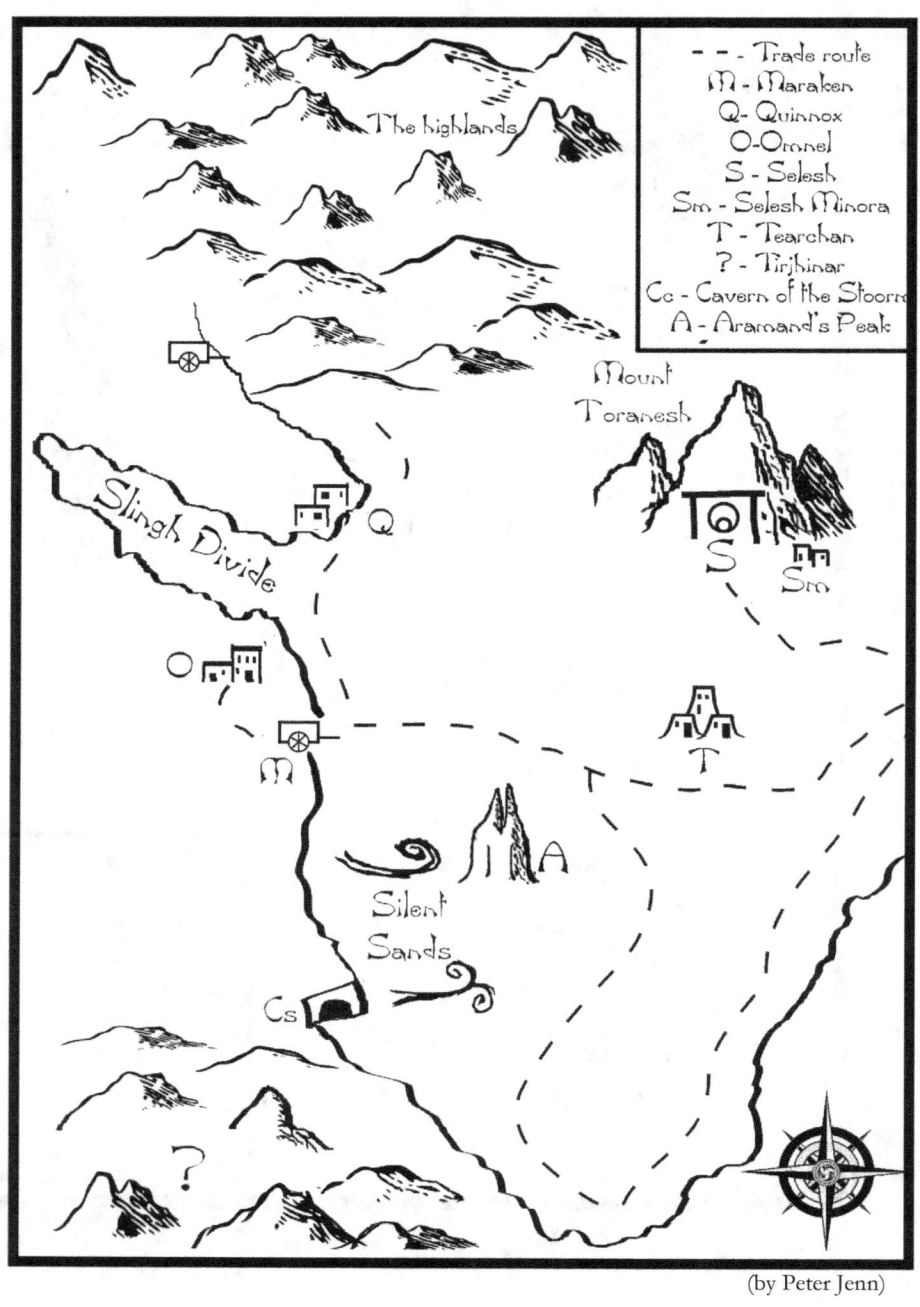

(by Peter Jenn)

(by Peter Jenn)

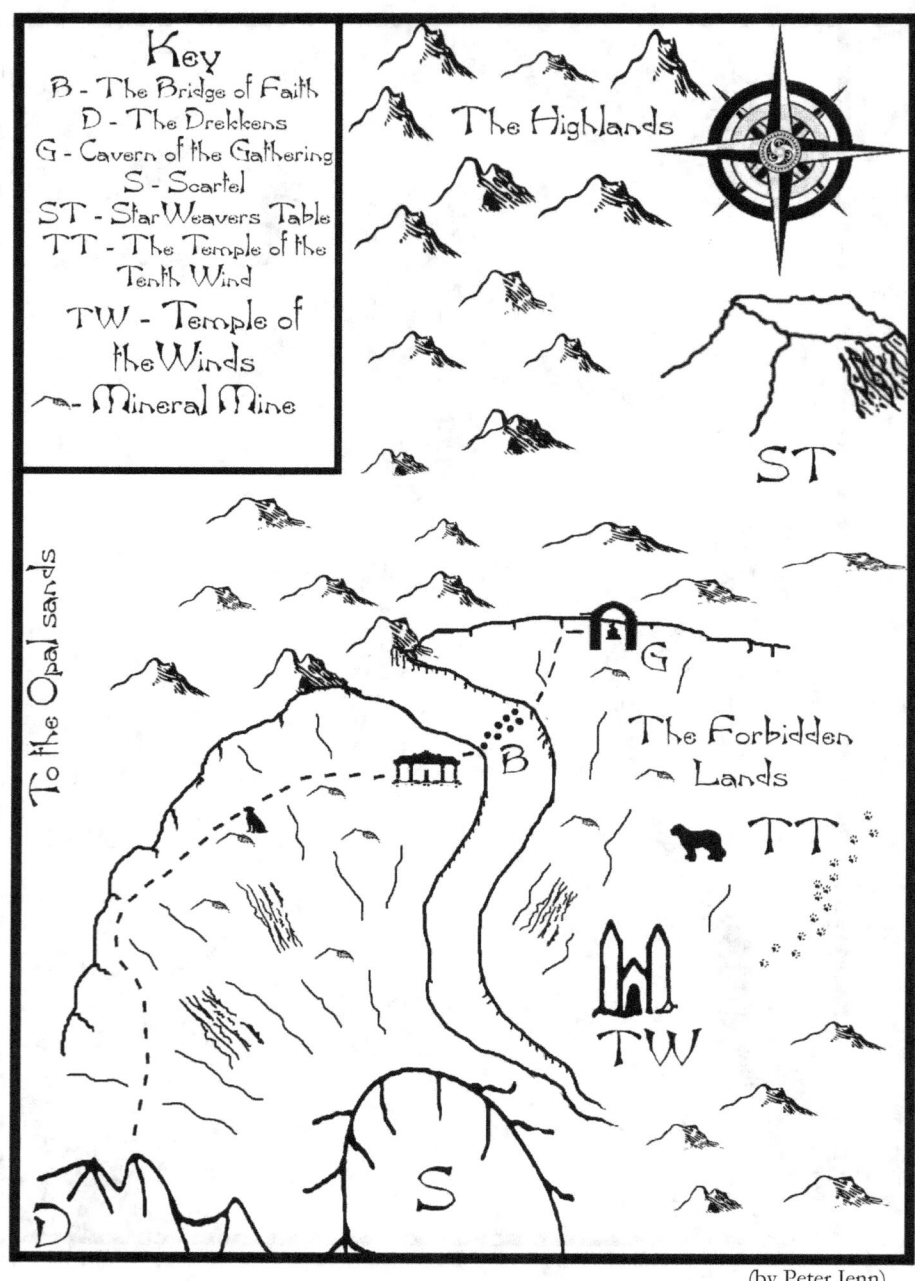

Key
B - The Bridge of Faith
D - The Drekkens
G - Cavern of the Gathering
S - Scartel
ST - Star Weavers Table
TT - The Temple of the Tenth Wind
TW - Temple of the Winds
— Mineral Mine

The Highlands

ST

The Forbidden Lands

TT

TW

G

B

S

D

To the Opal sands

(by Peter Jenn)

Pronunciations.

Note: Emphasis or stress should be placed on the underlined syllables.

Characters shown **bold** should be hard, e.g. **g** as in **g**o, rather than g as in gesture Syllables in brackets are soft. e.g. (g) as in gesture.

Characters separated by an underline follow the previous syllable with no change of emphasis.

Word	Pronunciation	Description
Aramand	Arraman	Ancient Sandsinger (Opal)
Adruna	A <u>droon</u> a	Sorceress Elect (Amethyst)
Anempor	Ann em <u>paw</u>	Capital of the Azure Sands
Ashgenar	<u>Ash</u> **gu**nn are	Wilderness
Beneva	<u>Ben</u> evver	Guardian of Knowledge
Carolus	<u>Carol</u> us	A wandering Apothecary
Czerezin	<u>Cherra</u> Zin	Clan of the Cynabarr Sands
Cynabarr	Sinna Barr	4th Sand of Pelshar
Dinajh	Dinnar(g)e	Invisible water tracts in the Sands
Diras	<u>Deer</u>ass	Daro's bodyguard
Djellim	Jellim	Library established in Selesh
Drecon or Drekken	Dreckun	Dragon (legendary animal)
Feydora	Faydrah	Mysterious Sandsinger from the past
Fronish	FroeNish	Healer Halt on North Eastern Border
Gresshe	Gresh	Clan of the Malachite Sands
Greeeyn	Gree <u>yain</u>	Academic/Artisan caste, city dwellers
Hukvah	Huck va	Headdress like an Arab Keffiya
Ikella	<u>Eye</u> kella	Sorceress/Guardian of the Way
Inesh	In <u>Nesh</u>	Second Clan of the Opal Sands
Ivinish	<u>Eye</u> vinnish	Master Herdsman at Selesh & Tregeth
Jentaroth	Jenn ta roth	Winter Rite of Passage
Jhirelle	<u>Jirrelle</u>	Clan of the Amber Sands
Kora-Mai	Corra My	Clan of the Onyx Sands
Koth	Koth (as in moth)	Evil High Priest of Gatta

Malos	May loze	Capital of the Malachite Sands
Maraken	Marra ken	Trail stop where the story starts
Myst Cat	Mist Cat	Puma sized feline with arcane abilities
Nahamida	Nuh Hamm idda	Sorceress of the Onyx Sands
Nishanawa	nih SHANN awa	Mysterious sect of the Ashgenar
Nishan	Nishun	Dedicated to the Guardians as warriors
Othervoice	Other voice	Magically empowered voice
Olneth	Oll_neth	Sybillsce warrior refugee turned spy.
Patris	Pattriss	Trader & Daro's second Songfather.
Sandsinger	Sand Singer	Higher class of mage
Shalhanhi	Shallarni	Ruling clan of the Opal Sands
Shenamai	Shenna my	Caverns with strange crystal roof
Shjaratel	Sharra Tell	Ancient city in the crater of Scartel
Shiarjha	She ara	Guardian of Powers
Shilinch	Shill Inch	Market town N. W. Fringes (opal Sands)
Skyrrh	Skirr	Temple of Gatta (Amethyst Sands)
Soloria	Soll orya	Late Sorceress of the Amethyst
Suraya	Surr rah yah	Ikella's successor
Sybillsce	Sibillsh	Clan of the Amethyst Sands
Tearchan	Tier shann	Hospice at the crossing below Maraken.
Timmisandro	Timiss Sandro	Sandsinger Carnelian Sands
Tirjhinar	Tier rinn are	Fabled lost city of the Sandsingers
Tregeth	Treejeth	Zeglure Breeding ground (S.E. Azure)
Vetali	Vitt arly	Trifoliate plant with magical properties
Zeglurs	Zegglures	Donkeylike Pack animal
Zenitheon	Zenith_ee yon	Summer Solstice

Zephryn horses	Zefrin	Legendary single horned storm
Zurias	Zurry ass	Clan of the Azure Sands
Yaydoran	Yea Durann	Last female Drecon surviving in stasis

PART ONE - CLOAK AND DAGGER

Prologue

One Rotation after Sowdin's death, locked behind the magical barrier created by Ikella Guardian of the Way, the Amethyst Sands still writhe to the rage of Adruna, Heretic Sorceress of the Sybillsce. Deep below the ninth desert of Pelshar, long corridors lead to the torture chambers, where Drex (erstwhile Recorder of Skyrrh) languishes terrified of Adruna's cruelty, yet fascinated by her power. Here, memories still flinch from the young heretic's rage as she paces and plans to overthrow those who imprisoned and rendered her impotent. Determined to impose her heresy on her world, she turns to the forbidden knowledge of Pelshar's past, as she seeks a weapon to use against her own kind.

The prisoner ignored his manacled hands, facing Adruna warily. So extreme had been the anger of the Dark Sorceress over his failure to destroy her Sisters in Sorcery, that the erstwhile Recorder of Skyrrh trembled as one flash of her lilac eyes seized his soul with malicious ease.[1]

As indelible images of the frenzied bloodletting that followed his failure crossed his mind, Drex shuddered, and then the fearsome grip of her power swamped his senses. He sweated grimly, resisting the compulsion to reveal his secrets, as she forced him to relive that aftermath. Entire Halls had been silenced. Funeral pyres branding her fury into the desert floor, while he waited in terror for his own torture to begin; now it was his time to pay.

"Tell me what you recall of your final incompetence." she demanded silkily as Drex drew breath, painfully aware of the hostility smouldering below the surface of her voice.

A soft footfall interrupted, (the entrance of his cell darkening) as Koth, the tongueless High Priest of Skyrrh was admitted. Adruna whirled, eyes sparkling, but Drex only caught a sense of something dry and deadly rustling past, as his terror escalated. The tip of her prisoners tongue wetted his lips as Adruna turned back, pinioning the unfortunate Recorder with a stare devoid of all humanity.

"Speak!" she commanded, then (as Drex fought the renewed compulsion to reveal all, Adruna reached out, tracing the elaborate tattoos that branded Koth, with a passionate absorption that spoke of a relationship too close to contemplate.

As Koth purred under these attentions, Drex recoiled, physically forcing himself to describe what he'd 'seen' (without mentioning his source), until he had their undivided attention.

He spoke humbly.

"Lady, Sowdin was worthy of our trust. He learned much in the short time available and prepared well. The Bleckoned Driands were delivered to Tirjella's table at precisely the right time. By all the indications Sowdin should have succeeded, but for one thing. Someone recognised him! He called her Jalni, Healer and Grand-daughter but she destroyed him nevertheless! Lady, she is no

---

[1] See Song of Sorcery ©Julia Cæsar 2011

Sorceress, but what manner of Healer could tell a man to die, and then watch him burst into flames at her command?"

Koth's new sycophant hesitated on the brink of speech, and Adruna whirled as his breath hissed between suddenly clenched teeth.

"You know something Bahgra?" she demanded, and the junior priest whitened as Koth's eyes fell on him also.

"Most High.", he whined, "I only just connected two separate reports, neither of which individually made any sense.", his terror seemed to ease a little as he spoke, and perhaps the High Priest (whose flickering finger language Bahgra interpreted, realised that the man was still thinking out some theory, for he nodded, fingers flying in silent communication as they withdrew to discuss their thoughts privately. Adruna returned alone not long afterward, with an expression of cool calculation on her face.

"Unchain him!" she commanded the custodian, then Drex trembled violently as the iron cuffs fell away, revealing wide bands of scarified flesh beneath the cruel kiss of metal.

The dark Sorceress spoke conversationally.

"Drex, I cannot believe that you would dare to play me double, but to ensure that you don't, henceforth, you will be confined within the Black Tower of Aryphnia, where you will search the records for the meaning of a word, (success being the price of your continuing survival)".

Drex shuddered as he recalled the immense obsidian structure, poised on the rift which created an impassable barrier at the far western limits of the Sands. Reputedly the library of some ancient race, it had been used to confine dangerous heretics in the historic purges before Cataclysm. Impenetrable walls, narrow slit windows, its forbidding aspect had combined with rumours of powerful enchantments, to save the scrolls it hid. However intriguing, faced with a darkened, solitary imprisonment without access to artefacts he had (through painstaking research) learned to use, Drex foresaw this as a death sentence. His terrified comprehension showed in his face as Adruna laughed cruelly.

"Don't worry little man.", she taunted, "Koth survived it, and so can you. I'll transport your apartments and their contents for you. Request any aids you need without reservation. The search for truth must be supported."

She lent close to the shivering Recorder persuasively,

"You can have anything within reason. Just find the meaning of a word." Her lilac eyes flickered hypnotically, her sibilant voice seemed to be a long way away as she said softly.

"Drex, you will tell no other living soul what you are looking for. You will find the great tower inhabited by the remnants of Soloria's court, but you will not speak with them. Your task is to search the Library of Lurann and discover the meaning of the word Sandsinger." her voice dropped to a mere thread as Drex's eyes closed and his head whirled.

He woke shivering, lying on the floor of an immense room with her voice ringing in his ears.

"I also want to know of this Healer Jalni! Succeed and live, Fail and your flesh will shrink from your bones and crawl to Sundreth's deepest mines without them!"

Her voice carried the threat impersonally, adding to the horror of his situation as Drex (skin clammy with foreboding) saw the evidence of Dark Sorcery looming above him. He lay beneath a circular repository, through which a breeze seemed to rustle the parchment of scrolls, thousands of scrolls, Rotations old stretching into infinity filling the shelves above him. He whimpered, realising he was already in Aryphnia, and as Adruna's savage chuckle mocked him, he moaned despairingly and fainted.

Chapter 1 - Discovery

Olneth smiled grimly to himself as he left the welcoming gleam of the travel stop behind, and set off into the night. His hardy Zeglur chuntered softly under its breath as the Master Spy caressed the donkey-like creature's neck and whispered to it soothingly.

"Sssh Matanas settle down," he murmured, tugging one of his ungainly steed's comically large ears. The Zeglur grumbled softly, enquiringly, as its rider turned south, heading between a lonely massif and the forbidden zone skirting the spy's home sands, and the man gentled the animal as it shifted into a lumbering trot.

"No Matanas," he whispered into the listening night, "we cannot go home.", and the sand seemed to shimmer under the Zeglurs hooves as they trotted slowly into sight of the sinister glow that surrounded the Amethyst Sands, a glow that proclaimed the magical barrier that separated those sands from the society of Clans, and physically imprisoned Adruna and all those Sybillsce who followed the dark path to power.

The Zeglur rocked and swayed, panniers full with trade goods, and Olneth relaxed in the saddle, used to long sand crossings at night in pursuit of intelligence for those who had given him a home through the long Rotations of exile.

Once Soloria's Captain of Guard, he had wept as he buried his dreams along with the girl he'd reluctantly identified as his wife. Then, he had turned his mind to their child, following Subtle clues ever onward, raising hopes of reunion, defeated by age and injury until these annual journeys became additional indulgence in pain. This cynical self-realisation did nothing to slow the spy's progress; rather it inspired him to look about him critically examining his impressions of the southern path to Selesh, even as he passed the forbidden trail to the Sherrol Pass.

His Zeglure snorted softly but the hand that guided it was inexorable, turning the beast north around Aramand's Peak, a lonely outcropping named after some long dead Lord of the Opal Sands. He hugged the shadows of the oddly banked rocks, grateful that they soared above him, shuddering as he thought briefly of being observed from the Amethyst Sands, however unlikely that possibility was.

There was a wind rising, quavering hollow tones through the narrow divide, so Olneth dug his heels into the Zeglur's flanks, and urged the animal onward, wondering what freak of temper had made him set out so late on this particular path.

He had just turned up his collar, settled his traditional hukvah so that the cords binding it to his brow bit more firmly, (one side of the drape covering his mouth), when the Zeglure reared back squealing in fright. It took all Olneth's skill to remain mounted and some time to stop the terrified animal bucking and leaping about the concealed body of a man, buried to his neck in blood-soaked sand. Eventually, the tall Sybillsce gained control, but nothing would persuade the creature back along the path, so wearily Olneth turned away toward a sort of cove against the towering rock above, hobbling Matanas and placing a soothing feedbag over the restive animal's nose, as he returned on foot to discover what he might.

Only the man's head remained above Sand. Olneth lit a shaded lantern, studying this hapless traveller grimly. Every muscle in the spy's body tensed, the restless probing of the wind stirring the sand in an uncanny rolling motion as he stared downward.

This death was old, possibly a full Rotation since this traveller had breathed, but still there was evidence to gather from the pitiful remnant of humanity. He was Sybillsce, enough of his traditional tattooed neck remained for Olneth to gather the fact that this man had been married, fathered a son, and had died most horribly, head damaged, neck dislocated, and as the taciturn Clansman dug the body free, it became obvious that no clue remained in clothing, for the body was naked, shrunken in sand, semi-mummified, pathetic in its solitude. Eventually Olneth carefully covered the body in his own serape, lowered it into the grave he had dug, and covered his fellow Clansmen reverently, before sending a prayer winging into the star speckled night for the soul who had perished here, before turning back to his tethered steed.

The animal dozed in the lee of a rocky pinnacle, hardly noticing as his rider extracted a cape from his saddle-bags and set off on foot seeking somewhere clear of the stench of death in which to relieve himself.

There was a sort of path between two tanbark bushes, and the spy slipped through the gap and silently ascended a small rise leading to what had clearly been a man-made platform. His darkened lantern gave out just enough light to see the path ahead, so curiosity overcoming sense, Olneth ascended silently, stealth being one of the many tricks of his trade.

He passed odd shapes in the sharp incline which made him think of caverns, but disinclined to make the close acquaintance of a sleeping seobra, he pressed onward and upward until he could take a moment to make himself comfortable, before deciding to continue as far as he could. This close to the border of his own home Sands, the pain of his exile hovered close by, but the excitement of finding a secret rendezvous for informants, made him persevere until, rounding a bend he nearly missed the precipice at his feet.

For a dizzying second the pale gleam of his lantern disappeared, then as his feet slid under him, Olneth realised that the faint gleam of light was reflected from the far side of a deep chasm into which he was falling. He flung out a hand, scrabbled at the ground wildly, then his toes found a foothold and he managed to secure a handhold, grasping at what felt like a piece of rope.

His breath whistling noisily in his ears, the spy twisted this about his upper arm, clinging onto the ledge until strength flowed back. Somehow, he'd saved his lantern, so, tightening the rope, he swung himself up to the edge of the path from which he'd nearly crashed to his death below.

For a gut wrenching moment as he swung, he realised that his rope was actually not plaited, just a twist of fabric caught into the edge of the drop. As he recovered (kneading sore muscles back into some semblance of normality) the hysteria of shock bubbled to the surface borne on a single thought.

"Saved by some old curtain flapping in the wind, a thousand Rotations since life fled this place!"

Hysterical tears flowed as he laughed with relief, then a whisper of thought crossed his mind.

"No ordinary weaving could have survived so long. No fabric exposed for Rotations could have supported my weight.", and half afraid of what he might see, he looked down.

His hands were wrapped in Amethyst silk, shot through with colours so vivid they made his eyes blur and his throat hurt. He peered down disbelieving, it was dark, and his lantern had guttered and failed as he fell, yet he could see the cloth clearly. His mouth suddenly dry, he turned the fabric very carefully, and it untwisted itself, falling without a crease into the recognisable shape of a cloak. It glowed, not brightly (as a beacon), but subtly as a darkened lantern as his hands sought to uncover the half that appeared to be buried. Gradually, using his dagger, the spy uncovered it, and it seemed to him that it came into his hands with a sigh of relief, as though it wanted to be found. Now all he had to do was to get it back to Selesh, where those practised in the craft of magic could examine it closely. His hands seemed to work on their own as he draped it over one arm, allowing the faint gleam from it to guide his feet back to his impatient Zeglure. He was shivering by the time he had packed it into his saddle bag, but he never once considered wearing it. Too weary to care about how he seemed to have been led to his discovery, he headed swiftly for Selesh, where Sorcery and Sandsingers could make sense of the problem, and spies could sleep, untroubled by the artefact or its potential to cause disaster.

He passed into the great underground fortress without hindrance. His Zeglur plodding wearily now, the night chilly, turning toward winter leaving its traces in frosty air, droplets of moisture on stone walls as the great door was rolled open for him. Inesh warriors eyed him without suspicion, so used were they to Olneth's mysterious comings and goings, and at least one of the lean tawny women raised a welcoming hand in salute as he passed down the tunnel, through into the Gathering Square, and up to the huge doors leading to a strange underground pasture in which the spy had his quarters. Half a sector later, (the weary Zeglur turned out into the lush grazing) Olneth laid his saddlebag aside as he entered a comfortable tent in the rear of the strange cavern, headed for his bed. He would sleep until Seleus rose and warmed the Sands of his adopted homeland, then he would examine his strange find, and report to Ikella (if the aged Sorceress was well enough to receive him), or to Beneva, Guardian of Knowledge who would undoubtedly know what to do with his discovery until his Sandsinger returned.

He rolled himself into his blankets and slept, unaware that he had brought danger with him, a tool so powerful that it had been shunned, stored away from sight and forgotten before it could once more wreak havoc on a society not prepared for its use.

Chapter 2 - Tears for the Singer

High above his sleeping Master Spy, the Lord of the Opal hunched in misery surveying his options. The magical city of Tirjhinar called to him, but his duties to the Shalhanhi Sorceress who'd adopted him, held him prisoner. He was restive, unhappy, and anxious to be anywhere but at Selesh, yet he didn't know why. Leaning back against a rock contemplating the Sands which he knew would be gleaming faintly beneath the twin moons of Pelshar, the blind Sandsinger wept, in a fit of anguished self-pity.

Fighting down the urge to give in to maudlin sentiment, he forced himself to count mixed blessings. Wasn't he the only man to tread the path of power for a millennium? Hadn't he also found love and respect from the Clan whose Sand he would ultimately rule?

As he slid down to sit on his warded ledge, his mind turned to Jalni, his lover of a few Rotations. Briefly touching on their future together, he gazed sightlessly from Mount Torrenesh, where as a boy, he had looked down on the growing grounds above the underground fortress that riddled the massif like a honeycomb.

Recalling the simple place it had been before Ikella opened the Hall to welcome potential Healers to train under her tutelage, he sighed longingly as memories were evoked. His lips curved as he remembered running across tough pastures at the sound of the Summoning Bell. Late for supper again, the rhythm of his younger self's body washed over him as he remembered how it had been. The joy of jumping down stepped paths in full pelt still echoed in his flesh: also his foster-mother's peremptory challenge as he ran like some wild animal through the corridors of the Healer Hall.

"Daro bin Selesh! Here we live in peace, quiet and tranquillity in order to heal those who are sick. How can healers study and learn with a demon tormenting them?"

Then he was filled with guilty recollections of nights when he and Ahnell had groaned and shrieked through the ancient passageways, until the Sorceress had unleashed her faithful warriors to hunt them down. Smiling ruefully, Daro remembered how silently the tawny women had encircled them; Jashell suspending Ahnell, (only eight Rotations old) high against the rocky wall, teeth and spear blade gleaming in the dark. For a moment the memory of Jashell joyously applying a slipper to Ahnell's backside almost made him chuckle, then, the loneliness swept over him, unbearable grief nearly overwhelming him as he thought of them both, long Rotations dead. Trembling, he fought the compulsion to howl like some bereaved animal until, the battle won, he subsided against his rock, staring with unseeing eyes over the great expanse of Opal Sand, as he quieted.

He must have slept, for he certainly dreamed. Strangely split between watching the events unfold, and experiencing the sensations of those who played within that scenario, he leant forward to get a better view.

In his mind's eye, a group of people wearing the Colours of the Sands came onto the promontory that fronted Selesh. There were many Shalhanhi, dressed in Opalwear, then it seemed every Colour was represented in the nine within their midst. In the centre of this gathering was a man who could have been himself. Tall, lithe, olive skin glowing against garments that blazed every shade like the living Opal itself, he walked along with the group, yet separately, as if high rank divided him from his entourage. Behind him however, something unusual gleamed in the rays of a setting sun, and Daro stared intently, for what he "saw", was not sand, but water!

Water like no living soul had seen in a thousand Rotations, water that danced and sparkled into the horizon of his dream, and as if to ensure his belief in this vision, the man who strode towards the water's edge, surrounded by courtiers, turned and Daro "saw", dazzling opalescent eyes, compelling magical eyes, the eyes of a Sandsinger. As he watched in disbelief, a strange vessel came into sight, great sails spread as it rocked below the promontory, and came to rest with a succession of cries from men, clinging to the tall masts, and hanging in the shrouds.

Although he longed to shrink back against the safety of his rock, he felt himself running forward to the edge of a wall, below which a huge flight of steps led down to the water's edge. Peering over cautiously, he realised that no-one had noticed him, so he stood and watched the Sandsinger and his retinue board the strangely graceful conveyance as it turned, and made back into the water. Somehow, he felt the rock and surge of the craft as it began to move off. Oddly he could hear music, a thread of sound so familiar, so dear that his throat ached, and with that he knew that the Sandsinger was in magic. He felt the slap of the sails as they tightened, heard the cry of the men hauling in the sheets, and felt the lift of the sailship as it swept out to sea.

The tune sounded in his head and heart, something hard and wheel-like spun under his hands, and Mirayen filled the sails as they sped away. Completely overwhelmed by a succession of strange sensations and unfamiliar yet comprehensible words, Daro's dreaming hands clutched the wheel of the ancient sailship, and his lips framed the words to the song in his heart.

He leant into the wind, feeling the ancient sea lift him forward as the cries of sea-birds and his dream crew drowned all sound from his mind, and thus thralled, he relaxed against his rock until natural sleep overtook him, leaving him to wake, sad but determined, knowing what he must do if Pelshar was ever to return to that way of life again.

It was in this mood of melancholy that he entered his Eyrie, walking silently past his guard, who (with innate understanding) came to their feet, but made none of the traditional stamping salutation due to his rank. He nodded grave but silent appreciation, and glided on, led only by his glowing Staff's powerstone which threw out a subdued opalescence around him. The door to his private apartment opened at a wave of an empowered hand as he slipped into his great-room, and over to his treasure wall. He came to a stop, close to but not actually touching any of the shelves, running a glowing hand along the length of ancient Torrenwood shelving until he found what he sought. It was an elaborately crafted pendant, made of a blue stone set in crystal and framed in some silverwork. He held it for a moment, warming the stone, and then he held it against the similarly crafted Opal at his own throat, and whispered a single word into the silent night of his world.

"Rishenara", he commanded.

In the sleeping chamber beyond, the woman who shared his bed opened great glowing jewel-like eyes, before rolling over to sleep once more.

Chapter 3 - On Shifting Sands

For days after this, Daro remained in the Eyrie. He seemed to have little to do (other than annoying all who came within his orbit), and Jalni was almost glad when finally, he decided to go and see some relic that Olneth had taken to Beneva for examination. She had endured a kind of oppressed gloom, into which Daro kept asking after her well-being, in such a pointed way that she'd decided she must look ill. He hadn't given up, even after a glance in her mirror had told her that she looked perfectly well.

She was tired and irritable after nights of nursing half of the first year Healers, who'd unwisely, crossed a patch of thornbush in a vain attempt to find salt grass for a remedy. She'd experienced first-hand evidence of Daro's contradictory mood after she'd slid into bed, having salved the last pair of sore legs, when he'd complained bitterly about the smell of soapwort that clung about her.

She'd only responded in her usual light-hearted manner, when the stiffness of his expression told her that he wasn't teasing, that the temperamental display he'd exhibited had been for real, and she'd stared at him, wide-eyed and very aware that there was a lick and a roll of thunder along the horizon to underscore his savage reactions.

She'd crept away, not into the bathing room (as he'd demanded), but into Tobin's sewing room, winding herself into some quilted material, until her lover's body servant had appeared the following morning.

Tobin (without a word) put his fingers to his lips enjoining silence, and brought a winter coverlet, tucking her in firmly, where she'd fallen asleep once more. Later, he'd amused her by describing one of his former lover's moods.

"Ooh yes.", he confided brightly, "My Andrau was like that when something he'd planned didn't turn out the way he'd wanted it… and after he was paralysed you can imagine the frustration level just went up, and up.", he sighed heavily, remembering his recent loss, and without self-pity accepted the gentle pressure of her hand on his arm as she extended silent sympathy.

"He was always what you'd call "a man's man.", he said, unaware of the double entendre his words conjured for the Healer, but she understood what he meant. His lover had not seemed obviously homosexual, but the skilled Weaver had kept his secrets until he met gentle Tobin, and their love for each other had been strongly determined, despite the terrible injuries inflicted on the Weaver because of their mutual devotion. Long after Daro had rescued them, their experience of intolerance had made them overly discreet and withdrawn. However, Tobin had gained popularity with the Inesh with his skilled personal service to Daro. His knowledge of hairstyle, clothing and appearance had been shared willingly with the warrior women who had championed the slender servant to the amazed gratitude of his crippled lover. Soon, Andrau's bed was frequently rolled out into the Gathering Square, where Tobin had often displayed his unparalleled talents in the traditional plaiting of the women's hair.

Even the Senior Healers had smiled at the chuckles evoked from the sick man, and as Summer succeeded the first Winter that couple spent in Selesh, Andrau's fragile health had recovered enough for him to continue dictating a book of Weaver techniques, watching all the while as Tobin settled into the fabric of Selesh, satisfying the promise of the young Sandsinger who had given them his patronage. The Inesh had more than repaid Tobin's sharing of skills by the enthusiastic searches they carried out in the abandoned older sections of Selesh.

Great bales of specialised weaving were unearthed. Boxes of fine trimmings were revealed, old looms liberated, and in the wake of all this, the Weaver Guild were invited to oversee the removal of these treasures. Occasionally, some more personal items came to light, but Daro (after glancing over them perfunctorily) dismissed them as being of no account. He permitted Jalni to retain a couple of trinkets, but forbade her to wear a pair of anklets she'd uncovered on which, mounted on chains at the heel were tiny silver bells.

His swift response as Jalni paraded the tinkling anklets was stiff, frowning and unyielding, startling Jalni with a harsh "No!", as she'd turned towards him laughing, and so, the anklets were removed, but an air of discord filled the Eyrie, depressing poor Tobin further, and leaving Jalni discontented.

She began to feel that Daro was devoted to "junketing" about, visiting one village after another for no reason other than getting out of Selesh. She was struggling herself, mentally returning to her own Sands night after night as she dreamed of their recent journey to Scartel, re-visiting her memories in the period after Height of Sun, while everyone rested in the shade.

Even Daro seemed happier there, planning with the Rangers as they located the remnants of their childhood homes. As the Ranger Children of Scartel started rebuilding, Jalni leant against a cool wall in Selesh, with the memory of the lingering passion that had re-ignited within the flooded cavern complex burning in her blood, which only served to make her more dissatisfied with her day to day existence in Selesh.

Here, she felt stifled, unable to express herself, clumsy and unequal to the task of supporting the blind Sandsinger. Inevitably the tension between them grew, until Jalni positively yearned to get back to her own Sands and a pattern of existence where she was able to understand her place in the scheme of things.

With Daro absorbed in some project involving Olneth, Jalni wondered glumly how long they would be in the Sands, for she had seen obvious signs of preparation (despite her Lord's best efforts to conceal them). She leant against the bare rock wall of their apartment, head resting on her arms and wished that they were Azure bound once more and drifted into a light doze, remembering…

Chapter 4 - The Mirror Pool

The Rotation was coming to an end when the Sandsinger and his love accompanied the Children of Scartel back to the Sands of their birth. However, reality (instead of mirroring the dreams that had overwhelmed her night after restless night), was less than the triumphal parade she had envisaged.

As they descended the long sweeping track and turned toward Scartel itself, there had been a long, threatening roll of thunder. Having amused herself picturing this moment, Jalni had dreamt them riding the trek cart resplendent in their new cloaks with those who followed them on Zeglurback, or on foot, cheerful in Clan Colours. Somehow she had not pictured anything like the reality of fatigue and fear. Trek cart and driver bolting along the well-worn track to shelter; everyone soaked to the skin, teeth chattering with the shock of the sudden cold downpour, terror struck by the awesome display of raw natural power. Nor had she thought that mindful of finding their own place of safety, the settlers would have abandoned the Opal Sandsinger and his lady, leaving them to fend for themselves as the skies opened and the lightening streaked groundward.

Thankful for the brilliant flashes that seared across the darkening skies, Jalni simply grasped Daro's hand and ran. Forgetting his blindness, forgetting the path that led to the Lower Caverns, whipping hair obstructing her vision she ran, towing her awkward companion.

As lightening hissed to ground behind them, they reached the base of the towering crater walls then somehow her hand pierced a wildly whipping curtain of strangleroot, revealing in a narrow fissure, an entrance to an ancient cave.

They huddled together laughing ruefully, then Jalni started to look about her as the storm (cheated of its prey) rumbled furiously, caught in the circle of mountain peaks that soared perilously skyward around them.

Despairing of ever being dry or warm again, she leant against the cave entrance and stared pensively across the crater floor, to where the deepening gloom hid the emerging sprawl of the new township. Daro, propped on a man-sized boulder, turned his face skyward, and in one of the sustained flares of lightening Jalni saw his lips twitch in a smile and knew that he was remembering another night in this place, another storm, when he had danced on the plateau beneath the peak with the Zephryn of ancient legend. Her own lips curved when she recalled his taming of Araneus, (the baby of that herd), who was probably rolling in the underground pasture back at Selesh, dry, warm, and not missing them at all.

Shivering, she sneezed suddenly, causing little echoes to 'ping' around them rather disconcertingly, and Daro's attention was suddenly diverted. The storm was gathering strength, the wind plucking at their wet bodies, as he turned to the exploration of their situation.

He held out his left hand and in its wet brown palm there was fire. A faint trickle of power stirred Jalni's skin; and she turned to stare past her lover into the depths of the cavern beyond. Steadying his hand she gasped as the light intensified, flashing on something ahead that reflected the light back. Somehow changed, the light danced into the void, bluer, suffused with a myriad of sparkling reflections that seemed to be swaying, far into the distance. The light streamed and reflected, till Jalni turned to Daro and said,

"I thought I could see a mirror. Perhaps there's something else that shines through there, but it's strange. It seems to move. I'm so cold, wet, and tired that I can't think straight. Perhaps I might see more if we follow this path, we will have to move soon anyway, there is water positively pouring through. We'll drown if we stand here waiting for someone to rescue us."

As the same thought struck Daro, he came bolt upright, cursing as he briefly lost his concentration (and the handfire he was conjuring). Swiftly regaining his balance and encircling Jalni with his free arm he made a complicated pass with his other hand unleashing a burst of pale light high into the roof of the cavern. It lit up, like the heart of a fire cracked gemstone and Jalni stood rooted to the spot as the flare revealed the caverns true enormity, and the lake that mirroring and reflecting all sources of light, stretched from about twenty spans in front of them, in every direction, as far as her eyes could see.

Daro, aware of her stillness said only mildly,

"Not more trouble?", then as his aura cloaked both of them in opalescent lambency, the Sandsinger drew her with him as he walked forward. Jalni trailed her free hand along the wall of the short passage, a dim blue fluorescence spreading out from under her warming palm. Fascinated by this, she was nevertheless aware that Daro was 'humming', a trickle of power was tickling her as though some conductive element cloaked her, and then their feet found a paved pathway, and Jalni gasped as around her there was a buzzing, and a crackling, and like some archaic machine coming back to life, the cavern lit up around them.

Immediately in front and substantially below them the path led directly to a swiftly flowing current of water. The outer walls of the cavern were entirely natural in appearance, soaring high above the flooded interior, where century old stalactites plunged into the immeasurable depths of the pool, creating mysterious archways that disappeared into the distance ahead. Only dimly perceived at first, lights were now appearing to the right of the precipitous pathway down to the water's edge, and Jalni tugged at Daro's arm, trying to guide him away from the direction of the lake, but somehow her feet were overwhelmed by the urge to stay with him, and turning to look at him Jalni was aware that his eyes were fully opened, the deeply hooded orbits filled with the elemental Opal shimmer that she recognised so well. Deep 'in magic' Daro glided effortlessly down the steep gradient to a set of steps that were lapped by the swiftly flowing current of the underground lake, and as she was drawn into the protective shelter of his arm, and caught to his side she felt an undercurrent of mystery, heard a stirring in the depths beyond them and a kind of tingling expectation electrified her skin.

Lost in the moment Jalni became aware of an insistent rhythmic throbbing and turned her head to the left a little, peering past Daro far into the shadows on that side of the cave. Was that water slapping that she could hear? No, it was a rhythmic driving sound that made Jalni's hair stand on end in apprehension, someone, no, *something* was approaching them, and a sonorous drone heralded its arrival.

There was a pallid glow on the water now, and heart beating wildly in time to the melodic throbbing that perfused Jalni's very blood, she leaned a little forward to see the most remarkable conveyance approaching them. Gliding out of the shadows, a high prowed boat; great sweeping oars propelled it towards them, and it was the gentle creak and sway of the oars that had come to Jalni's ears as the intricate thrum and beat of some musical instrument. There was no-one on board, and yet the oars moved constantly as it swept towards them, as though summoned, and as it arrived she could not but notice the lavish hangings of Opal weave, the sumptuous piled cushions and throws that adorned the platform of what looked to her suspicious eye, as nothing less than a bed. It came to rest, rocking easily at their feet, and it seemed that there was nothing more to do, than to step down into it, and settle, feeling their wet clothing, clinging clammily to their soaked and weary bodies as they did so.

Daro seemed distant, distracted by something, and yet, however absorbed he was very powerfully present, warm, vital and alive beside her, and Jalni ached to hold him. She was exhausted and hardly had the great boat moved out on to the lake again, when her compulsion to lie down on the bed and sleep overcame her natural instincts. Daro's encircling arm was comforting, but she trembled with cold and fatigue and her numb fingers plucked uselessly at her sodden garments, till it was only with his assistance that she succeeded in divesting herself of them, and rolled herself into the pleasantly warm covers and lay cushioned on the bed. She was aware of sound, a combination of the gentle rocking of the vessel, a pounding in her blood, the rhythm of the sweeps as they were driven powerfully forward, under an archway of stalactites and then they passed through a kind of veil, nothing more than a shiver of sound, a shimmer of light and everything about them changed. They were bathed in warm light, here there was a confusion of colour as a cloud of flyby's swarmed suddenly around them, flickering in and out of vision in the most disconcerting way, flashing all the hues of the sands on their wings. Jalni saw Daro's face relax, saw the smile flash across his features and dimly realised that he was no longer cloaked in the aura of the Opal. His eyes were still open, but the sheen of magic had left them and she watched him warm and languid, nestling in her cocoon of acquired finery, as he cheerfully shrugged off his soaking cloak, his travel wear, and his boots and stood naked and unashamed, glowing in the warmth of this magical place. He sat on the bed, shaking the tangles out of his shoulder length hair, and then with one fluid motion he slid under the covers into her warm burrow and gathered her into his arms.

'Can you hear the music?' he questioned her softly, bending his expert mouth to hers and stifling her reply – but he was right, crushed against him she could hear it too. A rippling cascade of notes reverberated in her head resolving itself in a rhythmic pattern that matched the movement of the boat through the water. She could hear the enfolding of the song of flybys and the splash of the oars in that throbbing persistent melody, yet entwined in the music were notes that soared, that gathered them in; notes that she felt would flow through her soul, heart and mind forever. Was it the river she could hear singing to her, or the cavern? Who possessed her - the music, the river or Daro? Whatever held her captive, she was borne away on a gliding, floating trill, created by no voice, or wind, or flyby of this world and swept away on a torrent of musically enhanced passion, Jalni surrendered herself. Time stood still, sensation, sound, and the driving rhythm of their love took her, launched her as if she was the boat, floating in one moment, soaring down rapids in the next, until dizzy and pleading she was brought to shore, safe with her sailor, rocked in the depths of his love. She remembered trailing a hand in the water, watching the lake flush from midnight black through every shade of blue, with overtones of gold, till Daro roused himself and took her hand in his, bringing it up to his lips and kissing the palm dry murmuring,

'That's for another day love' and she curved into his warmth and nestled as the music in her subsided and became just an echo, and her eyes flickered and closed in sleep. Daro, his head pillowed on a cushion, stretched his aching body luxuriously, reached out with those magically enhanced senses and could detect no danger nearby. He still held Jalni's fingers in his hand, and he moved, careful not to rouse her and stroked them gently; wondering if what he had heard and felt in their strange journey had conveyed itself to this wilful mate of his. She moved trustingly against him, and he slipped an arm protectively around her, aware of a feeling that something had changed, something had happened here. He puzzled over it awhile then slid into deep and dreamless sleep, the answer eluding him in his exhaustion.

Chapter 5 -Revelation

Was it only four moons later in the heart of Selesh that Jalni woke in the huge bed she shared with her lord, tense, unrefreshed and strangely restive? Lying in the luxurious sheeting she wondered lethargically what was wrong with her. She'd been "out of sorts" ever since they returned from Scartel, and she considered it likely that the same sense of detachment was affecting Daro.

He'd been grumbling aloud to himself for days, irritably taking himself off without a word of explanation other than the muffled comment that if he didn't get out of Selesh he'd suffocate, at which Jalni had let him go without protest. There was, after all (she reasoned to herself), a huge difference between the crater of a long extinct volcano and this vast underground fortress, where in the silent corridors only the gentle murmur of the Healer community served to brighten the day.

She rose, padded across to their private bathing room and slid from her wrapper into the warm pool served by the underground spring far below Mount Torrenesh. She floated, languidly spreading her limbs in the water, surprised at her own lethargy, faintly aware of an uneasy nausea.

"Perhaps I'm sickening for something?" She rolled over, supported herself on the edge of the pool, and reached for her basket of toiletries. Sorting out soapwort scrub and a jar of carrenna oil, she became aware of avoiding the heady aroma of kerflax, shocked by her unreasonable response to the familiar and sought after scent.

"I've probably got some nasal infection," she decided later, pushing away the bowl of milta grain she had been offered for breakfast, and taking only a small cup of stemmis, she wandered back into her bedroom, where she was startled as a curtain was swept aside and her unsmiling lover stalked in, two paces ahead of his personal servant.

The blind mage held a staff loosely in one hand, swinging it effortlessly as he found his way to his chair, allowing Tobin to pull off his boots without a word until the servant enquired calmly,

"Can I be of further assistance Lord?"

The Sandsinger's brows drew together savagely, and Jalni flinched, knowing that the thunderous skies above Mount Torrenesh reflected her lover's mood.

However the expected snarl of frustration died unborn as a sound from beyond the curtain attracted his attention and as quickly as a fleeting shadow Daro's scowl melted, head turning quizzically and Jalni sighed with relief as Diras (Daro's bodyguard) announced the visitor.

"Master Olneth, Ichspeller."

Tobin's eyes caught Jalni's as the Sandsinger rose, summoned his Staff with a flick of the hand, and greeted the Master Spy.

Discreetly withdrawing, Jalni slipped past Tobin into the ante-room, and smiled ruefully at the bodyguard on duty, before turning into Daro's great-room and picking up a sand tablet and enscrasure. She left a brief note, and then fled to the Infirmary where she took up her workwear and went to change.

She had just sat under a glowstone lamp, tucking her feet up as she picked up the list of remedies required, when the nape of her neck tingled, and she looked up at the slap of sandaled feet approaching. The light voice of the Guardian of Power quivered with laughter, then Shiarjha appeared with a gaggle of student Healers, coming directly down the long room to greet her.

"Dommichspeller," she said hopefully, "We brought you some interesting plants found only today on the growing grounds. Could you identify them for our class?"

Glancing around the group, Jalni saw that these second year candidates were all avidly staring at the seeds she had been collecting, and smiled at Shiarjha though her own head was aching with the effort of concentrating. Putting aside her own work, she took the small collection of plant matter from Shiarjha's hand and laid them out neatly on a clean linen cloth. They were all of the grass family, and Jalni looked at them thoughtfully as she divined Shiarjha's reasoning for this class.

Taking down a fine spill made from a dry reed, she carefully separated one sort from another then turned a questioning glance on the attentive students.

"Look at the roots of every plant first, see if they spread like a mat, or if they pierce through the soil and grow downward." she advised. "Those that spread can grow on weak soil or sand, binding themselves to each other to resist being uprooted. However, they don't produce much food, and are only good for animal fodder, bedding, or literally to bind sand together. The ones for food pierce the soil looking for water, and have stronger stems and well fed leaves. They grow taller, and might be harvested for seed or grain, or even for the stems which can make thread, or be split for basket weaving or roofing for shelters." she paused, then added mysteriously, "Then again there are other uses for common plants that only we Healers learn."

She looked at the simple plants critically, and murmured,

"Harburnroot for joint ill, ruedwort for dry skin, and barksweft for fever". She swept up the two remaining clumps of plant and handed them to Shiarjha and said sweetly,

"Mossroot and bermout however are used only in the creation of potions for magic users. They contain or absorb from somewhere ingredients that can greatly assist with the preservation of ancient records, and I am sure Guardian Shiarjha will show you how to identify plants with magical properties as opposed to those used for medicine."

Shiarjha took a sheet of the new writing material that junior apprentices in the new Guild of Recorders had created and suggested that the group split up into two and take up seats at the long table under the brightest glows. She smiled as the girls scrambled to obey, then she took over one group of nine, and Jalni took the other.

"Take a spill, separate the plant matter, looking for roots, stems, and leaves that match. Tease out individual plants and carefully lay them on the recording card. When your plants are all separate, you can wet your finger in the durun gel in the setting bowl and moisten the thickest stem and a couple of leaves with the glue. Lay the plant on the card and put a weight on top of it to secure it firmly. When you have your samples ready, you can identify them for us, and we'll show you the symbol for that plant. You can copy the symbols on your own notation tablet and take them away to learn. Your plant records will be left to dry, then you can collect them, and practise drawing the plant and adding the symbol, so that in years to come, you can prepare medicines from apothecary slips, recognizing the drawing and symbol before you identify the substance in the packet".

Shiarjha's voice encouraged the students and for some time there was a pleasant buzz of activity as they worked over their identification cards, then a tall girl of about fourteen Rotations held up her hand, and rather ruefully Jalni responded.

"Yes Halima? What do you want to know?"

The girl considered for a moment, then said quietly,

"Dommichspeller, when the medication is prepared it will look nothing like the original plant. The picture will tell us what the plant looks like, the symbol will confirm the name by which it is known, but how can a Healer know what the slip contains unless they have prepared it themselves?"

It was a common question, one that Jalni appreciated for she had prepared most of her own medication during her travels in the Azure Sands. She smiled encouragingly.

"That's a good question Halima. Most of us will prepare our own medication. Apothecaries are rare animals these days, but you know how it is. Some things don't grow in our own Sands, others we send off-sands ourselves, but they all have to conform to a standard. When we use medications we have not prepared ourselves, we are trained to identify by eye, by smell and by taste, then by specific attributes of each medication. Believe me, as you grow stronger in the Craft and your othervoice develops, you will find that you can match the vibration of the ill or injury with the resonance of the cure. Sometimes the reverberation between the two is so strong that the Healer must lower the pulse of the patient so that they can receive the cure, other times you have to excite the humours of the blood to carry the medication to the injury. That's a little like the opposite of cooling the humours to reduce temperature."

She watched the liquid brown eyes of the student widen, and then she said gently.

"It is a long training, but one that you will be able to rely on always. Just don't rush it. Let your voice develop naturally, don't force it, and obey the rules implicitly. Healers who fight the rules or don't learn their set work thoroughly can't meet the unexpected when it happens. Remember that and you won't go far wrong."

She brushed her hair back, her Healer braid (a narrow plait bound with Opal and Azure ribbons) swinging against her cheek as she did so, then his voice sounded in her ear.

"Jalni, I have left with Olneth. He needs to show me something which isn't that far from Tirjhinar." the name of the fabulous lost city of the ancient Sandsingers tripped off his lips as though he spoke of Selesh Minoria (the local village). He continued with the wry chuckle that told her that even her thoughts were not entirely her own.

"We will be gone four nights, but I have sent for Marran, so Terris will be happy to hear that. It may be that I have to journey again shortly, but I think you'll not miss my sour moods. Perhaps I need something to engage my energies; after all, you have your baby Healers."

His voice had taken on an abstracted air, and as Jalni looked up to see Halima greatly absorbed bending over her plant record, he said softly:

"That child should be tested for Sorcery I think.", then he was gone.

She had only stilled for a moment, but Shiarjha caught her eye, and discreetly began assembling their class, coming up behind Jalni as she stretched her taut neck, and relaxed.

"Don't tell me he's off-sands again?" the Guardian said softly, but Jalni shook herself laughing.

"No, not exactly," she said thoughtfully, "Olneth needs him to see something in the far south-west. I have no doubt this is some kind of men only junket, but he's sent for Marran, saying he's not going to be away that long. I confidently expect the High Pasture to be knee-deep in Rangers before the night is out, so I will have to go and make arrangements with Diras and the guard. Please excuse me Shiarjha, but I must go."

She swayed as she stood up, and the Guardian steadied her, noting her sudden pallor and the beading of fine dew on her upper lip.

"Great Sands child…" she exclaimed (forgetting Jalni's exalted rank for the moment). "Are you sick? You should go and see Ikella or Beneva straightaway. There's no good in hiding the obvious from yourself. You look wretched, probably feel worse, and what are you doing about it? Nothing but fretting over Daro's excitements and excursions. By the way," she swung round on Jalni thoughtfully,

"Where in the Nine Sands is that wretched Apothecary? Ikella isn't getting any younger, and quite frankly my dear, she hasn't made the recovery we were hoping and praying for. I'm glad that Suraya has turned out to be a bright student, and is taking on her responsibilities properly, but I'm uneasy, I don't mind telling you. Now, promise me that you'll consult Beneva if you don't feel any better soon."

Her voice was interrupted by the ringing of a bell, and the Guardian fled after her students muttering crossly,

"Sorcery and Sandsingers! Height of Sun already and no time to chatter!", as she shooed her flock into the dining hall, going gratefully to the Djellim and her own work thereafter.

Jalni went back to her apartment in the Eyrie. Scarcely noticing the salute of the guards, she went to her bathing room and was thoroughly sick. Dosing herself with a mixture of barrisweed and holmbrush, she brewed a cup of stemmis and drank it slowly, then curled up on her bed and drifted off to sleep, resolving to seek Beneva's advice after Height of Sun.

She dreamt. A cool breeze brushed her cheek as she looked across from the caverns of Scartel. In her dream, children ran about playing, a soft tinkling sound chimed from the populated caverns above, and she smiled, listening to the wind chimes that decorated many of the cavern openings in the human rookery that filled the extinct crater.

She smelt the homely aroma of firestones heating as the kitchens prepared for evening meals, the sharp scent of citrines as a group of young men carried a net of fruit past her, and knew peace. It was so different here in her own Sands, she thought, envisaging the endless roll of Azure blue encircling the ancient crater, and dreaming, she continued to look out towards Gateway where the side of the crater had collapsed, leaving only the suspended rim of the original wall, the structure of which some ancient technology had reinforced, forming a massive entrance through which the outer Sands glimmered into the distance.

She felt almost light-headed with joy as she saw below her, the industry of building. There were men, women and children working to erect a village, she supposed, but it was on a scale unprecedented anywhere else. They seemed tireless, and as she watched buildings of stone rose from the ground, dwarfing the builders in basalt beauty. It seemed as though they had the help of magic, a blue mist gathered in the streets as they formed, then she heard herself singing...and woke.

She was confused, sweating, and as she sat up her head reeled for a moment. Turning onto one elbow to drink, she decided that this would have to stop.

"It's ridiculous," she grumbled inwardly, "I'm not sick, but I feel dreadful. I simply must go and see Beneva (for all the good that'll do me!"

Reinforcing her decision with action, she rose, stripped her sweat stained workwear off, bathed swiftly and re-dressed, unconsciously pulling on an Azure tunic as she did so. A sector of the sand-glass later, she passed into the Djellim, and made her way to Beneva's new apartments, which had been opened up when the new Master Builder discovered yet another corridor off the mighty Library.

The little Guardian didn't seem too surprised when Jalni appeared, but listened to the catalogue of all her woes carefully. She only had one question to ask,

"Why child didn't you go to the Infirmary? Suraya is a fine diagnostician, and she is your own age besides. Why come knocking on the door of one who has hardly used her skills in your lifetime?"

She noted Jalni's deep blush with amusement, then said briskly,

"Ah well, you young things allow love to get in the way of almost everything, particularly common sense." she referred obliquely to the well-known rumour that the new Sorceress elect seemed to have developed a crush on the Opal Sandsinger, which his lover actively resented. Jalni's eyes flashed a shimmer of Azure fire, and Beneva relented, sighing and picking up an enscrasure and wax tablet.

"Go through to the next room Jalni. I'll wash my hands and come and have a look at you. Then, you can wait for Felova or Misanra to come on duty if you need medication. It isn't the end of the Opal child, don't look so forlorn!"

However for once Beneva was wrong…for Jalni it was the beginning of the end, and the knowledge she carried back to the Eyrie was to be bitter indeed.

Chapter 6 - Complication

For a long time she lay on the Healers couch, hardly listening to the Guardian of Knowledge as she muttered to herself.

"I'm sure that I never heard of any Sandsinger having a child before, we assumed that they couldn't regenerate, which eventually led to the entire race dying out. This is amazing Jalni, won't Daro be delighted? He's so good with his orphans, and Ikella will be overjoyed."

Her voice failed as Jalni sat up and said curtly,

"Beneva, I implore you not to tell anyone that I'm pregnant yet. You must agree that this is my business, and that I have the right to decide which Sand my child is born in?" she rolled over, taking for granted the Guardians acknowledgement of sand-rights, as she continued.

"Daro has never asked me to jump the trave with him, we are not permanently partnered, and he is restive. I could not endure to foist on him an unwanted child, we have never discussed parenting, and even I don't know his wishes in this…let alone my own!"

Her voice had dropped dramatically as she remembered her own reaction to the strange prophecy that the Oracle of the Temple of the Winds had spoken. "You will become the mother of the Tenth Wind, and with his birth will come many changes."

"I must think, and the time that Daro is away is fortuitous." she said slowly. "I heard prophecy at the Temple that has bearing on this, which demands considerable thought before I tell anyone, including Daro."

She had drawn herself in, tucking her chin down in a pugnacious attitude that brought back memories of her tumultuous arrival at Selesh and left Beneva, going back to her retreat in the Eyrie. Not long afterwards, she was joined by her Apothecary friend Terris, two joyously noisy Rangerlings and her husband Marran, now Ranger of Scartel.

Depositing the children on one corner of a huge carpet cluttered with toys going back to Daro's childhood, the Ranger and his wife joined Jalni, who swiftly told them her news. However, such a cloud hung over the great room that Terris frowned.

"You have to tell Daro how you feel Jalni!" the young Apothecary expostulated. "You can't run away all your life, and you can't run away from your pregnancy, that's for certain."

Marran shifted uneasily.

"Jalni, you don't have to return to the Azure to give birth. Your baby automatically has both sand-rights, twin heritages to claim. Neither Ikella or Tirjella would deny him or her either, and Daro must be told how you feel. He has rights too you know, and as Sandsinger, how in the Nine Sands would you go where he can't find you? Why would you want to leave him? Is there something that you're not telling us?"

Jalni flushed, and then said in a small quiet voice. "He's bored, he feels constricted, can't wait for any excuse to get off Sands or out of Selesh. I don't know why. He won't talk about it which makes things worse. I can't even tell if it's something I've done. It's like living with an unpredictable animal. One moment he's sunny and smiling, the next he's growling and baring his teeth. I can't do anything right lately, talk annoys him, quiet makes him suspicious. He's generally fractious, lacking direction, and frets over his disablement in a way he never did before. I can't see him settling down to fatherhood willingly."

The tall young Ranger sighed, and then said heavily, "You still have to give it a chance. You never know, this might be what he's looking for. When he gets back, tell him, and then we'll see. As for your idea of having your child at Scartel; We still don't have a permanent Healer base, but by the time you're due that will have changed, and besides that, I can't see Sushanna, Terris and all turning down that opportunity.", he smiled, but his steady brown eyes were concerned as he said quietly, "You know we'd help you do anything Jalni. We will never forget what you and Daro did for us, but to take you back to the Azure, I'd need my Sandsinger's permission."

Too late Jalni remembered that Daro had bonded the young Ranger by blood-brotherhood, joining the ranks of his ranger patrol. Too late she recalled that the first Ranger Dorenard had served an ancient Opal Sandsinger, she winced. Marran however caught the drift of her thoughts and said hastily,

"I pledge to assist you return to your homesand if as you fear, your relationship has soured, or if you have your Lord's permission. I will not speak of your condition for I have no right to do so, and my wife is bound by Apothecary traditions. Sleep on your thoughts Dommichspeller, and we'll meet again in friendship, once you know your Lord's intentions."

That promise hung in the air; coming back to haunt him several nights later when the Lord of the Opal returned in no mood to listen to anyone.

Chapter 7 - Separation

During that interval, Jalni continued to worry about her pregnancy and grew evermore restive, longing to share her news but fearful of Daro's reaction. Outwardly, she answered the Summoning Bell promptly, performed her duties with silent efficiency and to those unrehearsed in Jalni's history, all was well. However, at least Daro's trusted inner circle of Inesh warriors drew together in the guardroom whispering uneasily as their Dommichspeller glided past, eyes averted, and face inscrutable.

When their Commander said uneasily, "Ichspeller Selunsanni seems to be always from home lately." the underlining tension in her voice made even the newest recruit apprehensive.

The tension ramped up when Diras's Second remarked.

"Three sectors to Watch End, are you sure you really want Lord Daro to return now?" at which her companion exclaimed abruptly.

"If World's End is nigh, then I for one would rather get it over with than wait indefinitely. I can face my death if I know it is imminent, it's all this uncertainty that spoils my appetite."

She scowled, stretching long limbs and prepared to muster her Command. Clad in her loose fitting desert pants and over robe, she wore the insignia of Daro's household, a single tear shaped Opal bound to her brow over the oath cloth that caught up her hair, shadowing her face and making it mysterious. Lifting her spear and assuming the posture of command, instantly silenced her cohort as they fell into expectant ranks.

It was only a whisper of sound, but suddenly, framed in the doorway of the guardroom there stood a slender figure. She was serene, her ancient eyes fathomless, as she lent heavily on a strangely winged Staff of precious Hojawood. Diras fell to one knee, smiting her bosom with the flat of her left hand.

"All Hail Ikella!" she cried and her faithful troops saluted the Sorceress as she glided into their guardroom with only a slight halt in her movements despite her obvious antiquity. Waving them back to their duties, Ikella advanced purposefully towards Diras.

"Is there any news of Ichspeller Selunsanni?"

Her voice was still liquid with the resonance of power, but Diras shook her head mutely, reluctant to disappoint her Lord's mother.

"He said only that he was about the business of the Sands my Deshun. Adding that he might accompany Olneth to investigate another Sybillsce murder and that he would return before this ninenight is out."

The Sorceress nodded, saying softly to herself,

"The One grant him the intelligence to read the Sands. There is trouble afoot…" and turning abruptly she wended her thoughtful way back into the community that was Selesh. Diras passed amongst the other women, ignoring for the moment friendly remarks about the best way to polish spears, and stood looking back down the entrance tunnel to where the light fell haloing the ancient ruler of the Sands, and wondered what trouble to expect now.

It was not long coming. Just after Height of Sun, a pair of sharp eyes picked out a plume of dust, then it was reported that a single rider on a Zeglur approached from the south-west. By the time Diras and her second reached the fabulous Gate in the Rock, The man who had felled it with a single touch was striding angrily into the entranceway, and with a muttered curse and a wave of a hand had completely disabled the new field of energy that protected the healer settlement from disaster.

Diras kept silent, but her disapproval must have radiated from her tense eyes and mouth, to the punishingly inexorable stance she took, spear gleaming hostility at her Sandsinger's retreating back. At the bottom of the entranceway he gave a shrug, bowed his head minutely, and then, gestured at the great Gates behind him. However, it was not until the lights around the circular door glowed, flickered and steadied, that Diras relaxed.

"I'm glad we're out here." she murmured to her second, then withdrew into the Guardroom and busied herself about Guard business.

However, in the Eyrie high above Selesh, a rising wave of annoyance engulfed Daro's great-room as he examined the artefacts that ran along his "Treasure Wall". There was nothing missing, nothing out of place, and yet his hand lingered for a moment over a strangely shaped shard of pottery. A faint inscription showed up, sparkling against the age-darkened surface so ephemeral that the letters might have been simply mica chips come to the surface, but Daro knew differently. He hesitated, the hand that "read" the ancient words still, then, his sun bronzed face tightened, brows arched and his eyes opened to reveal a whorl of opalescence. Along the shelf containing the many magical artefacts he had retrieved from the depths of Selesh there was a distinct rustle. A thin chiming of awakening, and as the blind mage swept the shelf with his empowered othergaze his hands rose "sensing" (for want of a better expression), some other magically empowered being that had entered his private domain.

After a few moments however, he turned away, (a puzzled expression on his face) and thrusting his Staff ahead of him called the powerstone to light.

"Exos", he commanded, rather gruff in tone as he used the unfamiliar term., then pivoting on his heel, he brought the gleaming powerstone to bear on every corner of the room. His robes flared out around him in a glorious whirl of Opal cloth. The very air in the room seemed charged, clothing crackling, his long dark hair swirling like some aureole around his shoulders as the blazing stone pulsated its magical trail around the room. Any observer would have recognised a hint of impatience twisting Daro's expression from its normal relaxed set. Any observer might have seen trouble coming, but there was no-one watching, his bodyguard were all intent on keeping a safe distance, and the one person who could have answered the question as to "Who has been in my room?" was sunk in the depths of sleep.

She woke groggily, aware of his presence before he made his way into their sleeping area. She could feel strange little pinpricks like some current of excitement running through her skin. She sat up, wrapping a throw around her shoulders, aware of a faint buzzing in the atmosphere, and then he was in the room, angry eyes searing her flesh with his power in full display. He came right up to the edge of the bed, and then sent his Staff away with an irritable flash of one hand. It soared, spinning and singing in a weird thrilling note, and then he had both hands on his hips and he was positively snarling at her.

"Can't you find something more suited to your calling to do, rather than interrupting me when I'm engaged on the affairs of these Sands?" he demanded furiously, as Jalni stared at him, blank incomprehension on her face.

Stuttering with sudden rage, (fury fired by fear she supposed later), she replied.

"I summon *you* my Lord?" she exclaimed wrathfully, "Did it not occur to you that I lack the power to summon even your interest these days? How then without magic could I call you back from the business that takes you out of Selesh?"

That her bitter tone had its effect she had no doubt, for the mage flushed and bit his lip, however if Jalni had scored a point, he wasn't about to admit it.

Unwisely, she continued goading bitterly.

"How is it possible my Lord? You choose to depart when I am otherwise occupied, leaving me without knowledge of where you were."

The atmosphere in the room was electric as she rose to her knees on the bed, rage flushing her face and making her eyes blaze Azure.

"I can't believe that you have turned out the Guard, while summoning up a fine storm to frighten guests and their animals, just to berate me for something I couldn't do if I tried. Whatever brought you home my Lord, it was not I!"

She found herself regretting her bravado almost as she spoke. His robe, (or was that a cloak?) swirled ominously, almost like a living entity as his brows drew together and his mouth thinned.

"When I say that I distinctly recognised your touch on my treasure wall when I have warned you never to interfere with any object placed there, are you going to call me a liar?", he threw back at her, and Jalni stilled as she remembered her uneasy dreams of the night before.

She had dreamt of standing before a wall of treasures, dreamt that a voice had told her that she could choose only one. She recalled touching nothing but a shard of pottery because it glittered suddenly, but only in a dream.

Before the anger in his eyes, her stubborn streak flared.

"Is anything missing Daro?" she enquired sarcastically. "Perhaps you should search the Eyrie, search my belongings too if it suits you!" she fired at him, matching ferocious scowl for scowl. "You've left me alone with your treasures often enough. Why do you question my honesty now?"

The look she turned on him forestalled his next comment.

"I thought I was your partner, your lover." she challenged. "However, when you are here you can't leave me to work in peace. You've been fussing me constantly, too busy with your own intrigues to spend time with me, yet never leaving me to my own devices. What is it that I'm supposed to have done? Don't I live here too, or would you rather I didn't?"

There, it was said and although she could have bitten back the words, she hadn't. Now, she stared at his suddenly subduing aura, at the curve of his cheek, noting the muscles of his face harden under her gaze. So, it was over, she thought bleakly. Then he sighed, winter icing his voice.

"No Jalni! It is only over when I decide its over!" he exclaimed abruptly, voice edged with malice.

"I really don't think I do want you prowling round behind my back anymore. I'm too busy to concentrate on your activities while I'm from home on Clan business. I rather thought you'd want to stay in Scartel with your Ranger friends the last time we were there, but that's not you is it?"

She stared at him as he strode about the small area between the bed and the door to his great-room, oblivious of his Staff which hovered a hand-span from his grasp.

The cloak he wore shimmered and swirled angrily as he snapped,

"No, you'd rather drag me back here, exhausting a good Zeglur, wasting my time and energy to deal with your tantrums, then pretend that you don't know what I'm talking about, wouldn't you? Well, I'm not making scenes for nothing. I was engaged on important business when I received your call. I came, and you say that you didn't call me, but that isn't what magic tells me. There is a distinct trace in my room, I sense something different about the entire place, as if I don't belong here anymore and I don't like it!"

His face had darkened ominously, she was drowning in his eyes, nerves at full stretch when her own grasp on reality shifted and for a moment she blazed in fury.

"Well Ichspeller, never let it be said that one of my low rank stood in your way. You want security in your Eyrie, not to be disturbed when you go about Clan business, so you can have your wish. I'll return to Zurian territory as I'm plainly not good enough for a prince of the Shalhanhi. I only wish that you'd thought of that before you entangled me in your web. Now you can do something for me. Stop sharing my thoughts, invading my privacy and denying me the peace to go about my chosen tasks. Take your bond from me, for I want none of you, Sandsinger or no!"

She wished the words unspoken almost as she said them. It was ridiculous, irrational; inevitable… she sighed and hung her head defeated. However, he seemed to be fired by spite, his brows grew together as he said maliciously,

"Oh no, Jalani bin Selesh; you were adopted by the Healer Hall on behalf of Mina bin Attwa. You are bound to this Clan, to these Sands and their rulers. You can refute my claim on you as mate, you can travel where you will, I'll exert no compulsion on you to return; I'll be too busy having fun to bother you!"

In his hand was an orb which danced and sparkled before clearing to reveal a scene which left Jalni sobered out of all anger. In it dancers pirouetted, hips swaying suggestively, naked belly's ornamented with jewels twinkling as they writhed and thrust to the insistent beat of drum and tambourine. Astonished, revolted yet fascinated, Jalni saw men breathing fire, balancing great spinning disks in mid-air, and realised she was viewing a group of Wanderers entertaining in some other Sand.

"Go about your business Healer." his voice commanded her. "Go freely into the Sands and work if that is what you want, for I want none of this."

Then he vanished, leaving no trace of his ever being there. His Staff hung in the air, humming mournfully, then the powerstone dulled, closing down almost apologetically before it too vanished with a faint "pop".

She sat quite still for a heartbeat, then stood abruptly, caught up a carrisack and started to pack.

She left before Tobin could find her and start her tears. She had taken nothing Daro had given her; even her clothes were placed in her dressing cupboard as she prepared to leave. Eventually, dressed in her Zurian Colours she stood before the great mirror that adorned the bathing room, taking grim pleasure in the image she presented. Hair bound, Healer braid plaited only with Azure ribbons, skin unadorned, just two sets of workwear taken from the Healer Hall in her carrisack, a day's food, a full scrip, her precious tools, a flask of water and her pride. She left a sand tablet for Mina, asking her foster-mother's forgiveness, and then walked up the sharp incline to the growing grounds above the complex. Gathering sweet marjoram as she went, she followed the track up to the high pastures where the Rangers were encamped, seeking Terris and her children.

If the guards she passed had any idea that she was leaving, she didn't know, but she was glad to be out early before the questions and the sympathy started. She owed a farewell to the Guardians, but she thought they'd understand, and then she was brought to a halt, heart thumping as she "heard" a voice in her head.

"I see that my son has finally come to his senses!" the old autocrat spoke sharply, and Jalni sat cross-legged in the pasture, head bowed and listened without expression on her face.

"Quite properly he has seen that you are far too good for the likes of him." Ikella snorted disapprovingly, and then added (to Jalni's shocked amusement). "Well, at least he's given you some valuable experience and as you don't need your virginity as a Healer, he's done you no lasting harm."

The ancient Sorceress continued calmly.

"I don't know what you young things are about these days, but the Hall owes you a debt of gratitude. Therefore, before you leave I have arranged for your onward travel. My son's Ranger has a pouch for you, in which I have placed certain instructions. Wherever you go, you may call on Selesh for providing a mount, food and shelter if you need it. You also have my pass on which to draw in emergency. Go safely Healer, remember your own Clan and Hall, and remind me to your Sorceress when you meet. May I live to see your return?"

The voice faded, but Jalni suddenly felt tears prick her eyes as she thought of the indomitable spirit she was leaving behind, and bowed her head, whispering, "May I also live to see you once more my Deshun.", and knew her words had been heard.

So it was that as Spring Rites filled the settlement with visitors, both the Sandsinger and his lady departed Selesh in opposite directions to face the future apart.

Chapter 8 - A Succession of Sorcery

There was a buzz running through Selesh two nights later. The Guardians were meeting in the magically shielded Council Chamber, the Sisterhood of Sorcery (with the exception of Adruna) had preceded them into the great Djellim, and even now were congregating around the developing map of their world (which yet unfinished), rested on an enormous table in the centre of the room. Every one of them was pre-occupied, examining the extent of their own Sands, commenting to neighbours about the singular clarity of drawing, the fine execution of borders, scrolls and other elaboration, to the high satisfaction of the one who had called this conclave.

About this gathering, the "Little Sisters of Sorcery" stood ready to act as messengers on behalf of the women they would undoubtedly succeed. These, dressed with care in their Clan colours, waited nervously for their first introduction into the life of rule, watching their home-sand Sorceress avidly.

In the Council Chamber, nods of satisfaction passed between the three Guardians as they studied the gathering discreetly, using one of the attributes of Jocasta's Mirror, which passed from hand to hand as its Guardian smiled grimly.

"Well Shiarjha…" Ikella commented, "I'll admit that I thought you mad when you suggested this, but I agree. There should be nothing hidden from candidates to Sorcery. Learning the control of power is not only fundamental to our continued existence, we have to accept that magic on its own has little value, other than as a method of drawing notice to ourselves. The Gattarene was an example of the extremities to which heretics will go, in order to subjugate those whom we should protect. No, I think you've struck a blow for change my Sister, just look at Nahamida for example. She's just convinced Matandra that not only is she qualified to enter the Sisterhood through command of power, but as she knows the Sands so well, she is competent to talk to Clan leaders with her own degree of expertise. I guarantee you that her confidence will be much improved after this, for which I am more than grateful."

Across the table, ancient eyes smiled at Shiarjha, then the redoubtable Sorceress - Guardian said in the practical manner they knew so well,

"Of course, after I am gone my girl, there's no way that you can accede to the Staff. With all your responsibilities in Guardianship well established, my Sand must pass to Suraya!"

The voice that had ruled the Opal for more Rotations than she cared to think about was level, still liquid with music, still absolute in its finality. A cool breeze seemed to stroke Shiarjha's cheek as she struggled to comprehend what her fellow Guardian was saying. She lifted her head defensively and was stilled by the tender expression on Ikella's face.

"Child", she sighed, "I knew and feared this moment, for from the time that Jocasta sent you to me, I recognised that your path lay in another direction. It is what kept me from welcoming you as I might otherwise have done. Your true path lies in containing and controlling what my Sisters will do when they realise that the Way has nearly come to its natural end."

Her hand, almost diaphanous in its frailty was raised to silence Shiarjha's protest, and then she continued slowly.

"Believe me, I do not yet feel my death upon me, but yet I do not recover as swiftly as that fool Apothecary would like. All of my Sisters walk around me on Drekken shells, and I am sick of all the attempts to bring me ill-disguised curatives for nothing worse than a terminal case of old-age. Time moves ever onward and I do not propose that I should ignore the opportunity Spring Rites afford, so I will say once more, Suraya should become my successor. She was born empowered, came into my hands like the affirmation of continuance itself. I agree that she has battled her demons and has won, not only that fight, but the approbation of this Hall and those who serve the Opal. She is strong in the craft, a fine Healer, yet she is young enough to reach out to those I could never win, the young of this Clan. They already follow her, my own son told me that, so even if she has other struggles to overcome, her nursery mate will protect her and the Sands she must rule."

She sat back in her chair, one hand absently straying to her winged Staff, awaiting her fellow Guardians comments.

Beneva was first.

"She has experienced a long training," she said contemplatively. "I think that has done much to undo what a spoilt childhood might otherwise have produced. She has shown herself to be reliable, more than a quick student and remarkably loyal. She should certainly be considered as having potential."

Ikella shook her head firmly. "That's not good enough Beneva. As Guardian of the Way, I do not seek to harness either of you with more responsibility than it is possible to bear. Suraya will never be Guardian; even I have no power to choose a Guardian once I take my Long Journey. As you both are well aware, that choice has been pre-destined for all time and only the wristlets choose their next bearer."

For a moment each one of them felt (rather than saw) the ephemeral glow of the mysterious silver brands imparted to their wrists by the insignia of their rank, then Shiarjha nodded.

"We will have to strengthen Suraya's training soon anyway. Is it your intention to bring this matter before open Conclave Sister?", and for a moment Ikella frowned.

Eventually she said quietly, "No! It would only raise concerns amongst other-sands. No, this is a matter to put before the Opal, but I felt it only right to address the matter between ourselves first. No, I am only thankful that the One in his wisdom has taken that madcap Olneth a-wandering, and for companionship, he has taken my son."

If she noticed Beneva's eyes widening the Sorceress made no mention and presently the Guardians turned to discussion of other things, however, Shiarjha cornered Beneva a few sectors of the sand-glass later, demanding explanations.

If she was surprised by Beneva's evasiveness, she made no comment, but when she heard that alongside Daro and Olneth, her fellow Guardian had missed the strange artefact brought in by the Spy only a ninenight or two ago, her eyes narrowed.

"Well, I hope that if there's magic afoot, that young man shields himself effectively." she said, then added quickly,

"I wonder if Jalni's with them. I looked for her when Tirjella arrived, but she wasn't in the Eyrie."

Beneva spoke softly,

"Sssh. Don't say anything Shiarjha, but I rather think that Daro and Jalni have exhausted their relationship. He doesn't want to settle down and she's finding the hard part of catching a Sandsinger, is holding on to him. If my studies tell me true, theirs was a love that could never work. She's left Selesh my dear; I think going back to the Azure with her Ranger friends will be better than staying here with Daro. His path is so uncertain, his task still unknown and Jalni needs more than he can provide."

The younger woman shook her head despairingly.

"I had hoped she would settle him down and stop him fretting over his lost sight." she murmured. "Does Ikella know? She'll be disappointed."

For a long moment Beneva considered telling Shiarjha about Jalni's pregnancy, but remembering the girl's insistence that she told no-one, she simply grimaced and turned towards the Djellim and her own quarters, saying softly,

"I don't think she knows, but it's difficult to tell. Daro is such a source of anxiety to her; I tend to keep off that subject. At least we've managed to send him away before we summon the Sands tomorrow. He's determined to know more before we break silence on the subject of Sandsingers. I suspect he wants to establish how long it will be before others of his status emerge, and when we last spoke he said that he was searching for ancient Seguidor. He has his own it seems, and one other, but there are seven more to collect."

She paused, aware that Beneva was indulging in a fit of giggles.

"Well then, perhaps one fine day that boy will try trusting others with his endeavours. ", the Guardian of Knowledge spluttered,

"Who has the keeping of most of the regalia pertinent to our ancestors?", and Shiarjha grinned,

"All of them?", but Beneva shook her head. "Not all, but a fair few I think. The rest of course may be in Tirjhinar ..." she paused, frowning.

"Do you think that's where they've gone? Olneth and Daro I mean?", and the two women eyed each other cautiously, not daring to speculate further.

Meanwhile, the object of their concern was en route to re-join Olneth, who camped halfway between Selesh and the turn to the western Fringes. Arousing no interest from fellow travellers, he selected an area shaded by a modest outcrop of bronzed rock, tethered his Zeglur, and prepared to wait at the point where most chose to take the central paths across the Opal, in preference to the old main route to the forbidden Sybillsce homesands.

He squatted on his heels in the lee of a rocky outcrop, which gave him blessed shade from the blazing orb that was Seleus, and watched the thin trickle of smoke rise from his campfire. Long ago, he had been taught the trick of focussing the rays through glass onto dried plant matter to start a fire. Now he was pre-occupied, not only by his trailstop meal, but also with the enquiry that he had been asked to conduct. Too many times of late, Sybillsce refugees had been found dead. From simple traders, to exiled members of the Clan Council, at least seven had died under mysterious circumstances and Olneth glowered as he suddenly realised that he could account for one more.

His mind had flashed back along the trail to Aramand's Peak and the lonely traveller he had found on the night he had uncovered that peculiar cloak that so fascinated his young master. He shifted, groaning as his knees cracked, then fed the fire with some thickened grassroots, stifling back a cough as an unexpected draught blew the pungent smoke in his face. His eyes watered, then the wind dropped and the fire steadied, allowing Olneth to pull out his provisioning sack. He set a new pan (blackened by the forge Master to prevent reflection), on flat stones in the centre of the fire-pit, pouring enough water from his flask to brew his evening drink.

"There," he told himself with more than a touch of satisfaction, "The water will heat steadily, my dish will sit on top of that, and my meal will be cooked by nightfall. All I have to do, is to add stemmis leaves and the job is done."

He leant back against rock, stretched his long legs until his muscles relaxed, and settled down to think.

The first incident occurred just south of Quinnox (a Greeeyn city on the central Highland belt that enclosed the western border of the Opal Sands. At first, nobody had thought it suspicious that a Sybillsce Clan leader had died along with his family, when the cart he had been driving was buried in a landslide. Master Doloran (now Guild Glass Master) had reported the deaths to Ikella almost a Rotation ago, after other travellers had come across the evidence. It was initially assumed that this was just a tragic accident, then a crop of incidents had been reported across the Sands of the New Union. Without fail the victims were Sybillsce, refugees like himself, often those who had succeeded in settling best outside their homesands when the borders were closed.

Olneth sat forward, noting the bloom of bubbles in the water he was heating, and set a blackened dish to rest snugly within the pan, supported by a thin rim hammered about a third of the way down the inside. He cursed as his thumb came into contact with the hot metal, but soon, he was able to drop ingredients into the dish, adding a little water now and again as his stew heated slowly.

He considered other cases coldly and clinically, listing common attributes, discarding gossip until all seven cases were laid bare in his mind's eye. He enumerated them slowly; a trader who had mysteriously sickened, dying in agony far from home in the care of Tirjella's Healers; the case of twin brothers who had become lost just outside a highly populated area of the Onyx Sands. They had died of dehydration in the desert, despite that both knew the area well and had full flasks (totally untouched) on their belts when found.

He sat like some carved bronze figurine, the long shadows of evening gradually creeping from his small rocky enclosure to mask him from casual view, and continued his grim task thoughtfully. From the Tourmaline Sands (he recalled), a report of a young Sybillsce Healer becoming allergic to a common medication, followed by another case from the Malachite Sands. There, an aged Apothecary had attempted to treat a Sybillsce star-gazer who had been brutally beaten and thrown down outside the old Palace stables.

The latest report was rather closer to home, and Olneth's eyes narrowed as he considered the facts. A married couple, having decided to travel separately had parted in Caranchar. This Highland city, once reduced to little more than ruins in his youth, was now a central marketplace for all the wares of the Opal, so it was not unusual for traders to travel backward and forward between workplace and market, together or separately as their lives demanded. In this case, the trade was in herbs and remedies produced in the north of the Opal, and Sybeera, (the wife) who was an old friend of Ikella's had brought rare lasrin oil into the Healer Hall as she passed en route to their growing grounds. She had arrived sick, only six sectors after parting with her husband and had died within a day of arrival. Shock and distress had given way to anger and suspicion when, the herbalist's husband had also been found beaten to death his body hidden on their growing ground along the Fringes north of Selesh.

They had counted that as two incidents, and as Olneth started to stir his evening meal, he wondered bleakly if he knew of an eighth. He hunkered down by his fire as the shadows lengthened and shivered, superstition whispering in his ears.

"Only one more incident like these makes nine…and I shan't be looking in any mirror soon, in case I see the next victim's face", he thought, settling down to wait for his Lord patiently.

It didn't take long. After a series of sullen thunder rolls, the Master Spy became aware of the Sands reverberating to the pace of a rider approaching at speed. He rose, removing a sand rooted ball of grassroots and letting the air freshen his fire. Under the shelter of the rocks he'd picked, he knew that would only give a hint of occupation, but it was enough for him to loosen his dagger, mindful of the fact that the approaching rider might not be Daro.

He needn't have worried. The steady drumming of hooves changed to a trot, then he saw the sands at his feet glisten, flush and glimmer ahead of a glowing aura. The blind mage was grinning, apparently impressed with his own abilities, he brought the animal to a quivering halt, then slid from its back as the opalescence faded completely away. Olneth eyed him sourly.

"I hope that glow of yours protects my Zeglur Lord?" he said firmly, "I should hate to answer for your intrepid adventuring when your Songfather specifically forbade night-time excursions. I only own half the herd and if I let you ruin precious breeding lines, that half will be forfeit to Carolus under our business arrangement."

Daro made a rude gesture, at which his spy blinked, but hardened his heart, sternly telling his Lord,

"That's all very well Ichspeller Selunsanni, but Sandsinger though you are, I would sooner be a thousand Sands away, or on the other side of that barrier than face Carolus with a wounded beast!"

He watched as the young mage shrugged, then squatted to make stemmis as the Lord of the Opal ran suddenly anxious hands over his beast enquiringly. The animal snickered, tossing its mane contemptuously as the mage checked its legs carefully.

"Legs cool, breathing steady, just a little sweat from the exercise Olneth", he protested, "I took him round the High Pastures cloaked in my aura before I ventured out onto the Sands", he pacified, as Olneth relented.

"I know nothing of magic Lord," he said uncomfortably, "but think boy, think of how not knowing about something has already nearly killed you once! I remember the Drekken Claw even if you don't and I saw what that did to your Songfather. Tell him that his Sandsinger came to grief falling at high speed from the star of our breeding stock, then tell him I was forced to cut the animal's throat with my old dagger to release it from pain, then tell me I'm welcome in the Opal."

Daro stared at his spy, hearing the tension in his voice, regretting the impulse that had prompted him to quicken his mount's paces. He straightened, facing his spy and deliberately "tuned in", listening to Soloria's last Captain of Guards most private thoughts. He watched the man who stirred a pot over the fire unsmilingly, and noted the unusual gravity in the man's dark eyes.

"The One protect this young fool!", he was thinking in a disgusted tone of voice. "Carolus will certainly remove his Clan braid if he continues like this, and then how will we save my Sands from the Gattarene and her predations?"

The spy, unaware of Daro's "eavesdropping " grated a little porrisroot for sweetening, then thought sadly, "o, if only I had one such as this for a son, I could cuff his silly ears and make him muck out stables for half a Rotation in payment for such folly! However would I tell Ikella that I killed the hope of the world by letting him borrow the first Zeglurtun that Master Carolus ever bred? Why ever did I listen to Shiarjha? He'd have been safe in Selesh!"

If he still had his sight, Olneth's drooping shoulders would have told Daro that he harboured grave concerns about his ability to advise his headstrong companion, but overhearing such dismal thoughts filled the Sandsinger with shame. He stood silently as his retainer approached, and said awkwardly,

"I'm sorry Olneth, I didn't consider for a moment the dangers of the night-time Sands, or of your obligations to the Clan and my family. I'm too ignorant of our duties I know, too ignorant of cultural diversity, but if I can't go out without a minder, how in the One's name am I to learn? There's nobody to teach me, no books to learn from. That's why I have to fight free from everyone advising me how to proceed."

He watched as Olneth placed his drink and a meal down, then sat, spoon in hand while Olneth cut the bread with his dagger.

"See what I mean? I must always have a body servant to help me dress, cut up my food, or wipe my arse."

The tone of deep disgust brought a chuckle from his companion, who greeted this information with derision.

"Lord, I thought you were a Sandsinger! If I had a tenth of the powers you seem to have, I'd deal with those problems magically."

He leant forward, digging his dagger into the sand to clean it, then returning it to its sheath he said quietly,

"I'll bet you haven't even tried that, have you?", and Daro was immediately reminded of a day when chests had opened for him, clothes had slid from their hangers and buttons had fastened themselves. He shook his head mutely, and Olneth laughed, taking a whetstone from his pouch and attending to his dagger.

Having forced his meal down, Daro sat miserably at first, listening to his spy's activities. He heard the 'ker-slap-thunk' as Olneth's blade (suffused with shades of amethyst fire) spun from hand to hand as he worked the blade down the whetstone. The prickle of power (manifesting itself in subdued flashes of colour) continued, but oblivious to magical signatures, Olneth worked on, unaware of his Lord's wakening interest.

He was grumbling softly to himself.

"Poor old thing now aren't you?", he asked the dagger and to Daro's ears it sang back to him, a thin, weak tome, but it was there…the sound of magic, old magic.

"Yes," said the Lord of the Opal, and the dagger flew across the two spans between the men, straight to Daro's hand, thrilling to his touch as he cloaked himself in his aura.

Olneth started, seeing a flush of violet infiltrate the Opal screen flickering around his Lord. He shook his head bemused and as he did so, a thread of sound escaped from the area that Daro had protected. The spy sat back, head on one side and listened carefully, remembering from a long time ago, a woman's voice singing softly.

He stared down at his feet, not noticing as the mage strode forward, until he too was surrounded by a glimmering shield, as his Lord commanded his attention. He could hear voices, just below the level of true hearing, a throng of voices seemed to surround both of them, as though they walked through some market place. Occasionally a voice came to the surface, a few words made sense, and then disappeared again. It was very disconcerting, and then there was music.

Low throbbing insistent chords, played with supreme skill on some instrument other than those the spy was familiar with. They rippled throatily, soft strumming in the background, as the rhythm built to a crescendo, then died away to a soft sobbing note that seemed to question the Sandsinger, who stood staring down at his companion's old dagger.

Olneth stirred, whispering softly.

"Part of me feels that I need to follow a trail to where that music is playing, yet part of me rejects that idea. My child would be a woman herself if she lived and I, (coward as I am) feared to track her too closely in case I bring down the wrath of the heretic on my family. I don't even know where to start looking Lord, so I stopped looking to avoid the pain it caused me. Without Carolus and his care I would have been a madman by now." His voice trailed off uncertainly as Daro fussed with the hilt of the dagger, pressing his fingers lightly in the rhythm of the cascading notes.

He watched as a film of Opal filled the mage's eye sockets, then threw up an arm, protecting his own sight against a wild flare of brilliant light. He sat frozen with terror as swirls of colour shot from Daro's hand, and then there was a soft "snick".

"Aah…" Said the mage with a sigh of satisfaction, holding out his hand in which a circle of silver bound crystal surrounded the deepest Amethyst he had ever seen. Olneth stared, fascinated, as Daro threw back his head and laughed, his aura dissipating as their campsite reverted to normal once more. Staring at his dagger in bewilderment, Olneth saw that the silver mount on the hilt of his dagger was missing, and the tang was exposed. He sighed, knowing that his dagger needed replacing anyway, and turned to see his companion placing the jewel in his scrip.

"I suppose I shall have to replace your old blade with a new one Olneth?" Daro exclaimed, "But where did the original come from?"

Olneth stood and assisted the young mage to sit, while he reheated their drinks, then he said easily,

"Oh, Lady Soloria was very kind to us when she knew my wife was pregnant. She gave me my old dagger, and my wife had quite an elaborate hair comb, both jewelled and bound in silver. She was so pleased that we liked our gifts, that she urged us to keep them with us always in remembrance of her."

Daro chuckled,

"O yes indeed she would!" he exclaimed fingering the strange little jewel he had removed from the hilt of Olneth's dagger. He turned a thoughtful glance on his lieutenant, then said deliberately,

"Were you not given instructions for these gifts my friend? Perhaps she suggested that you bring the comb and dagger to Ikella if anything was to happen to her?"

Olneth sighed.

"No Lord, she only said that I should pass them on to my children or my children's children one day, but I know that my wife bore a girl child. Of what use is a dagger to a woman, who would not be allowed to wear it on her belt?"

"No use at all!" said his Master settling down on one elbow, "but although I know what this is, it doesn't tell me where the other parts of it are, nor does it tell me how to find them."

Olneth spoke across the feeble flicker of the banked fire. "I don't think I like magic much Daro, I would have thought it might explain itself a bit more, it must be like wandering round the desert in the dark!"

Daro's lips quirked in a grim smile, then he yawned.

"That's why I'm blind Olneth!" he said suddenly. "Blind people are good at working things out. I know that if I got lost in a maze, a blind companion might do more to get us to safety because they pick up on clues sighted folk can't see. The world of magic is a hidden world and it takes someone who can interpret all the clues to unravel its mysteries."

It was a profound realisation, and Daro ought to have been very excited by his discovery, however, he was tired, dog tired, so warmed by the gentle heat of the fire, the Lord of the Opal slept, the Seguidor of the Amethyst Sands clutched loosely in one hand.

Chapter 10 - Sand Song

As usual, Daro woke with the first ray of Seleus when the crystals in the sand roused. In the near dark before dawn, his eyes opened, aching for the sight of the caramel coloured rock Opal that surrounded them, but as usual there was nothing as he sat up, re-orientating himself. He brushed sleep-tousled hair from his forehead, nostrils flaring as he scented the morning breeze. Then, before he was crushed by his yearning for the sight of the dazzling Sands, he forced himself to suppress his daily groan of dismay, remembering the strange conversation of the night before.

"Was that true?" he asked himself silently, even as the tingling roar of the Sands began. Struggling to his knees, he knelt upright, one hand extended toward sunrise, his strange eyes closed in prayer.

When Olneth awoke, Daro was quiet, withdrawn and a little wistful as he waited for the spy to fan their small fire into life. Olneth remained silent, observing his companion discreetly as they made a simple breakfast, then prepared to rejoin the trail south-west. He recalled the Sandsinger's words perfectly, and thought about their evening as he rolled his blankets, unaware that the mage was focussing on his innermost thoughts once more.

"That's why I'm blind Olneth..." Daro had said, and from the long silence afterward, the spy had deduced that this was in fact a revelation that he had been privileged to share. He wondered silently when Jalni would join them and was shocked when a bleak voice said bitterly,

"She's not coming Olneth, she and I have parted trails, as if I needed any reminder how to get things wrong, it seems that I can scratch personal relationships off my list of things to wreck!"

Turning his head fractionally, Olneth could see the Sandsinger sitting cross-legged on the Sands, his blanket draped over his shoulders, cloaking his head in anonymity. At his throat was a simple jewel strung on a thong. It glowed gently, reminding the Sybillsce that beneath the blanket-cloak there was a leather belt supporting an intricate buckle on which was mounted a fabulous Opal clasp, and his eyes narrowed thoughtfully.

"Was that what Daro had meant when he'd commented about "other parts of the jewel he'd retrieved from the hilt of Olneth's old dagger?", the spy couldn't help wondering. Daro's face gave away nothing. Supremely indifferent to the opinions of others, he was calm, relaxed, and almost serene. Then he opened his eyes, great lambent fire Opal eyes, and Olneth's brain whirled as he slid into darkness.

He was walking on brilliant crystals, each one of them fired into life by the glowing figure at his side. Turquoise, flame red, white, green and black, great flares of colour surrounded him as the Sands sang. There were deep harmonics, sparkling fountains of sound and colour, thrilling chords and cascading arpeggios which tingled his skin, stirred his soul, and released emotions that he didn't know existed. He was thralled, swimming in a rising tide of joy, shaken with sobs of the deepest misery, plunged into a nerve jangling, sensation blurring tide in which he must swim or drown. He felt as though he glided one pace, then struggled to stay afloat the next, and so, alternating between despair and ecstasy he floated until he woke to the sound of his Lord's voice.

"Olneth, wake now and tell me you understand what I'm trying to show you. What you hear is Sand song, what you felt was the power of the Source, all else was magic my friend, and that is what I experience every second of the day and night, yet I do not have sight to help me interpret it. Now do you understand how truly different I am?"

He woke, his tongue tasting of ashes, fingers curled painfully into his palms, eyes burning in their sockets. He sat still, letting go of the experience little by little, knowing that he would examine it more carefully when he could concentrate in peace.

Rising, they sought some shade, slaked their thirst on Daro's flask of Opal water, then resumed their journey, Sandsinger to the fore, Olneth riding to the rear, determined to investigate Aramand's Peak and seek the origins of the cloak that Olneth had found. The day crept onward, the Sands warming until Height of Sun made it impossible to continue. Olneth pulled up, took a couple of oddly shaped sticks from an extra-long bag slung on his ungainly steed's flank, then using a blanket contrived a miniature tent under which they sheltered until in the later part of the afternoon, they set out once more.

Daro was nervy; probably more so since he had slept the zenith away, leaving a watchful Olneth to protect both of them. He had dreamed that a voice called him, yet he hadn't heard it… which though odd, made perfect sense somehow. Wondering if he was to meet yet another of his shadowy mentors, he kept silent, without realising that the shadows under his eyes were darkening, telling their own story of tension and unease. On the other hand, Olneth was almost loquacious, telling Daro about the Amethyst Sands he loved…as the journey drifted onward, turning south west as the shadows drew in. Through that twilight Daro thought back along the path he had taken. Wondering why he had resented Jalni calling him back so much, why he was so intent on following Olneth, and what (if anything), he would gain from this experience.

Days before the adventurers slipped out of Selesh, Daro had been very specific with his instructions. As they planned, heads lowered over a reading desk, shadows jumping on the smooth walls of his great-room, the mage had been reminded of Ahnell's last journey, going along much the same track at his behest.

Voice strangely roughened, the Sandsinger said softly,

"Olneth I want no comment being made on our absence, no drift of thought following us, for we go into danger! This time, I need no innocents tracking our path either."

Then as Olneth realised that the vision of another trusted confidante had crossed the Sandsinger's mind, he changed the subject. Without a glance at his Master Spy, Daro continued speculating about their intended destination.

"I rather fancy that Aramand's Peak is named for someone who once lived there, or for some ancient who discovered it. Whichever it turns out to be, the cloak that you brought before Beneva must accompany us. There are signatures in magic that might give me some clue as to its purpose, the Guardians having no knowledge of it."

He had remained enigmatic about the whereabouts of the unsettling artefact and Olneth wisely asked no questions, just placing a large carry-sack next to the saddlebags he was packing, with a significant rattle of its buckles. The blind mage grinned wryly, wondering privately if Olneth would notice when its shape changed once he summoned the cloak to him.

However, that event didn't occur until the plodding Zeglurs had put two days distance between them and their first encampment. Only two sectors of daylight remained, when Olneth (riding to the rear of the Sandsinger) noticed the bag was rounded and full. He shivered, aware that he (the trained observer) had seen nothing, further discomforted by the ironic chuckle that drifted back from his lord.

"I know I'm sneaky, but don't broadcast that so strongly my friend!", Daro's voice said clearly, then the Lord of the Opal kicked his mournful eyed steed on, as they made their way towards the furthest reaches of the Sands.

The next sector of the sand-glass brought them to an intersection with a faint track leading due west. Here, as they left the main trail leading to the Sherrol Pass and the blighted sands beyond, the young mage's head lifted as some alteration in air pressure warned him that they approached one of the dramatic outcrops of rock towering over the palely sparkling Sands.

Olneth saw him stand in his stirrups, then was amazed (and somewhat shocked) as the young mage pursed his lips and let out a peculiarly haunting whistle that bounced and echoed around the rock face towering to their right. For a moment the Sybillsce was convinced that his young lord could see once more, as his face tilted, sightless eyes straining upward, but then Daro's head inclined as though listening, to the faint "pinging" sound that resonated through the sand. The mage scowled, concentrated, and then emitted another whistle, lifting his head to launch the sound skyward. Olneth grunted as he came alongside the Sandsinger's steed and prepared to dismount.

"You'd better hope the Gattarene has no way of observing us Lord.", he commented softly, "or are you perhaps seeking to scare away any who might lay in wait for passing travellers?"

Without waiting for an answer, he slipped the Zeglur's reins over its head, drew its nose-bag over its comical face, then quietly padded to its rear legs and proceeded to hobble it, so that it could not wander. He attended swiftly to Daro's mount, standing still as the blind man slid from its back, patting it as both animals fed contentedly.

Hoisting saddlebags easily enough, Olneth guided Daro to the start of the trail upward, but as they passed between the tan-bark bushes that disguised the ancient path, Daro raised a hand. Both men froze in their tracks, then, an echo of Daro's whistle bounced off the rocks above and sighed into darkness.

Astonished, Olneth shot a quick glance into the night sky as a feather fluttered groundward. Standing a hand's breadth from each other, Olneth saw the gleam of Daro's teeth as he smiled, enigmatic as ever.

"It's safe Olneth," the Sandsinger announced, casually holding out a naked hand from which the unusual lilac blue handfire of magic users glowed.

"I'll light the way, if you lead on!", but Olneth frowned, hesitating until Daro confessed.

"You won't see them until morning my friend, but I summoned others who can be of assistance to adventurers. They have kept the heights here under surveillance for me this past ninenight, during which nothing unusual has occurred. The first cavern homes only Nightlingbys so we have somewhere warm to camp tonight."

He made no other illusion to the "friends" he had summoned, but submitted to Olneth's commands placidly carrying his own bags behind the spy who reconnoitred the path ahead. During their brief shuffling scramble up the faintest of tracks, the blind man produced (from nowhere), a Staff, complete with softly glowing powerstone, which seemed to lead him as surely as sight ever had, behind his lieutenant and into a low cavern and comparative safety.

So it was that the first Sandsinger in a thousand Rotations made his way to the foot of Aramand's Isle, unaware of the looming crises that his visit would provoke.

Chapter 12 - The Dawn of Power

The day dawned fair (but careful of tempting the wrath of the winds) Olneth kept the campfire he contrived, to a meagre handful of flaming shards. It was enough to make a warming sweetdrink for both men, but doused with damp moss before even a morsel of bantbread could be toasted, it drew a scowl from the young mage who shivered as light rose over their unfamiliar surroundings. He had placed a hand on the dull brown cavern wall as Seleus woke the crystalline shafts that permeated the rock Opal walls with an ethereal chorus of power. Conscious that the Sandsinger was communing with his Sands, Olneth contented himself with menial tasks about the camp, returning only when the faint echoes of his nearby homeland ceased to trouble him and dawn was breaking over the Opal desert.

As light grew, Olneth turned his attention on the cavern itself, gathering his impressions with a wry satisfaction that amused his lord.

"Planning on using this on your travels?", the blind man asked slyly, and Olneth grinned.

"Am I that obvious Ichspeller?", he enquired tentatively, but Daro only laughed.

"Probably only to one who knows you well my friend, I could hear the smile in your voice!", and the tall Sybillsce was saddened as he remembered the physical power in the youth that Daro had been, and they both sobered.

The Sandsinger stood abruptly, shook himself out of his cloak and stretched, easing into a routine of exercise that Olneth had never witnessed before. Powerful bronzed limbs moved rhythmically, gliding from set form to set form, gleaming with the glow of health as Daro displayed his prowess. Learned from the Ranger children he had helped to rescue from Scartel, the leaping, twirling, postures were part of a daily routine that he had never forgotten to practise, and as he came to a flushed, chest heaving halt, the young mage had reason to be grateful, for he tingled with regained warmth, ready for action.

Olneth was suitably impressed, recognizing some of the forms of self-defence within the elaborate ritual, and as he observed the mage towelling himself down, he began to see the man who had emerged from the youth Daro had been.

Dark hair (worn unfashionably long) swung heavily onto his shoulders. A serious face perhaps, made all the more so because his eyes were always closed, high cheek-bones above a sensual mouth, edged with a carefully trimmed beard that seemed to merely shadow his face and render it mysterious. The spy swiftly scanned the trail below their base, then cast a glance at his travel companion, who was replacing his discarded tunic over a rippling chest.

"I must move the Zeglurs Lord", he suggested. "They are creatures of habit that must graze. I have arranged to take them round to the travel stop west of here, from which they can be retrieved later, when we return perhaps?"

Daro nodded in tacit agreement, thinking that after all, no-one knew exactly where he was, and that no-one would associate Olneth's travels with his disappearance, should it ever be noticed… then became aware that Olneth was speaking again.

He forced himself to focus.

"If I travel back on foot, I'll get here quicker on my own Lord, but it will still take me one night to return. Will you stay in the cave where I know you are safe? We can explore together after that."

There was finality in the older man's voice, and Daro, (who knew well the voice of command when he heard it), did not demur, after all if he said nothing he could not be accused of lying.

Olneth was standing in the open outside the cavern which faced east, set into an overhang of bronzed Opalstone. A dense cover of strangleroot hung above the entrance like some bushy eyebrow, concealing it from casual view, and so long as the Sandsinger remained in the cavern he would be safe indeed. However, Olneth was well aware that Daro was unlikely to adhere to the route of discretion, having rescued him from many an escapade.

"Don't worry Olneth!", the young mage surprised him by saying rather gruffly, "I have no desire to risk life and limb on my own. I realised I would need to wait for your return, so I brought several items to study in your absence. There is water here, I heard it trickling inside the cave last night. If we find that, and you can leave me with a fire, I can manage very well. Remember, I am used to sand-walking and I have magic with which to defend myself."

Before Height of Sun, all those arrangements were in place. Rations had been divided, Daro had walked the cave and knew its outlines, and Olneth had provided Daro with a latrine, a sleeping area, and a small supply of the desiccated fungi for burning. Surprisingly the Sybillsce found a small seam of firestone, collecting enough to provide a few days warmth before it was time to depart.

They stood on the low promontory outside the cave, as Olneth gathered his saddlebags, but as he hoisted them onto one shoulder he couldn't restrain the natural enquiry.

"I'm a fussy old man now Daro, but you told me that you have friends around. Do you remember? You said they could help adventurers?"

He was stood a little below the mage as Daro raised a hand from which it seemed that force emerged. To Olneth, it appeared that the air in front of his young companion "thickened", a bar of some light glinted in the sun, then a vortex appeared, spinning silently from the palm of the mages hand.

The spy gulped, then as the mage indicated, he looked up to where two giant snow ravens twirled, circling overhead plumage glistening in the rays of the sun high above them. Daro's soft chuckle reminded Olneth to close his mouth, which was hanging open in shock, then he understood. A man who could summon the legendary Cuirax from thin air needed no nursemaiding, and so content with his appointed task, the spy turned and made his way down to the Zeglurs, coaxing them westward, leaving Daro quite alone.

The Sandsinger sat on his blanket, his back resting comfortably against the wall, and pulled his saddlebags towards him. He fumbled at one of the catches, cursed under his breath, then (grinning to himself) flicked a finger and thumb together. The catch flew open with a chink of metal, allowing the mage to take (from the depths of the bag) a fine linen wrapping in which two small books were nestled together. He selected one, as easily (as though he could see the ancient bindings) and it fell open beneath his uplifted hand. His head bowed over the fine script as though his sightless eyes could read, he prayed earnestly that his wanderings would find favour with the One and then his eyes opened.

Fire Opal orbs gazed out across the Sands, drawing power while his downturned palm seemed to glow as the characters danced on the page. He sat cross-legged contemplating a list of names cautiously testing his memory of names used within the Clan at that time. He knew his own name to be unique, but could have listed a dozen Ahnell's, Mica's, or Torio's. However, he had never heard of another Aramand, Darius, or Loran and considered that although it seemed unlikely, he might just have found a list of Sandsinger names, then thought that he had no idea if these were the names of Sandsingers past, or those yet to come. He shook his head as he realised that he didn't even know if the prodigious list of names referred to the Singers of all Sands or just his own and caught himself chuckling. For the One's sake he didn't even know the gender of the names he held in his mind, then caught himself wondering if there had ever been a female Singer of the Opal Sands. There was just so much he didn't know.

He sighed, wondering idly how so much information could be packed in so tiny a space as he carefully wrapped the Book of Rule away with its companion. He had not attempted to read the other small book, and considered that his own might take him a lifetime to complete. He stood stiffly, stretching and yawning as he stepped cautiously around the perimeter of the small cavern to the latrine that Olneth had dug for his use.

Relieved, he carefully returned to the shadow of the cavern and prepared to sleep through Height of Sun where he had been studying. So passed Daro's first day alone; alternately sleeping and reading until the shadows lengthened and the chill of approaching night made his teeth chatter. He lit the fire left by his spy, using his skill in magic to ignite the snarflin chips and control the wisp of rising smoke. He decided to try adding to the meagre stock of kindling by reciting Ikella's own duplication spell, but he failed miserably. He carefully filled his pan. A handful of dried stemmis leaves, three mugs filled to the brim with water from the spring he'd detected, and a scraping of porrisroot for sweetening provided much needed warmth, however, the task seemed to take forever and he was thoroughly disgusted by his inability to pour cleanly from one vessel into another. He smiled as he sucked a small burn on his hand, and wondered what he should eat. He'd decided to keep his small stock of cheese for tomorrow, didn't particularly want to try cutting the small loaf of bantbread, and was yearning for some sweetened milta grain topped with dried fruit, when he felt his bowl tilt under the weight of food, and a glorious aroma filled the air. He sniffed, lifted the bowl, and had to stifle his chuckles as he realised the significance of the moment. He'd actually managed to supply himself with a meal by some sort of natural magic! He ate hungrily, savouring the rich, full flavour of the milk soaked grain, then realised that he'd also topped it with honey-cream, a sugary delicacy that he'd hardly eaten since childhood. He carefully used a hand to elevate the pan containing his sweetdrink and thought of his mug filling slowly, and heard the liquid pour. Ignoring the pain of a burnt lip, he wished it hotter, then curled into the furs that had silently appeared on his bed. He tucked the carry-sack with its precious contents under his head as a pillow, and resting his arm on the saddlebags he slept and dreamed of a high peak and somehow, flying.

The following day was cool and Daro thinking that Olneth would return early, decided to explore. He put himself through a punishing routine of exercise while the cavern mysteriously cleaned itself, and then, having warded the small cave against unexpected visitors, Daro summoned the Cuirax and his Staff, lifted the carrisack, slung it over his back and began the treacherous ascent. He knew the risks and fought to minimise them, taking extra care to swing the Staff in a wide sweep ahead of him, making a mental map as he went. It was torturous. Every step he took, he braced himself for a fall, proceeding in small sections, emitting the piercing whistle that conjured up the mind-map that he'd used so successfully during his journey to Scartel. He could picture a small straggling village strung along the edge of the towering cliff as he made his way up the steep incline, but where he imagined the path should widen out for the next part of the ascent, the fluting calls of the Cuirax changed to agitated shrieks as he neared the precipice that had nearly claimed Olneth's life.

He stopped abruptly, checked the ground about him for solidity, then sat, poised above the rift and considered his options. He had planned to see if any habitation survived on the Peak. However, his path was frustrated by this enormous precipice, so, knowing that the chances were that any remnant of a building, Temple or even cavern dwelling, lay at the foot, buried under the spoil, he thought about the cloak instead.

Supposing that it might have belonged to an ancient mage, he started to wonder just how old it really was. There was no clue to be found on its surface, he knew, and as if it heard what he thought, the carrisack shifted under His hand. He wondered what upheaval had created the rift where he sat, even considered the possibility that the mage might have perished wearing it, for but some reason, Daro still couldn't approach the thought of Cataclysm.

"Surely nothing could have survived here that long?", his treacherous mind whispered, and reason argued his defence.

"We have a dry climate. If no-one and nothing animal survived here, anything might have lain buried for years without degrading."

The next thought surfaced.

"But surely the winds would have disturbed it?", and again his reason argued back.

"The weave is a technique unknown in our time. Though damaged, the Guardians agree that the cloak has a residue of power about it, however, they cannot trace the origin and have been reluctant to examine it. I must either find its locus of power, or consign it back to where it came from."

He had already privately decided that the best place for the cloak might be in the vastness of the rift where it could do no harm, but a whisper at the back of his mind said firmly, "Nor could it be of use to you Sandsinger!", and in that thought the die was cast.

He never remembered removing the cloak from the bag, it just settled about him, meshing its magic with his, as he realised his power for the first time.

He was the Opal. His power blazed forth in a throat catching, dizzying flare that enveloped him totally. Where strong bronzed limbs had been, he glowed jewel-like, opalescent in the morning sun. Something surged against his lips, tickling the back of his throat, filling his body with an awareness of infallibility, then his mind recoiled as the enormity of understanding washed over him like rolling thunder.

"There's nothing I can't do", he breathed, "Nothing that can stand against me, change me or force my direction."

So shocking was this revelation that his body wobbled uncertainly, and he shrank back against a rail that teetered on the edge where he sat. Involuntarily he clung to it, not noticing that under his hand it straightened, grew solid as it silently extended along the heights reforming as a barrier to those who might pass this way.

"If I am impervious to injury," thought the Sandsinger, "I might be able to cross this crevasse, although I can't see how. He grinned as realisation dawned, then his face grew bitter as he added savagely, "In fact, I can't "see" any sand-blasted thing at all. I wonder if that will limit what I can achieve forever?"

He folded his legs under him, and rested, contemplating the enormity of this question, thinking,

"If only I could ask someone any of this", totally unaware that he sat enfolded in a cocoon of blazing Opalwear as the cloak spread its influence about him.

He was still sat, a chillingly remote expression on his face, when Olneth returned. The spy had made good time, having set out at dawn, back-tracking his path along the massif from the crossing where he had left the Zeglurs at the trail stop. He had checked the cavern, dismayed to find his charge absent, and the cave warded. He had climbed up the steepening trail at a reckless canter, determined to find his Lord (if only to chew his ears off), and had been frozen into silence by the icy stare that calling Daro had provoked.

The Sandsinger's eyes were open, his face a mask of anguish as he sat, staring sightlessly towards the eastern horizon. One hand held on the rail that newly fenced the edge of the precipice, the other was buried in the soil, as if the young mage had sought to find out where the cloak had been buried and still he sat, as if carved in living Opalstone, immoveable, inscrutable, alone.

Olneth left him bathed in the light of Seleus approaching Height of Sun, taking shelter in a cleft beside their cave and slept. High above him, Daro dreamt of a Voice which tugged at his very soul.

"Remember…" it whispered softly in his ear, "Remember my voice, and my memories will always be here for you…" and a long sigh swept the desert below.

Unable to protect his fragile human soul from the power that enveloped him, he was swept by a torrent of longing,. Tears started, searing his eyes and scalding his cheeks as he grieved for a world he had never known. The Voice, deep and melodic drowned his own emotions, searing him to the heart with a pain that was almost physical in its intensity, yet the music filled him with deep and certain joy, for he was listening to a Sandsinger, caught in the thrall of ancient magic, and with that knowledge came a flood of insights that he had somehow missed in his short span of life. The life that he had wished on himself, he suddenly understood, the life of a Sandsinger.

As the words of the song framed themselves on his own lips, phrases seemed to turn tiny keys in his mind, clues that had been there, but from which he had shied like some nervous boy, reluctant to face the reality of manhood.

"Remember us, we'll always be here, We live forever…", the sobbing ululation of a mourning woman entangled itself as the husky tenor strengthened, then Daro himself was in magic and the world as he knew it, faded and slid away in a rush of brilliant colour.

As an unfamiliar panorama re-assembled itself around him, he was gazing out across a great expanse of water, from which green forested peaks thrust themselves skyward. Not far away, a great cloud of fly-bys erupted chirruping as they swooped and swirled around a distant cloud that even as he watched was resolving itself into the most fantastic creature Daro had ever seen.

It hung in the air, advancing swiftly with each down beat of enormous wings, its great scaled head lifted proudly, where perched high on its neck was a saddle, in which a figure sat, robes streaming in the wind. Around the enormous beast and its rider, the flock of fly-bys chattered fearlessly and Daro marvelled as the play of light reflected from its scaly hide. Almost metallic, its myriad scales caught the light of a spring dawn, enhancing the opalescent figure that sat comfortably in the great saddle as they floated lazily to land.

Daro stared incredulously, as the beast back-winged, strong legs extending clawed feet which the creature used to grasp a rocky ledge, where its rider dismounted.

"Drekken", said the Sandsinger's mind, acknowledging the reality of what he saw, as the fabulous creature leapt skyward, disappearing into the clouds. Then with that thought everything changed, the sky darkened, thunder rolled, fire erupted from the ground at his feet, and the water seemed to boil. Steam rose, bringing with it noxious smells, as though he smelt the deaths of a thousand creatures on the wind. Now he saw the Drekken again, this time listing as it struggled to fly with a badly damaged wing. It was bleeding, crying out with bellows of pain and fury, then came an ear-splitting roar and fire seared its remaining wing.

From overhead a massive shadow cut off the light of Seleus, then, as the young mage's dreamscape extended, he saw that the shadow was in fact a gathering of black Drekkens. They had blood-drenched scales, teeth and claws, red lights glittered in malicious eyes and flame leapt from their savage mouths as they screamed into battle with the sole silver Drekken in sight.

The battle was so unequal that the poor beast had no chance. However, it paused in flight long enough to set down its plainly injured passenger, before leaping skyward with a snarl of defiance. The man tottered, summoned a Staff, and threw his arms to the skies where his wounded beast was even then flaming, skin seared and twisting as it fell out of the skies into the waters below.

Then the very world erupted in flame. The ground shook, the air thickened and shimmered in the heat that was boiling the water away.

In the depths of this vision, the blind Sandsinger screamed and clung on to the rough sparse grass as the rift opened up below him, swallowing the village and all who had lived on Aramand's Isle. The sky turned blood-red as the water withdrew, leaving only the sea floor and the dead, marooned creatures there, including many of the Drekkens who had done combat in the skies above Aramand's Peak.

It was there that Olneth found his young Lord, deeply unconscious. Wrapped in the cloak he had purloined from the Djellim deep within Selesh, his hands torn and bleeding where he had tried to dig them into the bare rock opal itself, he lay like one dead. Only his even breathing told the spy that outwardly he bore only minor injury, but he muttered in his sleep and his anguish showed in his face.

Staring down at him, the Sybillsce refugee spoke roughly.

"Whatever have you gotten yourself into now boy?" he demanded gruffly, then, pulling his own blanket out of a backpack, he threw it over the Sandsinger, excluding all light from the cloak, then (before he lost the courage to attempt a rescue, bent, and slung the unconscious man over his shoulder. For one horrible moment the spy teetered on the edge of the rift, then he grabbed the new rail, and keeping Daro's inert form balanced, slowly made his way back to the cavern. Mercifully, it had unwarded itself when Daro had passed out, so Olneth did everything he could for his difficult charge, even unlinking the catch of the cloak, eyes averted, hands trembling as he pressed the catch together through the old woollen blanket, fearful of touching the magical thing himself.

He lifted the mage clear, rolled him into his own blankets and fed the fire through the night, until a mournful howl announced the arrival of help.

PART TWO – SEERS AND SANDSINGERS

Chapter 14 - The Forge of Truth

After Spring Rites passed uneventfully and their visitors dispersed, the Guardians gathered in the Council Chamber at Selesh. The two older women pored over scrolls heaped onto the great table in the centre, while the youngest sat at a separate desk, making notations on a heap of sand tablets. She thoughtfully bit the end of her, enscrasure frowning then sighed as she failed to get her thoughts in order.

Recalling the reaction of the Sisterhood to Ikella's choice of successor, she considered things had passed off very well. There had been no dissent, even the senior members of the formidable Sisterhood of Sorcery recognizing Suraya's rights willingly. Smiling as she wondered how the Lord of the Opal would react to this change in the Way, she looked up to find that Ikella was gazing at her searchingly.

"Daro would do well to recognise the female path to power with less than his customary cynicism! ", the Sorceress said, apropos of nothing in particular, but Shiarjha blushed, knowing full well the unsettling effect of Ikella's uncanny perceptiveness.

She regarded the Guardian of the Way steadily.

"*Can* he object my Deshun?" she asked respectfully and with a glance at Beneva, Ikella said shortly,

"I'm sure he can, but less sure that he will."

The aging Sorceress sighed, and then continued rolling scrolls as she spoke.

"He knows that he is better off with three Guardians protecting the Sisterhood. He also knows that you have been my Elect for long enough to guide Suraya in my stead. Thankfully, they have exorcised their childhood demons and he accepted her right to my Staff long ago. The only trouble we might have had, departed with the Rangers at Sunfall taking Chrysim and that mystcat with her. May the One protect her path!"

For a moment her expression softened, then she continued briskly.

"That animal has been causing mayhem amongst the villagers stock, sitting out at Emblem Rock and yowling the night away."

The other women smiled at the thought of the panther-like creature crying for Daro, but Ikella said firmly,

"It's better he goes back to find a mate and rear some kitts, not hang around here frightening the villagers. He'll come back to Ichspeller Selunsanni's call."

Mouth twitching with suppressed laughter, Beneva busied herself over the scroll she had brought before this gathering. Peering at the ancient script she hazarded a guess.

"I suspect this script is shielded, or damaged by age, it appears to mention a place known as the Forge of Truth, which I have found no other reference to in the whole Djellim! Perhaps this place no longer exists. It could have been abandoned, renamed, or sent into oblivion during Cataclysm. The One forbid it lies in the province of the Gattarene, but I have certainly never heard of it, and it may be crucial in our search for the Tapestry of Tten. I just don't know if I'm reading this correctly.", she paused, passing a weary hand over her eyes as the Summoning Bell sounded sonorously through the great Library outside the Council Chamber.

"I'll get this packed away.", she said slowly, raising her hand towards the chest at the side of the room. Around her wrist a silver torc blazed against her skin, and the parchments on the table glittered in response.

"Vantera", said the Guardian of Knowledge, and the scrolls filed themselves away into the Sanctuary Chest. The pile of sand-tablets shimmered and vanished with a soft tinkling sound, and the great map that Shiarjha had been working on earlier, appeared on the newly emptied table.

"There!" exclaimed the Guardian with pleasure, "All back where they belong my Sisters, now let's about our own business, then supper!"

Ikella regarded her with faint amusement.

"Do you think our visitors left us anything to eat my dear?", she tilted her head, one eyebrow raised sardonically and the party broke up with gurgles of amusement as they warded the precious Council Chamber and went into the Healer Hall chattering.

Far along the rift known as the Great Divide there was an odd shuddering. Not a sandquake, nor anything caused by the soughing of the Winds, but something *other*. There was a low rumbling, a shimmer that one might catch from the corner of an eye, then it was gone and in the distance, across a horizon of rolling Azure Sand, there was a final susurration as the Rangers poured from the Sheer into Holmgarth.

There were cries of welcome, followed by many hands assisting visitors to alight from the backs of Sheerwolves, bewildered guests accepting the friendly guidance of complete strangers to comfortable caverns and welcoming cots. Amazement greeted the last to dismount, as amidst admiring children Chrysim and Echo walked up the short incline together.

At first both Rangers and Mystcat had been doubtful that the enormous Sheerwolves would tolerate the presence of a feline. However, Chrysim seemed so positive that he could persuade Echo to behave, that Draille Skellin permitted the experiment.

The great cat, dwarfed by the Rangers wolves, hugged his companion's side, whiskers twitching. There was enquiry in the rumbling noise the she-wolves made and Draille (watching closely), allowed a wolf to step forward and lower her head towards the cat.

Echo kept very still as the enormous creature sniffed his scent, then he lowered his own head submissively and the encounter was over. Disinterested, the wolf returned to her cubs, as Echo rolled over in the Opalescent sand, wriggling to stop an itch on his back. He sneezed violently, and Chrysim grinned, reaching down to scratch the offending part of the cat's hide. Draille was taxed with explaining to Chrysim that his cat couldn't travel the Sheer, unless he was carried by a Sheer wolf. Here there was an impasse, the cat refusing to enter a cage. Eventually the Ranger decided to sling the hapless creature across his own saddle and secure him there encased in a soft Irix hide bag, much in the way they transported young Dorowen back to the Garth to provide milk for their own children.

The cat was outraged, but Jalni laughed so much at his snarls of protest that eventually Echo settled, arriving (none the worse for wear), in the strangest place he'd ever seen in his young life. They were poised over a giant rift in the sandstone rocks of another Sand. Around them Rangers bustled, women stood in the entrances of small caverns (which to the cat's eyes) appeared to go on forever. The group who had been detached to Selesh, were even now greeting their families and the cat's ears flattened as it took in the number of man-kitts. His tail lashed warningly, as a stranger approached, but the Ranger passed by, seemingly intent on welcoming Jalni (who had travelled with them). Staring, Echo stood still, nostrils flaring, ears twitching wildly, until Jalni took pity on him, reaching into her scrip for a calming chew. She touched the crown of his head gently, forcing her own exultation at being back in her homesands to one side, concentrating all her efforts on calming the mystcat, who, after a moment gave a throaty "Puhrr", accepted the titbit willingly, then followed Chrysim to the single visitors cavern more calmly.

Turning back to greet Garald, the Healer grinned. The Dream Walker's eyes were riveted on the mystcat as Chrysim was shown how to lower the leather curtain for privacy. As some of the younger Rangers set about inducting Daro's protégé to their temporary quarters, Jalni wondered what tale was forming in her friend's mind, even as she watched him, eyes narrowed, lips moving in silent recitation as yet another "dream" was born.

Garald grinned sheepishly at her expression, admitting that the Rangers had dismissed tales of a tame mystcat at Selesh laughingly. He shook his head in wonderment as Jalni explained how the cat had followed her, how Chrysim had become his liege lord's "cat-keeper", and how the creature communicated with her sometimes. He listened avidly, filing away the tale for winter nights, before conducting her to a cavern within the Ranger family area.

She stared at the luxurious furnishings, then said in a small voice,

"Garald! Surely this room is Ichspeller Selunsanni's province? Perhaps you'd better know that I am no longer with him. He has sent me away."

The bitterness in her voice surprised the Dream Walker, who said cautiously,

"Perhaps not permanently?", but Jalni steeled herself to reply earnestly,

"He told me that I should go about my business, leaving him free to go about his. He didn't want me calling him back at inconvenient times. He seemed to be having fun with a troupe of dancing girls when I last spoke with him.", and despite the misery in her voice, her lips twitched with amusement.

Startled, Garald said instantly,

"Well Lady, you know what fools men are!", then added hopefully, "He'll come to his senses one day you know?", but Jalni was wandering the cavern, stroking a soft fur, touching gently the carved semblance of a leaping Storm-horse.

"Do you like it Jalni?", a woman's voice enquired eagerly, then Terris and her children were in the doorway, and the mood of wistful introspection was over.

"When you said you needed somewhere to rest and think, Marran decided to use this area for you, or Daro, or any of the others to come and stay with us. We are only in the next cavern to your left, and that won't be for long. We have to be back in Scartel before this moon wanes."

Jalni stared at her solemnly, she hadn't thought of that when she volunteered to help Sushanna for a while. She'd just assumed that Terris and Marran would be staying here with her. Terris broke the little silence brightly.

"Don't worry. We will be back frequently. We can't expect much of a harvest this Rotation, but we must get the land ready, plan our next plantings and gather what we can from the hills. The men must hunt game, the women must prepare our homes before the settlement can fully re-open. Not all the Children of Scartel have returned yet, but we have a list of would be Zurian settlers already. Lady Tirjella is planning to call on us next Spring Rites and we hope to have a Guardian present as well."

Jalni thought sadly that it was unlikely that the aging Ikella would be able to make the journey, then a niggling idea crossed her mind. If the Guardian of the Way could get here, she would need the support of her son to do so. She would be a mother herself by then, and the One defend her child from his irresponsible father!

Somehow, she kept her face still, somehow she hid the panic from showing, but her heart was hammering. She had to get out of here. She had to leave again. Now!

Terris observed her friend's features still, noticed how Jalni's hands instinctively flew to her belly, and suspected that things were harder for the Healer than she knew. She hid her concerns behind the bright instruction to her children to "run along home now boys", then with a brief hug, left Jalni to her own devices.

The Healer sat on the bed thinking furiously. Where in the Nine Sands could she go without Daro finding her? Why was she so afraid that he would casually wrest his child from her and insist he was raised in the Opal Sands? She settled back against the high mound of pillows, raising her knees to ease the tension in her back, allowing the warmth of the furs to ease the penetrating chill of the Sheer. She sank her head into her hands, twisting long fingers through the strands until she touched the thin Healer braid that denoted her calling, immediately beginning a self-diagnosis as Ikella had instructed her class so many Rotations before. She fancied that she heard the precise tones of the Sorceress once more.

"If any Healer finds themselves doubting their own well-being (either mentally or physically), it is incumbent upon that Healer to check all her symptoms, list them, then have her findings checked at the earliest opportunity.

Under no circumstance may she attempt to heal either herself or another whilst unwell."

She grinned faintly, then listed her symptoms softly.

"Fatigue, morning nausea, odd aches and pains, the loss of the cycles of the moon, loss of appetite, painful breasts, and the odd feeling that I'm being watched all the time."

She recalled her odd fits of temper, attacks of tearfulness, and thought dismally,

"I'm probably irrational due to my condition. I might not have rowed with Daro if I hadn't been pregnant ..."and promptly burst into tears. She was still sobbing when the curtain was swept aside and Sushanna entered quietly.

"Come now Jalni," the Ranger's Apothecary said firmly, "You are tired, emotional, and Garald tells me that Selunsanni has sent you away. What nonsense is that? Terris thinks he's insane, but I suspect you know the reason you left Selesh so willingly, so are you going to tell me?"

While she spoke she had drawn back another curtain on a tiny cooking area. A pan filled with water was stood beside an oil burner and with swift dexterity the Apothecary busied herself, setting a frame over the burner, lifting the pan into place, sprinkling a greyed brown powder onto the warming liquid, and then stirring vigorously. Jalni was so far gone in misery that a familiar aroma wasn't recognised until she took the first sip.

"Deo me!" she exclaimed abruptly, "Why do you give me the Sandsinger's own restorative?", but before Garald's wife could answer her, the curtain was slid back again, and a familiar voice said cheerfully,

"Probably Because I prescribed it, young woman!"

He could have finished his sentence with the comment;

"Along with a tasteless sedative that you won't recognise!", restraining the impulse at the sight of her woebegone face. He took her hand instead, testing pulses as his remedy took effect.

"Oh!" she said sleepily, "I didn't know you were here Carolus." wondering why she felt so lethargic.

The old man turned to Sushanna and raised a finger to his lips.

"Sssh!" he cautioned, "We must let her rest. She's been on an emotional tightrope for ninenights. Once she wakes naturally, I'll see what I can do."

He lit a lamp, setting it where Jalni would see it when she woke, and then half-drew the curtain that led to a compact wash-down and necessary.

They left quietly, slipping from the cavern (to walk along the ledge above Holmgarth simply) the Master with his apprentice at his heels. They were not as discreet as the Ranger who waited a few curtained doors away, and who slid into his chosen position like some flicker in the dark. Draille Skellin sat cross-legged, wrapped in his travel cloak, his patch dyed blues blending with the soft summer night as he kept guard on the only woman he could ever truly love.

Chapter 15 - A Spirit Wandering

Jalni slept so soundly that she was unaware of the flurry of agitation right outside her door in the mid-watch hours of the night. For once, her fingers were relaxed, stilled against her bedclothes as others ran on Healer business. Subdued voices passed her door, but she was sunk in that dreamless kind of sleep that takes the utter weariness of mind and body far away from any sense of recognition.

Whilst Rangers slid into the night-time wilderness of the Azure, she floated in her cocoon of comfort, unheeding of the rippling shiver as her hosts plunged into the Sheer, once more speeding a-wolfback to the encouragement of an ancient call to service. She was still sleeping when they returned, and so didn't see the worried looks flitting across the faces of her friends or hear the cautious tone in the voices of her attendants.

It was late morning before she roused, staggering (sleep-drunk and dehydrated) into the small private necessary, before she really woke. Scarcely had she emerged however, when she became aware that someone had been keeping watch, for she could smell fresh bread, and on investigating the small tray that had silently appeared on the narrow table beside her bed, she discovered a break-day meal fit for a queen.

Her pillows had been banked up, and shivering slightly, she discovered that it was quite pleasurable to climb back into bed, settle herself so that she could reach the pale golden roll, and think only of herself for once.

She felt relaxed, happy not to be forced into putting on appearances when mornings left her lethargic and nauseated, then came to the astonishing realisation that for the first time in ninenights, she was neither. She grinned to herself, hugely cheered at the thought that she had at least passed the first trial of motherhood, then scowled, refusing to give in to the demands of a child she had no intention of rearing. Satisfied that she was at long last rested enough to make decisions about her life, she leant back against her pillows, ate five pieces of the bread roll, lavishly coated with some fruit preserve, drank the milk (which she would have normally refused), and found herself smiling as she recalled Mina's maternity lectures.

"Encourage young mothers to eat wisely, meat for muscle, milk for bone, fruit for clear skin and bright eyes.", the Senior Healer had chanted and as she thought of her erstwhile foster-mother, a tear sprang to Jalni's eyes.

"How much Mina would have loved this!", she thought wistful for her old room in Selesh, but she dashed the tears away mutinously, and refused to let her wandering emotions get the better of her, then

"Time to get up sleepy-head!", a bright voice announced at her door, as Terris arrived, bringing with her a set of clothes.

Jalni stared as she realised that these were the clothes that Daro had provided for Terris herself, once a young pregnant bride.

"Ranger blues," her friend agreed cheerfully, "You'll feel better if you fit in, and you'd better keep these."

The Ranger Apothecary grinned hugely, as Jalni struggled up to try on the gown.

"They are amazing Jalni. Not only did Daro somehow find out about patch-dyeing, he must have "enchanted" them, so that no matter how big you get, they'll still fit. I always felt at my best wearing those, so let's have no nonsense about his having provided them. His own child and you should benefit as well."

Jalni stared at her friend in surprise. There had always been an air of quiet competence about the young Ranger, but since qualifying as a fully-fledged Apothecary, she had become much more confident and more assertive. Jalni (who was fairly forthright herself thought she liked this new Terris all the more for it. She lifted the garments gratefully, and in a moment was staring open-mouthed at the stranger in the mirror opposite her bed.

Her outline shimmered blue, all the shades seeming to shift as she looked at herself critically. Long legs folded under her as she smoothed the top down over the gentle swell of belly, then Terris silently handed her the traditional three-quarter length pants that went with the tunic. They giggled as Jalni pretended to have too big a bump to get the strange leggings on, but once in place, she could feel the oddly elastic material supporting her belly like a gentle pair of hands, and relaxed as her friend tied the waistband carefully.

She refused to admire herself until her boots were laced and her hair brushed and re-plaited, then they both stared bemused by the way Jalni's clothes now seemed to match the disconcerting shade of her eyes.

"Blue!" said the Healer firmly, "Azure Blue," agreed her friend, "Sure is.", said Jalni dryly, then giggled before saying deliberately, "A-Zurias in fact!", before they set about re-threading Jalni's Healer braid with a fine piece of Azure tinted gauze.

They made the bed, removed all traces of food, then left the room to explore Holmgarth and look for old friends, but although she kept an eye out for him, Jalni didn't see Carolus in the Ranger's Garth although she was sure she remembered him being there previously. She dismissed the idea that the Rangers seemed a bit guarded around her, recalling that they had unreservedly accepted Daro's standing, and supposed that they felt a bit awkward giving her even this temporary refuge. What she didn't see was the glances of wonder as she blazed pure Azure fire from sparkling eyes, shimmered all the shades of blue, from turquoise to midnight as she walked innocently through the heart of the old Azure where the Rangers had found refuge after Cataclysm, completely unaware of the startling gleam of her "blues" against theirs.

She found (with delight), that several of the girls she had known as awkward teenagers had matured gracefully and had become part of the Ranger base. Nimah had married a Ranger and seemed determined to set up a school for the children. She listened avidly to Jalni's advice, showing her with glowing pride the cavern that Rigg Skellin (her husband) had prepared for her. She giggled when

Jalni confirmed that she and Daro had been mated, then looked absolutely heart-broken when Jalni told her that they had parted.

"Perhaps your lives will cross again someday." The younger woman had suggested, but at the familiar pucker of Jalni's scowl, she said hurriedly,

"Or perhaps you'll settle for somebody who can be yours entirely and not mixed up with magic?"

She had sighed romantically as she spoke, and Jalni saw (as she turned away) that behind her, a huddle of Rangers was grouped around Draille Skellin. The Healer paused, considering, then she shook her head and continued looking for Asher or Rianna.

So the rest of that first ninenight continued. Sushanna and Terris insisting that she sleep late, nap during Height of Sun, and get to bed early, until with the beginning of the new ninenight, she felt able and willing to offer to help earn her keep. She listened (without resentment) as Sushanna decided that Jalni should not undertake any Healing during her pregnancy. She was a normally healthy active woman, and for a time was absurdly annoyed with her own lassitude. However, she remembered how incredibly ill she had felt when only using the Source to sort herbs.

Her unnatural queasiness had proved the touchstone on which she had made the decision to consult Beneva, whose counsel she valued. The Guardian had said cautiously,

"You will have to be guided by your own body Jalni. This child's father is steeped in magic remember. We have no idea of his powers, he has no one to consult, even I (as the Guardian of Knowledge) am completely in the dark!", and so Jalni had come to recognise that for her child's sake (if not her own), she must remember the things that immediately nauseated her, or made her unwell. As one of those things seemed to be any attempt to harness the Source, she kept her own counsel and settled down to wait for the return of Carolus, hopefully wondering if one of his miraculous potions would suit her.

However, it was to be the Rangers who discovered a method of giving her life some meaning with the opening of Nimah's little school. The young Ranger was not to presume on Draille's tutelage but to select subjects that would widen the education of the Rangerlings in her care. They would measure ingredients for cooking, make decisions on what to plant and when, in addition to reading the girls would learn to count and cook, the boys to read, write and tally to keep records.

Until the little class was settled, Jalni kept well clear, but once she met them trooping along the ridged path out to the hills beyond Holmgarth, she took a chance and asked Nimah brightly, whether she could do with a class assistant. Nimah was delighted with that idea, having recently suffered through having too many children attending, and not enough hands to keep the class occupied, so not long after this, Jalni began to teach the girls how to recognise medicinal plants, then how to gather them and take them to Sushanna.

The days passed, Nimah (now supported by her close friend Motri) showing the girls how to undertake simple mending tasks while Jalni taught the boys how to oil the thread their mothers used to stitch winter clothing. She was thinking that this winter would be very different if she joined Marran and his contingent at Scartel, when she became aware of a most disconcerting event. Her stomach "fluttered", all by itself and unable to restrain her gasp of surprise, her hands flew to her belly, as it happened again.

For a moment she felt quite faint, then Bortran (a lad of about eight Rotations) said gruffly,

"Don't worry Healer, it is only your baby kicking. It won't hurt you, he's just stretching!" She turned so white, he slid a chair under her as he spoke.

Motri looked up knowingly, then chuckled.

"Didn't you expect that Jalni? Even Healers have to go through all the things they've studied once they decide to jump the trave!"

Jalni (mortified and feeling desperately alone), bit her lip, accepting the responsibility of birthing her child alone.

She wended her way back to the guest cavern she occupied and sat, glumly thinking that she would so much have liked to share this moment with Daro, biting back the bitter taste of disappointment as she caught a glimpse of herself in the mirror.

She was in glowing health, her skin peach blossom, her hair glossy and glowing in auburn shades against her shoulders. Her breasts had filled out, the patch-dyed blues swung easily from her body, never getting torn, never getting dirty, a joy to wear at all times. She looked and felt the part, a young woman in early pregnancy, full of life, and yet the bitter taste of ashes was in her mouth and mind.

A swift step outside alerted her to another's presence, then Draille Skellin asked permission to enter. He was smiling cheerfully as Jalni welcomed him, one glance showing her that he brought gifts with him.

He drew back the leather curtaining so that he could be seen clearly from outside, and accepted the low seat that she offered him before revealing his purpose.

"Lady," he began respectfully. "I do not presume to ask questions about why you have come back to your Sands before your Lord's child is born, but rumours say that your paths have parted permanently."

His deep brown eyes showed only gentle sympathy as he said quietly,

"I once hoped your affection could fall on me, but that not being my joy, allow me to protect you as you go through the next phase of your life alone. If I cannot persuade you to take my name, perhaps you will indulge me by appointing me as your Ranger, so that I can honourably stand by your side whatever is to come. I cannot simply stand by and allow you to roam the Garth like some spirit wandering!"

The expectation of a terse rejection was in his face, but Jalni saw only the man who appearing like a shadow out of the night had saved their lives and reunited the Children of Scartel with their Ranger past. She remembered the shock Draille had instilled in them as he materialised out of nowhere, his easy familiar laugh, the crinkling of the skin around his eyes and mouth when he smiled and the deep resonance of his voice. She thought hard, sighing as she said softly.

"Dear Draille, had I not met him, I would be honoured to take your name. Had I no idea of his power, I would still be honoured, no I am honoured by your offer, but I do know him, and he sent me away with the warning that "It's not over until he says it's over".

I would risk my own life, but he knows nothing of his child to be, therefore I cannot risk my child's or your life just to be safe, happy and loved. I hope you understand what I am saying my Ranger. I am no great Lady, though you do me honour by using that term, but I will happily accept your offer of protection while I am here or at Scartel. Ranger Dorenard has his skiel of Rangers to protect, and cannot risk all to help me, and I have a plan for this child, which does not involve a restless, resentful father influencing it. Will you protect me until I can carry out my plan Ranger Skellin?"

To his credit he didn't move or show his disappointment, but a muscle quivered at the edge of his mouth, making Jalni wonder for a second what it would be like to permit his kisses. However, she pushed the thought away brutally, as Draille stood sketching a salute.

"I hear and obey my Lady." He spoke vehemently,

"However, I am advised that it would be unwise for you to travel through the Sheer at this time and that if you hope not to be here at Jentaroth, plans must be put into action soon."

He laid on her bed an elaborately hand carved baby board, swaddling wraps, each one of which had a hand carved bone pin securing them and with a lump in her throat, Jalni realised that the news of her baby's quickening had run through the tight-knit community. She fingered little wraps of hand -made materials, from which she would contrive her baby's first clothing, and could restrain her tears no longer.

Comfortingly Draille laid his hand on her arm, then slipped once more from her cavern, and made his lonely way back to the large one in the range above her own, from which he trained those who would be Rangers.

She went to bed that night troubled by dreams of a figure endlessly searching for her soul-mate, hearing the lament of a lonely wind as it bustled past her door, with a haunting call that sounded in her dreams as though it cried "Remember…", then fled into darkness, love unrequited.

Chapter 16 - An imminent Sand Crossing

The following morning Jalni consulted Sushanna. The Ranger Apothecary was sensitive to her patient's moods and she soon "tuned in" to Jalni's frustration.

"I can see why you want to be anywhere but the place your Lord might stray," she acknowledged gravely, "however, you cannot go galloping off having adventures while you carry his child. Have you thought that his occasional lapses from grace are as much a symptom of his status, as those symptoms of illness? I take it that he had already taken the mantle of the Sands before you met him?"

Her gentle fingers measured the progress of Jalni's pregnancy as she spoke and Jalni was so caught up in the wildly fluttering movements of her baby, that she didn't measure her response with her natural caution.

"Huh! Running around the Sands with a troupe of dancing girls doesn't seem like any illness I've ever encountered!", she exclaimed wrathfully. "I felt as though he was challenging my presence in his life and when I asked him if he still wanted me to be with him, he said that he wanted me to get on with my life and leave him to get on with his!"

She sniffed miserably, a tear sliding down her face, then Sushanna expertly taking Jalni's wrist pulses said firmly,

"Well, he had no freedom as a boy, shut up in Selesh with all those Healers. He hardly came to manhood before offending Deshun Ikella, then as I understand it, he lost his sight. Hardly a recipe for a well-balanced man, then there's all that power to contend with on top of everything else. I'm quite sure that under similar circumstances I might want to run away and put my head in the Sands like merribirds do when seobra's chase them. He's running away from responsibilities too great to contemplate. I dare say, that when you broke the news of impending parentage, he panicked! He'll come round in time my dear, don't you worry."

Jalni said sombrely,

"He doesn't know, I didn't tell him, he was acting so unkindly, so irresponsibly. I just took the opportunity to leave and left. I did tell Beneva, but she is sworn to silence. Only the Rangers know and that was a grave mistake. I should never have involved you with my problems. Now my Lord has a target in his sights if ever he finds out."

Sushanna whistled through pursed lips and presently a girl with straight blue-black hair came in quietly with a tray on which she carried steaming horn mugs containing an aromatic liquor which seemed familiar to Jalni, although for that moment she couldn't place the aroma.

"Shanberry juice.", the Apothecary offered, "It's a little tart, but it has properties which will protect you against winter chill."

Jalni blinked, thinking furiously,

"If my timing is right, I will come to birth before Spring Rites," she muttered, sipping the pungent fluid slowly. "I don't think that's enough time for me to consider having my babe at Scartel. I heard that they won't have a resident

Healer until the village is formally opened, which isn't likely until at least next Zenitheon."

Sushanna nodded, eyeing Jalni askance:

"Won't you consider going back to Selesh my dear? By that time, your Lord might have come to his senses and be missing you badly. Haven't you thought what you are denying your child?", but the hectic flush and mutinous scowl on Jalni's face made further conversation on that point useless, so the Ranger Apothecary left Jalni pulling on her walking boots, saying lightly,

"Never mind me, I only worry that you'll be unhappy with your decision one day Jalni.", her voice was calm, but her face betrayed distress. Jalni stared up at her, then Sushanna said quietly:

"Garald and I lost our firstborn. There were no Healers to help me and I was too long in birth. Our daughter lived only long enough to draw breath the once, then the One took her back. Since then I've never conceived and Garald dreams other dreams, afraid that if I tried again, he might lose me as well. Think long and hard Jalni, we all want your happiness, your child's happiness, even Daro deserves to have some choice in his child's future!", then she was gone, the leather curtain swinging closed as she departed Jalni's sleeping area, then the outer cavern stilled, as Jalni stared after her, saddened by this confidence.

Pulling a lightweight woollen shawl round her shoulders, she left her cavern, moodily swinging down the steps that took her to the Ranger's growing ground, then turning onto the path up to the high land beyond Holmgarth, she began (out of habit) to fill her scrip with leaves and berries from the hedgerow as she walked. She had lost all sense of time when the sound of water running caused her to pause in mid-stride, and she touched her workbelt (now slung over a visible "bump". The baby kicked hard, then Jalni chuckled, realising that she was indeed thirsty.

"I don't need you to tell me I need to drink," she aimed the thought at the baby in disgust, glancing around her for the source of the sound. It was a small spring, trickling from the rocks above, it had been channelled along to a rocky basin around the corner of the path, where she could dip her horn travel cup. She unhitched it from her belt, but first dipped a finger into the ice cold liquid, raised it to her nose and sniffed.

"Test by smell", Ikella's voice sounded clear in her memory, "Test by sight", the Sorceress had instructed, so obedient to the Way, Jalni scooped a handful of water and looked at it critically.

"Clear, no evidence of contamination.", she muttered to herself, and touched the tip of her tongue to the liquid in her palm, and gasped.

"Its outstanding…"

Her hands were shaking with excitement, she'd never tasted anything so refreshing and even the small quantity contained in her palm seemed so pure that it almost evaporated into the sides of her mouth before she had time to swallow. Amazed, she placed her horn mug under the trickle from above, nearly jumping out of her wits when the distinctive tinkle of crystal's filled the air. She withdrew the mug doubtfully, checked that the contents were unchanged, then lifted it to her lips and drank deeply.

Why she wasn't astonished when the voice said,

"That's water to beat anything in the Opal!", she didn't know, but there he was, her faithful shadow, standing less than two spans from her, elevated on a slight terrace above the spring.

Jalni, filling her cup to the brim again, asked absently,

"Draille, have you set yourself the task of making me faint with shock every time you appear from nowhere, or are you trying to impress me with Ranger magic? I don't impress easily you know!", then shading her eyes against a sudden brilliance, turned her head to look up at him.

He was grinning at her amiably, offering a hand to swing her up beside him, as finishing her drink, she carefully shook out the last droplets on a nearby flowering plant, before joining him. He spoke instructively.

"I'm glad you enjoyed your walk and the water. Would you like to know more about the area and its legends? The spring has been there for Rotations, as far as Garald can tell it was part of the original settlement. The first families came hard on the heels of Cataclysm, over mountain passes that no longer exist, and down through a series of valleys that ended north of here, where the mountains burned."

He had somehow steered her onto a narrow track which led away from Holmgarth itself, up and around the area that sheltered the Sheerwolves, and onto a broad sweep planted with grain crops. He pointed out strips of unfamiliar vegetation, naming several medicinal plants that were traded with Selesh, before steering her beyond these growing grounds to an immense grassy depression.

She stared, noting the profusion of basalt rocks jutting from the ground, then spoke hesitantly.

"A fire-pit?", she looked at the area carefully, realising that the area was simply too great to be man-made, visualising how the huge depression would look afire, then her colour faded as a remnant of her strange vision at Jerritol drifted into her memory. A flaming mountain! Scartel, but somehow not Scartel! She moistened suddenly dry lips whispering…

"A caldera? You're insane Draille, only madmen and wizards play with such fire. Are you telling me that the Rangers deliberately settled themselves and their children where a fire mountain might ignite once more? What in the One's name tells you that it will never happen again?"

He was standing still, an enigmatic smile on his face as he said slowly.

"Lady, there will come a time when all your questions can be answered, but that time is not now, nor am I the one to answer those questions. However, our legends say that there are plants that grow near Fire Mountains, some of which only existed in the Southern Sands before cataclysm. We believe that several pain relieving medications which only grow here now, have been saved because Rangers brought seed to a place which remains warm in winter. We have a subtly warmer climate, mineral laden soils, water so pure that it sinks into living tissue or plant cells despite chronic dehydration, isn't that enough to minimise any risk?"

She studied his profile as he spoke, his eyes gleaming with the joy of sharing his heritage, reminded by the constant tattoo of unborn limbs unfurling that here was a man whose depth of vision could help her drive the demons from her door, and yet she could not deny her love for Daro, though she fiercely wished she could.

She thought about her Search vision again, seeing in her mind's eye a connected chain of fires across a mountainous range, the massive cauldron that was Scartel, then she found herself remembering the Azure Tapestry. In the unusual light of Tirjella's Staff various motif's had been thrown into prominence, others virtually obscured. Weaving techniques using double threads had added to this effect, so again her mind raced across that strange two-dimensional depiction of the Northern Azure, until she found what she thought she had seen. Another mountain, wreathed in smoke, far greater than any she had seen so far, but apparently one that was far beyond those in the foreground of the weaving. She bit her lip in frustration. The ancient weavers must have misunderstood the relationship of the mountains because no place that immense existed anywhere on Pelshar that she knew of and certainly not in the Ashgenar as depicted.

Her shoulders drooped, and Draille looked at her with concern. She was tired, her lips trembled with disappointment and he had to swallow the thought that she had been about to say something interesting. However, he had been able to draw her out of her shell for a brief moment, and with that thought the Ranger had to be satisfied, as he carefully brought her down into the settlement once more.

They were going (via a short flight of stone steps) up to the next level of dwellings, when a step set into a corner of the stair caught Jalni's eye. She paused in her ascent, certain that she had never been that way before, then there was a soft "shirrh", as a leather curtain was drawn aside, then Kilda Pagthorn, ritual tattooist of the Rangers was standing there, framed in a doorway that Jalni must have passed without seeing many times. She smiled, but Kilda seemed withdrawn, thoughtful and for some reason Jalni's heart seemed to leap into her breast, beating double time.

Kilda spoke softly,

"Healer Jalni.", she inclined her head sideways, then Jalni realised that she was being invited to join the Decrian as she stepped through the narrow doorway into an extraordinary room.

It was long and narrow yet lofty. One wall featuring the odd window apertures covered with the fine vellum panel's common to both Ranger lofts and the cabins used by the herders of the Southern Azure. The wall opposite, shrouded behind a highly decorative curtain. Following Kilda, Jalni watched as Kilda turned, pulling on a cord mounted on the wall. Silently, the curtains parted, revealing a fresco painted directly onto the rock face.

Jalni gaped. Along the wall was a scene as yet unfinished. Near the floor, life-sized wolves were depicted, lying as if waiting to be called. Facing her (head bowed) kneeling on one knee was a Ranger in patch-dyed blues, but in the forefront of the fresco was a woman in blue. Waist length auburn hair cascaded down her back as she stood at the entrance to a massive cavern. About this image little jewel bright stones glittered oddly, giving the illusion that the woman moved. She seemed to have an aura of radiating blue, gold, turquoise encircling her, her eyes were set with brilliant flecks of Azure, but the image that stopped Jalni's breath was plainly unfinished for it showed half a man that could have been Daro.

His hands were raised to the woman imploringly as he appeared to be falling from a small ledge, reaching out to the Ranger who knelt by the lady. That hand had somehow grasped the hilt of the Rangers sword, which was slung on the Ranger's back. There were tiny flecks of brilliance along the unfinished part of the work, so Jalni (suspecting that a vein of mica had made fixing the paint to the wall impossible) moved one of the Zeglur shenn panels, then cried out as the shaft of light caught a wall set with tiny faceted crystals.

Shielding her eyes, she crept closer to the fresco, stroking the hilt of the sword with wondering fingertips. Caught in the thrall of discovery, she didn't notice the hilt flush Azure, but Draille and Kilda certainly did, as their visitor turned bewildered eyes back to the depiction demanding,

"Have any of the Guardians seen this? It's utterly amazing, and how odd that this poor man looks just like Daro!"

She was inclined to ask the Decrian if Rangers wrote down prophecy, but laughing Draille explained that Rangers rarely used script anymore and that these frescos referred to the time in which Holmgarth had first been settled, that there were probably more of them, but that with many mouths to feed, they tended to leave such mysteries to reveal themselves, while Rangers fed their children or planted next Rotations plants in preparation for hard times ahead.

He persuaded Jalni that she could come back another time to see what else she could divine from the painted wall, laughed at her when her stomach rumbled, then suggested that they ascend to the levels above and eat as they made plans to travel.

They planned into early evening. By Sushanna's reckoning, Jalni could safely travel until summer. Although she knew her skill would be welcome when the herders gathered at Tregeth, Draille warned her that going so far from help might put her baby at risk. She would have to travel the desert crossings just to get to Scartel, but at least, towards autumn other Healers would have arrived in the new settlement, and Jalni had the idea that she'd like to birth her baby there. Inevitably her mind turned to Daro, and she fiercely repressed those thoughts, anxious that she should not reveal her whereabouts should her Lord seek her signature in the Source. Parting from Draille, she packed, ready to go whenever her Ranger said it was time, then climbed into bed and slept.

In her dreams she saw a strange place. All high halls and glowing walls. She walked slowly, running her hands against a marbled wall of such vivid hues her mind wandered as if following the tracery of some mystic river as she scanned the seams of living crystal in the rock. Her heart pounded as she turned a corner, seeing another figure in the distance at the other end of this wondrous gallery. He was framed in the archway of some great entrance, the sky visible beyond him, but as she approached, he reached out to a kneeling figure whose sword was cradled in its scabbard on its bearer's back.

As the man's hand touched the hilt of the sword, it leapt into his hand glowing opalescent against the night sky beyond. Then she saw that the figure was Daro and as she stood rooted to the ground in shock, he vanished into thin air and was no more.

She woke gasping, the sound of a bell shivering through her body. Sitting up, still cradled in the furs from her bed Jalni thought savagely.

"What manner of Sorcery could dematerialise a Sandsinger?", knowing in some way that what she had "seen" was no ordinary dream, and that although she'd seen Opal gleams from the sword itself, nowhere had she heard or felt Daro's unmistakeable signature, indicating that he was responsible for his own disappearance. All she could think was that someone else had intervened with a Sorcery unknown to current magic-users, and remembering the events that had so nearly killed Tirjella and Ikella, she shuddered, chilled to the bone by fear.

While Jalni rejected every thought of Daro, Beneva was crossly stomping around the Djellim, wishing for once that her tricky charge would return. Ikella had been busy working with the fourth year students and had severely over-reached herself, falling asleep at the High Table in the refectory, displaying for all Selesh to see, the frailty of extreme old age. After she had been carefully removed to the Infirmary, Beneva had summoned both Shiarjha and Suraya to a meeting in the Council Chamber, where they could discuss matters of import without interruption. While they talked, they worked tirelessly, picking their way through yet another box of scrolls and sand-tablets retrieved from the depths of the great underground fortress. Having set Suraya to search a box of sand-tablets for any notation she couldn't understand, Beneva set up a table with two scrolls to examine, then turned a worried face to Shiarjha, muttering direly.

"Well my dear, our Sister Guardian is failing I'm afraid. Dear old Hannah was in tears when she told me, but its natural at her age I suppose. She needs to rest more every day and I fear greatly her Rotations are limited. One word off-sands and we can expect deputations from everywhere. I cannot see how we will deal with them. I had Tirjella in conference when the call came, Suraya was superb, but I still had enquiries this morning. They were discreet enough I suppose…", she broke off frowning as Diras approached them at the run.

"Where's the fire Commander?", she demanded tartly and the Inesh warrior slowed her pace and contrived to look guilty.

"No fire Seris Beneva," she remarked shortly, "However, I had word through from Shilinch on the north-western border that Olneth has wandered afar. To Tregeth in fact, where he intends to stay and help Carolus through the breeding season with his Zeglurs. I thought you might like to know".

"Thank you Diras, I'm certain that I can use that information.", the Guardian of Knowledge turned to her companion.

"There!", she said triumphantly, "At least we know where some of our missing coatans have strayed!"

Shiarjha nodded, tiny lines at the corner of her eyes crinkling as she scowled down at the record she was reading.

"Diras didn't mention Daro by name." she stated flatly, re-rolling the scroll she was holding onto a plain dark rod, clapping her hands together irritably, sending up little puffs of dust from the ancient vellum as she did so. Beneva watched the unwanted scroll dematerialise with a click of her fellow Guardian's fingers, then said in mild admonishment,

"Sister, we were tasked with the observation and recording of magic-users, not to emulate them, or waste our own powers doing what a pair of perfectly good hands can do!", but Shiarjha (the irrepressible) chuckled.

"Beneva!", she exclaimed cheerfully, "I *was* using my hands, and you must have seen me doing so!"

Beneva joined in the flicker of merriment, but she felt the eyes of the young Sorceress-Elect on her, and took the time to explain the laughter to Suraya, who was busily counting sand-tablets into a brush basket.

"Seris Ikella was very unsure that Seris Shiarjha would follow her to the Staff.", the ancient Guardian elaborated. "She told us that small magic was to be avoided if we didn't want to get so fat that we couldn't travel anymore."

Shiarjha took up the story willingly,

"She made me sit and work my way through hundreds of old maps of the Sands, to prove that I wasn't lazy. Eventually, I got interested and started to map the Sands, as if they joined together. Forming the Great Map of Pelshar has proved a lifetime's work, but has encouraged me to sit in the Djellim for sector upon sector, rather than walking round Selesh keeping thin! As a direct result, my bottom is growing to match the shape of my chair.", she grinned across the Council table at the next Sorceress of the Opal and said provocatively,

"The Way is changing, women do the work of scribes, Apothecary's act as spies, and for all we know we are missing a Sandsinger!"

Heavy lidded almond shaped eyes regarded her seriously.

"Seris Shiarjha, Lord Daro was with Olneth when he left. He has been gone four ninenights now, which isn't long for sand-crossings. His Songfathers are both at Tregeth during this season, what could be more likely than Ichspeller Selunsanni has accompanied Olneth to Tregeth?"

Suraya's face was solemn, though her eyes danced and Shiarjha blinked in surprise. Then the Sorceress Elect remarked quite calmly,

"Seris Ikella made me study the stories of simple lives. Of love, marriage, birthings and heroic death.", and coloured faintly as she confessed,

"I found the love stories boring. Who wants to remain cleaning and sewing while a man labours in the field getting dirty and tearing other clothes to grow food. I could have been a Healer, but I didn't find my inclinations ran that way. I would rather administrate for the Clan, create medications with the help of an Apothecary, making sure all the time that my people are safe, fed and well. After all, by so doing I win the admiration of many men, don't get grubby running after children, nor do I have to bear them!"

She gave an elaborate shudder, then grinning wickedly, produced from nowhere, three narrow stemmis cups, filled to the brim with the tan liquid and after handing one to each Guardian, turned her attention back to the ancient sand-tablets with a beatific smile.

Beneva rubbed her nose, sniffed at the homely brew, nodding appreciatively, then her voice sounded in Shiarjha's mind.

Beneva's use of "speech without speech" was limited, but the younger Guardian heard her clearly.

"Thank the One! At last sense has prevailed and Suraya is over her crush on Daro."

A wry nod was the only response, then Suraya held up a hand clasping a sand-tablet and they turned wondering eyes on the excited girl.

"I have a little knowledge of ancient languages." she confessed. "I got very bored in Mahkesh, and although Deshun Kerisima did her level best to teach, encouraging me to use my gifts appropriately, there were times when I longed for a way or a place in which I could indulge my interest in understanding what has happened to our world, and could not."

Beneva looked stricken as she thought about the way that Suraya had been segregated from other youngsters specifically her fellow Sisters in Sorcery, but Suraya just smiled gently, saying

"Seris Beneva, you had no choice! I was a brat, fully empowered, had I been left here in Selesh, or anywhere in the Opal, Daro might have been the least of your problems. By sending me to Kerisima, you gave me no access to my homesand, therefore no chance to make mischief. Besides...", said the next Sorceress of the Opal, "with me away, Daro was able to mature into power without hindrance, and Dommichspeller Jalni still lives."

This awareness of her own immaturity caught both the Guardians off-guard, and Shiarjha chuckled grimly, thinking of the unmistakeable threat that had hovered (however briefly) at their door. She sighed, realising with a little jerk of fear, how very little they knew about bringing up potential Sorceress leaders away from the nullifying effect of Sanctuary.

Her frown grew as she tried to remember the monumental edifice, forcing herself to consider which Sands it had stood in, realising eventually that it had (apparently) not stood in any Sand, but on a great ledge, poised above Sundreth's Chasm, which was crossed only on the Bridge of Truth, an ephemeral rainbow which could only support the rightful rulers of the Sands, pure in mind and intent.

She could not restrain her derisive snort, as she thought suddenly of Adruna the heretic. Fathomless lilac eyes, great swathes of dark hair, on a slim but curvaceous figure. She wondered briefly when the Sorceress of the Amethyst had been corrupted and by what means, for she had to have left Sanctuary pure or she would never have left alive.

She dragged her attention back as Beneva sighed, then Suraya laid the odd sand-tablet on the clear space between the Guardians, bowing her head and waiting for them to see what she had found.

They stared in silence, for the sand-tablet was unlike any other that they had found previously.

It was so slim that it needed a permanent support, and that was made from some form of ceramic in an odd shade of Azure. The tablet was so old it was virtually translucent, and to Beneva's astonishment, Suraya leant across the table and picked up a pot of the soft wax she had been using to re-surface old scrolls with, helping them to retain some flexibility. The girl mused thoughtfully,

"If this isn't needed desperately I might be able to reveal the words on the tablet by running a thin coat of wax over the tablet and taking an impression. I don't think the casing is complete and I'd hate to break the tablet easing it out of the cover its sitting in."

Shiarjha looked nonplussed, then Beneva said mildly,

"This is not a backing then Suraya?", and the girl nodded shortly, her attention caught by a word impressed deeply into the ancient sand.

"No Seris, I remember writing the word Selesh on my mirror at Mahkesh. I wanted to have some tangible target, some ambition that I could fix my ideas on. Then one day, I had a girl come and fix up my hair and I caught the word in my hand mirror. It read hseleS of course, which made me laugh because one of the girls at Kerisima's Hall is Sybillsce, and you know how oddly they lisp half their words? I did entertain the wild idea that Selesh had once had another name, but couldn't find any language that supported my theory. Therefore, I suspect that this tablet has been forced down into this cover upside down, which means that it should be read from the other side. As I can recognise the word "Selesh" written backwards, this is a conclusion that you might care to entertain."

The Guardians looked carefully at the tablet. It was only about the size of a woman's hand, but incredibly heavy. The "sand" (usually sand mixed with wax, and compressed into a "former", would have been baked semi-dry in the heat of the day, before setting in the chill of night. The resulting "tablets" were remarkably strong, but had largely gone out of use since the Great Storm preceding Daro's birth. During that, the upper levels of sand had been incredibly contaminated, rendering it difficult to obtain clean tablets to take the imprint of the sharpened enscrasures used by Healers, scribes, and recorders alike.

The discovery that a superb hard wax could be extracted from the living trees of the Malachite sands, had not only promoted a cross Sands industry making the lighter wax tablets, but had been instrumental in resurrecting old ideals. Ignited by the discovery that additional pots of wax could be supplied with a wax-tablet, very few users failed to see that they could make notes on a wax tablet for temporary use, then, when the notes had been transferred to a scroll, or the new writing material processed from discarded linens by the new Guild of Scribes, the wax could be melted and the "former" used to create a replacement. However, this was definitely an old tablet, heavy in Sand, which glittered oddly, fused together in some way…

"Like Master Doloran's glass?", Shiarjha muttered, running a shapely fingernail over the semi translucent back of the tablet thoughtfully. Then, Beneva brightened,

"Could we not hold that up to a glass and see the words Suraya?", she asked slowly, but Suraya looked doubtful. She glanced at the tablet briefly, then explained that she thought the dully blued cover might not have sufficient contrast to show the words clearly where the glassy substance of the sand tablet was thickened.

They touched the ancient words wistfully, each determined to spend the evening considering how to free the tablet from the cover to which it seemed fused without irreparable damage to the artefact. Whether it would then be possible to read the inscription no-one could tell. However, they parted, each of them determined to try (and at least one felt that she had an advantage none of the others knew about).

That night, Suraya slipped silently into the Djellim. Crossing to the work table where Beneva had left the basket of sand tablets, she gazed down at the odd one thoughtfully. Her bare feet were cold in the chill of night, and she glanced around to find somewhere warmer to sit. Deciding on a corner which still had a curtain hanging from an elderly rod, she discovered Beneva's comfortable old chair, and a nearby glow basket which she was able to angle, so that light and a little warmth provided the comfort she sought. Positioning a small work table nearby, Ikella's Elect gathered up an enscrasure, then settled down. Mouthing each character as she studied it, she managed to copy each word painstakingly onto the new wax tablet in her lap, then she sat staring at the words in silence, utterly dumbfounded by what she held. Then she placed the tablet and the transcription together and went to find Beneva, quite aware that she was likely to cause a stir in the annals of Sorcery when she revealed what she'd found.

Beneva stared at the Sorceress-Elect for a very long time, then she looked down at the translation Suraya had made. The frail writing was old, set in a far more elaborate script than she was practised in using on temporary writing surfaces. She cleared her throat, then spoke clearly and deliberately.

"I hope I don't have to tell you that no word of this must reach the Sisters of Sorcery until I have decided what to tell them, how to tell them."

She looked down at the strange sand tablet then murmured in a softer voice,

"I hope that before he died, he knew how much she was prepared to give up, how much she must have loved him!", and her hand was particularly gentle as she traced a line on the original.

She read aloud,

"If I must walk the halls of Selesh alone for the rest of my life or even beyond, I will be with you my love. I hope only to bring word of our world to another generation of Sandsingers, so that they are forewarned. Tonight, I will lie with my love, die with my love if I am wrong, but if I am not, then …"

The Guardian said softly,

"My dear Sister in Sorcery, I can only hope that in following the Way, we have not restricted the lives of all those who followed Adaria. We have remained celibate in order to focus our control of the Source, but it seems that once a Sorceress didn't have to do so, and still remained powerful enough to reach beyond the grave to carry out her promise."

Many Rotations before, she and Ikella had told Suraya the story of Feydora's appearance, now she stroked the name that finished the diary board (for Suraya had identified it as such), then she whispered,

"This belongs in the Azure Sands, where I have no doubt Tirjella will treasure it. She will likely draw parallels with our current situation however, so I'd like to play this down until Jalni and Daro come to their senses. If I am right, then Feydora's story has some bearing on the return of the Sandsingers. She obviously died with her lover at Selesh, probably during or shortly after Cataclysm."

She paused thinking about the words she hadn't spoken, then Suraya said gently,

"What seems obvious however Seris Beneva, is that she was once a Sorceress, probably of the Azure, but you say that she claimed to be a Sandsinger. Is that translation possible? From one sort of mage to another?"

Her face was solemn, her eyes watchful, but Beneva had the last laugh.

"Of course it is my dear!", she said firmly. "Adaria proved that point herself. Once a Healer she became a Sorceress. So did I, then at Sanctuary they gave me another option, become a Guardian. Like Seris Ikella who was Healer, Sorceress and now Guardian. Yes, I'm afraid we've had some things terribly wrong, or the Source and magic have changed course in our lifetimes!"

Thinking about this and all the promised future that this laid bare, the two magic users went soberly to bed, praying that they would never face the type of choices that now yawned before them like a hungry trap.

By unspoken consensus, neither the wise old Guardian of Knowledge, nor the young Sorceress Elect spoke about Feydora's sand tablet when they rose. The rituals of the day had to be performed, the rounds of the patients within the great Infirmary completed, so it was comparatively late in the day when they again assembled in the Djellim. This time they were not alone, for their new Infirmarian had been brought to meet them, so the news (and the translation) had been thoughtfully placed into the Sanctuary Chest which was stored behind the strange energy field surrounding the Council Chamber.

Hannah, soon retiring from the position she had enjoyed for the last twenty-six Rotations, brought her replacement towards them smiling.

"Davina... I knew that Hannah had something up her sleeve to surprise and delight us.", Beneva said warmly, looking at the new Infirmarian with a welcoming smile. "So, the healers of Caranchar have finally let you go!"

She indicated another seat at the large study table where Shiarjha was contemplating a recent addition to her Great Map, and turned back to the side table where the reports of the day had been assembled.

"How do you like our Infirmary now?", Beneva asked simply, aware that in the intervening decades, Davina had built up her own Healer Hall at Caranchar and that to leave that legacy only a day's brisk walk away must have been a wrench. However, the mature woman that faced her wreathed in smiles didn't seem reluctant at all, so the conversation ran on matters medical for some time until they turned inevitably to their Sorceress.

Davina spoke impulsively leaning forward, hands (which had sketched images of the town where she'd practised as Healer since the Great Storm) at rest.

"I don't wonder that Ikella's exhausted Beneva! She's Guardian of the Way, Sorceress of this Sand, Leader of the Clan Shalhanhi and she's worn to the bone. It took complete collapse to bring her into the Infirmary, she's practically working in her sleep. She's either fretting over this, that or Daro! Still, it might have taken one of my best concoctions, plus one of dear old Sanra's combined medications to effect true rest, but at long last she appears to be sleeping naturally. Now, I might only be a day away from Selesh, but I might have been on the other side of the Amber, for all the gossip I hear, so please someone, put me out of my misery and tell me about Daro's adventures, before I die of curiosity".

It was Hannah's turn to grin, albeit wryly.

"The Clan have protected Daro so fiercely that very few outside the community here at Selesh know the whole story Beneva.", she explained. "I thought of this when I recommended Davina to Seris Ikella. Davina of course, was there when he was born. She saw the changes right from the beginning, and she has earned her place in Selesh as a tutor of trail medicinery."

Shiarjha blinked, thinking about the comparatively short time in which everything that she had expected from a life devoted to the recording of magic had changed. Now, in the blink of an eye, the young student Healer that they had left in Caranchar had matured far beyond Ikella's wildest expectations. Here (she found herself thinking) was a worthy successor to Mina when she retired), then the task of bringing Davina up to date yawned at her feet like a pit, as sighing, she began the long thankless task.

The glows burned late into the night as they talked. Once or twice a servitor was summoned to bring food and drink for the company assembled, but at long last a very sober Davina faced those who had sent for her speaking quietly.

"Thank you all for trusting me with such wonderful news. may I ask, who else knows of these events? How in the Ones name have you managed to keep everything secret? Oh, I wish I could have seen it all!"

It was a simple enough comment, but they had all renewed their own sense of wonder as Davina stood transfixed on the threshold when Beneva opened the discreetly shielded Council Chamber. They had Surrounded her as the Guardian revealed Jocasta's Door, bringing to life the scenes of Daro's emergence as Sandsinger in its mysterious depths. As Davina collapsed weakly into a chair at the Council table, she confessed shyly.

"When Deshun Ikella Summoned the Winds at Caranchar, I thought I heard voices! Now I'm certain! I always thought I heard someone say, "Master of the Winds...the Voice!"

She trailed off uncertainly, unaware that her face was glowing with fervour, then Beneva's inner voice spoke directly to Shiarjha.

"My dear Sister, we seem to have added another name to Daro's tally of lovelorn Healers!"

Shiarjha made no comment, her serene face never showed any perturbation as the little group broke up and headed for their beds. However, as Beneva turned into her own room, her fellow Guardian's voice sounded clearly in her mind.

"Yes, my dear Sister!", she agreed pleasantly enough, but beneath her normal gently respectful tone there was a tinge of concern. "What bothers me however, are the truths we seem to have discovered about Sorcery today. How do we know that Feydora wasn't both Sorceress *and* Sandsinger? It occurs to me that we know so little of our magical past that we have a very complicated animal by the tail, of which a very little knowledge is a dangerous thing!" Before Beneva could respond to that sober thought, Shiarjha's door closed on the long quiet corridor, leaving the Guardian of Knowledge thoughtful, and just a little afraid.

Chapter 19 - The Black Tower

Far from the influences surrounding Adruna's court, Drex drew an unsteady breath and looked around the familiar apartment. He had been exiled scarcely three rotations, yet here he was, considering the odd idea that he was actually happy for the first time in his life.

All his belongings had been magically transported with him. Every book, scroll, or paper note he'd ever written seemed to have been filed neatly into his miniature parody of Skyrrh's Great Library, so jealously guarded by the dark Sorceress, that even Koth had difficulty obtaining unrestricted access. Drex smiled to himself. His clothes, curios and the odd collection of insignia he had hoarded were all in their places, everything was as it had been at home, but he only had to peer from a window to discover that was half a Sand away from here.

Below the basalt tower, the rift dropped away into inky blackness on the southern flank of the desert. All light seemed to stream into an unnatural void,, sucked down so that the uncanny fear of falling asserted itself as he gazed over the deepening purples of his homesand. He gulped, averting his eyes from that dizzying aspect, relieved to find his apartment hadn't shifted, although the sensation was so tangible that a light dew of sweat beaded his brow. He swung the shutter across the narrow slit, returning to his high stool and perching there, mechanically adjusting his robes so that his sleeves wouldn't brush the surface of the scroll he was reading.

Adjusting his glowstone lamp, he reassumed his normal reading position, and then returned to his work. Time passed silently. No sound carried from the desert outside. No sound penetrated his peculiar concentration as his hands (carefully sheathed in white linen gloves) traced the lines of fine old script, fingers occasionally tapping where the one-time Recorder of Skyrrh found something of interest. Occasionally the glowstone flickered, sometimes a breath of wind stirred the huge banks of scrolls that lined the ancient walls of the tower, whispering through the galleries like some trapped presence fluttering through the words of yesteryear.

Below them Drex made notes, listed words he didn't understand, then passed on to the next scroll without questioning how the scrolls came to his workbench, they just came. Made of fine vellum that seemed to resist time, age and handling, he nevertheless handled them with the respect he believed they deserved. He permitted no part of his body or clothing to touch these precious relics of the past. No food or drink was ever allowed into his reading room, no direct light was cast across the flowing scrip, and with the pure exercise of his calling, the Recorder kept faith with the ancient who had left this staggering history of a world long gone.

Every day Drex rose with a jolt of joy at the thought of his task. Every night, (understanding a little more of the script) he learned of the world they had lost, falling into bed so exhausted that he never remembered eating or bathing, although he woke clean, refreshed and willing to return to his task again, his prodigious memory at long last put to good use, as the twist in his personality corrected itself unseen.

Once a day there was a tap at his door and a woman would bring him food. It was simple fare, bread, broth, sometimes a sliver of cheese or meat, sometimes a piece of fruit. He nodded gravely, ate sparingly, anxious to return to his reading. At Height of Sun he would bathe, wiping his body down with the water he found in his bathing area. He never saw the one who cleaned and tidied, refilling his flask or lighting his lamps. These things simply went on happening, as Drex studied.

Piles of wax tablets grew as he came to a fuller understanding of Pelshar past, yet he still hadn't found what Adruna hunted. He was about to celebrate his fifth Rotation of silent captivity when he woke from a light doze, to hear Adruna's petulant voice demanding his presence. Scrambling to his feet, he found his door ajar and the dark Sorceress standing in his anteroom staring around her.

"Drex", she acknowledged him impatiently. "What news do you have for me? Speak up man, I haven't got all Rotation!"

Fighting down the compulsion to hurl himself from the window, he spoke slowly as he registered the absence of her shadow on the stone floor. She chuckled softly.

"You surely don't think that I would travel in person to talk to you worm!" she said contemptuously. "No, I just got bored playing with Koth and his keepers. I thought I'd look in to find out what you have discovered. I hope you haven't been sleeping Drex. I should hate to kill you too early in the game. What have you found out about Sandsingers eh? I don't want to discover that one of the Sands has some sort of advantage over the others."

He felt her gaze crawl over him and shuddered inwardly, aware suddenly that in this place she had little power over him. Determining not to let this show, he bent his head obsequiously, turning towards his reading room and indicating that the Sorceress should precede him. However, it seemed that the Dark Tower had other ideas, for the door obstinately refused to open. Drex ran anxious hands over his short cropped hair, watching Adruna's face pale in fury.

"By sinking Sand and Drekken shells", she swore impatiently, eyes blazing hot angry lilac. "Koth was right; no magic seems to work here. I especially wanted to see the ancient scrolls for myself!"

She turned away muttering, but Drex (strangely unaffected by her fury) took careful notice of the weakened shadow of her aura, comparing it inwardly with the odd tingling sensation that forced ordinary mortals to flinch away from her fearfully.

Cursing, the woman turned to him imperiously.

"Well then, report!" she commanded brusquely, so wise to her innate cruelty, Drex drew a deep breath and obeyed.

He kept his comments short, but to the point, telling the truth, but not revealing all of it believing that somehow he had to protect the great repository at all costs. She listened, dark head on one side considering his every word as he explained respectfully.

"Exalted One, I have studied long and hard just to understand the written words of these ancients." he said gravely. "Their language is so different from that used today, it has taken me Rotations to be sure that accuracy of translation can be maintained. With no understanding of the way the scrolls are organised, I then discovered that I was dealing with ten different dialects not including some specialised terms of reference, for which I have no key."

He watched Adruna's eyes glaze over with boredom, and then added temptingly, "However, I have persevered, working mainly on those records that I could understand, beginning with familiar place names."

He had her interest now, the glowing shape shifted position slightly, then she said softly, "Go on..." as the Recorder took up his story once more.

"I found a reference to Selesh, apparently written before it was inhabited. My interest was sparked by a mention of an impending danger. The person who wrote that scroll may have had knowledge of disease, but it occurred to me that it meant slightly more than that. They do not mention Healers specifically. I have been searching mainly for repeated words that I could then identify with certainty, but I find little mention of magic, no mention at all of power and nothing to suggest that anyone was unusually gifted. However, I am beginning to wonder if the person who wrote these scrolls was a Talent themselves. Of course if a scribe wrote them, he could only write what his Master dictated, but some of the writing is so poor, that I believe whoever wrote the scrolls originated the very words written. There are no maps, no drawings, no pictograms, only script, and a lifetime of script." He tailed off miserably.

Adruna eyed him suspiciously, and then sighed, her image beginning to fade even as she spoke.

"Drex, you know the penalty for failing me. I shall however give you a little longer. I may be able to get a report on matters at Selesh, so work on that scroll you were talking about and we'll confer later. Don't forget to look for anything that relates to ceremonials, Clan or otherwise, or descriptions of the layout of Selesh. In particular look for anything that would allow us to direct an army into the old caverns".

Her eyes flashed brilliantly for a long moment, but Drex felt none of the old compulsion to obey, none of the breath stilling fear, none of the stir of wicked delight that surrounded her. Despite this, he bowed his head in tacit obedience as she faded from view. Her voice was the last thing to dissipate, echoing dully in the anteroom to his chambers.

"Don't forget, wherever you are in my Sands you belong to me. Body and soul I own you Drex. Your mission is simply to keep body and soul together for as long as I permit you to do so. Remember my promise? The price of your life is success."

Her voice altered horribly. The precise diction, the melodic tone faltered as Drex recoiled from the blood curdling snarl that it became.

"One chance you miserable excuse for a Recorder. Find out about those Sandsinger references. Now, this instant, I command it…!"

There was a weird howling noise in Drex's head. He couldn't work out whether it was outside, in the room, or in the Great Library. He felt a light-headedness, a sensation as though someone of great import had entered the Dark Tower, and was not overly surprised when shortly thereafter there came a light tapping at his door.

Chapter 20 - The Lamentation of Loran

The young man who stood there smiling, held a tray laden with Drex's meal. A piece of cheese, a steaming grain and vegetable mix, a slice of dorbourn fruit together with a tall glass of sherbet, which fizzed deliciously as the Recorder took it doubtfully.

Never having spoken to the other unfortunate prisoners within the Tower, Drex found himself suddenly shy with this boy, not knowing what to do or say. He took the tray awkwardly, knowing that conversation was barred, but tempted by Adruna's apparent lack of influence here, Drex found himself murmuring,

"Thank you."

'There,' he thought triumphantly, 'That's done, and I'm still here!' before he realised two things. One, he had never thanked a mere servitor before and secondly, that by sending him here, Adruna had lost her influence over him, he was free! Emboldened by this thought, he added,

"I haven't seen you around before, what's your name?"

His visitor grinned engagingly, "Oh, everything from 'Oi you' to 'Bastard' usually," he answered sincerely, "but today, if you please, I'm Tanneus!"

The recorder didn't remember feeling faint, but suddenly there was a roaring in his ears, something like the tolling of a huge bell claimed his attention and he felt the dark pulling him down. Someone took the tray from him, someone lifted him onto his couch, and then the boy was raising a glass to his lips. He sipped, then drank until the glass was taken away, and a firm voice said gruffly.

"Sir, forgive my impertinence, but you are tired. Exhausted in fact, and I cannot believe that you got this way alone. Perhaps I speak out of turn, but we hear things in the night that made us think that you work endlessly towards some task imposed upon you. Can you not rest sir? Could a Healer help you? We are fortunate enough to have a healer amongst us, and she might help you sleep a little."

The dark eyes so close to his own were full of concern, the hands that steadied his frail body were gentle as the young man laid him back on the pillows that had been carefully piled behind him. Drex, truly wordless in the face of such kindness nearly wept as his mind took him back to the man he had been once, and he trembled, astonished at the man he had become. Something had stopped the voice in his mind, halted the canker in his soul and given him a purpose. He smiled into the face of his visitor and said firmly,

"I'm sorry if I disturbed anyone, but I have a task, one that just might set us free of the Heretic, who believes I am under her control. I suspect that once I isolate the scroll I need I will be able to identify someone who will make her power seem like the toy candles on the trees at Jentaroth."

There was a minute hesitation in Tanneus's voice, but he eventually said softly,

"Sir, if I offend by asking, would your task be easier if you had an assistant? I'd be proud to help the Keeper of the Scrolls."

As that title left the other's lips, Drex drew a long shaky breath, for his reading was far more advanced than he had dared to tell Adruna. Only that day he had realised that his current task had made him one with the legendary Ambrill (Keeper of the Scrolls at World's End). This character had appeared on the pages of a book entitled "The Lamentation of Loran", which Drex had found on his bedside one morning. Because of his peculiar lonely imprisonment, Drex had been drawn to read what he'd firmly believed to be a fiction. Somehow comforted by the thought that the mage who'd constructed his prison had created a tale in which Ambrill, (the legendary Recorder of the Scrolls) had been forever trapped in this lonesome place, after his Master had died in some ancient catastrophe. Drex, (unusually captivated by the tale) identified strongly with this fictional being, viewing his own situation in the same light as he too searched for a means of escape from the Black Tower. Now it seemed that this boy also knew the story, as Drex (suddenly chilled to the bone) simply stared at his visitor and wondered what was happening to him.

Tanneus was leaning over him again, helping him to eat his evening meal as Drex frowned trying to remember where he had seen that name before. He was aging fast, he was immensely tired and there was something soothing in the young man's companionship. He smiled, comfortably warm and safe from Adruna, as the next Lord of the Ninth Sand of Pelshar drew the coverlet over the legs of his Keeper of Scrolls.

"Why don't you sleep now?", the soft voice said, and Drex slipped effortlessly into sound healing sleep.

Tanneus smiled as he closed the door to the Keeper's quarters. Something had called him here, he was certain about that, but what on the Nine Sands was going on? He thought glumly that he was going to become a seer, so strong had been his dreams of other sands, places he had never seen, and he fretted that Adruna would find out, and persecute the pitiful remains of Soloria's court for his strange abilities. He had learned to hide the fact that he could double their rations with a wave of his hand, although some days he wondered how long that would last. He sat in one of the empty apartments and tried to gather his thoughts. He had managed to befriend the strange silent Keeper of the Scrolls, who had appeared in their midst with quite basic instructions. He should not leave his quarters, was expected to perform a search of the repository, and was not to be diverted in any way. One meal a day was to be allotted to the new prisoner, no conversation was permitted.

Telandra, his mother said instantly, "I'll take his meals to him poor man. He must have offended the Heretic greatly to have ended up here.", but the other prisoners had shunned them for obeying the instruction. In vain she'd pleaded for contributions towards the Keepers food, then she'd grown defiant. She'd told Tanneus since he could remember about his twin sister, now she rounded in fury on those who'd greedily assumed the rights to her missing daughter's ration.

"Tanneya would have been twenty five this Rotation, and likely would have married and had a child herself but for the fact that we were separated. I will never know if my child died when Olneth went for help, but I rely on the One's mercy, that wherever she is in the Amethyst, my husband will return one day and help me search for her. In the meantime, I claim Tanneya's ration as the head of her household. No-one else will lose to feed the new Keeper of the Scrolls, because I will feed him what has been my child's rations from day one. You who have divided her food amongst you may lose a little, but consider this, the only person who knows nothing about Tanneya's disappearance is Adruna. If you report this to her, how do you think she will react? Better keep faith with the idea that both Olneth and Tanneya escaped somehow and pray that she never finds out!"

Tanneus frowned as he thought of the vehemence in his little mother's voice standing as she was against men who had been Soloria's household guard and women who had served the previous Sorceress faithfully. He wondered briefly what anyone outside this unusual society of prisoners would make of the remnants of Soloria's court. He had grown to realise that each one of them had clung on to their previous positions, guarding jealously anything they had salvaged from the ruins of their former lives. Rank was the one thing they all seemed to believe they kept, but it was not long before the exigencies of their common experience took a toll on that idea. He had little memory of the times when a demand from senior Clan members had provoked near fist fights, but his mother had told him sternly,

"We are all one people Tanneus. No one of us greater, wealthier, or more important than the other. Whoever makes life miserable for another must be shown the error of their ways then, they must be welcomed back into our society without blame. We all have to live with less food, less joy, and no freedom to leave. Each one of us is like a building block on which the others might depend, so you must adhere to the Way, follow its strictures closely, believing that the One in his mercy will show Adruna the fault within herself, letting her heal."

He had often thought his mother overly ambitious in her evening prayer, but as he heard her earnest plea to the One for the soul of their Sorceress, he began to realise that he was greatly blessed to have such a woman in his life. As he grew older, he heard tales about his beloved father, how she missed him and how she had entrusted a gift of Soloria's to one of the women who had been picked to accompany the young Sorceress-Elect to Selesh as she succeeded to the Staff. He didn't find out until much later that she'd also entrusted his twin sister to this woman, in the firm belief that this way, Tanneya would be reunited with Olneth. Convinced of her husband's loyalty, she had no doubt that Olneth would choose to offer his services elsewhere, but what of their baby daughter? For many days she had wept, then she had taken heart from the slow arrival of those who had returned from Selesh. She had heard the story of how many Sybillsce had settled in Selesh, heard that Olneth had been seen in Caranchar after a squall of some kind had prevented his meeting with Adruna and her prayers rang out every evening for the child to find her father and return to those who loved them.

Tanneus had long since given up telling Telandra that her wishes would require magic of a far stronger kind than that available in their locked and lonely Sands. Since childhood, he had prayed for the power to avenge his Clan, once and forever binding it back to the Union of the Sands, clear and clean of Adruna's heresy. In the last nineninght he had dreamt of music, a kind he had never known, but his hands had trembled, curving as if to hold some instrument, and wondering if his twin was trying to tell him something, he had prayed earnestly for some sign that his dreams were about to materialise. Only that morning he had persuaded Telandra to let him help her and at the moment he entered the Repository, he had understood that this was his time, and that Adruna could expect no mercy from him.

He stood, rubbing sore legs earned while running up and down the stairs of the Black Tower, serving those too lazy or old to wait on themselves, then strode off to the kitchens, where his mother toiled. Today he had relieved her of the long haul almost to the top of the Tower, knowing that tomorrow he would do the same thing, for he would be working with the Keeper from now on. His spirit soared as he thought of learning where he could make a difference and he was whistling melodically as he entered the kitchens to find his mother frantically sorting sacks of grain and filling the capacious stoneware bins.

As he paused, mouth agape in surprise, Telandra swept a tendril of hair behind one ear and glared at him.

"I don't know what's going on my lad, but instead of being here when I needed you, I expect you've been up to fine old mischief!"

He grinned engagingly,

"Surely you don't hold me responsible for this?" He indicated the produce as it grew around them and Telandra stared at him blankly.

"You mistake my meaning son," she said, looking at him oddly. "Didn't you hear the horn sounding? The delivery was expected last nineninght. I have been frantically reminding Mishanndra at Istakan that we needed our stores. It seems after all that my message got through, although I don't seem to have any record of what they have sent again. I live in fear of some recorder demanding our numbers, for it appears as though they've taken no notice of our latest headcount, thank the One!"

He assisted her with the storage, smiling to himself as he realised that he'd been dreaming of food when it had appeared, then falling into his bed, slept dreamlessly, until the desert woke him, singing to itself as the dim light of Seleus penetrated to the floor of the chasm below the Tower.

Chapter 21 - Legacy

After observing his morning rituals, Tanneus was bewildered by his own apprehensions as he approached the repository Tower. Strictly speaking, the Black Tower was not one building, but two abutting each other. The building (now occupied by the main body of prisoners) might well of once housed guards. That building (square, like other barracks) nestled up against the ancient more imposing round Repository Tower. Built from the same obsidian stone, the edifice glistened wetly against a backdrop of dull Amethyst, where the light penetrated through a perpetual cloud that darkened the sands. Telandra had spoken with awe about the beauty of their homesands in her youth, but Tanneus had never seen the places she remembered, for born after the Great Storm, in a desert shamed by the heresy of its new Sorceress, he had always lived beneath the magical barrier imposed by the Guardian of the Way.

He remembered hearing others rant and rave against this imposition, but shortly after his fifth Rotation, Adruna had decided to confine the last members of Soloria's Court in the far South-western corner of their homesand, since which time he had only been exposed to the opinions of his fellow prisoners, and the dwindling number of guards necessary to imprison them. He dimly remembered a long journey by wagon, then the miserable days waiting in tents for the guard to clear the quarters where they now lived. He had been frightened of the Black Tower then, but as he'd grown, he'd woven fantasies around its grim exterior, even creeping through the passages into the lower rooms inhabited by their guards to peer cautiously into the massive Hall which joined the two buildings.

The little boy had been a favourite with the cohort comprised of the remnant of his father's command. Stripped of their privileged positions and rank, sequestered with the previous elders of the Clan, they had formed a distinct threat to the young Sorceress, so they had been overwhelmed by Koth's terrifying priests, and forced into exile as the High Priest had assumed more power over their wilful Sorceress.

The little boy had wandered the ancient buildings, finding friends amongst the guardsmen who missed their families, gradually realising how impotent the Elders of the Clan had become. He listened to the opinions of the men, hearing with bated breath the comments about vengeance, aware of the bubbling hatred of the girl that they'd entrusted their sand to. More particularly they had reviled Koth, who had been brought out of seclusion at Iskatan, where Adruna had insisted on setting up her Court. In vain, they had protested the changes that Adruna had inflicted. In terror, they had attended Clan Council's to find themselves struck down by mystery illnesses, sent out into the Sands on spurious endeavours, gradually whittled down to a number which Adruna could handle, then separated from loved ones and confined at Driearstorn, where Loran's Abyss prevented them escaping physically and the threat of Adruna's revenge held them prisoner mentally. Twenty-five Rotations after the barrier was imposed, Adruna the Heretic still had the power to hold grown men and women willing prisoner in fear for their lives and families whilst her depraved followers still worshipped Gatta in rituals of blood sacrifice. "Now (said the voice in his mine), I am come of age in my Clan, wear the braid of a warrior and am worthy to do battle for the honour of my Sands.", but still his hand trembled as he passed through the great arch between the lower hall of the barracks and the tower, to knock on the door of the man he had dubbed "Keeper of the Scrolls".

As he waited for the instruction to enter, Tanneus thought about the odd book that he'd found as a child. Filled with drawings of the Black Tower, it had been hidden in a little cubby-hole with an oddly carved plaque concealing it. With no other children to play with, he had been a lonely soul, creating games for himself, talking to an invisible friend throughout his formative years. They had not been able to bring much with them, other than Telandra's herbal, he had seen few other books, yet his mother told him that the Black Tower held a great repository of scrolls that someone, one day would read. He grinned as he remembered demanding a book of his own to read to himself, smiling tenderly as he thought of his mother writing a story all by herself, and drawing the pictures that had so entertained him that he still looked at the craftsmanship in the sketches and wondered where she had learned such skill. He was still mulling this over as a silent Drex opened the door and indicated that he should enter.

Curious, Tanneus put the tray he carried onto a low table and glanced around. The Recorder looked at his breakday meal in surprise.

"I'm not used to eating so early young man, but I confess to being quite hungry today." Drex cleared his rusty throat irritably, before picking up the steaming beaker and burying his nose inside it.

"Stemmis!", he sighed happily, "It' has been Rotations since I drank Stemmis! What has been happening since I saw you last? Where has that come from?", he pointed at the thick slab of honey cake in his dish, suspicion in his eyes, at which Tanneus hastened to explain.

"We get few luxuries here, but when the supplies arrive, my mother always makes sure that we use the most perishable goods as soon as possible. You arrived at the end of our rations, so you had to put up with what we had, and we had run out of most things by then. We had no allowance for you, but we made do, which is why you've been eating and drinking so miserably up to now. However today Mother says that there will be fresh bread, vegetable stew with seasoning from the east, and a fruit pudding as well."

Drex smiled at the young man's simple relish, then thought of the lavish banquets he'd enjoyed in his time, before looking at the boy closely.

Typical of the Sybillsce, Tanneus was tall, slender and tanned. He had dark brown liquid eyes, long unruly hair which clustered around his brow in midnight black curls, a straight nose, well defined mouth, and a proud tilt to his head. His parent's sigil was tattooed onto his neck, but without access to the Clan records, Drex couldn't draw any conclusions as to the importance of his parentage, so he sat, allowing this strange young man to wait on him as he breakfasted.

There was no conversation, Drex (normally uncomfortable and suspicious around other people) relaxed as his visitor looked about with interest. He watched Tanneus, surprised to find himself amused as he saw the boy's brow wrinkle over the book he was reading. He briefly wondered what his self-appointed assistant would make of script, thought it was unlikely that Tanneus could even read, then considered (with dismay) that he might have to teach him, before he would be of any use in a search for something he might just recognise when it arrived on his desk. Unaware of this, Tanneus collected up Drex's dish and beaker, crossing to the door to place the tray on a table outside. He returned with a flask of water and a clean beaker, then stood indecisively, trying to work out if Drex wanted him to take the refreshment into his reading room.

The Recorder caught his eye, shaking his head as he spoke.

"If you wish to become my Temporary Assistant Tanneus, you must learn several rules. These are rules that cannot be broken by anyone, for any reason. One, the scrolls kept here belong to all Pelshar. They reside in a repository designed to keep them in the condition that makes them accessible to the future generations of this world." He frowned, seeking the words he needed, looking for a moment incredibly severe, then continued slowly.

"At this moment I'm not sure that I can take you into the Repository, but assuming that I can, you must swear to obey the rules I set for the protection of us all.", he said firmly. "We will come to that later, but initially you must not divulge by word, action or writing anything that you encounter in the confines of the Tower," he said earnestly. "It is my contention that what we are looking at is nothing less than Loran's Legacy and while we know that the ancients had a different view of our world, there is a code by which all Recorders operate, and that defines the records that I make, the records that come into my care, from their inception to their committal."

Tanneus stood stock-still as Drex spoke softly, the words obviously learned by rote, seemed to echo oddly, with the ring of compulsion behind them.

"No scroll that we set our hand to is ours. The words that we record are in the governance of their originator, belonging only to him or her, unless they deem otherwise. Each written word must be understood before a letter is formed. Each word committed to letter must be legible, every word true to the originators will. No change can be made without the originator's mark to approve that change, each alteration must be validated separately, and the validation stored with the scroll. No scroll must leave the repository unless the originator permits. No copy of any scroll can be permitted without the originators permission. Any sub-notes made must be destroyed if they leave the repository." Drex drew breath, then looked at the rapt face of his young companion.

"Drekken shades! Everything is secret?", said Tanneus joyfully, as Drex stood and crossed to the door of his reading room. He carefully unlocked the heavy metal door, which swung open silently as though expecting him, then, suddenly Drex stepped aside, permitting Tanneus to enter before him. The boy nodded awkwardly taking two paces into the silent Tower as (from nowhere) a clarion call rang through the building.

Drex saw Tanneus straighten, felt the air "swoosh" around them, then saw the glow around the boy. A Subtle luminescence cloaked him, lilac flickers seemed to charge his dark hair like static and as he watched his companion in awe, even his stature changed, broadening, defining, strengthening him to stand like one of the ancient warriors from which the Sybillsce were descended.

There was music, rippling chords wrapping around Tanneus like some embellishment of his aura, then as a peculiarly sweet arpeggio thrummed into life, the young man turned and saw that Drex also saw what was occurring.

"Remember…" the untried mage whispered laughing, "If Recorders keep secrets, so can I, particularly in this Tower!", he said cheerfully, then with a subtle flick of a finger, Drex's stool slid under him, supporting his frame as he sagged in shock, rallying only to learn more about this anomaly

He looked at his "assistant", then said heavily,

"I don't know what to say or do now!", he confessed, asking abruptly, "What manner of mage can you be?" to Tanneus's obvious joy.

"I don't actually know Master Drex," he confessed, "but I have an idea. Shall I tell you about it all, and let you be my guide?"

The invitation was tempting, but Drex recoiled in horror. "You can't…!", he shouted, "You don't know in what terrible danger you walk, because you don't know about me. I'm treacherous, dangerous, a threat to all of you.", he was sobbing, suddenly needing to confess his past life, his laziness, wickedness, evil thoughts. He fell to his knees, shattered and shaking as the young man listened silently to the recitation of Drex's former evil, then sighed, gently raising the man, reseating him safely.

"It sounds like you've had a bad time." he said gently, "but since you came here, the Tower has worked its magic. You've found your calling in pure research, you've resisted the evil in the Heretic, perhaps it's time for you to stop punishing yourself and move on my friend. Today has been a revelation for you. I've shown you my secret, you have bravely shown me yours. Now, why don't we both forget what we've learned? That way, you can learn to trust me, as I must trust you. I know what kind of animal you've been in your former life, now you must help me find out what kind of animal I'm becoming, so that I can help the Sybillsce expel the Heretic and regain our place amongst the Union of the Sands."

Drex stared at him, hope lighting his drawn features. He saw lilac flickers in the eyes of the wise young man facing him and suddenly knew what Loran's Legacy was to be used for.

"Lord," he said humbly, "I suspect that there is great power here, and exposed to it for many Rotations, it has settled on your shoulders.", he sighed as Tanneus looked at him enquiringly.

Drex spoke solemnly, "I was sent here to find what the word Sandsinger meant, but I suspect I've done rather more than that, for I found you. If I'm right, you are Loran's Legacy, and will become Sandsinger of the Amethyst Sands."

Tanneus shuddered, suddenly cold to the marrow of his bones, then he said simply, "If the One wills it, but will I be able to stand against the rampant evil of Koth and Adruna?"

The room shuffled and sighed, papers rustling along the scroll boxes towering over them. As the first scroll of the day swooped to Drex's gloved hands, another pair of linen gloves appeared at Tanneus's elbow. Drex smiled ruefully,

"That would seem to be the answer we seek Tanneus." he remarked, and began his assistant's first lesson.

Chapter 22 - The Lake that Sang

Three days ride from Tanneus, Daro woke but couldn't tell where he was, so he lay, quietly absorbing what he could from the clues around him. Warm and comfortable, yet tremulously fearful, he felt utterly powerless, nothing here under his control as his eyelids fluttered open. Vaguely disappointed at there being no discernible light source he stretched lethargically, curling back down into the deep well of unconsciousness he had momentarily left.

In his sleep he was visited by visions of a tall lithe man, with the unseamed skin and clear eyes of the ageless. He "watched" the stranger go about his business, hands gentle on the limbs of a disabled child, hands busy mixing ingredients, eyes watchful as he dispensed medications, always accompanied by a faint thread of song as gradually the thought formed that he was watching some sort of Apothecary.

However, after a period of confusing images showing the same man star-gazing, he began to doubt his earlier assumption when he saw the stranger consulting with others engrossed in scrolls bearing star charts of great antiquity. Murmuring to himself Daro considered warily. Surely ancient history had always been a closed subject? The Stranger of his dreams was no Greeeyn, for he wore the braid of a Clansman, but he acted like a student of science. Finally, after "watching" his stranger making copious notes in a fine script, he understood the nature of the one he watched, when he "saw" the great outer gate of Selesh open automatically at a single gesture of the man's hand!

He tried to withdraw from his dream, Wrenching away from the insistent beat that infused his awareness, forcing it to slow, unsuccessfully seeking escape from the images that assailed him.

He heard confused sounds, running feet pounding through the passageways of his childhood home. He tried to call out, to find out what was happening, but instead he found himself drawn by the magnetism of the man he followed, into the most intimate encounters he had ever experienced. Fragments of conversation showed that an imminent crisis was at hand as weeping women ran past him, laden with food, bedding, clothes, water, moving it down into the deeper recesses of the cavern system. Then, amongst them a familiar face appeared and Daro chuckled bitterly as Feydora sped past, flinching as she returned to peer up into his face doubtfully. She murmured,

"Dearling, my memory cloak suits you, but somehow you look different…Less sure of yourself, yet more commanding!"

He didn't try to make sense of that, for in the next second she was kissing him, and his mind reeled under the passionate assault of her tongue and lips. There was a sound like a hammer-blow, the very passageway under him leapt, doors to right and left burst open, and then a terrifying roar of falling stone filled the air followed by a billowing cloud of dust & debris.

The world tilted and turned black, visions blurred and faded under a sense of overwhelming pressure then amidst a swirl of sparkles, Daro "saw" the

Assendarium open ahead of him, and found himself walking out onto the lowering tongue of rock as it pivoted into place in the great Hall. He felt himself hold out his hands to the assembly below and glancing down, saw that these were not his hands at all, but those of another. Panicking, uncertain of who, where or when he was, he tried to struggle out of the swirl of cloth that imprisoned him, intent on escaping from memories that were definitely not his and in so doing, encountered a pair of hands that gripped his firmly. He clutched at them desperately, hearing a warmth in the voice that echoed in his mind.

"Hold on Sandsinger. Hold on to my memories… They will save your world. Don't fight the cloak, it will help you see what you are." The voice choked with emotion added softly, "What we were." Before returning to command him forcefully.

"Hold on, help is coming."

Then he was falling down a deep well of silence into a black void where no light penetrated and the visions massed to ambush him again.

For a time he had respite. He lingered in the dark, skirting the edge of thought, fearful of anything that might provoke the visions he didn't entirely understand, but inevitably a wave of black sleep rolled him helplessly, thrusting him into trance where the experience of others filled his mind.

When the sound came, although half prepared for it, the volume of the ringing bell took his breath away. He could see women, sat in ceremonial war canoes, which lazily floating on a great underground lake, seemed like a flotilla of sleeping water sharls, mythical water beasts of the distant past. Daro felt rather than saw the expressions of fierce concentration on the faces of the leaders. They (like the others) knelt in the belly of their canoes, one at the front, the other at the back and with the shock of recognition he saw the elaborate tattoos of the Nishanawa stand out embracing long graceful spines, shimmering brightly on wrists raised to bring the immense paddles down into the water.

He gazed down (it seemed from a height), as the sound gathered, swirling around the immense cavern that held this secret lake, listening to the rising crescendo of sound, and watching the water starting to rise. Then, as he watched the singing lake in awe, the charged water rose abruptly, as he flinched away in fright. He supposed fleetingly that he feared water, didn't understand its principles never having been exposed to more than a bathing pool's depth of it. This place was different to the world he inhabited. Water was as plentiful as sand (and as Daro knew full well) one could drown in sand.

As the thought struggled to the surface the canoes leapt forward, racing across the boiling lake as it heaved as though trying to escape the confines of its cavern. A deep sonorous groan rang from the walls, the water climbed higher, then the object of the canoes course became evident. An enormous tunnel set high up on the walls was rushing towards him.

Truly horrified, Daro gripped the sides of the canoe he now appeared to be in, trying not to scream as the craft was catapulted into the dark. Frantically he "reached" for his powers, but they were gone. There was nothing he could do or say, other than cling on, desperately hoping that those who paddled knew what they were doing. He was aware of the grim smiles as their craft bucked and shuddered under the pressure of the torrent as they surged around some great underground bend, then the muscles on the arms of the oarswomen bunched and they were thrusting down into the river's depths again, paddles lifting and falling to some inner rhythm from which he was excluded.

He found himself counting the craft. Nine canoes were shooting the rapids and for a while his mind floated free, aware of the rock and sway, the nail biting surges, the pain in the ears as they streaked through ever decreasing apertures, until he heard a distant roar, a great thundering shook his body as the leader of his canoe raised her voice in some arcane chant.

The effect on the oarswomen was electric. Heads lifted, arms rejuvenated they plunged the great paddles into the water, hurtling the craft forward, chanting in unison as the other canoes swung in behind them. He struggled up, sitting frozen in terror as he took in the roots of trees penetrating this tunnel, the black depths below as an impossible tide swept them over the edge of a precipice, swirling them down a darkly glistening tunnel toward impending death. The rhythm of the paddles both drove and lulled his anxiety, the surge of the water was matched to the surge of the women's chanting, there was a pounding in his ears which matched the pounding of his heart, then beneath him, the lake sang.

He opened his eyes as they swept from a tunnel into an enormous cavern. Great arches soared into the remote heights of the roof as they swept past a landing, on into another tunnel, water billowing and surging behind them as though assisting an escape. The rocky confines of the tunnel they had entered glittered crazily as they bucked and swayed to the elaborate syncopation of the women's chanting, the splash of the paddles and a dull booming from far behind them. There was a growing sense of urgency, the blood thundered in Daro's ears, then an exquisite pain shook him, the tumult in his blood rose as the toll of some great bell echoed through the cave system and Daro felt the land around them buckle under insupportable pressure.

When he surfaced he was lying on sand, Opal Sand. Around him was utter devastation amidst which a small flotilla of canoes was beached, so far from water that they might never have floated. Numbly, he watched the women he had travelled with, form up on their leaders, totally ignoring him as they marched away. Physically and emotionally drained. He slept, waking in the dark as another dream began.

He was no longer alone. Someone, no, "something" was curled in sleep not far from him. He sat up cautiously, turning his head to try and penetrate the absolute darkness of his surroundings, anxious to find out where he was. Gradually he became so frustrated that he clicked his fingers the way he usually did when engaging "truesight" and focussed. Beyond him lay a huge supine form, so large that even when he stood, the creature topped him by his own six spans in height. There was a strange, yet familiar scent in his nostrils, and Daro whirled to see the familiar cavern opening that looked out over Scartel's monumental crater. He was in the Lookout Cave, and yet he felt at home, as though he was in the Opal Sands, and looked down to see that the floor of the Lookout was covered in a deep carpet of Opal Sand.

He ventured into the room that he and Jalni had shared during their rescue of Solana's orphans, and he wondered (if only briefly) how this had come about, then shrieked, clapping his hands to his ears then crouching to hide as a voice filled his mind with the information he needed.

"I brought your sand when you were sick Ichspeller.", the voice said apologetically. "You needed your Sand, we needed you, and so my rider instructed me to bring sand while the Healers treated your wounds. You are better now?"

Daro was nonplussed. He had never heard of an animal that talked, and wished he could see this one clearly, but there was not enough light.

"You may touch me Ichspeller," the voice in his head commented quietly, "I am bond to another so your touch will not cleave me to you".

The suggestion was so outrageous, that for a moment Daro's head swam. Where had this beast (whatever it was), come from that it knew the inherent dangers of a Sandsinger's touch? How in the Holy Nine Sands was he to explain this to his mother, and explain it he must for he was lurching far from the Way in his activities and must seek the guidance of the Guardians. He hesitated, thinking wildly.

"This is just a dream. The information this beast offers is just in my head, besides, I've never accidentally bonded anything I didn't want to bond!"

There was a soft rumble (like the thunder of a thousand sands), and the voice remarked acidly,

"Dommichspeller Jalni might disagree with that my friend!", then Daro's truesight froze him to the spot in terror as he gazed into the eyes of a Drekken for the first time.

Hours passed as he communed with her. He had instinctively cloaked his inner self, raising augmented shields against the unknown, but as time passed, the flagging Sandsinger leant against Yaydoran's flank, stroking her glittering hide with oil as she requested, listening to the soft croon as the Drekken told him her history. He heard about the rise of her kind, the hatching of many small Drekkens, then of her pride in being the one chosen to bear the Opal Sandsinger when he travelled the Sands. He heard the increasing tension in her voice as she told him of the world she remembered, a world with one moon, safe overland travel, and seas. Daro's mind whirled, then steadied as Yaydoran' explained gently.

"My last clutch had left me weakened when the call came. We were to carry my Lord Aramand to a conclave at Sanctuary.", she confided. "My clutch were still in stasis, so were safe to leave with my mate, so I was detailed to fly my Lord Aramand and his Grandfather the Star-Weaver from Selesh to Sanctuary. The Sandsinger said they were to discuss "preparations".

It was clear from the way she spoke that the Drekken was not privy to those preparations, but she said thoughtfully,

"Bad weather made it a difficult flight. The conclave didn't go well, and both the mages were very angry afterward. We flew straight to Lord Aramand's holding, but we were attacked as we arrived."

Daro nearly choked, he had "seen" that attack, watching in horror as the man he now knew as Aramand plunge to certain death, as his Drekken was torn to shreds by the vicious black Drekkens. He shuddered and Yaydoran's head lowered as she studied his grief stricken face.

"You're a strange man my Lord," she stated, hissing as she moved what appeared to be a wounded wing. "I never came across a Sandsinger who didn't know he was immortal before."

Daro bit his lip, then said quietly,

"I never came across a live Drekken or another Sandsinger. What you are telling me seems hideously impossible. Sandsingers died out a thousand Rotations ago, Drekkens were believed wiped out at the same time. I am the first of a new race of Sandsingers..." then he was interrupted by a long shivering sigh from Yaydoran as she lowered her head in despair.

"Then my Lord, I must be the last of my kind, waiting for you to find me and my clutch, so that together we might reverse the damage and prevent the fall of Gatta."

Her brilliant eyes dimmed as she lowered her snout, drifting off to sleep, but not before Daro heard her closing thoughts.

"Either he's too young to take on this challenge, or I am too old. Besides, Sandsingers don't die, they can't. Perhaps he's mad, perhaps I'm mad. No Sandsingers? No Drekkens? Perhaps we're both dreaming?"

There was a roaring in Daro's ears, he had to lie down or he would fall down. Feeling sick and dizzy he went slowly back to his bed and slept like the dead. Again he woke to darkness and the residue of exhaustion. He lay, quietly recalling some of his dreams, replaying them to himself wonderingly. He was vaguely aware of someone else present, but chose not to engage with them, although he was grateful for the small attentions he was receiving. He felt a cooling cloth on his forehead, smelt a sweetly pungent odour that he dimly associated with his childhood, as his lips were wetted with warm fluid. A spoonful of liquid warmed his throat, (the dryness of which astonished him), then he felt the darkness creep up on him and slid into dream ridden sleep again.

He was running. Searching for something or someone when he heard the bell. It was low toned but seemed (like some vibration) to be summoning him personally. He stood stock-still, chest heaving with his previous exertions and he felt rather than saw the prickle of his aura surround him. He could only surmise that somehow he was endangered, as he sought to master his ragged breathing, but soon he knew different. He heard the excited yips and yowls of the Sheer wolves before the Tawn found him, then he was being thrown up onto the saddle of a magnificent beast, gratefully taking hold of the reins as a familiar voice declared,

"He's still in shock! Can he travel like this?", followed by a deeper voice which emitted a wry chuckle.

"He'd better. There's no faster way to get him off-sands and if his mother finds him in this state, she'll flay Olneth alive!"

No more was said but the Sheer Wolf glided into that place known only as the Sheer, but Daro was far from them, sleeping and dreaming of another time, another place, while the memories he had absorbed found their lodging in his mind.

He rode out the memory dreams, gradually learning to distinguish his own from "the others". With no way of determining dreams from an altered state of reality he relied on common sense to keep him sane as he wandered in this strange state of somnolence.

Vague childhood recollections of poisoning himself with a scratch from an ancient Drekkens claw, reminded him of anxious eyes watching over him, so much so that rousing in between dreams, he persuaded himself that his current "minders" must have been present at that earlier event.

Now, a strong pair of arms lifted him whilst another tipped his head back, nearly drowning him with a preparation so foul that he retched helplessly. That one, he mused darkly, had been ruthless to the point of extremity, refusing to let him slide deeper into the dreams which dogged his heels. Slapping his cheeks sharply when he slipped into the mellow warmth of memory, his tormentor ruthlessly cut him off from the sweet smell of new-mown hay, closing down the dream world to which he was clinging. Aware that he had clenched his hands on cloth, he felt an ephemeral impression of a woman's body against his, even as he fought both the hands that attempted to unclench his grip and the voice insisting that he,

"Let go".

Fighting an odd compulsion to obey, he heard a faint ringing sound and struggled up losing his precious trophy before fainting clean away with the pang of its parting. Then he woke!

The eyes that surveyed him coolly were not human. They were huge, lambently gold, angled strangely along a snout richly endowed by silver fur. He "felt" the colour, knew with certain understanding that somehow he was seeing through another's eyes and reached out as a well-remembered voice said softly,

"So help me boy, but if you frighten me like that again, I'll suspend you by the heels from Hadda's Rift until you beg forgiveness for your wilful stupidity and arrogance!"

The threat was not issued lightly, but hissed between the clenched teeth of a man who fully believed that he could carry it out with no fear of reprisal, despite the young mage's skill in magic. Fierce but loving hands grasped Daro's upper arms, lifting him to a sitting position as someone else slipped a rough pillow behind him, then he was lowered back to rest. He breathed in slowly, separating scents as he attempted to work out who was present.

The sharp tang of vinagared saltberries warned him that Carolus was to be approached with care. The odour of mingled saddle-wax told him that Olneth stood guard... but still there was another, then there was the wolf. He shot upright, nearly colliding with the solicitous form hovering over him, then the warm, slightly amused voice said clearly,

"Steady Daro, you are not out of this pass yet!", as strong young arms caught and held him with brotherly affection. A rush of something like panic touched

Daro briefly, then he focussed his own memories, seeking the voice, confusing himself by recalling it in a younger, lighter tone.

"Rann? Is that you?", he tilted his head, listening as the deeper adult voice chaffed him.

"Yes my friend," the tall young Ranger laid his fellow Nightlingby back on his pillows, then stood aside to let Carolus fuss over his Songchild. "Someone had to stay with Grey..." he broke off as the Sandsinger was lifted and resettled in preparation for a meal, then continued smoothly as the others removed soiled bedding and went to prepare food.

"...she wouldn't leave your side. Boy, did I ever get a scolding from Draille!", he exclaimed, some of his youthful exuberance spilling over, as delicious aromas rose from the small hearth.

"He bawled me out for bringing her along. Told me she was too young for such a haul, but she settled easily with the Tawn, and Garald said it was necessary!"

The Sandsingers hands had quite naturally captured the Sheer wolf's snout and as she sighed against his palm in contented drowsiness, he soothed her himself, whispering little endearments that told the young ranger that he was privileged to witness this lowering of Daro's habitual guard.

The men at the hearth murmured softly, a lamp glowed warmly, then the mage felt himself drifting and fell asleep, quite naturally, quite restfully, and for the first time in two ninenights, completely dreamless.

When he woke, Grey and Rann had gone and the disappointed Sandsinger lay in a kind of torpor that proclaimed his utter bone-deep weariness. He managed to drink another of the Apothecary's remedies (this time not so foul), and nibbled a softened biscuit until he fell asleep, rousing only when Rann returned, face grave, body language serious.

He heard the discussion, feeling that he should do something to help, but too tired to concentrate, he drifted as they spoke quietly amongst themselves, listening as the apothecary sorted through his seemingly endless stock of medication.

"Take these restoratives to Hanna," the old man instructed. "She'll know best how to use them, but make sure that Deshun Ikella rests. She's had one too many of these turns and will feel out of sorts for quite a while. Her Sisters in Sorcery should be told, but gathering immediately is hardly necessary. Beneva has the right of it and as soon as the young lunatic recovers himself, I'll stop by and help sort out the old one!"

Far from being incensed by the old man's disrespectful words, Daro first felt comforted by the knowledge that the apothecary wasn't particularly alarmed, then amused by the tone he had taken. However, sense told him that Jalni would nurse his frail Sorceress mother and he stopped worrying abruptly, concentrating on tickling Grey's tummy fur, while Olneth pretended that he hadn't noticed the sudden stilling of the apothecary's hands, nor the gesture which seemed to redirect his young Lord's interests away from their conversation. He wondered gravely why he hadn't noticed things like that happening before...then forgot those thoughts as a pair of steady eyes levelled at him.

"Since Daro was a child I've been able to hypnotise him into forgetting those things that frightened or upset him.", the old man confessed. "Don't you remember the underground pasture's odd crystalline roof Olneth? I noticed that animals kept there seemed unusually calm and when Daro was injured on that damn Drekkens Claw, I used one of the crystals to keep him calm while I worked the poison out of that wound." He produced a strangely subdued crystal out of a capacious pocket.

"Here... Let me show you!", Olneth and Rann looked at the uninteresting shard as Carolus turned it to the light, then, as it flashed green, they bent closer...and forgot...

The evening shadows lengthened as Daro woke to the realisation that this was not the original lower cave that he and Olneth had discovered. There had been little enough room for two in that, he supposed sleepily, listening to the echoing "plop" of water dripping somewhere slightly removed. He had become aware of a breeze earlier in the day, then understanding dawned, he was facing an entrance which seemed at odds with the shape of the cave he remembered. He roused himself to shuffle backwards into a pile of pillows, and grunted in surprise as his hands encountered fur. It shifted, something rumbled briefly, as Daro froze, and then a warm tongue gently swiped his cheek. This was not Grey he decided, then he sensed another as a gently hypnotic voice invited,

"Share your dreams with me brother", followed by what he later described as the weird sensation of travelling. There was a low toned harmony surrounding him in a cocoon of comfort, yet he was quite aware of hands touching him familiarly. Somehow, he was unable to resist the oddest sensation of a tempo building in his blood, and succumbed to the rhythmic kneading and the lightest of feather touches at his temples, the crown of his head, even his throat.

He felt gentle fingers probing his feet, his legs and ribs, and suppressing the urge to move away, surrendered his body to the lassitude that enveloped him. Then the fingers paused, there was a grunt of satisfaction, and then the fingers found a sore area. He flinched, but the practitioner (of whatever dark art was being performed) ignored him, pressing hard onto the very edge of his rib-cage with one hand, and his shoulder with the other. Swiftly the hands seemed to pulsate various points or positions on Daro's chest, neck even his forehead and fontanel. Daro quivered, feeling almost like some ancient ritual sacrifice as he felt each part of him quieten and attune to each other. His breathing slowed, his heart matched the tempo of life, his pulses steadied. Heart, stomach, kidneys and lungs began to work together. The relentless thrum of life ceased to batter itself against the fragile shell that held it, and started to flow with renewed vigour, and through it all he felt the tidal surge of something too strong to deny, too subtle to define, and too ephemeral to grasp in his hand.

He woke finally and fully in the deep quiet of early evening and sat up. He could hear the chink of spoons against bowls, smell the tang of biroots stew, yet he was nothing like as hungry as he ought to be. He rolled over to face the area from whence the sounds had come and was convinced that the others who sat grouped together were eating.

He raised his voice, shocked at the tremulous sound he made remarking to no-one in particular,

"I seem to have missed dinner?", hearing the sharp intake of breath from the others as he spoke.

Garald's voice said calmly,

"You have made a very quick recovery, but I think it unwise to feed you instantly. Your Songfather sleeps, and until he wakes naturally you must make do with milta grains soaked in milk. Will that do?", to which the responding growl of Daro's belly only raised a low brotherly chuckle from the Rangers gathered at the hearth.

Afterwards, Daro remembered little of the treatment that Garald had performed, accepting that the Dream Walker had thought it better that he didn't, however, given that his powers seemed to have slept with him, he considered privately that perhaps his own understanding of magic was different to the command of power that Garald obviously enjoyed.

Sensing his own acceptance of power in others not typically associated with talent of magic marked a significant change in himself, he swore softly.

"That's it! Rangers are possessed of a kind of natural magic!", he decided, then another thought intruded. "I wonder if that has anything to do with their constant interaction with the Sheer."

Subsiding on his pillows, back pressed against the familiar warmth of his own Sheer-wolf he pulled his blankets up and rested as his brain started to grapple with this mystery, unaware of the knowing smile on his Songfather's face.

The following morning he was permitted to join the others for their breakday meal. It was simple fare and listening to the low chatter, Daro began to realise just how long had passed since he had swung the ancient cloak around him. He listened quietly as Carolus proposed his next course of action.

Assuring him that Ikella was also on the road to recovery, the apothecary sighed, then reminded Daro of his own duties at Tregeth. He drew Daro back to his bed, pointing out that the young mage's legs were shaking. There he lowered himself onto a spare bedding roll as the members of the Tawn withdrew discreetly and Olneth started to clear and clean the cavern. The old man's voice was low, but vehement.

"I don't pretend to know what happened to you," he announced brusquely, "but you nearly succeeded in destroying yourself. Your curiosity must be tempered with more care Daro!", he warned peremptorily. "Your foster mother is aging fast, Suraya isn't yet ready to step up to the Staff, and you seem too ready to risk everything on a whim! We don't know enough to help you, yet you are Sandsinger, expected to set others an example."

He sighed heavily.

"Well my lad, we have to consider others before ourselves. You've shown that you can do that, so I'm begging you to understand how dangerous magic can be in the wrong hands, or at the wrong time for just two out of two billion examples. You need to come to terms with ordinary life as well!"

His voice grew serious, and Daro suddenly knew that he had disappointed the old man yet again, then the apothecary took up the theme.

"you have a long way to go if you can't remind yourself that there's a whole world that needs to be fed, sheltered, watered and taught. Women make magic, lead and teach us. Men work for food, shelter their children and bring their women to bear the next generation, and then there are Sandsingers. What do they do young man? Do they exist to torment old women with worry? Do they exist simply to provide problems for hard working Rangers who'd be better off looking after their own, or dragging me half a world from my duties at Tregeth? What exactly have you gained with all this nonsense Hey? A bad experience? A near-death experience? What would you do with that? Just what have you learned from it Daro?"

Severe old eyes surveyed Daro narrowly, and hearing the censure in his Songfather's voice, even Daro shifted uncomfortably before replying. He sat cross-legged on his blankets considering, his face drawn and uncommonly pale with great dark circles (like bruises) beneath closed eyes. Then sighing, and licking suddenly dry lips the mage said gruffly,

"I gained a glimpse of Pelshar as it used to be. I saw wonders (and horrors) and more water than I ever believed possible. I saw Selesh as it prepared for some disaster but…" his voice lowered dramatically as he whispered hoarsely, "They confused me with someone else!"

There was no sound, no breath of wind, not even the faint "plop" of dripping water as Carolus took in the import of Daro's last words, then the apothecary hissed as he exhaled a long quivering breath..

"Hadda's balls boy! In what company have you been walking?",

In the moment that Daro sensed the apothecary's concern, "the other" spoke softly.

"Remember Sandsinger, only gather the courage to remember and we'll be here to guide you, for we can never really die. Remember …put the present from you, then reach back and share our past!"

Carolus saw Daro pale still further, and gasped as the younger man made as if to rise before falling limp and unresponsive at his feet.

There was a clamour of voices, helping hands lifted the blind mage from the sands, then a jumble of comment and protestations as the party rolled Daro into a hastily prepared travelling sling. To the dazed young man in the centre of the huddle that stripped the cavern and prepared to leave Aramand's Peak, only one voice seemed clear and consistent.

"We are going Olneth! Remember what I told you? Lay a trail north, then join us when you can, but leave no hint of our visit here. For Daro's sake, I need to get him off-sands and away from whatever besets him. He has a long road to recovery ahead of him, and needs complete rest. That can be arranged at Tregeth where I can look after him and my other duties simultaneously, whereas here, I can do nothing!"

Vaguely Daro was aware of being lifted, heard the soft sound of Grey's snuffling, then he felt movement, cold ripples passed over him as the Sheer wolves surged forward, disappearing at the edge of vision as Olneth clucked to the snickering of Zeglurs as he led them away in the opposite direction.

The shadows lengthened in the cavern they had occupied, a breeze swept the sands below until with the daylight fading there was nothing to suggest that the company of Rangers (and others), had ever been there. Overhead a low fluting call echoed, two shadows detached themselves from the highest peak and with a strong beat of down swept wings, circled once then followed the mage into the Azure Sands and beyond.

The first thing Jalni knew about changes to her plans was heralded by Draille's absence just days after she began to pack. She had been busily weaving a length of cloth on a hand loom in the afternoon rest break, and looked for Draille to knock out a stubborn peg on the frame, so that she could lengthen the warp. When she discovered no sign of him in the settlement, she cheerfully accosted Sushanna who having assisted her, decided to look at Jalni's hands.

They entered Sushanna's quarters, and Jalni sat looking about at the Ranger Apothecary's workroom with a sudden pang of nostalgia for Selesh. Kneading her patient's wrist, Sushanna gave a rueful grin before asking,

"Any tingling? Do you suffer night pains? Perhaps you've discovered that holding your arm up vertically helps?", all of which she answered in the negative. Sushanna pursed her lips, turning each of Jalni's wrists back and forth then taking her pulses contemplatively as she murmured reassuringly.

I don't think you've got week wrists Jalni. It's just that we have experience of a particularly uncomfortable problem that sometimes affects pregnant women. However, you say you're not suffering transient pain or tingling, and that weaving frame *did* have a very tight peg. There's no other sign of pinched wrists thankfully. It's a miserable condition, and I'd need Garald and Kilda to fix it, so that's fortunate because they're away just now."

Jalni stared at her. It had been very quiet for the last day or two, but she hadn't realised just how quiet Holmgarth had become.

"Hunting?", she surmised, and was amazed when Sushanna blushed faintly.

"Some of them are ...", the Apothecary said (carefully minimizing the amount of information she gave out, then added swiftly, "Others are taking plants to market, and more have departed about their own business."

Jalni succeeded in restraining her curiosity, but couldn't fail to note the absence of Sheer-wolves when she came on a disconsolate Chrysim who was keeping company with a gaggle of Rangerlings. They were busily grooming Echo (much to the Mystcat's disgust) when Jalni sat down to pass the time of day. Conscious of the cat's link to Daro, she had been avoiding all contact with him, but she was touched when the great sleek animal put a paw over her foot, rumbling softly. Chrysim nodded slowly to himself then said clearly,

"Healer Jalni, we know you're in kitt but we won't tell Daro. He's too full of magic to trust these days. He said he would go adventuring with Olneth, and we told him that we are bound for the Ashgenar. I want to see the mines. Echo wants to find his Clan, and Daro thought that was a good idea if Lown or some other older joined us."

It was a huge speech for Chrysim, and Jalni (somewhat taken aback) said faintly,

"What do you want with the mines Chrysim?", and the boy coloured.

"Father wanted to give Deshun Ikella a gem to thank her for the home she has given us. He thought that he could find something appropriate in Drayshall, where the best Zurian gemstones are mined. He has saved every credit towards this end, saying that once he has this last part, he can fashion a jewelled map of the Sands as a book rest for the Book of Rule. He retires from shoemaking this Rotation, my half-brother will carry on his business, while Father takes a long deserved break. He will keep a workshop, lease part of it to Master Farandel's son, and they will work on this gift together."

Jalni was overcome at the thought of her old friend Duvell retiring. The blind shoemaker had seemed ageless, and she was used to finding him as a useful confidante. She knew his older family, knew of his re-marriage and the subsequent birth of three more sons, and had been present when Daro had taken Lown as his first Sandsworn. Undeniably linked to this humble little family, she had journeyed with them, broken bread with them, and yet she knew so little about them, other than the old shoemaker was Zurian himself.

She sat in the sun of late afternoon helping one of the youngsters plait a reed basket, perfectly at peace, wishing that Daro's first enquiry wouldn't find her here, putting her friends at risk if he took umbrage against them. Suddenly Chrysim leapt to his feet, padding off towards the narrow cleft in the hidden fissure that was Holmgarth. Echo, rolling over to watch his companion depart yawned lazily, eyes narrowing and ears twitching. His throaty purr however, gave his level of excitement away and for a moment Jalni stilled, filled with a horrible idea.

"What if Daro had followed her?", she thought wildly, but Echo just blinked and licked his paws. Turning, she fixed him with an imperious stare, unaware that her eyes were blazing Azure fire, hair sizzling in a copper aureole around her head.

"Who?", she demanded.

Echo twitched his ears uneasily, lowering his head. Struggling to look innocent, he failed dismally, and eventually allowed Jalni to turn his head and peer into his eyes.

"Just one man comes", was the thought that she fastened onto.

"One man?", she questioned, as the cat's purr intensified, "Puhrr raorh!" he agreed, then she caught sight of him. Broad-shouldered and light on his feet, grinning from ear to ear, her Uncle strode along with Chrysim bouncing in his wake. Immediately she noticed his Weaver's surcoat, now proudly topped by his Master's broad-brimmed hat. She gasped as she took in the pins adorning its crown, Master Weaver and Holder they proclaimed to the world, but next minute she was swept into his smiling embrace as the lads scampered off to admit the small pack train.

Several hours and a meal later, Jalni broached the subject of her situation with Orto, who was much more adept at conversation now his deafness had been all but cured. He listened carefully without interruption as Jalni described what had happened. She gave herself no quarter, openly admitting her own faults, but Orto sat grim-faced as she told him of her plans.

"You can't imagine that the most powerful man on Pelshar is simply going to forget you?" he spoke heavily.

"I knew him long before you did sweeting, long before he came into his power, and he was scary even then! My Solana told me what was coming. She believed in Sandsingers you see Jalni, and though she died before I could return to Scartel, I comfort myself by believing that she knew what he was before she went to the Sands."

For a long moment Jalni's breath was stilled as she recalled that heart-breaking moment when Solana lay against her Sandsinger, concentrating on passing on her Song Spells, then she bent her head and told her Uncle how it had been, admitting simply,

"She knew Orto. He told her before she died, I heard it myself. He supported her to the end and almost beyond. I assisted him, and I suppose that's when I fell in love with him. He cocooned her in his power. Took all the pain and fear away, and gave her easy choices to take. When the One took her, Daro was so committed to keeping her safe that he nearly didn't disengage in time."

Her brilliant blue eyes sparkled through her tears.

"We had to force him back, anchor him to the Sands or he might have died then and there.", she spoke simply. "I think the Healer in me engaged too much then. I already admired him for his courage, but I didn't quite understand his power and now I do, I wish I didn't. Oh Orto, what am I to do?"

Her Uncle surveyed her gravely.

"Well, I think we should finalise my trading here, send the boys back to Jerritol with messages for Edrith, Orana, and Madiv," he paused smiling as he added teasingly. "Then, I'll persuade your friends to house me and a couple of pack mules before we go seeking miners with young Chrysim."

He held up a hand at Jalni's astonished outburst, and resumed his planning, without any sign that he was thinking "on his feet".

"Look my dear, it's quite simple. Chrysim wants to help his father. I want to secure some unusual dyes and you want to avoid confrontation with your child's father. The cat wants to find a mate and it can all happen in the Ashgenar. I remember someone telling me that no Healer or Sorceress would travel there because the abundance of metals and minerals in the soil stopped magic -users tapping into the Source. That's why large permanent settlements have never developed there." He leant forward, eyes bright with cunning,

"Don't you think it might also make it unlikely that yon lad would seek you there? In addition, if my continued interest in Mystcats tells me true, even over a short distance they can't communicate with their own kind easily. In the old days when there were hundreds of them, they were hunted nearly out of existence. They escaped to the Ashgenar and survived, but man didn't follow them, because of the terrain and lack of water. Now we know better than to hunt the cats, have located water sources, and can mine the minerals."

Jalni thought silently. She would have to be careful, but she was fit and well, only five moons gone, and her Uncle had missed another advantage, and another place she could consider home.

"Yes!", she exclaimed on a rising tide of excitement that caused her unborn child to kick in enthusiastic agreement. "Besides everything else, we are both seasoned travellers, and if I'm not mistaken there's a way through to the Temple of the Winds. The Oracle predicted this birth, she also offered me a home there with the rest of the Clan. Now I can escape my difficulty and she can be a witness. If I am right and my child is male, he will be fostered along with the other children born to the Nishanawa. He will be one amongst many, so if my lord was to seek either him or me, he'd have to follow an invisible trail, then sort out which child is whose!"

So it was left and that night Jalni slept, confident that she could make the journey. She'd be safe in her chosen companions, and able to fulfil her plans..

On the far side of the Opal Sands, many of her friends conspired to keep Daro safe without revealing any of his lover's plans. He had been hoisted (half asleep) into the cunning slings that Rangers used to transport game after a successful hunt. Packed against bass-grass padding the young mage had succumbed to the drug infused sweetdrink without a murmur. One of the larger she-wolves carried Carolus as she padded in Grey's wake. Close to the Sandsinger's mount, Garald watched the first journey of the silver Sheer wolf cub with the eyes of a Bard and none that saw that party assembling doubted that this ride would go down in Ranger history. Deeper into the midnight blue Sands the Rangers swept, past Ranger Falls they turned south again, heading for the Zeglur breeding grounds at Tregeth where the Lord of the Opal could recover far from the resonance of his own Sands and the subtle persuasion of an ancient cloak.

Close to the range that enclosed his forbidden homesand, Olneth sighed deeply, feeling the pull of old loyalties and older loves. His hands caressed a small pouch containing a locket holding a curl of his missing child's hair. Silently praying that the Wind of his desert would waft his love to the hearts of those who still lived beyond the barrier, he turned north clutching the leading reins of his Zeglur stock, and made for Shilinch, the market town on the borders of the Opal and Tourmaline Sands. Here, he could dispose of his animals profitably, gather news and trade for rare ingredients, keeping his eyes open for a cure for his Sorceress who languished, in peril of her life thanks to a mere sliver of poisonwood.

PART THREE – SWORD OF SORCERY

Chapter 25 - The Unknown Territories

In the warm glow of a huge log fire, Carolus cleared his throat carefully then turned to address his Songchild firmly.

"From the moment we are born, we are all on a journey into unknown territory Daro. Who knows which beast the herder will choose for slaughter? Who knows what will happen the next day my boy. It is only by repeatedly seeing the results of another's actions that we learn not to stray into danger and as you very well know, danger comes in many forms, not all of them recognisable."

The hunched figure on the bed stirred restively, then from the dark a harsh voice said abruptly,

"I grant you that Songfather, but I can't understand why Jalni didn't stay at Selesh to look after my mother. The One only knows where she's gone and with my powers at an all-time low I can't raise the strength to scry for her. Women are damned inconvenient animals don't you know!"

The voice suggested exhaustion as his Songfather lifted a pan from the hearth and stirred it, sniffing appreciatively.

"What sand-blasted muck are you playing with now?" the querulous voice demanded. "Don't forget, I can recognise by taste and smell most of the potions you brew!"

There was a low chuckle as Carolus replaced the pan in the embers, approaching the bed with a beaker in his hand. He held the vessel up to the light, watching a distinct swirl of bubbles dissipate, then he said gruffly,

"If you want to recover sufficiently to return to Selesh for Jentaroth Daro, you have to make an effort. Yes, you are safe lying here, you don't hear the voices of times past while you are here, but you must return to Selesh sometime and for Ikella's sake, the sooner the better. You profess your love for your foster-mother, but you don't seem willing to be with her when she enters that journey from which none of us return. Would you have her die alone?"

Daro had been scolded by Carolus many times in the past, but there was a hard edge to his voice that the Sandsinger had never heard before. He gulped, rolled onto one elbow and sat up slowly.

"Is she really dying?" he asked, voice shaking with desperate weariness, as the old man carefully placed the beaker in his hand. He regarded Daro with sympathy, adjusting his robe and sliding a chair near to the invalid's bedside, before continuing softly.

"The One only knows." He said shortly, but added by way of explanation, "However that infernal piece of poisonwood got into her foot, in the end, it will kill her. Her age is against her, she has marvellous resilience but there's no cure for it Daro, no cure at all."

He sighed heavily, causing Daro to conjure up a picture of his indomitable mother, green eyes blazing, silver hair crackling with fury as she faced him down the length of the Healer Hall on the night he took his powers.

The Sandsinger echoed the sigh, then said slowly, "I can hardly believe that she has weakened so swiftly. I must speak with Draille about this poisonwood. The Healers might have stood a chance had they known what they were dealing with."

The Apothecary shook his head deciding that his charges hold on magic was so advanced, that ordinary mortals failed to take into account that Daro had led a sheltered life. Furthermore, he had lost his sight right at the time he might otherwise have been travelling the Sands increasing his general knowledge. He settled back, easing his knees with a rueful shrug and explained.

"Long ago, back in Adaria's time, there were regions so polluted by the effects of Cataclysm that they were declared blighted. We believe that the plant from which the poisonwood of today developed, may have connections to one of these regions. Of course, travel was so perilous in those days, that the Guardians of those times had no trouble at all in issuing a list of circumscribed areas. As you know, I have been the messenger of the Guardians for most of my lifetime, yet it is only during comparatively recent Rotations the Rangers have permitted us to take observations on their culture. As you know, poisonwood is unique to the Rangers. Its use, traditions and the ethics surrounding the practise are completely foreign to us, even abhorrent to most Healers. Nevertheless, I believe that there are times when we all consider the end of our lives and contemplate what we would do in the face of extreme and terminal illness or injury. You have already been in that position more times than is good for a young man, yet you didn't hesitate when you had to do the kindest thing for your friends, for Brus."

Daro sat up abruptly. "That's not fair Carolus! Both times I was out in the wilds with nothing to help me. I am not a god! I'm only a Sandsinger, and a pretty poor one at that.", he added (sotto voce).

Clambering out of his bedclothes, he huddled into a robe, swinging to sit on the end of the bed facing the fire as Carolus stirred it into life once more. Unable to see the satisfied look on his companion's face, he nevertheless listened attentively as the old man re-settled his pan on the trivet close to the hottest embers and set about refilling their beakers.

While the Apothecary hummed under his breath, Daro said shortly,

"I hear you old man. Do you think I don't know that you have a power of your own? For the One's sake, I might be blind, but I'm not completely addled! You've been at it all of my life, spinning a protective web around me. You and Ikella are a formidable team, don't think I don't know what you are doing, but I'm not sure that I can bear it much longer."

These last words were uttered with such despair that Carolus reached out, touching the young mage, lightly ruffling his hair.

"There isn't a normal man or woman that doesn't feel the same way my boy," the Apothecary said sympathetically, "However, when the time comes, you will deal with it, just as we all do, in our own way!"

The Sandsinger sighed, then said gruffly,

"I apologise. I've been selfish, stupid to the point of arrogance, expecting all my friends to carry my baggage, instead of growing up and doing what I must.", his eyes flickered open, the deep opaline gleams visible, but sleeping, his powers still resting after his long illness. He tilted his head as though listening for something, then said miserably,

"I know so much you would think that the One might grant me a chance to save her. Can I really do nothing for her?"

Carolus straightened and turned to face Daro, deep set eyes gleamed as he saw the young mage's unshielded face, then he said soberly

"You can prepare yourself to face the world with your head held high, my boy.", he said softly. "It will be a comfort, not only to our Clan, but to all the Union of the Sands if they learn that there will be no loss of power when our Deshun takes her long walk. It will undoubtedly send a message to the Heretic who has her spies amongst us.

She may in point of fact feel marginally safer on her side of the barrier once she knows that there is a Sandsinger in Selesh."

"Do you think that wise?" Daro sounded intrigued, so the old man prepared drinks, and returned to his chair while they considered his rationale.

"We will have a period of time during which we will have to manage with a new Sorceress, and only two Guardians. Obviously I can't predict who the wristlets will choose, but there must be stability in the Sands during that time. It is the one thing that Ikella has lived for, dreamt of, and fought every obstacle to achieve. Peace, stability, and healing for a grossly damaged world. These have to be the goals of High Magic if you are going to improve the lives in your hands."

Daro sipped his drink and grimaced, "One day I shall forbid you to infuse my drinks with that damned Vetali.", he drank the stimulant reluctantly, then lifting his blind eyes heavenward, he struck his forehead with the palm of his hand.

"That's it!", he cried exultantly. "Just before this incident with that sand-blasted cloak, I summoned my Azure."

The silence of total incomprehension filled the homely room, as the Sandsinger continued, voice filled with enthusiasm. "Sorry Carolus, you wouldn't know what I'm talking about, but let me explain.", he rose as he spoke, and stood warming his hands before the fire.

"I assume that you know that a mage may consult with others, or read portents and omens to decide on a course of action?" he continued briskly, face alive with the memory of those moments, unaware perhaps that both the elements of the Seguidor and Anduigor were gleaming fitfully at his throat and waist.

It was the right time to summon the next Sandsinger, following the ancient Order of the Sands. Using what I know of ancient ritual, I woke the Azure, but as yet, there seems to have been little or no response, so assuming that I might need to return to Tirjhinar, I proposed an expedition to Olneth, taking in the puzzle of that confounded cloak at the same time."

He paused, obviously thinking aloud, unaware of Carolus's keen eyes following the gestures of his hands as they left his belt, sketching his very frustration on the air. The husky voice continued grimly,

"I admit that I hoped it would be Jalni, but it seems that all she can think of is returning to the Azure, I no longer feel that I have any power to retain her love, or even her presence in Selesh. In the end, I felt so restless that I decided to precipitate matters, telling her that she could lead her own life if she wanted, for fairly obviously she wants nothing of me".

As Carolus watched, Daro's hands flickered up to his throat, then down to his waist where his powerstones glimmered faintly, perhaps seeking reassurance that if his power slept, at least he was still empowered. He found himself wondering (albeit briefly) if Daro would ever be able to face Selesh again after his mother went to the Sands, then firmly boxed those thoughts away, as Daro returned to his current situation.

"I'm sorry to burden you with matters of magic Songfather, but even Ikella cannot advise me further. Do you suppose that Jalni's desire to go back to the Azure could spring from my actions?"

The Apothecary cleared his throat, rumbling suggestively,

"If I could deduce the thinking of women I'd be the greatest mage that ever lived Daro!", the old man said scornfully. Ruled by the moons, always pulling in two directions simultaneously, why do you think I travel alone? Give me ten Zeglurs to herd and two Sands to cross in search of a compatible mate, and I'll guarantee you my absence!"

Daro grinned, white teeth flashing against his tanned features.

"Yes, I grant that they have a peculiar sense of what is important, but I'm not asking you to solve the normal problems of gender conflict!", he exclaimed laughing, "just to tell me if you think that what I would call "the Awakening" requires the subject to be on their own Sands?", his brow wrinkled as he tried to remember how it had been for him. Failing dismally, he smiled as Carolus answered doubtfully.

"I think that Sorcery shows us that being in contact with ones powerstone might be the key, but then again, I don't know if it works the same for Sandsingers.", he answered briefly. "Remember, although I've been backward and forward to Sanctuary, I never saw anything that magical. The only time I was present during a succession was when you were a child, and I was mainly behind the scenes.", his fierce old eyes glinted as he said firmly,

"Very glad I was of that as well young man! What I saw that night in the Hall of the Healers makes me think that magic is just too dangerous to play with. You already know that yourself, but just following your line of thought, I think you've become depressed, self-absorbed, and just a little afraid of what you've got yourself involved in since your investigation of that cloak turned sour. I've a mind to tell you to forget magic for the time being, get well and don't worry about Ikella, she's in good hands with Hannah and Mina fighting over her care.

Jalni will surface when she's good and ready. I believe she's got Orto looking after her right now, so you can rest easy on that account."

Daro struggled to stay awake as the mellow voice rolled over him and thankfully the Apothecary saw that the choice of herbs and natural ingredients that he had concocted was finally working.

"Come along my boy," the old man steadied the exhausted man as he guided him back to bed. One hand touched his charges belt, the other sketched a simple symbol in the air as Daro gave in, snuggling into his bed with a sigh of relief.

"Rest, repair, mentally and spiritually. May the One in his goodness protect you against your own frailties and follies."

The simple prayer reached the blind Sandsinger as though from an immense distance. Then finally, he surrendered to sleep and began to recover.

As Daro began to take more notice of life, Carolus fretted. His entire hold was full of visiting traders and Rangers, the herders and crew were working dawn to dusk manning the precious breeding pens and yet the old man had a distinct feeling that he was needed elsewhere. His mind turned to Selesh where so much of his life belonged, but he didn't think he would be needed there for a while, and so he fidgeted and paced, until his frustrations became obvious. Tregeth was bulging at the seams, he couldn't leave any more than he could stay, so grumbling mightily, he decided to walk off his frustrations. Ascending through the pastures he stopped regularly to talk to his herders, examining a few cuts and bruises, and then looking at the new Zeglur colts as they gambolled around their mothers. He stretched, luxuriating in the pleasure of just being alive, but still something niggled, like an itch at the back of his brain. Nearing the edge of the plateau above the Unexplored Territories to the east of Tregeth he saw a figure sitting on the ground, back against the rock where he remembered Jashell leaning on her last visit. He peered at it doubtfully, recognizing one of Daro's Ranger protégés, sitting alone, apparently absorbed by deep distress. Pausing only to wonder if his Songchild should be involved before he interfered, Carolus used his walking Staff to lean on briefly while he observed his potential target, but when he saw the torment in the young face that lifted to greet him, such thoughts went out of his mind.

"Good day Ranger Godway.", he murmured soothingly, noting the tension in the young body as he fumbled absently in his scrip.

"I hope I'm not intruding?"

He didn't wait for a reply, but brought out his flask, tipped the paper screw he had just retrieved over a travel mug, watching as the powder settled into its depths. He measured the water he added by eye, then said in tones of mild exasperation,

"Well, bless my Sands…I seem to have forgotten my spoon. What an old fool I've become!"

With the courtesy characteristic of his origins, the Ranger boy proffered a thin strip cut from some plant, saying gruffly,

"It isn't a spoon Master Apothecary, but you can stir your medication with that. It's only a tanbark peeling, so it shouldn't destroy the medication's efficacy."

Carolus blinked in surprise, then smiled, taking the strip and stirring the mixture until (with a blossom of bubbles) he was content. He added more water from his flask, washing any residue from the strip as he did so, gravely returning it to its owner,

"Thank you Ranger Godway, but this isn't medication…" he lowered his voice conspiratorially, "It's a special treat which I reckon I thoroughly deserve!"

He sorted through his scrip, locating another slip then offered the mug to Rann in formal invitation.

"Want some? It's a great pick-me-up! Puts the world to rights and lets you get on with your day, even when you feel down, out, unloved and unwanted. Here, give me your mug, I can see you could do with a pick me up!"'

As the young Ranger hesitated, Carolus beamed at him.

"There's no Ranger law preventing you from accepting trail hospitality is there? You've completed Holonogarth I know, saw you invested three moons back didn't I? You're the third First Class Ranger since Marran aren't you?"

The old man twinkled at him and suddenly Rann was holding out his mug, gratefully accepting the shared drink. He gazed at the Apothecary, watching as Carolus tilted his mug, throwing down the restorative and joyfully smacking his lips.

Apparently contemplating the monolithic rock stacks beyond the yawning chasm that lay below his neatly terraced plateau, Carolus rose, relaxing gratefully as the tall young Ranger dutifully drank. He watched surreptitiously as the hectic flush on the boy's face vanished. Waiting until the dew of sweat receded from his brow, he judged that imminent action had been avoided, but only until he was sure whatever tumultuous passion had brought the Ranger to this precipice did he speak.

"If what drove you here can be helped young man," Carolus said mildly, "you only have to ask and I'll do my best. Nothing can be gained by such destruction; you might not succeed in your chosen path, doing irreparable harm, not only to yourself, but to the whole of Pelshar."

The old man didn't need to turn his head to know that the young Ranger was riddled with shame; the wracking sobs told him that. After a moment however, the strong, deep voice continued,

"Why have you held this within yourself, how have you hidden this from Kilda Pagthorn, Draille Skellin or the other Nightlingbys? Why didn't you consult me? What have I done that you wouldn't trust me with your grief?"

Rann's face was haggard, his voice cracked and colourless as he said hesitantly.

"I can't share any of my wild dreams with Rangers sir…I might have trusted Daro, who after all is my blood brother, but he holds the future in his hands and can no more single out a friend for comfort than I would burden him further with my confusion.", he gave a wry chuckle,

"Draille is too busy with his responsibilities to help me, and Kilda thought I was insane when I told her that I couldn't stay a Ranger, that I had to go to my mother's homesand. I tried to sort it out, went solitary for a full moon, then I was needed to help Daro get here, so I volunteered to look after Grey."

His chest rose as an enormous sob shook him, "I thought that with something to do I'd get over this depression, but then, all I did was to love Grey, and made her love me"

He flushed, hanging his head as he whispered painfully.

"I've been sent away, so that Grey remembers her bond with Daro and forgets me. I'm not permitted to ride with the Tawn until she settles again; I'm no use to anyone, not Ranger, not Zurian, though I've lived all my life in these Sands. I can't go forward, can't go back, and I dream Master Carolus, oh how I dream! I can't stay awake, dare not go to sleep, and all I see is pale green Sand as though I was being called to go somewhere that I can't go!"

He slumped against his rock and whispered painfully,

"Please Master Carolus, what shall I do? What is happening to me? Why must I feel as though the trail has melted beneath my feet and I've nowhere to turn, no-one to love, nothing left in this life for me!"

The Apothecary moved quietly to the distraught Ranger's side, and under the guise of taking pulses, caught the boy's wrist in one hand, forming human contact with this despairing soul. He bent over, brushing the hair from Rann's damp forehead, saying lightly,

"Well, my boy…You've got a fever, so let's get you back to base, get some good food and medication into you, then we can perhaps make sense of this. Daro will be glad of some company by the way. He's so much better that I think He's almost ready to return to Selesh. Perhaps you'll be able to accompany him there, I know that you enjoyed the Djellim and talking to Seris Beneva, besides…"

His voice providing a hypnotic background to the action, he raised the Ranger to his feet, and guided him away from the dizzying heights and down the track towards his homestead, all the time talking in a low monotonous tone, until he was handing Rann up the steps and into the arms of his blood-brother.

Once he'd settled Rann into a chair by the fireside, he busied himself lifting the lid on pans already set on the trivet. He stirred, tasted, seasoned the food, then went into his small workroom, and took down a flask containing an oily liquid, which when poured proved to have a fruity smell and the deep burgundy hue of berries. Daro, who had been keeping a watchful ear on their exhausted guest, appeared in the doorway, one interrogative eyebrow raised as Carolus decanted the thickened liquid into minuscule drinking vessels.

"Right…" proclaimed the Sandsinger in a mildly puzzled tome, "Rann runs away from the Tawn in disgrace, Draille came looking for him with Garald just now. You disappear for the day with nothing but that new restorative of mine, I get a summons from Beneva, who thinks I ought to come home, and you appear to be celebrating with redberry liqueur! Perhaps you'd care to explain?"

Carolus grinned, his own fatigue only just beginning to hit him.

"I went to walk off the feeling that I was urgently needed elsewhere, which I suggest was the case." he laid the three tiny goblets on a tray and went back to stir their evening meal. Rann was sleeping sat upright, head nodding gently as the Apothecary continued sombrely.

"I found Ranger Godway trying to decide if he could fly off the edge of the precipice." he said bleakly, as the Sandsinger's eyes opened in surprise. "He seems to think the alternative is to live with an agitation of the blood, which he thinks will drive him mad. He can't think, sleep, or function, and appears to feel that not even Grey (whom he loves), would really miss him if he died in the attempt. Incidentally, He's dreaming of pale green sands, despite the fact that he's half Ranger and doesn't remember living outside the Azure."

Daro's head tilted expressively, eyes widening at his Songfather's insinuation as he said softly,

"Can you be saying what I think you're saying?" he questioned sharply, "I know I raised the Azure correctly, but she hasn't responded yet. Even if another comes, they would have to be Azure wouldn't they? Rann is a Ranger, I know Holmgarth is in the Azure, but I believe he would take the Sand rights of his mother and she came from the Tourmaline. Or..." he said slowly, absently corralling one of the goblets, "could I have summoned any potential Talent in range Carolus?"

The Apothecary was ladling stew into large bowls as he spoke and his voice was unusually muffled as he turned to cut bread.

"My dear boy!" he exclaimed, "Why ask me? I'm only a lowly Apothecary, doing my best to earn a crust by breeding the most stubborn animal on Pelshar. I'm too stupid with sleep to answer that question with the degree of scorn it deserves. Young Rann is heartsick with all the conflict he is enduring and I believe that he could do with a blood brother to help him along. Why don't you take the poor boy away from the Tawn and listen to what he tells you. I think you might recognise some of his problems, the others you might lay before Seris Beneva. He knows Selesh, loves the Djellim, and you could engage him to assist the Guardians with their research, while I finish up here and follow on behind. I felt the pull of the Sands this morning, so if you think you are up to taking young Rann on alone, I expect Draille will authorise his release to Selesh."

The old man sipped his liqueur, gently rubbing one wrist with the fingers of the other hand. Daro took a little of the potent drink and blinked at its power, feeling it warm him, blossoming through his throat, momentarily stilling the steady thrum of magic as the old man chortled.

"Why don't we make a race of it boy? That'll take the stress off your Rangerling. He'll be too busy sorting out a path to worry about his tangled emotions. Yes blast it! Let's drink to new adventure!"

The Sandsinger grinned across the hearth at the enthusiasm in the old man's voice, but his strange eyes glinted suddenly severe, then he relented.

"Yes indeed. New adventure!" he said, but his mind thought bleakly,

"At the end of which, I will still be blind and alone!"

Chapter 27 - Daro's Dilemma

Throughout the remaining cycle of the moons Carolus avoided Daro's questions, removing himself to the pastures with no hint of his previous restlessness, leaving Rann with Daro. However, the expected dialogue between the two failed to materialise, and Daro was forced to accept that quite possibly it never would. Rann, who had always been the silent Second of the Nightlingby Patrol, seemed even more withdrawn, but Carolus seemed quite relaxed and ready to wait until natural confidence returned.

Draille Skellin was more difficult to read. His reaction to the proposed journey was fairly predictable, but Daro sensed something else driving the man. He too seemed edgy, and the Sandsinger had to face the fact that quite possibly Draille harboured a grudge against him over Jalni. Oddly, Daro sympathised with the taciturn Ranger, although it was hardly his place to do so! He listened gravely to the Ranger's bewilderment over Rann, nodded sympathetically when Garald enumerated Rann's divergence from Ranger philosophy and culture, then said (sotto voce),

"Dream Walker, look at your man! He is seriously incapacitated by whatever troubles him. This is an illness, not some assault on your culture. He can no more control his confusion, than I could resist the lure of magic! He is your Ranger I agree, but he is my blood brother, a fellow Nightlingby and I take responsibility for him. You have closed your eyes to the code regarding avoidance of magic in order to support me, now do the same for Rann I beg you. I will take him to Selesh with me. He has lived there before and trusts the Healers. It may be that a period of retreat, peace and quiet will resolve his problems, or if not, the best treatments known will be at my fingertips. Be assured that Rann will be as safe with me as Grey is with Trailfinder Grobold..."

His voice, although quiet was implacable. Shadows haunted his eye sockets but the strange opalescent eyes were open, disturbing flickers of colour swimming in their depths as he raised his head. Despite every intention of persuading the Sandsinger that Rangers solved Ranger problems, Garald and Draille found themselves leaving the main settlement at Tregeth without Rann Godway. Afterwards neither of them was prepared to discuss the matter, nor could either recall exactly what had happened until they found themselves turning into the hidden approach to Holmgarth, half a sand away.

"Strange!" thought Draille, "I will ask Kilda about that." and returned to planning his intended visit to Scartel.

"Peculiar!" sighed Garald, "I must recall this to add to a legend later...", but neither ever did, forgetting quite how their return journey had started almost the moment they'd arrived.

Daro had turned to Rann, laughing.

"Oh dear, so now it really begins.", he said cryptically, knowing that Rann had seen his hand inscribing arcane symbols even as he'd "instructed" the Rangers to leave. Looking at Daro, Rann asked curiously,

"What did you do Daro? I saw something shimmer, but they didn't seem to notice. They were in such a hurry to go, they didn't even give me a chance to say goodbye, or wish them safe trail finding!"

His astonishment at such behaviour was palpable, as Daro grinned.

"Exactly!" said the mage in deep satisfaction.

"Oh!" said his companion, glancing sideways at the Sandsinger as they set about packing, quietly absorbed in their own thoughts.

In the early light of dawn Daro faced Carolus, as Rann completed their preparations outside.

"I'm in a thankless dilemma!" the young mage announced gruffly.

"I will have to teach him won't I?" he spoke softly, aware that his own awakening had commenced with enhanced hearing. The Apothecary added ingredients to the pot he was stirring, scowling over his concoction as Daro slid carefully wrapped books into the bottom of his capacious carrisack. The Apothecary nodded glumly.

"That would be the usual route,

He said in an entirely neutral tone of voice, "Only I'm not sure that it works that way with magic."

He lifted the pan off the flames, steadying it momentarily on a blackened metal sheet, and then poured the thickening mixture into a shallow pan, where the surface wrinkled as it began to congeal. Daro sniffed, and then smiled.

"Perenroe toffee for Jentaroth?" the young mage suggested, at which the Apothecary snorted in disgust.

"Fine Apothecary you'd make…" the old man cackled, "Gall root drops for worming Zeglurs! Go on with you, get about your magic and don't forget to tell the Tourmaline boy that becoming a Clansman isn't all bad. He's got a decent Sand, a more than competent Sorceress and I'd stay on his good side if you want to add honeycream to your porridge!"

Daro grinned, it was plain that the old man was in high good humour, which he assumed came from the planned return to the Sands, unaware that his blindness had prevented him seeing an expression on the Apothecary's face that told the rest of Pelshar that Carolus of the Nine Sands took his joy in returning a healthy Sandsinger to his people.

Daro stopped to speak to Patris, who (though stooped with age) was still the strongest man he knew. His other Songfather hugged him in delight, slapping his back with pleasure as Daro indicated Rann.

"We're going to race Carolus to Selesh!" said the Sandsinger cautiously. "We go by the Ranger trail; he'll go by the Sands, whoever gets to the doors first pays "penalty of task" to the other!"

Ivinish the beast handler who spent his summers helping at Tregeth, hummed cheerfully.

"Can't see the old man getting you to muck out the barn at your age!" he quipped, at which Daro shivered, suddenly sobered by the memory of the accident with the Drekkens claw. He turned gesturing at Rann.

"Do you remember Rann?" he asked Patris solemnly, "He's going to come back to Selesh to study with me." he announced, watching the Wagonmaster closely, hoping that his inference would be understood. Patris didn't let him down.

"Really?" he tilted his head in a nod to the Ranger. "Well, we've survived one parcel of Dolcans with you and Ahnell, I guess we'll get by with another tricky trader, but he doesn't seem ready yet. Still in training is he?" at which Daro chuckled.

"Not even started an apprenticeship yet Harmeister.", Daro revealed softly, gently turning Patris away from the subject of their conversation.

"He may need someone to trust at Selesh. He'll appreciate some company that grounds him in ordinary things, but this is not for everyone's knowledge. He's easy round animals and might feel at home in the pastures where nobody will trouble him."

He watched the easy acceptance, saw the brightening in his Songfather's eye, and knew that he had done the right thing. When the task was tough, when the Ranger wanted nothing more than the peace and placidity of natural things, he would be certain to find the Underground Pasture at Selesh an escape that would also protect him, as it had Daro in his early struggles. He said his farewells, clapped Rowbet on the shoulder and left Tregeth swinging (as ever) his walking staff ahead of him, aware (as no-one else could be) that hidden from all but another Sandsinger, his powerstone glowed comfortably, leading them across the Azure sands to the old Ranger trails amongst the lower Drekken Heights.

Rann set a steady pace, watching the mage, intrigued by Daro's reliance on the Staff. He'd seen him navigating the ancient halls of Scartel like this, apparently aware of his proximity, but concentrating on the messages received from the slim shaft.

'Tap and swing, tap and swing', he could almost hear the words accompanying the action, subconsciously fitting his own pace to Daro's as he did so. He thought about that Staff, remembering how the strange friend of Solana had struggled round the Lookout Cave at Scartel using an old broom to begin with, wondering whether Daro had found the Staff at Scartel. His mind flicked over the episode, failing to recall any time in which that could have happened, although as one of Jalni's foraging team, he certainly remembered the finding of the powerstone.

They were emerging onto the sands proper now, but Rann was so caught up in remembrance that he failed to notice the slight smile on Daro's face. The day marched on towards Height of Sun, the heat bouncing off the firm blue sand, bathing their faces in sweat. Daro paused in his stride to let Rann catch up, suggesting that they'd better find some shelter before midday, and the Ranger scowled.

"We're a little off course to strike Minla Rocks.", the young man advised, "but if we follow the older trail, we'll come past a really ancient oasis that all but disappeared long before we settled Scartel."

He watched the Sandsinger consider this and when Daro nodded, he crouched, sketching lightly in the sand.

"There are three "bumps" along this edge of the Sand." he said instructively. "I can match those with the shadows thrown down by the peaks behind us." he held up a hand to prevent Daro protesting.

"I know you can't see them, so you'll just have to trust me, just as I'll have to trust you." he continued his explanation,

"We wait here until Height of Sun, when the central peak's shadow lines up with the central ridge, so that they look like a bird's wing, and then you head for the position at which they join."

Daro's brow wrinkled, then he smiled holding out a hand as if assisting the Ranger to rise.

"Mmmmn!" he said thoughtfully, "but why don't you do it my way?", and it seemed to Rann as if the sands themselves spoke in his mind. The Sandsinger threw back his head and whistled, a high fluting call that pealed and echoed around the trembling Ranger, then the very sky shuddered as spiralling above him, twin vortexes sprang from Daro's hand.

Rann's face whitened as Daro took his left hand, passing the twirling mass of energy directly into his palm.

"O Medraneus!" said the Ranger mage in a whisper, "O Yaydoran! What have you done to me Daro? I'm alive... I feel really..." he paused struggling for words as his friend's eyes opened showing a blaze of Opal fire.

"Connected?" suggested the mage smiling as (for Rann) the sands turned Tourmaline green.

Chapter 28 - The Crossing Begins

"What's happening? Deo mi! Am I dying Daro?"

The Opal Sandsinger might have laughed as Rann (the Silent) became Rann the garrulous, but for the awe and joy in the Ranger's voice. He considered Rann's innate quietude, his respect for his Ranger heritage and sighed. How difficult it must have been to choose a path between Clan and Ranger cultures? How much harder must it have felt to discover he had made the wrong choice (after gaining the highest accolade possible to a Ranger?) No wonder that his very soul had been rent apart at the thought of such betrayal.

The Sandsinger listened to Rann's relief in sympathy, remembering the first flush of power soaring through his own body, intoxicating, overwhelming, tantalizing. As the Ranger leapt and twirled to the rhythm of the Source, Daro didn't need truesight to witness Rann's awakening, for his companion's excitement bubbled over. However, before relief became hysteria, Daro's hands described a symbol and Rann began to calm.

Amused, Daro considered his own childhood, recalling Ikella's hands flickering when playtimes got too rowdy to tolerate. He sat quietly, while the energies Rann had awoken sparkled around them, one part of his mind listening out for Rann, the other sorting images closely, filing significant events that had invoked his mother's intervention.

Eventually, Rann's ragged breathing slowed until Daro could picture him gazing skyward at the vortex pirouetting from his hand.

He called softly,

"Rann? Do you remember Brus?" knowing that this memory was one that no child who'd accompanied him from Scartel would ever forget.

Rann's voice shook as he said huskily,

"I fix his image in my prayers every day Ichspeller. It is the only thing that has anchored me to life in recent times; just the thought that I might experience something like that once again has held me here. Why do you ask?

Daro's face relaxed as the faintest smile touched his mouth, then, he said gently,

"Why don't you call him Rann?" just remember the last time you saw him, think only of the new life I found to give him, and see what happens. Clear your mind, close your eyes and just 'see' the Cuirax. You can imagine your voice calling him by name, but don't speak, just let yourself want to see him above you."

The Ranger frowned, obviously processing the suggestion, and then he said suspiciously,

"How do I know that you haven't called him yourself?"

In answer, Daro quietly laid down his Staff, sat in the sand, hands in his lap, no aura visible. He smiled encouragingly as Rann first gulped, then asked in a very small voice,

"Should I concentrate my thoughts on this….This….?" his free hand waved ineffectually at the vortex, but. Daro supplied the missing word confidently.

"Chelyth. A magical vortex that can transport items with magical properties to your location", he intoned in the manner of a tutor, only just restraining himself from exclaiming "How in Hadda's Caverns did I know that?"

There was utter silence for a moment, and then Rann repeated the answer carefully, making it obvious to the young mage that at least Rann accepted his instruction.

"Ichspeller? How do I begin? Do I just think of him", Rann's voice prompted.

"You could, but be careful. You need to fix the memory on the Cuirax, think of Brus and summon his presence simultaneously but without force. It isn't a fight for supremacy, the summons isn't urgent, just think of a Cuirax floating lazily and see what happens."

There was a slight susurration, the sand shifting as Rann settled himself. Daro heard a long intake of breath, then a sigh as a tingling awareness began. The mage felt the lightest breeze brush his face as the atmosphere changed, charged with a flickering impression of water pouring down his spine. Rann gasped, a shiver running through him also as Daro caught the honeyed scent that perfumed the air. He stood gravely, hands uplifted as a well-remembered call fluted from above.

"Brus, Brus.", the snow raven sang and for a moment Daro felt a pang of grief over the fate of the boy who had given his mortal life to lead him, then a wave of joy filled his heart as he bowed to his fellow Nightlingby, the Ranger who would become Sandsinger himself.

"Welcome brother." he said quietly, "We both have a long trail ahead of us, but if we walk it together I think you'll find this crossing interesting enough. You might like to begin thinking about your new name while we walk. You have to understand that at the end of our journey both your life (and mine) will become very different. Once we return to Selesh the Guardians have decided (in the interests of long term stability) to reveal my position (and yours)."

Daro's teeth gleamed in an ironic smile as he continued soberly,

"As in Adaria's time, the Clans will have to get used to the idea of magic reasserting itself, which will inevitably pose strains of its own. We will be a small group, like the Sisters of Sorcery are and as yet we have no specific Hall to call our own, but for the moment there will be room at Selesh. I only know a few potential Talents at the moment, but it is not the way of the Sands to reveal ourselves to outsiders too early. Just remember one thing Rann, the Way is of itself change, and this crossing is more than a crossing of the Sands."

He stood, shaking the sand from his clothing and taking up his Staff as he spoke, then, led only by the glow of his powerstone and circled aloft by a snow-raven he began the lonely walk from anonymity into the bright blaze of Seleus, making the crossing from youth to maturity, as at the same time others were making similarly momentous crossings of their own.

In the relatively close confines of Holmgarth Jalni was confronted by Draille Skellin. He was his usual imperturbable self, but beneath his outwardly calm manner, the Healer detected his emotions seething. He listened to her newly laid plans silently, only a small muscle ticcing at the corner of his mouth betrayed his inner agitation.

She turned a quizzical face to him, catching for a moment a sense of stern resolution. Putting a hand on his arm, she spoke affectionately

"Dear Draille. Don't you see that my idea takes the weight of responsibility from you, from all of the Rangers? I can't stay here any longer, yet following my personal inclination to journey to Scartel isn't an option either. I was frightened at the beginning of this venture, but I've learned so much from all of you that I think I can manage alone."

She stopped his protestations with a finger laid softly on his lips, saying quietly,

"No, I won't tell you where we intend to go. It would be better if you knew nothing. Don't follow me, don't shadow me that way you can't betray me should my Lord come looking."

He said nothing, but a look of pain crossed his face as he caught her hand to his mouth. His brown eyes were expressive; his mouth soft on the back of her hand and suddenly Jalni was filled with the conviction that she might never see her Ranger again. She stared at him, anxiety written large on her finely boned face, but Draille shook his head and laughed.

"Lady, you show me too much favour. I came to tell you that I have urgent business of my own to deal with. My position makes me responsible for others too dear to me to fail. I would have asked you to start your journey as you plan, with your Uncle, your Mystcat and the boy, but I would have joined you, once my obligation is fulfilled. However, I bow to your superior understanding of Ichspeller Selunsanni's way, I am proud to have served you while I could, now it is time to hand over my responsibilities to another! I wish you safe crossings, straight trails, and the blessing of the One to keep you always."

Jalni hoisted her light pack onto one shoulder, then struggling not to weep turned and followed her Uncle who had struck out determinedly, taking the trail east towards Simlan's Gap where she had watched the Ranger fly over the fire and out of her sight for the first time. For some strange reason, she forced herself to march on, refusing to look back, certain that her Ranger had melted into the undergrowth that hid the entrance to Holmgarth. However, before she turned north-east to pick up the trail, she heard a call.

"Amar ar Ru….Amar Ru inay …Amar dey Ru…", and as the voice faded into the distance, she glanced back.

He was Poised on the far side of the rift, silhouetted against the morning sky, as the call pealed out, shivering along the valley below. One arm was stretched skywards in farewell, the other whirled a lure as the hawks flew around him shrilling, jesses trailing.

Her Uncle grunted in surprise. "Well lass! One Sandsinger, one Ranger, and I know a Weaver..." he paused, mentally testing the words he'd just said, then muttering "Mmmh... there's a song in there somewhere!", he strode off,, following Echo and Chrysim into the challenging route to the Ashgenar, trailed by a bewildered and very pregnant Healer.

In Selesh the day progressed steadily. Beneva worked tirelessly over a large scroll that had been unearthed from a box in Ikella's bedchamber. Shiarjha had taken it into her head, that Ikella would be happier in her own apartments, and had overruled Mina only that morning, persuading Hannah and several of the retired Healers to assist her tidying. Beneva (having found this scroll was of little use at all, spending every ten sectors peeping under the scroll cover until her fellow Guardian relented laughing.

"The big desk in our Deshun's study is clear. It's also clean, so I don't want you making it a muddle again dear. Take a rest (and that wretched scroll), then when you find it's not a Scroll of Prophecy perhaps you'll turn your talents to more suitable occupations."

For a moment Beneva looked bewildered, but then, she stood up frowning and lifted the large scroll onto the workbench in the study. She had no need to ask if indeed this was a Scroll of Prophecy, for she had already seen the flicker of ancient script under the cover. Hands shaking she adjusted the glowstone lamps that Ikella had been so proud of and bent her head to study while the sounds of preparation for her fellow Guardian's return continued unabated.

Shiarjha and Suraya's preparations had only just completed when sounds from the Gathering Square attracted Hannah's attention. She disappeared, returning with a sniff to say that Olneth had suddenly arrived, and seemed to be getting the underground pastures ready for other arrivals. She sounded disapproving.

"I know he's high in our Deshun's approbation," she said gloomily, "but he and that Carolus always seem to lead Daro into mischief and I can't bear her anxiety over that scamp! She's been distressed quite enough over the last few Rotations, why can't these men give her enough time to recover?"

Shiarjha said thoughtfully,

"Hannah, our Deshun is failing, it's true, but not from Lord Daro's doing, not from worry or anything other than the frailty of extreme age. She has survived things that would otherwise have seen her passing these many Rotations and more. Now, don't you worry about anything? She's safe within our care, and for as long as it takes we'll be there for her. You are tired, that's all. Go and eat, then rest and come back at Sunfall."

Hannah nodded, adjusted the sash that proclaimed her to be one of the Council of Nine and retreated (still sniffing).

Suraya stared after her, round eyed.

"I've noticed that many of the Elders are aware of our Deshun's frailty." she stated flatly. "How are we to stop the rumours spreading Seris Shiarjha?" at which Shiarjha's eyebrows drew together ominously.

"We are going to ignore the situation for at least the next three nights." she said firmly. "Seris Ikella is strong enough to withstand the move back to her own apartments, and with the help and support of Davina, the nursing skills of

Mina and dear old Hannah, we may yet see a turn for the better. I have it on good report that Carolus is already on his way, that's what brought Olneth back to ready the pastures. I gather that Patris and his company will arrive later tomorrow, so although no-one has mentioned him by name, Daro should be along in a short time."

Suraya sighed and nodded slowly, not betraying by any flicker or comment that her own sense of unease was building to crescendo. She simply slipped away at Height of Sun and went to the Hall of the Healers to pray.

On the second day of preparation Ikella's attendants cleared and cleaned her day-room. Working tirelessly around the call of the Summoning Bell, they sorted her cupboards, found homes for medications, even persuading her personal Guard to move furniture as they went room to room.

Sorrill surveyed the finished apartments, astonishment written over her face as she observed her own daughter lifting chairs and removing a bin of litter, but she said nothing and so the second day finished, with the planned move taking place on the third.

The Inesh chose to close ranks about their Sorceress. Though outwardly unchanged, there was a luminescence about Ikella that proclaimed the glamour of magic adhering to her countenance. She accepted (too meekly in Mina's opinion), the offer of a carrying chair, but the Guard turned the procedure into a ceremonial progress, which in turn charmed and enchanted the Sorceress. As they passed her devoted attendants, Ikella called cheerily to those who had thought they would never see her again,

"Here I am…back again.", and to the obvious joy of her Clan, she was conveyed, smiling amongst them once more. They paraded her out into the Gathering Square, where (with Mina clucking around her protectively) she was raised up to the small dais below the Summoning Bell, where she gazed towards the entranceway expectantly. At Diras's command, her bearers raised the carrying chair, until she could strike the Summoning Bell herself, to announce her return to the Clan, then it was time to take her back to her apartments.

They settled her into her favourite chair, tucked coverings around her, supported her with pillows and left her to rest, flushed and happy to return to normality. She dozed, subconsciously aware that she was not alone, that her Healers were constantly checking on her for signs of decline. She grimaced to herself as her thoughts turned towards Daro.

If, as she thought likely, he was with his Songfathers, he would be here tomorrow, stirring up trouble in his wake as usual. She sighed, wondering when his potential would be revealed, thinking back to the bedside conference she had called with her fellow Guardians. They had feigned shock and disapproval when she told them that this was so that she could make her dying dispositions, but in her own heart and mind she knew that her power was failing and had said brightly,

"Well my dears, you may be right, but I don't deal with chances. If I return to health, then it's one less task to contend with, if I do not, then it's one less task left undone!", and so they had given in.

Of course, so much was written in the Sands, she knew that. Her own small collection of possessions was easily dealt with, most of it going to Beneva, Shiarjha, and Suraya. She passed on her own book of medicinery to Mina, invited Hanna to take a memento from her small box of treasures, and then said she would like to leave Jalni something wrapped in linen and stored in a box, lodged in her ceremonial cupboard. A scribe faithfully recorded all this for her, Beneva attached her seal, and Ikella pressed her sigil into the warmed wax before Beneva bore it away to lodge it in the Djellim. She snuggled into her pillows as well remembered footsteps sounded in the anteroom outside her door.

Of course he came straight in, straight up to her chair, and lifted her wrist, seeking her pulses. He ignored her plaintive protests completely, signalling to her Inner Guards to lift her bodily and take her to her bedroom.

She grumbled crossly that she had been comfortable, warm and content, but he brooked no argument and when she realised that the gathering darkness was the onset of night, she was dismayed to discover that she had no memory of the afternoon passing at all.

Gathering her strength was impossible for some reason. She found herself longing for Daro's return, hearing the quavering in her voice as she asked Carolus his whereabouts.

"He's well my Deshun." The Apothecary said comfortably, mixing some powders into a small mortar and grinding them slowly. "He's been at Tregeth, helping young Rann with some problem these last two moons, but he's already on his way back, though I'm pretty sure he won't be pleased to see me when he returns.", he grinned at her over the rim of a cup, as she considered this last statement warily.

Eventually, as water boiled on the small trivet set in the hearth she struggled up and said wearily,

"I surrender, tell me what the bet is this time!", and he chuckled richly.

"Only that if I get back before he does, he owes me a task!" he said, innocently reprising one of his natural ploys. She regarded him severely.

"You men are all the same!" she countered flatly, "If I had a box of you, I could shake you up and you'd all come out of it defending each other!"

She accepted the cup of stemmis he'd brewed, wondering a little at the flavour, until he said kindly,

"You need some sleep my friend. Daro will be here by Height of Sun tomorrow, so I have added some wild valerius, cranwort and slauroot to your drink."

She drank deeply, held out her cup, and then as he took it from her, sighed, then lay back to sleep. The Apothecary rose and came to stand at her bedside, listening carefully to her breathing. He laid a hand on her wrists, finding her pulses humming gently under his breath as he did so. One humorous eye opened as Ikella regarded him fondly.

"Afraid your concoctions will send me to the Sands?" she queried and he chuckled softly.

"I'm not sure if I'm that competent!" he chaffed affably, "but I do wonder if a stimulant might be of benefit?" he laid her hand on the coverlet, picked up his scrip and prepared to depart, hanging back only to say sternly.

"Now, go to sleep do…There's nothing for you to worry about, that brat of yours will be here soon, and you'll need your strength just to listen to his discoveries, let alone some of his mad plans!"

She smiled drowsily at him, the lines in her face smoothing as she relaxed into sleep, and for a long moment the Apothecary looked at his old friend, then he turned and tip-toed out of her room. In the anteroom Shiarjha raised a weary smile for him, but his expression was grave. He slid into the chair next to hers; not speaking and the young Guardian straightened her shoulders before she spoke.

"Is it time to call the Clans?" she asked steadily, and the old man nodded.

"I'm afraid so my dear, she's leaving us. Not immediately the One willing, but soon, too soon." he heaved a huge sigh, and then said soberly.

"Set a watch for her. Experienced Healers only, and make sure I'm called will you? I have to go look after my animals; they've never been driven as I drove them to get here. None of them has ever been quartered inside and I can't leave it all to Olneth. I'll be over in the pastures, may catch up on sleep and I'd advise both you and Suraya to do the same thing. Will you tell Beneva to call the Clans or will I?"

There was no hesitation, the hand she placed on his was firm as she said, "Carolus, we are all indebted to you in ways too numerous to mention, but I know my duty. I will tell Beneva immediately, then I must prepare the Clan." she consulted some inner memorandum and said slowly,

"I have never asked you about your antecedents Carolus, but in all my time I have never come across a name like yours in Clan records. Am I correct in assuming that you took another name in order to disguise yourself? Or perhaps it was necessary to do so when you travelled for Sanctuary? I believe you are the Elder of our Clan but you never wear the Clan braid."

The old man relented suddenly, sharing at least one of his secrets in a voice barely above a whisper.

"I was named after an illustrious ancestor, but that name was erased from Clan records after I went to work for Sanctuary." He leant forward saying softly, "I am the tenth great grandchild of Darius Selunsa but for the Ones sake, don't tell Beneva!"

She stared at him open-mouthed as she recalled past custom. Each child bore the name of its grandparent in whole or in part. If your line continued directly, the tenth grandchild bore the name in full of the first patronymic. She shook her head wonderingly as she watched the old man leave, crossing her fingers in awe.

Had she heard that correctly, she wondered, setting about her sad task. No wonder he kept that secret she thought, heading for the Djellim to break the news. Should Carolus have to admit his full honorific; a man called Darius Selunsa would once again walk the ancient Halls of his ancestor's home!

As anxious eyes watched her, Ikella dreamed. She had fled the pain in her old joints, left behind the pain in her heart, discarding rank, ceremony, rules, or fears for succession. She floated free as a bird, high above the sands of her rule, wondering dreamily what festival the travellers were gathering to celebrate. She drifted, watching Seleus travelling through the night, waiting for him to light her way to the cavern again. She saw the towering rock islands of her Sand, watched the precious network of water courses thread the desert floor and felt the crystals warm beneath her feet as she walked steadily into the cavern where Daro had been born. At her touch the strange crystal formation hanging from the roof transformed into a waterfall, then, as she knelt to drink a voice said gently,

"Welcome sister.", then he was there again, the one who had pinned the wings to her Staff and called her "Honoured Mother".

She knelt at his feet, seeing him clearly now, seeing the Seguidor at his throat, the Anduigor sparkling at his belt. He took her hand, raising her to her feet, and murmured reassuringly,

"You are safe now, and can rest at last. The babe has thrived and comes at last into his own. Your love and protection has given our beloved world a chance, a new beginning. Come now, there's nothing more to fear, death is merely the door to a different Sand."

That dream faded, but he was still there, holding her hand, weeping. It was very strange she thought retreating from the bed; hovering to pass loving hands over the child she had loved as he wept for the woman who lay on the bed. Ready for the trail, hair braided, hands clasping a wonderful Staff of rare Hojawood, topped by crystalline wings. Even as she watched, the powerstone flushed, wakening to brush past her at another's call. In the doorway, Suraya appeared, as if she answered a summons, then the Staff slapped into her hand, and Ikella felt her bonds loosen and fall away.

Her guide still waited, his hand beckoning, as without hesitation she turned and followed him into that other Sand.

Chapter 30 - Sandsinger

Daro raised a haggard face to Carolus demanding angrily, "How has this happened old man? How could my mother have contrived to slip past two Guardians, forty trained Healers and the combined Guard, passing from life without word or struggle? How?"

He continued wearily,

"Why didn't anyone call me earlier? I may not have prevented it, but I could have tried, or said my farewells at the very least."

The timbre of his voice changed as he said indignantly,

"How could you all conspire to make me let her down again...?"

They stood just inside the doors to the private apartments, Daro doubled in pain, his chest heaving with suppressed sobs, Rann looking as though he wished himself anywhere but here, and Carolus (who had greeted them as they sped in to the dying echoes of Tekrun's Bell), was simply Carolus. Solid as a rock, apparently unmoved, he patted Daro's shoulder with one hand, while checking the Sandsinger's pulses with the other.

The Gathering Square was filling as Daro straightened, still feeling the great shuddering reverberations flooding through him. He'd half collapsed; supported by Rann, as the pain, the desolation had told him he was too late, as Carolus reached them. Now, he clutched the wall groaning, as the Healers, tutors, the men from the forge, cooks, drovers and traders apparently all sensitive to the greatest change to beset the Sands in living memory) flooded into the settlement. Then Daro heard the steady tramp as his Inner Guard surrounded him protectively.

Someone placed Rann into Olneth's care, and then he was stumbling into Ikella's day-room, only to find it filled with the Council of Nine and Ikella's Inner Circle. Diras (grasping his arm firmly), had tucked his hand into the crook of her elbow, leading him through the open door into Ikella's bedchamber. Then Carolus was taking him into the deathly silence beyond, and his anger dissipated in the calm dignity of Ikella's deathbed.

He had sat suddenly, the strength in his legs failing as he realised that Ikella was gone and there would be no farewells. The Apothecary leant against the wall behind him somewhere he supposed as he took up his mother's hand. A vision of her descending from the Sacred Circle, green fire in her eyes and scorn in her voice shook him, even as he felt hands combing out his trail tangled hair. He sat, head bowed as the tears fell, and then he heard her voice.

"Sandsinger? Well, if you claim our Sands now, they might believe you. Remember that it is not just you that has paid the penalty to prove your rank! You must do as I have Ichspeller Selunsanni. Lead by example, prove your worth to them, they will follow but they are lazy and belief takes hard work, however, you can show them the Way!"

She was leaving; withdrawing, but still he heard her,

"Daro, you are the one thing I have lived for, remember me, remember..."

His ears buzzed, darkness beckoned, then a voice said sternly,

"Selunsanni, if you faint now, I'll disown you. I'm too old to be lugging a lump your size. Here, take a deep breath."

Something stung his eyes, filled his nostrils with an acrid smell until he thrust it away from him gasping, and then the Guardians were there, clad in their silver robes, indicating that the men should withdraw so that they could dress Ikella's body, and take her to the Hall of the Healers. He rose reluctantly, and then steadied himself at the foot of the bed, remembering his foster mother's beloved face before he turned and left the room on the arm of the Apothecary.

Somehow he controlled himself, somehow he got to his quarters before he threw back his head and howled in despair and somehow he restrained himself from striking out as strong hands grabbed him.

"Dear boy, hold on, just hold on." Carolus enfolded him, bracing him against the storm of grief as it shook him. Expert hands threaded themselves into his hair, touched the back of his neck, the crown of his head and just when he thought he must drown in the flood of anguish, the storm passed, leaving him shaken but calming, clinging to Carolus as another wiped away his tears.

He shook his head, tentatively struggling to find his balance, and then Garald said gently,

"I felt great disturbance of mind, and when Trailfinder Grobold brought Grey to Draille in deep distress, I decided to bring her with me. I soon found out that I was needed, young Godway met me at the Gate in the Rock, and Sorrill passed me in."

His dreamcloak still hung from his shoulders, the rime on it betraying the mortal cold of the Sheer that he had ridden through, but the question was in his eyes as he faced Carolus over Daro's bowed head.

The Sandsinger pre-empted the Apothecaries response raggedly.

"O Garald, she's gone. I never got to say farewell, I will never hear her voice again or give her another kiss or apologise for my scrapes!!"

The Sandsinger's voice was desperately sad, although he felt drained of all emotion. Garald continued taking pulses that Healers didn't recognise, and then gave an encouraging nod to Carolus before asking cautiously,

"I've left Blue and Grey in the old herder's hut, where Echo and Chrisim stay. Can I bring them down to see Daro? Grey can behave herself in closed quarters and where I go, so goes Blue. They'll be no trouble if Daro warns the Guard."

Two sectors later, the distraction worked. Garald was ensconced in Ahnell's old room. His Sheer wolf lying comfortably across a disused hearth. Despite the initial hysteria amongst the Inesh (which had been mollified with a promissory note to be drawn at the Cross-Eyed Zeglur), the inn nearest the barracks in Selesh Minoria, Grey slept quietly at the foot of Daro's bed. After counselling a surprisingly supportive Tobin, Carolus went back to the underground pastures off the Gathering Square to prepare for the obsequies and to catch up with Olneth's travels, leaving Daro to come to terms with his loss.

Steadily the Clans gathered. Beneva and Shiarjha watched them arriving together, first the Sisters of Sorcery, who would sit with Ikella's body through the night watch. Then the Council of Nine, Clan Councils, their own High Council, before every member of the Clan Shalhanhi who could get there. If they were surprised to see the refugees from the Amethyst Sands they didn't show it, although expressive eyebrows were raised as a Greeeyn contingent approached.

"Master Doloran, Craft Master Buren, Master Ilorin.", Shiarjha named the three she knew as they approached the Gate in the Rock.

"They represent the Glass Makers, the Guild of Scribes, and the Stargazers!" she said rapidly as the High City dwellers were introduced. Then, as the men walked quietly down into the Gathering Square she added softly,

"Ikella achieved more respect than she knew. All we need now are the Felmin, the Rangers and a gaggle of Wanderers for good measure!"

Her fellow Guardian rolled her eyes, but made no further comment as they silently welcomed visitor after ranking visitor, shaken by the reaction to Ikella's passing. By the time the Summoning Bell sounded for evening prayers, her speculative comment had been fulfilled. In the area normally reserved for the Jentaroth Gather, a small tented village had sprung up. In the Upper pastures the Rangers settled around the old herder's hut, Sheer Wolves running loose to provide extra security. The village of Selesh Minoria was over-run by the Felmin farmers from the Fringes, and then the Wanderers arrived. No-one saw them coming, but suddenly the road from Emblem Rock was thronged with silent travellers. They walked confidently, some of the Stilled wearing the forbidden facial tattoos with pride. However many they were, no-one lifted a hand to stop them, for every man woman and child wore the Clan braid proclaiming their birthright, every braid picked out with the deep tomes of mourning.

Daro waited at the Gate in the Rock to greet them. A goggle-eyed Guard Commander watched as the leader of this strange group embraced the Sandsinger,

"Kissing him on both cheeks like a brother!" she reported in her barrack-room later. He led them, a quietly respectful group down to the underground pastures, where they were to camp, re-appearing shortly thereafter at the guardroom door.

"My friends are to be accorded every respect." he stated flatly, "They have chosen to be here and they are welcome, however, no aspect of real security is to be ignored. My Rangers are on call, so are the men of the village. Our real danger comes from the fact that every leader of true significance is in one place, so you'll need every eye watchful."

He gave Sidera (the new Second Watch Commander) a lop-sided grin, and said lightly,

"Don't worry. It will be over soon enough. After tomorrow nobody will want to threaten our safety for a very long time."

The Guard Commander brought her Watch to the ready, promptly, but as she was too new to her position to comment, her command had to make do with the widening of her expressive eyes as she watched the Sandsinger walk out of sight, tapping his way back to the Hall of the Healers where he would stand the last watch for his mother.

By the time Dawn broke over the great underground fortress, Daro had walked silently around every place of significance in his childhood. He had paused for a while in the hidden stairway to the Assendarium, his memory drinking in the sounds and smells about him. He pictured his mother reading from scrolls too ancient to believe, remembered her singing to him during a storm, thought back to her flashing eyes and fearsome frown at some childhood misdemeanour. He recalled her holding him, scolding him and wept until suddenly he was calm, prepared, and ready to obey Ikella's last command. In the quiet robing room, he turned abruptly, and passed through a door into the ancient rooms beyond. He held out a hand as he stood in front of the ceremonial press, and a robe enveloped him, sliding over his body like a warm wave of confidence. He smoothed it down, sensing the adjustments being made as the robe lengthened, narrowed, ties fastening at the nape of his neck, wrists and waist. He pictured himself, tall, dark, tanned and dressed in flowing garments, boots, with a hooded cloak. The garment he wore adjusted to this vision, and then he felt his belt encircle him.

Suppressing an urge to grin, he hid the belt with his gleaming Anduigor under his cloak, as the Seguidor blossomed against his throat. He heard low voices and hurried, hands flickering as he made subtle alterations not only to his appearance, but also to a bemused Rann's, who had been stationed in Olneth's tent. When ceremonial garments replaced Rann's Ranger blues, he had stared at them enviously, wondering who was going to wear them. Olneth had growled crossly,

"Why don't you try them on and see if they fit you?" the spy said shortly, and left Rann with his mouth gaping in surprise. He fingered the cloth, recoiled as the material seemed to shift, then Daro was there saying softly,

"Try them Rann, but hurry do. I've so much to do, so little time to do it in.", then he was gone as though he had never been there, and with a strange ripple of acceptance, Rann supposed he never had. He reached for the robes, and they came to his hand, enfolding his shivering body in a cloud of confidence.

He found a bag containing boots and pulled them on, then Olneth was back again, his own colours shimmering as he prowled around Rann, observing quietly,

"You look good Lord Rann. I could hardly believe that you also are called to High Magic, but you look the part already! Now, we go to the Hall of the Singers, where Lord Daro will instruct you."

He moved towards a door that Rann had not seen as they entered the pastures, leading through a complex into a room that seemed to still and steady Rann's nerves. Recognizing the significance of this moment, Daro's new acolyte stood still, watching and waiting for some signal, listening to the buzz of conversation as the Hall beyond this, filled with those who had come to bid their Sorceress farewell.

Daro was talking to a scribe, the pure white vellum of the Book of the Dead was open between them, when Daro turned and noticed him.

"Come", he invited, "As next present in rank you should witness this.", then he leant forward, holding out a hand on which a splendid Tourmaline ring sparkled.

"Have you found your truename yet?" he asked solemnly, and then when Rann nodded he held the boy's gaze for just long enough for Rann to feel the lightest of touches in his mind.

"Ichta Solennsis will add his sigil to the document, then the Guardians can sign Brannith.", he told the scribe, and so it was, robed figures coming and going about the business of the day, until light pouring into the Hall and the hum of wakening Opalstone called them to the ceremonial events they had gathered to attend.

In its simplicity it was beautiful. All pretence of pomp and ceremony had been swept away, for Ikella the love spilt out, reaching beyond any exaltation of rank, simply enclosing her family, her Clan, her Sisters in Sorcery and holding them as her son said his last farewells.

When Shalhanhi eyes strayed toward the vaulted ceiling of the Hall, he simply walked from the Way of Challenge, followed by a tall man in Tourmaline robes. Near to the seated Clan Councils he paused, as a teenage girl in Malachite robes stepped forward to join them. For a long moment he waited by the Zurian group, then, he walked up to the barrier surrounding the Sacred Circle where Ikella's bier lay, surrounded by the Sisters of Sorcery, and without hesitation, *passed through the barrier* that no man should pass on pain of death, and stopped at the head of the bier, looking down the long aisle at the expressions of shock and puzzlement below him.

"All hail Ikella, Sharall Deir Opal, Guardian of the Way, Warden of the Winds, Keeper of the Heartstone of Daro bin Selesh, Ichspeller Selunsanni, Sandsinger of the Opal and Keeper of the Nine Sands!"

Sorrill's voice, raised to the familiar stentorian bellow of the parade ground rang out; every word clear, every syllable carrying to every ear tuned to the proceedings.

The shock was so great that it rolled like a wave down the Way of Challenge, to silence even the most outraged. Then, as each Sorceress in turn knelt, Daro bent, gently placing a kiss on his dead mother's brow. Somewhere a sob was stifled, and then, music began to rise. In the banked seats, the Clan leaders (who knew nothing of Sandsingers) leant forward as Daro stood, magical eyes alight with love as he sang his farewell to the only woman he knew as his mother.

As disbelieving voices hushed, the soft, tender, but nevertheless commanding tones throbbed persuasively, as the audience were gripped by the poignancy of the moment.

Daro was standing arms raised towards the great vaulted dome, which awash with colour seemed to be altering in some way.

The dawn light was permeating the Opalstone, making the rock seem insubstantial, ephemeral. The congregation were all gasping now, pointing and calling out as the flower strewn bier started to glow, the corners of the under-cloth rising to form a sling supporting Ikella's body, then the voice ascended, thrilling to new heights as a pair of snow ravens appeared *through the rock of the roof itself*, spiralling down to catch the sling in their beaks. As the almost dreamy, drifting *othervoice* soared into the vaulted gallery, gasps and cries of wonder echoed in its wake, then she was gone, the colours of the Nine Sands flaring in a trail as the Cuirax disappeared with their precious burden and were no more.

In her place, he stood, where no living man could stand. His robes (now shot through with all the shades of Opal; hood thrown back, his Clan braid visible for all to see. Behind him a girl in Malachite greens, behind her another man in Tourmaline colours, both attended by their Sorceress.

At the great doors, there was a stirring rattle of drums as a company of the Inesh brought Suraya to the Sacred Circle and necks craned as she knelt to the Sandsinger, then bowed to the Guardians.

A thrilling, whirring sound accompanied this last action, and then flashing through the air, Ikella's winged Staff flew to Suraya's hand. There was a roar of approval from the Clan, then Daro stepped forward, strange Opal eyes gleaming as he held out a hand summoning his own Staff with its blazing powerstone alight. He inclined his head in respect for the Guardians before speaking simply.

"You have known me as Daro bin Selesh, adopted son of the Shalhanhi and more particularly the son of their Sorceress, Ikella te Syrene; but from this day forward know that I am Daro Selunsanni, Sandsinger of the Opal Sands, Protector of the Union of Sands and founder of this, the Second Age of Mystery."

Chapter 31 - Truth, Lies or Legends?

If there had been a roar of approval when Suraya took the Staff that was eclipsed by the tumult of disbelief from the gathering below Daro. Those in the Sacred Circle listened intently, and the Inesh watched carefully, marking those most vociferous, particularly those who seemed to rebuff the suggestion that Sandsingers walked amongst them again. In the midst of this tumult, a man stepped into the Way of Challenge, and to Daro's dismay he recognised Olneth.

The Sybillsce refugee held up a hand until silence fell. Nervous glances were cast at the small group wearing Amethyst colours, but the silence extended until Ikella's Master Spy cleared his throat.

"You gave me, (a Sybillsce stranger) both a home and a chance to make a difference to society!" he stated flatly, "Why can't you give one of your own, (no less than the son of our late Sorceress) the same? What can you see here but a walking dead man?", he shrugged expressively, his dark hawk-like features taking on a wry humour as he said boldly,

"I've yet to see him walk out of the Sacred Circle alive! I'd go so far as to believe that's the hard part, and if he succeeds in doing so unharmed, we'd better believe him."

He stood (as was any man's right) in the Way of Challenge and as if he voiced the opinions of the nonplussed observers, a low muttered agreement ran round the Hall.

Daro wasted no time in making a decision. He stepped back, indicating to the Sisters of Sorcery that they should precede him, followed by Beneva and Shiarjha, then he strode out of Circle, leaving his Staff in the gleaming holder next to the great Book of Rule. Only his finely tuned hearing guiding him, he crossed the metalled rim of the Circle in ten strides, then standing in the central aisle of the immense Hall, he turned, pointing one finger at his Staff.

Something like a flash of lightening leapt from his hand, struck the powerstone into flaring life, then streaked upward illuminating the immense vaulted roof, where the long abandoned Gallery of Mages was only broken by the anvil of rock at its far end. As cries of wonder (and fear) rose from the gathering, Daro smiled gently, then he raised his voice.

"AnSurisha!", he commanded and from above the Sacred Circle dust motes danced as the Ascendariam started to pivot into place. He turned taking the Malachite girl by both hands, saying quietly,

"Thank you for coming Lallee. I haven't seen you in a long time, but I promise we'll talk later. Give me your kiss of fealty, then we're finished here and you can go back to your Clan."

She knelt solemnly, both hands in his as he leant forward, brushing his mouth against both cheeks in the kiss familiar. Raising her gently, he presented her to the Union of all Sands, as Deschima, her own Sorceress hailed her proudly.

Ichta Matrical, Sandsinger Designate to the Greshe.", she called, as the blushing girl was received rapturously.

Daro held Rann's gaze as he introduced him, but he need not have feared. Suddenly the Way was filled with Rangers and Clan members, then both acolytes were gone, and he was alone.

"Now Selunsanni!" said an autocratic voice in his head, so he dipped his head to the Guardians respectfully, then vanished, reappearing two sectors later walking casually down the Assendarium. Amid cries of wonder, he paused at the base, then said calmly,

"Surrisha!", moving back rather more hastily as the great tongue of rock groaned and closed.

"There you are Mother," he said dryly. "Wherever the One took you, I hope you're happy now." then he sat on the steps where he'd first felt the Source stirring his powers and wept for the friend who'd given his life to bring about this moment, for the Sorceress who'd loved him, and for himself as he prepared to find out what the Clans really thought of the day's revelations.

He paused on the threshold of the bedroom he had shared with Jalni, wondering briefly if she had heard the news, then dismissing the uncomfortable thought that maybe he had been unkind to her, he went in to change. Tobin (who was apparently storing clothes away in a press, said quietly,

"You made a deep impression Lord, I never heard so much conversation between folk who might only meet rarely. As I came from Hall into the Gathering Square I saw Healers and Guild Masters chatting with traders and Clansmen. If you did nothing else today, you've certainly given them something to talk about."

He bustled about, taking Daro's ceremonial wear and hanging it ready to return it to the mages robing room, before reappearing with a simple set of clothes. He regarded them doubtfully, shrugged and presented them to the young mage as he went to bathe.

"Are you sure that these are what you need?", he asked, neatly swinging a robe around the Sandsinger, who stood at the door of his bathing room.

Reaching out, the blind man touched the fabric smiling secretively to himself, then he departed into his bathing room with a flick of his fingers. Behind him, Tobin gritted his teeth, choking back the howl of disgust that had risen into his throat with the change the mage had inflicted on the clean but worn workwear that his body servant had been holding, as chuckling Daro lowered himself into the warm water.

That night many campfires glittered in the dusk as the Clans paid their own homage to Ikella's memory. Suraya walked amongst them, listening to their concerns as she joined them, Sand by Sand, Clan by Clan.

From the subdued Sybillsce, to the dusky Kora-Mai there was one question burning on every lip.

"What's he like this Sandsinger of yours?", to which she gave simple straightforward answers.

"He's just Daro!" to those who knew him well, to those who did not, she said sympathetically, "Like all men…a mystery at the best of times, however, he's very approachable, kind to those in need and calm in the face of danger. You need have no fear of him, just treat him as you would anyone." to which she received a variety of replies.

Her entourage milled around her, student Healers taking the chance to visit their families made shy introductions, watched by members of the Clan and a phalanx of hangers-on. She paid little heed, taking her scribe to note requests from Clan leaders as well as her Sisters in Sorcery, gliding (with the confidence that Ikella had seen in her), between confidants and combatants, ears alert for signs of dissent, as in her wake others travelled silently noting everything that was said.

An old man clad in the rags of a beggar leaned against one of the great war drums of the Kora-Mai until he was hastened away by the drummers. He struggled through the crowds listening to the accolades for Ikella, leaning on his stick heavily, limping as though he might not make it back to his camp (wherever that might be!). A tall young man, still not sporting his Clan braid, but clutching the tambourine of the girl he accompanied was also intrigued by the hostility of some of the speakers. He nodded as if in agreement with a rather pompous man who seemed to think that Daro's claim to command of magic still had to be proven.

"It's all smoke and mirrors you know!" this individual pronounced solemnly. "Those Healers have all combined to ensure his safety, now his mother has gone, he's nowhere to hide. I'll believe in Sandsingers if he shows me his magic when there's no Sorceress in sight! That's the other thing, the poor lad's as blind as a blemingal so I guess he's afraid. However you look at it, no man has the right to claim such things as truth. They are either lies (May the One forgive him), or they're legends of the past, which is where they all belong."

This man, clothed in the tawny shades of the Amber Sands gazed imperiously around, then spotting the ancient beggar called out sharply.

"Hoi, you, yes you old man. What do you think you're doing here hey? Get away, you smell of Zeglur dung. You're a total disgrace. How did you get past the Watch hey?", he turned outraged features towards one of the Inesh warriors who had infiltrated every camp, checking on security.

"Ho, the Guard, should this old vagrant be allowed into Selesh?", he glared at the cowering beggar, but as the Guard joined him, it seemed that he'd lost sight of the old man, reluctantly accepting that his victim had slipped away.

As dusk turned to night, weary children claimed their parents attention and cooking pots were placed on trivets as camps prepared for sleep. Only a few traditions favoured night time gathers, and so it was that the large fire-pit in the upper pastures remained lit as the communities of the Rangers and the Wanderers joined forces to tell their legends to each other. At the outer edges of their gather the Sheer wolves prowled. Again strangers mingled with the Tawn, the petite dancer and her tambourine, her stoical attendant, some hesitant

Healers, a young Apothecary and her Ranger husband, an ancient beggar, a Sorceress and her scribe.

The Dream Walker was in his element as he told the legend of the Sword of Sorcery, (missing for millennia.) This remarkable sword had the power to save a Sandsinger whose destiny was to prevent a disaster more deadly than Cataclysm. The watchers hissed as Garald explained that somewhere this ancient sword remained so sharp that it could cut through forged iron. Somehow its jewel encrusted hilt fitted only the hand of the one destined to wield it and the crowd sighed as the Dream Walker explained that without this magnificent weapon, no-one in all Pelshar could defend them from certain destruction. He told them that the Rangers had searched for this sword for centuries, evoking cries of "Shame" as he said that they had not been universally welcomed by all Sands to carry out this duty, then it was the Wanderers turn, and their leader told of a blind baby saved by the intervention of a mysterious stranger.

There was a discreet shuffling amongst the cross-legged Rangers sitting on the ground, then the ragged ancient tapped his way through the Gathering, holding out a pouch and whining hopefully for alms, or food. There was a pause as Garald caught hold of the beggar's arm, drawing him back out of the firelight, however, there was spirit in the old man, for he wrestled himself free, and marched firmly back into the glow, where he crouched by the warmth, flagrantly breaching all forms of hospitality as he rocked and screeched for alms, for pity, for food.

As the puzzled community frowned and wondered what they could do to appease this difficult visitor, there was suddenly a brightness surrounding him. A silver grey wolf was weaving her way around a figure that was unfolding from a wizened, ragged old man, into the form of their Sandsinger complete with Staff and Opal shot aura.

"In truth, lie or legend my friends," said the Sandsinger softly, "for whatever the purpose the One intended, I am here, and so are the Appointed." He indicated the dancer and her companion, as they too revealed themselves to the assembly.

"We seek only to serve those Sands who follow common belief, to educate where we can, and work toward healing our failing world so that all of us can live freely together in harmony. Will you support me in that ideal, now and in the future?"

The roar of agreement from the Ranger encampment would have woken the Sands themselves, said the guard at the Gate in the Rock, it certainly shook the one returning villager en route from the fortress to its satellite village. He lingered in the shadows considering his actions, then turned at the crossing and fled towards the Sands, and a place where spies gathered, determined to get word back to Adruna, whose beliefs he shared.

The following day (blessed by their Sorceress Leaders) the Clans departed at dawn, going on their way apparently reassured. As the camping grounds emptied, the villagers returned to work, and the Winds blew sand across the visitors tracks (wiping all evidence of their passing) until Selesh slept through Height of Sun.

Internally however, much was afoot. The Guardians had cleared the Djellim, rolling back the faded floor covering to reveal the lighter patch where the Book of Rule had once stood, setting out the seats that usually stood near desks in formal rows, returning the ancient Library to one of its historic appearances. To one side the long table for the High Council waited, to the other they had moved the Sanctuary Chest. The lights were glowing softly and only the presence of several Guards in formal finery gave any hint of ceremonial procedures to come. However, as the sun tilted off its Zenith, a small procession approached, led by Suraya clasping the winged Staff of Selesh, powerstone aglow. At the door, Daro (accompanied by Beneva and Shiarjha) stood to welcome the party, the walls lined by Suraya's Inner Guard, flanked by Daro's personal escort.

Diras stepped forward, bracing her spear diagonally across the path of the oncoming party (as tradition demanded), then paused taking breath before bellowing (in a fair imitation of Jashell's manner),

"Who passes this way?"

Sibrill, now elevated to the position of Suraya's personal guard gulped once, then announced firmly,

"Suraya, Sharall deir Opal, Protector of the Sands and her Sisters in Sorcery."

Behind Daro and the Guardians, the doors to the Djellim were flung open and as each Sorceress passed within, she was accompanied to her seat by a novice Healer from her own Clan. Soft murmurs of welcome were extended as the bemused guests took their places, then the High Council were brought up the corridor and welcomed as well. Two guards took them into the Djellim and saw them seated before returning to the doors as four Rangers approached.

Beneva turned her head to survey the blind Sandsinger, who seemed quite aware of her scrutiny as he said in a soft murmur,

"I've learned a lot since I last had time to talk to you Aunt Beneva. You will see where things fit together later, but please make Dream-Walker Garald Lightfoot, Ranger Leader Draille Skellin, Decrian Kilda Pagthorn, and Ranger Leader Designate Marran Dorenard welcome."

As the Rangers were accompanied into the ancient Library, two more figures approached timidly. Beneva, resplendent in her silver robes smiled at the simple dress of the couple, then took interest in the child (carried by Adriss, seconded to the Inner Guard at Daro's request.

"May I present my friend Bernot, his wife Trellin, and their son Daroden", the Sandsinger said simply, then blushed (to Shiarjha's amusement as the small boy leant forward, peering up into Daro's face demanding,

"Magic eyes Daro, do magic eyes!"

The mage chuckled, kissed the boy on the crown of his head, and whispered.

"Later, if you're a good boy!"

As they passed within, Shiarjha said quietly,

"Are the Appointed coming Daro?" at which his grin reasserted itself as he said impishly,

"They're already here." as both acolytes materialised in the previously empty doorway.

The younger Guardian said reprovingly,

"Magic is no toy Selunsanni. I wish you joy with your use of it, but don't use power where your own feet can take you. Seris Ikella (of blessed memory) taught me that, and you'd be a better man to remember it."

Daro smiled serenely murmuring,

"I'll bear that in mind Aunt Shiarjha!", as he shepherded the disconcerted Guardian before him and turned to the business of the day.

As he had requested, the centre of the Djellim was now filled with his visitors, facing the Sanctuary Chest where it stood, back against the wall, flanked by Beneva and Shiarjha. The low lights produced a comfortably intimate atmosphere, which Daro did nothing to dispel as he took his place. For a long moment there was silence, then, with a gentle tinkling of prayer bells, the Book of Rule materialised on its podium, right into the position marked by the pale patch on the floor of the great Library of the Ancients. Daro stood, then, turned and mounted the podium thoughtfully, his Staff (as usual) leading him. It quivered in his hand, slipping into the clasp intended for it, then flaring into life as (with a subtle gesture) the book opened before him, pages turning until silence fell and they settled to an open page as the young mage began to speak.

"I welcome to this first Gathering all those who represent the interests of our world." he said softly and into the light stepped the three Greeeyn Guild Masters, Bernot, Olneth and Carolus. There was a gasp which brought Beneva forward a step, but the rustle of robes subsided as quickly as it had begun, and the mage continued, voice and face serene.

"May we meet in harmony, with one purpose before all of us, which is to solemnly embrace the ideal of improving our world to support every one of our peoples in their endeavours. May we strive towards a world that can greet strangers without suspicion or hatred. To create a place where food and water is plentiful and to make sure that no child goes to bed unloved or in pain. May we meet before the gaze of the One in solidarity of spirit, determined to rescue from the wreckage of the Storm, a world fit for all of us, our children and the children yet unborn."

Tirjella looked up at the man she thought of privately as "her" Sandsinger, lips curving as she remembered his kindness to two of her Clan, seeing

Deschima smiling also. Nahamida nodded, eyes following the Sandsinger as he held up a hand commanding silence.

The air prickled as his eyelids flickered open, revealing fire Opal orbs, then he said softly,

"I have in mind one duty of honour to complete before this Gathering is handed over to the Guardians. May I request a scribe and two witnesses to come forward?"

At the High Council table Brannith took up a quill and set out a prepared sheet of vellum. Plainly involved in some secret, his lips curved in a smile as he laid a sheet over part of the wording, marking a point at which witnesses could sign, or attach their sigil.

Then Daro stepped from the dais saying gruffly,

"Olneth, Carolus, Draille, Marran, Garald, Bernot." He called, and then as they shuffled forward into line before him, he bent his head and kissed each one as he said,

"To each of you, I pledge support, safety, and a secure old age under my aegis. You have all contributed to save my life, to educate me in the unselfish nature of the best of humanity, and so in return I give you the freedom of the Sands. Wherever you need support, just show this mark, and you will receive whatever you need."

His thumb touched the centre of each man's forehead on which, a glowing Opal appeared to glimmer faintly. To Olneth he said quietly,

"Don't worry, that won't compromise your work, but it might just save your sorry hide somewhere."

Then he was clasping his Songfathers hands, commanding softly,

"Will you please get Tobin to fix your braid? You can wear all Nine if it suits but a high ranking Shalhanhi male must look as though he belongs to my Sandsworn!"

Carolus grinned then Daro clasped arms with Draille, with Marran, then Garald, who said severely,

"You must stop stealing young Rangers for your own Tawn Ichspeller!" Daro could hear the smile in the Dream Walkers voice as he acknowledged Rann's transition with another question.

"I suppose he's beginning another training now?" at which Daro blinked, considering.

"Yes," he agreed simply, thinking 'That's another problem Selunsanni!', but in his heart there was a sudden rush of recognition and in his head a voice said,

"For the sake of the One boy! You have the run of Tirjhinar …what do you think it was designed for? Magic users must live apart from the influence of family, friends and distractions, or they'll never learn."

He had a brief disconcerting image of the hall of High Magic in his head, which was swiftly replaced with the image of Sanctuary as his mother had described it, and then the moment passed as the Guardians stepped forward, silver wristlets blazing as they solemnly folded back their sleeves, revealing their rank.

Everyone sat, including Daro, whose ceremonial chair had simply slid into place behind him. Now Beneva took the dais, speaking quietly to the unusual gathering that filled her normally peaceful Djellim.

"Welcome Sisters, Healers, and gentles all." she said warmly. "We find ourselves writing a new chapter in the annals of the Way as we seek to find another Guardian to join us. From time immemorial there have always been three, guarding all Knowledge, all Ways, and all Powers, that they may be protected for posterity. It is our duty to scrutinise those of us who have access or influence over such matters, that they are not led astray by personal gain, or led into conflict with each other. We (who keep the record of every Rotation) are on the same path as every man, woman or child, seeking to undo the mistakes of the past, by learning so that we do not repeat them. This time we have decided to keep the ceremony private, amongst our own society, where our faith is understood, and where greed and jealousy cannot spawn such heresy as was displayed at the last accession to Higher Power."

She paused, looking to see if her words had found favour, then apparently reassured she added by way of explanation.

"Of course, the wristlets choose, we do not. Nor have we any influence over the choice. We will simply do as we have always done, pray to the One for guidance, then open the Chest and see if the next Guardian of the Way is amongst us yet. Please open your hearts and follow me in prayer."

She made a gentle circuitous gesture with her left hand and the Sanctuary Chest opened, brilliant light streaming from the silver wristlets lying on a sumptuous bed of black veluin within. Leaving the Staff of their Sand in the hands of Shiarjha, each Sorceress came forward, bowing their heads in prayer as they did so, before holding out their wrists ready to bear the weight of Guardianship should any one of them be chosen.

Each time there was a subtle dimming of the lights as the wristlets failed to recognise the chosen one, each time the Sorceress excluded stepped back, bowing to Beneva, before gladly retrieving her Staff and returning to her chair. Garald Lightfoot watched intrigued, quietly commentating for Daro, who smiled, one hand tracing the Source through his Seguidor, instantly aware of the process long before the Dream Walker.

As Nahamida turned back relief written large on her homely face, he began to wonder if the Way had come to an end, wondering what in the Nine Sands the remaining Guardians would be able to achieve if that was the case. However, he had nothing to fear, for even as Kerisima (the youngest) stood to make her way towards the Sanctuary Chest, he felt a tingle run through his fingers. He listened carefully, aware that Rann had suddenly sat bolt upright, then to a cascade of soft bell sounds, he felt the shiver in the Source as the wristlets flared, then closed softly around the wrists of the chosen one.

He rose; grasping his Staff as Lallee carefully took his hand and led him to congratulate the dazed new Guardian. He called Rann, using "speech without speech", taking the Ranger mage by surprise.

"Rann, go and congratulate Kerisima. She's your Sorceress, the first Quexoni Guardian in this Age of Mystery then swear your fealty. Kneel to her properly, and don't scowl so much!"

He almost laughed at Rann's expression, hearing clearly the mutinous comment. "Seems to me that a deal less formality would seem more sincere!", then thought about that. Brought up by Rangers, Rann was used to a culture where each man or woman had equal status. He remembered the rows he'd had with Ikella, his constant refusal to submit to her will and pondering this, waited for the formal acclamation of Kerisima's new status to subside before making a decision, just as the Summoning Bell sounded.

He waited while the Sisters of Sorcery and the Guardians departed to the Gathering Square to make their announcements, then, closing his eyes, rearranged the Djellim once more, using just the power of his mind's eye, and an odd "memory", which teased at his conscious efforts to recall what the Djellim had looked like, the last time he had seen it. Diras came to his rescue as soon as the sound of moving furniture ceased, clapping in delight as she re-entered the Library ahead of the returning party.

"That's amazing Ichspeller," she declared, "I like the way you've not allowed anyone to group themselves by Sand, culture or allegiance."

She moved to the centre of the circle of couches he had conjured, deliberately tapping the floor with her foot on the light patch where the Book of Rule had stood only moments before. "What happens here Lord?" she questioned softly, "It occurs to me that if a glow was placed here, the light could represent Seleus, shining on all present, as equals under one roof!"

She broke off as Daro's laugh rang out, then blushing to the roots of her hair she whispered apologetically.

"Forgive me Lord. I spoke only from my heart. I have no shame my mother tells me... I just open my mouth and show the Sands my empty head!"

Daro chuckled, admitting ruefully,

"My mother said much the same of me Diras, but there's nothing wrong with your heart!", he conjured the feel of a warm hug, added a brotherly kiss for good measure, then sent it after the retreating back of his bodyguard. He heard the hiss of indrawn breath as the sensations reached her, but Diras (true to her calling) didn't falter once as she passed through the doors to wait for the other's to return.

Daro's reorganisation was greeted with warm interest. From the dim resources of "his" memory a tall lamp was summoned, which when placed centrally cast a spectacular circle of light around the murmuring group, now seated "in the round". The young mage much encouraged moved to stand under the gleam of this lamp and as he did so, a soft note sounded, silencing the gathering, as he prepared to speak.

He called softly:

"Diras; Sorrill; Senida; please join us."

As the senior Inesh women came into the circle of light, the Sandsinger explained carefully.

"In all our endeavours, for some reason unknown to me, the Inesh have always been ignored. My mother set them free long ago, but we still ignore their part in our lives, yet we could not live here without their service. As I see things, we can no longer continue this way, and I therefore invite them to share our deliberations. In a moment I shall surrender this position to another, but first let me welcome all present to the Inner Circle. No Sand is supreme, all castes, Clans, cultures are equal under the Sun, while Guardians and Magic Users prepare for a search like none other held before. We seek information that will lead us to discover the whereabouts of the Sword of Sorcery, missing since Cataclysm. This search (both magical and physical will be unlike any previous search, and will require complete secrecy."

Somewhere a door banged shut, and then they all felt a shiver in the atmosphere as Daro said softly.

"My brothers and sisters in magic, here begins the Sifting of the Sands!"

Chapter 33 - The Sword Seer

The dusty traveller slipped from the trek cart as it pulled up just short of the halt in Shilinch. The old man driving adjusted his hukvah, shedding a stream of Opal dust onto his shoulders as he did so. She flashed him a smile, holding out her hand in which three copper pieces gleamed.

"Thank you Master," she murmured, drawing the edge of a rough blanket over her mouth to shield herself from the wind squall that had threatened to close in on the shabby cart as they travelled north towards the border town. He gave a dry cough, waving aside the proffered payment.

"You keep it lassie!" he growled, smiling back through a mouthful of blackened teeth. "I go on to Nustrowa to deliver dried grain. I had my orders and am only glad that I was able to find you quickly after that Gather," he muttered confidentially, leaning closer to add instructions, looking around cautiously, checking that no-one could hear them, despite the increasing howl of the wind.

"You can't go into the inn by yourself. Unaccompanied women are not permitted inside, but you can register for a room at the traveller's lodging house. You might try your luck getting work there if you've skills to sell." He looked thoughtfully at her, then said meaningfully,

"They're a funny lot round here. The Quexoni have elaborate courting rituals, and their women are treasured. There's no entertainment, no dancing girls, no whores, not even a little flirtation permitted. The other Sybillsce keep themselves to themselves poor souls, every one of them afraid they'll be put to death or sent through that barrier..." he cackled mirthlessly, "then there's our lot. Dead beat herders, exhausted traders, but the beer...! It's wonderful and I'm not permitted to stop! If you intend to stay, you'd better have some skill to sell... I mean cooking, cleaning, perhaps you might be able to offer repairs like sewing?"

His eyes had lingered on the swell of her breasts and she hugged herself defensively as he drove away, knowing that he'd glimpsed the ornate embroidery on her robe.

She turned away, clutching a small bundle to her as she passed the inn. Threading her way through the alley alongside the main building, she found herself in a courtyard fronted on three sides by accommodation provided for those attending the markets. She paused, eyes instinctively checking to see if her arrival had been observed.

Ahead of her a door crashed open and a man shouted angrily as he emerged into the sand strewn yard. He glanced at her once, lip curling as he took in her shabby appearance, and then she saw the guild badges on his hukvah, which he was struggling to adjust.

"Curse the snarrelled thing."

He flung it to the ground irritably, but the wind picked it up, bringing it to her feet, from where she retrieved it. Recognizing the elaborately embellished cords that proclaimed his status as Brewmaster, she peered at the crown, seeing that the braid was unstitched (and that his attempts to correct this had made matters worse). However, as she attempted to return the hukvah to its impatient owner, her blanket slipped, revealing her expert embroidery work. Immediately the man seemed more interested, coming forward, one hand held out for his headdress, the other guiding her inside out of the squall.

He apologised gruffly,

"I'm sorry Mistress, I'm at my wits end. My wife died recently, I'm only just getting sorted and Deshun Kerisima is about to descend on my inn!" he continued distractedly.

"We must ensure the linen is in order; that her retinue will fit in our newest guest rooms, and that my sand-blasted hukvah shows my credentials correctly!"

She smiled speculatively; fate must be guiding her footsteps, she thought as she produced her own credentials casually, along with a titbit of information she'd gleaned from the Healer post at the crossing point below Maraken.

"I was employed at Selesh for the last ten Rotations, during which time I sewed everything from alterations to ritual robes. I can make anything with material, or embellish what is already made! I can work to a pattern or design, freehand."

She watched his eyes grow greedy, then said in a tone designed to engage his sympathies,

"When my husband died suddenly, I only knew of one cousin who I believe is in Shilinch, although I haven't seen her in Rotations. With Seris Ikella's passing, I set out to visit her, as there won't be much call for my skills this Rotation of mourning. However, as I was about to tell you, fortune would seem to attend me, for Deshun Kerisima has acceded to the role of Guardian. I could assist your preparations while you await her arrival. Then if fate permits, I might engage to serve her further."

She gentled the damaged hukvah enticingly as he considered this news, saying lightly.

"I only have three coppers left to pay for my keep, but I would repair your hukvah, or even replace it should you be able to provide a room for me to work in. I could sleep on the floor, take my meals in the inn… the only thing is, would you be able to get word to my cousin for me?"

This last question brought him to his feet with a shout of laughter.

"Are you serious? Is it true? Deshun Kerisima is now Seris Kerisima?" Well, I'll drink to that, or at least my customers will, then I'll have a double celebration. Your arrival is timely indeed, and you shall have a room, with a bed, and a sewing area as well. You will eat with my family, and I undertake to contact your cousin. Who is she?"

She thought she'd lost his interest immediately she replied.

"My cousin is called Sencatja." She'd said seriously. "I haven't seen her in twenty Rotations but I know she lives hereabouts."

He had paled slightly, she thought curiously, and then he said slowly,

"That's an unusual name. Do you mean Sencatja the Seer?"

At her nod, he said cautiously,

"I hear she's good at predicting weather, but I don't hold with magic or anything out of the Way. If people are going to go about having visions, let them do so because of my brews! I don't mind them paying me for the privilege, but I don't hold with magic in any form outside Healing. We don't need to know the future, we don't need screaming, wailing women foaming at the mouth, and I don't hold with visions of weapons. I was fool enough to let my brother take me to one of your precious cousin's performances last Rotation and I'll tell you I was scared. All she could talk about was the time of the Sword...! However, a promise is a promise and Benjard of the Coatan's Plight Inn never goes back on his word."

She thanked him prettily, gave him the name she'd used in Selesh, and went to rest thinking grimly,

"It was as well that my father died before my mother could ink my skin. I'm lucky not to be obviously part Sybillsce and even luckier that it took only one thrust of that poisoned skewer to rid me of my late husband. Gatta only knows what Seris Ikella would have made of her private cook's death! Now, before I can lose 'Sennia' of Selesh and take on a more pleasing identity, I must make use of my cousin to tell Deshun Adruna the latest news!"

The next evening, as the animal pens emptied, Sennia slipped from the inn, following one of the guests (who said he'd come specifically to consult the Seer). She paused, taking in the strange glint of pale green Sand far to the west, her fingers clutching a cloak about her as the breeze tugged at her clothing. She ducked her head, scurrying behind the trader, trying to remember if she had ever met him before.

"Sandrigals..." she swore under her breath, "I'm too tired to think! I feel like I've walked too far, changed names too often and possibly killed too many husbands to care about myself, but all I need is to pass on what I know, and then I can rest!"

She struggled to keep up with the traders long strides, then, suddenly they were there. Many seemed to have the same idea Sennia thought glumly, but she settled down, prepared to wait for a private audience if necessary, wondering in the meantime if her weird cousin had become stranger with the passage of time. She shouldn't have worried. A low throbbing note sounded from the direction of a rickety stage and a dancer appeared, obviously intending to set the mood. Sennia tried to ignore the blatant sensuality of the woman, who postured and gyrated to the beat of the drum and the tinkling of finger cymbals. The lights flickered hypnotically, the dancer shuddered and stamped, hips rolling, belly undulating, limbs curving sinuously suggestive. Sennia watched the woman as she sank to the floor, seemingly close to a state of trance, then she realised.

She was looking at her cousin! The woman's eyes flickered, opening into a blank stare, as an attendant raised her, lifting her into a centrally positioned chair, where petitioners could approach her. To Sennia's surprise however, all that seemed to happen was that a basket of wax tablets were lifted onto a table where a scribe sat, enscrasure in hand, ready to record what Sencatja said. A darkly bearded priest hovered nearby ready to interpret, and Sennia sighed glumly. There was no chance that she would make her report this way, she decided and returned to the inn, before the burly trader who'd accompanied her here, finished his own business.

Stitching from dawn to dusk the ninenight dragged on. Every evening she raced to get a place at the front of Sencatja's stage, every night her cousin appeared in a different guise, so that even Sennia began to doubt her eyes, but thankfully she remembered the one skin pattern that her family had used for Rotations, and each night she fixed her eyes on the undulating body, as Sencatja danced herself to a standstill then fell into trance. Focussing on her cousins hands, Sennia saw the tiny sword again and again, She thought dully that possibly Sencatja belonged to some sect she didn't know about, but thanking the stars that she had avoided the ritual brands of the Sybillsce, she worked towards completing her task.

On the last night she wrote a list of things she needed to pass on to Adruna. She made it short, displaying no glee over the death of the autocratic old Guardian and taking care only to couch the news in a prayer to Brochayen (the Wind of the enclosed and forbidden Sands).

Her hands were shaking as she passed the wax tablet to the priest, her lips were icy, and her cloak seemed no protection from the cutting wind of this northern Sand.

She detested the Opal, hated the Shalhanhi cook (who'd bought her from the relatives of her previous husband and wanted nothing less than freedom for Adruna, working tirelessly to retrieve snippets of information for the heretic sorceress.

She watched avidly as Sencatja took the wax tablet and without reading it, placed it to her brow. She was muttering a strange language, eyes rolling and Sennia thought she caught sight of a flickering light surrounding her face, her lips.

There were no crowds tonight, she noticed as the Seer finally collapsed, energies spent, but as they raised her to the chair, the priest hurriedly brought a wax tablet back to Sennia. He just shoved it into her hands and scurried away, leaving her to open the cover.

There was absolutely nothing on the pad. It was as new, and for a moment Sennia struggled to make sense of what had happened. Then she understood, her words had been taken, worked into the web of knowledge that Adruna had woven, collected and absorbed by the Seer.

A shadow fell over her as she passed out of the main pathway back to the inn, and she looked up to discover that the tall trader had waited for her. He seemed quite serious, possibly quite sad, but his bulk was reassuring so she walked close to him as they passed into a particularly dark alleyway. He stopped ten steps in, and she looked up at him uncomprehendingly as his dagger kissed her throat, preventing the scream of terror welling up, like the blood that was jetting from her mouth.

He bent forward, catching the dying spy as she fell, laying her gently on the ground at his feet, before bending over her, hands doing something at her wounded throat.

Her dying mind recoiled, but he held her attention saying softly,

"Tell your mistress that others might not have seen you for what you are Sennia, but I never forget a face. I have watched you for Rotations, waiting for your one mistake, now know this...

He was changing before her eyes. His face altered, became younger, hair more elegant, and features no longer Sybillsce but Shalhanhi! Her mind raced ...a name came, then left with her dying breath,

"Daro!"

His voice took on a terrible intensity as he spoke again, all her attention on him, ignoring the bubbling of her last breath.

"Tell your Sorceress, that I live, and that while I live she will never be free. Tell her my name; say that Daro, Sandsinger of the Opal sends her this curse. If she sets foot on any other Sand, she will die, consumed by her own greed and duplicity, just as you die, pinioned by yours!"

He watched as she died, then he leant forward, holding a glimmering hand over the ground and whispering enchantment. The sand stirred and was cleansed, the blood vanished. Gradually, full darkness fell, then there was a brilliant gleam of light (as though from a torch), then the Lord of the Opal was standing in his great room, sadly running his hands along his treasure shelves. He found a gap where he thought the knife might fit, and took it from his belt where it had nestled since Olneth had traded it for a new one. He touched the Amethyst stones gently, knowing that when the time came, he held the Seguidor of the Amethyst Sandsinger. Tonight the knife had dispatched yet another Gattarene to the sands, but he wondered wearily, why did he seem only talented in death, when his whole being ached to contribute to life?

High in the hills bordering the Azure Sands, Jalni and her small party forged their way north, passing the growing grounds, leaving comfort and security behind with every footstep. They journeyed higher, passing beyond habitation, up into the old trails frequently used by Rangers for training, for hunting, the new colour in the day turning cold, the air harder on the lungs as they climbed into the Drekkens.

Jalni (pausing more frequently) felt the muscles in the back of her legs stinging as the others overtook her. She wondered briefly if she'd taken on too much at this stage of her pregnancy, but decided to ignore this thought, concentrating on where she placed her feet instead.

Echo and his minder played all manner of silly games up and down the sloping trail, pretending to chase each other, rolling down green pastures until, with savage splendour the rocks erupted from a gentle landscape into monumental splendour. They all quietened down as the trail grew harder, Orto (now walking in the rear) ready to assist Jalni as the mountain range soared to meet the sky, forming a closed canyon. Jalni (consulting that strange inner clock that all Healers could access), realised that Height of Sun was upon them and they needed to seek shelter. She called the cat sternly.

"Echo, where are you? We need to rest now, get yourself down from wherever you're hiding and help us find somewhere close by.", but to her intense dismay, she heard nothing.

Her uncle stopped dead listening, then, edged closer, tilting his head back, obviously concerned that their miscreants might have climbed higher.

Peering up the valley he frowned, but shook his head, obviously not able to pinpoint them either, so tired and frustrated, Jalni decided they should stop, looking about for a safe place to make camp for the night. She was aware that she couldn't walk the distances she would normally have covered (due to her pregnancy), but she had expected to get further on the first day of their expedition, so she was disappointed as they rounded a corner where the trail seemed to change direction.

She stopped so abruptly, that Orto trod on her heels, but instead of the silent amazement displayed by Jalni, the weaver let out a roar of surprise as they took in the monumental size of the cavern entrance into which the trail was taking them. The rumbling echoes of his amazement shuddered the walls ahead of them and Jalni flinched, concerned that they might have started a rockslide, but despite her fears, the basalt rocks seemed strong and only a small rattle of shingle sounded in the far distance.

Trying to pretend that her growing concern was for herself and her baby, Jalni prevented Orto from exploring further, saying comfortably,

"Leave them to it Uncle. Chrysim has Echo to protect him, this is plainly the way the trail goes and I'm sure that they will scout ahead, and then return. They won't be pleased if they come back to find we haven't prepared food for them.

It's far too soon to worry, come take a rest and drink; I'll open our packs and prepare a feast."

She found cheese, biscuits, (Ranger trail provisions) and dried fruit in her own pack and set these out on a ledge nearby. Casting a glance around, she saw that if she piled up her pack she could sit by this ledge using it as a table, so she invited Orto to share his rations and look for a spring.

He was gone only a few moments, returning with his flask filled to the brim. He had also found their missing scouts, who grinned happily waving handfuls of shanberries, their faces amply smeared with the dark wine juice. Jalni grinned as Chrysim held out his hat into which he had harvested the berries. He smiled sunnily as she scolded him, then said gravely,

"Sorry Jalni, we thought you wouldn't go into that big cave without us and we were so hungry we just ate, and ate till we were full, then we fell asleep."

The cat stretched and yawned, settling down to wash his coat, as Jalni shared out the dried meat that Orto carried.

She disliked the texture of the pemmican that the Rangers provided, still maintaining a diet based on fruit, nuts and grains where possible, yet that certainly hadn't always been the case, but it made sense when travelling. She thought wistfully of the stews that Terris had made with trail rations as they'd journeyed on the trail from Scartel to Selesh, then, as her tummy rumbled in agreement, she found herself responding to a cheery hail from behind them.

"Ho there!" called a woman's voice, followed by a rich male chuckle then Terris and Marran stepped into the mouth of the cavern from the tunnel beyond.

Jalni blinked.

"Ho there indeed." she replied carefully, knowing that Marran's first loyalty must be to Daro, his blood-brother (and honorary member of his first Patrol). He eyed her silently, as though reading her thoughts, and then as he squatted beside her, he said quietly.

"Jalni. I owe far more to you than I do to Ichspeller Selunsanni. Yes, he saved us, and we might never have made it without many more casualties if he hadn't come to our aid, but don't think for one sector that I've overlooked your contribution. You were risking your life to guide him before we were involved. Had we too succumbed to plague, you might have had to make the return journey with him on your own. We know that you suffered every bit as much as we did, and probably more when Brus could not be saved. You were the one who saved Daro, made us feel comfortable round him, and nursed Solana. Although his power has given our brother a different life, his arrogance and anger has caused you much pain. I have agonised over this, but I believe that in choosing to serve you and his unborn child, I am still serving him. Without my help, your child might not be born alive, and I would carry that guilt to the end of my days."

To Jalni it seemed as though they were alone. The others were grouped only a handspan away, but they seemed as though encapsulated in another world.

Here, there was only the kneeling Ranger and herself, the sun beating down, the buzz of a honey bug, the faint lonely cry of a bird. She sat straighter, one hand curved about her belly, the other extended to Marran's brow. She pressed her thumb lightly against the centre point as if seeking his "third eye", then the Sands rose within her and she felt the completeness of his joy as she said softly,

"Into my service then Marran Dorenard, First among Rangers to wear the mark.", then as suddenly as it had come, the moment was over, but Marran wore between his eyebrows a faintly glowing blue brand.

Jalni gazed in awe at the mark, then at the glowing tattoos on her hands, before leaning down to kiss Marran's cheek gently. She felt dreamy, as if her body wasn't her own, but she was certain that this was the right step, the right thing to do. The Ranger stared up at the girl that he'd thought of as a sister and gulped, hearing in his mind his Grandfather's voice, uttering his dying words.

'In the Gateway, an Opal blazes against my Azure Sand. My eyes must be failing, my wits are scrambled, or am I the Ranger thrice blessed by the sight of an ancient Anduigor worn on the belt of the Prophecy himself? With him comes another, shadowed, shaded but glowing still, the right and left hand of power, and unless I dream, the Lords of Sand walk amongst us again.

Now I am content, and my writing is done. Mereth I am ready my love, let death release me on Opal wings which flutter all around as the Wind rustles comfortingly in my loft, my hawking loft, my home..."

Marran stared at Jalni, awe written across his face, as he watched the Azure flush drain from her eyes. He could hardly believe what his subconscious mind had known for Rotations. Jalni would be Sandsinger and she had entrusted him with the responsibility of getting her to where her child must be born, without telling his Lord. He gritted his teeth, choosing to feel only the connection with his Grandfather, the joy that his recognition of their Talent had produced, making a vow to himself to guard, guide and protect both his Sandsingers, preferably together, but if necessary apart. He stood, aware that Jalni was looking pale, then, thanking the One that his wife was an Apothecary, he went to talk to Orto and plan the rest of their journey before night fell.

They had agreed to use the cavern entrance as a camp for the night, so as Jalni and Terris found a discreet corner to withdraw to, the men made a fire, setting up a trivet and hanging a variety of food to cook on it. Soon the warmth and feeling of security made Jalni so sleepy that she couldn't resist curling up to sleep. Terris had given her something sweet to drink, assuring her that all she needed was a good night's sleep to recover, so Jalni relaxed, slipping from weariness to dreams without difficulty.

Before night fell however, she was jolted awake by the clamour in her blood. Somewhere a bell was ringing, deep and sonorous it tolled a lifetime. She sat bolt upright, staring out into the summer sky in horror, knowing without any doubt that Ikella te Syrene was no more. Beside her Terris stirred and woke, her own senses telling her that something auspicious had happened. Marran appeared in the firelight as both women struggled to their feet and headed towards the entrance of the cavern, where they stared in wonder as the night sky lit up with a blaze of falling stars.

Tears were coursing down Jalni's cheeks as she thought of the autocratic old woman who had dedicated her life to raising a foundling. She thought sadly of Daro, who despite all their fights, loved his mother and would be devastated by her loss. She thought back to their last odd conversation, she sat in the pastures at Selesh, the Guardian of the Way lying on her sickbed in the confines of the ancient fortress below Mount Torrenesh. Perhaps she had known then that she would never see her reluctant mentor again!

Eventually, the cold night air forced them back into shelter, into their beds once more, but instead of avoiding all thought of Daro, Jalni's last thought was of her lover, wondering how he would go forward alone. About her a subdued aura of Azure bloomed, as cushioned by her Sands, protected by her ranger Jalni slept, en route to fulfilling her destiny once more.

PART FOUR – STAR WEAVER'S TABLE

If anyone had told Jalni that an entire ninenight could have passed in a blur of impressions, she would have laughed, but as they travelled through the amazing tunnel system that they entered the following morning, all sense of time and place disappeared from her reckoning. She became certain that without Marran and Echo they might have wandered here until they died of hunger. Thirst was a different matter, for springs of crystal water seemed plentiful.

They walked steadily, always on a slight downward track, carefully cleared of debris, plentifully stocked with low boulders on which they could sit at resting points. For the first day, her sense of time helped her to gauge when to stop, when to eat, when to sleep. However, as they journeyed onward through the vast tunnel complex of black basalt, she began to feel unnerved, oppressed, as if the very mountains above them could crush them if they proceeded. Silently, she began to feel that she couldn't breathe, couldn't take another step, had to run, had to get away from here, and it wasn't until the compulsion was on the edge of total panic, that she became aware of sweat beading her forehead.

Marran must have spotted her discomfort, for he caught her arm, slowing her increasingly erratic progress and turned her to face the torch he bore, concern in his gentle brown eyes.

"Healer Jalni," he pierced her rising panic with his formality, once again the boy she had so admired, his calm leadership steadying her as he said quietly,

"You are feeling the compression of the air at this point. We only have one short walk to make, and then you will be able to breathe more easily. Terris suggests that you drink from one of her flasks. There's a little restorative added to the water, it will calm you without affecting your baby. We can't have you upsetting yourself at this stage."

She gazed at him silently. The slightly shy boy had gone, in his place stood a faint echo of Draille and she looked at him with increased respect as she saw the tiny silverwork badges that the Rangers wore on their clothing, denoting their achievements.

She saw Trail Master, Tawn Leader, several she didn't recognise then her eyes widened as she saw (on a thong round his neck) the symbol of a hawk back-winged (as if about to land) two jesses trailing from its legs. She stared at it, mystified, until he said quietly,

"Yes, I didn't have time to tell you that I am Second Ranger Designate to Draille Skellin. He has many more than the forty summers we expect, but even though he is fit, alert and the epitome of everything a Ranger should be, he feels the need to leave us in good order."

Jalni stared at him, huge eyed and no longer aware of her earlier panic. She noted the breadth of her Ranger's shoulders, watched the throb of a pulse at his throat, and thought how lucky was Terris to have this well-grounded man at her side, sharing her life, loving their children. How lucky she was that her Ranger was taking them through the maze of caverns personally, and then she realised he was speaking solemnly.

"You will come to know all that we know and protect Lady, but the time is not now, the place is not here, I must insist that you take some refreshment, sit here for a few sectors, then we can push on, and tomorrow we should be on the other side and in the Ashgenar!"

She took the proffered flask, unstoppered it, and sniffed cautiously. She recognised vetali at once, grimacing as she remembered showing Terris how to make up "Sandsinger's Friend", Daro's own restorative, then she dipped her little finger into the liquid, licking the drop that formed contemplatively. Honey, vetali, redberry juice, blended with ginger, citrine and something else… she frowned but encouraged by her baby kicking happily, she poured out enough to fill her mug, then sat sipping as the others arrived breathlessly.

They laughed, seeing her absorbed face, but the winks that were sent to Marran made her realise that her sudden urgent flight had worried them. Hot shame flushed her face and she was grateful for the mug in which to bury her flaming cheeks as she drank the rest of the liquid.

They gathered around as Marran raised a hand to call them to attention, Jalni carefully placed in the centre of the group. The Ranger (returning Terris's flask) spoke calmly but firmly; raising a distinctly serious note to press his message home clearly.

"This is the most dangerous part of the crossing." he announced firmly. "We will be entering a great cavern, so immensely deep that even we Rangers hesitate to explore it. We enter along a wider passage which passes along what we believe was the route of the ancient Opaz River. Of course, the river was diverted during Cataclysm, emptying what seems to have been an underground lake, but we have only been able to follow this path, any others being too far below for safe undertaking."

He took from a capacious pocket a slate and soft marker, and proceeded to draw, tongue tucked into his cheek. Eventually he handed his sketch to Jalni who looked at it in surprise. It showed something like a circular pit, encircled by a large ledge on which minuscule people walked. He had even included the Mystcat and Jalni smiled approvingly as Chrysim and Echo peered down at it curiously. The large man cleared his throat,

"Big?" he queried, as Marran nodded, brown fringe flopping forward over his furrowed brow as he stressed the reply,

"Very, very big! Deep and dangerous!" his voice had taken on a darker tone. "No-one, I repeat no-one human or cat is to go near the edge of the bowl. You must all pledge to obey me instantly, and be ready to run if I give the word. No-one makes a sound while we are in the cavern, the echoes are thunderous and if we all started chattering, the sound would go round and round for days. It would be very dangerous, possibly hundreds of times louder than a normal voice as well. Draille believes that the sound of your own voice could even kill you."

His eyes were suddenly stern,

"Do you think that the cat understands what I'm saying?" he asked Jalni. "I'm deadly serious about this. He must understand no growling, no meowing, and everyone watching to make sure that sudden falls don't cause anyone to shout! I would advise we all take a drink, clear our throats and noses, and then, above all try not to sneeze!"

There was a wry chuckle as he showed those with hoods how to raise them, securing them over their ears with a thong, then he looked at the cat, perplexed. Jalni touched his arm,

"I can talk to Echo and so can Orto", she explained, "He seems to understand sign language, so I'll tell him what you said, although I think he understands the next walk is dangerous."

She squatted by the Mystcat, turning his head towards her, gazing deep into his eyes. She listened, hearing the soft purring throb of his breathing slow, and then she said deliberately,

"Echo we walk into danger. Even the sound of our own voices could hurt us, so we must be very quiet. No talking, no shouting, no singing!"

Almost immediately she was overwhelmed by a sense of sadness, of regret and the poignancy of it caught the breath in her throat, stopping her voice as she heard a thread of sound in her head.

"Daro…" she gasped, hanging on to the rock wall where she knelt, helpless in the thrall of his power. Then she realised what she was hearing and touched her hand to forehead, lips and heart, honouring the One as Ikella was lifted to her eternal rest. The others about her questioned with their eyes, then she touched Echo's forehead with her thumb and the cat lowered his head submissively. Orto said sternly,

"Look friend cat!" as the great head rose, watching Orto's fingers flying in sign.

"Make silent like hunting! No sound or no dinner", and to the amazement of the others, Echo's ears twitched rapidly in response. That matter settled, Jalni struggled to her feet and stretched, somewhat fearful of the next stage of the journey, yet entirely unprepared for what she saw.

The tunnel seemed to be increasing in width and height as they rounded a bend. Marran walking ahead of them held up his torch to illuminate huge seams of different colours streaking the dark rock face as the tunnel widened into a cavern the like of which Jalni had never imagined in her wilder dreams.

The walls rose high above them, the light of their torches barely penetrating the gloom that surrounded them. Marran paused, turning to face them, signalling absolute silence, and then beckoned them forward to peer into the cavern proper. Jalni gaped, thinking that this must be at least fifty times larger than the Hall of the Healers in height if not more, thanking the One for her head for heights. She gazed down silently; trying to imagine what this cave would have looked like filled with water, but could only picture a stream, which was the most open water that she had personal experience of. She eyed the dank walls suspiciously, her Healers eyes noting the signs of fungal growth nearby, before shuffling backward at the touch of Terris's hand on her shoulder. She fell into her place in the straggle of silent explorers as Marran raised an arm, then they were negotiating the great gallery around the bowl of the cavern, almost tiptoeing past, in case some immense slumbering beast should be disturbed.

It seemed to take a lifetime that last walk. Her legs were unsteady and she was shaking with chill fatigue as they threaded their way back into a narrowing tunnel on the other side of the cavern, but she kept plodding, kept silent until the Ranger turned, gathering Terris into his arms and hugging her close as he said quietly,

"Well done people. You did well.", then he solemnly signed congratulations to the Mystcat. Echo's ears twitched as Orto translated poker faced.

"Good! Dinner now?"

"Soon", the Ranger said enigmatically, then they marched on, keen to leave the cavern complex and see daylight once more.

"Take care as we leave the last cavern my friends." Marran instructed them cheerfully. "We exit high above a trail, to which we will be lowered by others. I have half a Tawn waiting to take us to the next stage of our journey, in a manner that could not be followed by random search!"

His grave expression softened Jalni's frozen heart as his eyes found hers. He seemed to be saying that in this direct disobedience to her Lord, he hoped for protection from her, until unaware of the ethereal Azure aura surrounding her, she gave a silent nod of acquiescence. She glanced around her as her feet carried her out of the small cave into which they'd emerged, aware of Orto's slightly dulled voice protesting from somewhere up ahead. Then she saw the narrow ledge, the sharp incline, and then the chasm that opened up below. Her Uncle had been persuaded into a sling suspended from a ratline anchored to the rocky outcrop above the cave and as she watched, was swung out into space by some cheerful Rangers, who obviously found this form of vertical travel entertaining. She emerged on the ledge outside on all fours, right behind the Mystcat, just in time to hear Orto whooping in surprise as if he found the experience enjoyable too. She gritted her teeth and closed her eyes as Echo bounded away, leaping the gap as though he'd been doing it all his life, then it was her turn. However, it seemed that Garald had other ideas, for there he was, helping her to her feet with a smile that reassured her wildly fluttering heart.

"Stand still Jalni," he instructed calmly, "Torvin will lift you up to me, and then we'll go a wolfback."

She glanced up at the tall man who held out his arms for her, then gasped laughing.

"Torvin, of course... You are kin to Garald! I remember wanting to ask you about that when we parted at Holmgarth. Now you are full grown, you seem to have shot up at least half a span!"

She accepted the assistance of a steadying hand, a bent knee, and then she was scrambling up into the saddle with Garald securing her firmly, as though he was taking a child for her first ride. He smiled down at her as the baby kicked enthusiastically, then he said quietly,

"We do not enter the Sheer friend Jalni, we simply skirt it, in a way designed for she-wolves to travel in pup.", then he squeezed his knees gently and the SheerWolf leapt forward. She was totally unaware of the drop below, absolutely secured against the Dream Walker as the great wolf bounded to the ground, then she was being handed down into the welcoming embrace of Marran, who had negotiated the cliff face via the ratlines, followed by an exuberant Chrysim, who raised a laugh from the waiting Rangers by hollering all the way down,

"Last man out, last man down!"

He received a round of applause as he landed (feet skidding and churning up some loose dirt), then he doffed his cap, and chuckled as the cat reclaimed his minder.

"Got to let the Rangers know that there's nobody left behind," he exclaimed cheerily, "otherwise some poor soul might not get out alive!", and Jalni saw how far this homely man had come from his blighted childhood, as once more she touched forehead lips and heart dedicating thought, word and life to the One as she did so. She discounted a slight uneasiness as the Rangers made camp, ate well from the biroots stew that they produced, then lay down to sleep as darkness fell, sure of her safety in this company, but hardly had she dozed off, when she jerked awake with a horrid realization. She lifted herself on one elbow listening. There was the muted crackle of the fire, the soft snuffling of the Sheer wolves, and the gentle snore of a sleeping man. The cat had left the camp to hunt and the night was only disturbed by the whispered asides of the Rangers, who kept watch, but still she listened, not quite sure of what she listened for, then it hit her. She couldn't hear the gentle rhythm which had governed her life every day since she left childhood. She pressed her Source beads hard onto her wrist, wondering what had happened to the throb of power in her bones. There was nothing. Just silence. The faint song she had first heard in the garden of the Weaver's Halt in Jerritol was just a hiss. The connection with her sands seemed stifled and she bit back miserable tears as she finally realised what she had done to Mina (her devoted foster-mother), as the explanation became clear. She was already in the unexplored territory known as the Ashgenar. Somewhere in the transition between the cavern and this sparsely grassed campsite she had left the sands and the source behind. She was alone, disconnected from all forms of magic and powerless to alter this, Jalni bent her head and wept.

If anyone noticed Jalni's inner distress, no-one mentioned it as they marched steadily into the wilderness. It was an odd place, full of stunted scrub, low growing bushes bearing blackening bulbous fruit unknown to Jalni and ignored by the single Zeglur that the party of Rangers from Scartel had brought with them. Torvin remained with their party, accompanied by a shy teenage girl called Nona, who attached herself to Terris, listening avidly to the young Apothecary describing the medicinal plants she sought.

Unwillingly subjecting herself to examination, after Terris professed concern about her low mood, Jalni was relieved to discover the baby was the least of her problems. She felt well, a new regime of short walks had noticeably increased the distance they covered daily and so, the unusual party progressed.

Torvin and Marran scouted ahead (occasionally meeting up with Chrysim and Echo), the three women walking in the middle of the patrol, with Villeth del Orto leading the Zeglur in the rear; (occasionally accompanied by Chrysim and Echo as the mood took them). They walked for nearly a full ninenight like this, and then they began to pick up signs of human habitation.

Jalni and Terris (who were taking it in turn to map their progress during rest periods) had already realised that the vast sprawl of pitted ground covered with vegetation had few discernible landmarks. All around them the uncaring Ashgenar rolled into the distance. A wasteland, filled with low mounds where mines had been worked out, deep in soulless silence.

They walked single file, not wishing to disturb plant or animal life, watching brightly hued sandrigals sunning on rocks, eyeing them with caution in case the serpents were venomous. Jalni saw hawks hovering, but these (according to the Rangers) were wild, unlike the hand-reared hawks they used for hunting. Now and again the Zeglur would plunge and rear (as if afraid to go on) but they never saw a reason for such behaviour, simply putting it down to the unnatural silence of the place, as they soothed the silly thing with handfuls of hempen plants which grew in the few clearings that they came across.

At the end of the seventh day however, the first sign of human habitation manifested itself in the shape of a dog, chained to a forged ring, set into a large rock quite close to the worn path they had followed into the wilderness.

It was old, grey about the muzzle, but well fed and cared fore according to Marran who knelt, checking it over. It seemed determined to welcome them, wagging a distinctive plume of a tail so fast, it shimmied. The Ranger laughed, looking around for the owner.

They waited, sitting aside from the track in a cleared patch, watching as Terris gave the dog a strip of hide to chew, saying cheerfully,

"He's had a lot to bark about recently judging from the sound of his voice,", then as Marran peered at the unusual rise in the ground to the left of the track, she caught a glimpse of movement. As though he rose out of the ground itself, a small stocky man came into view, carrying a carrisack and a flask.

He approached them warily, patently intent on feeding his dog, who barked happily, leaping around, bouncing and shimmying until the man pushed a cap to the back of his head chuckling.

"Good day Ranger," he addressed Marran in a cracked voice, obviously not used to talking.

"You're a long way from home aren't you?" he asked, continuing his duties, pouring water into a stone trough, then placing portions of a freshly butchered gulley-hopper where the dog could reach it. He busied about, draping an old piece of sacking to provide shade for the animal, before turning to face Marran, who'd waited patiently while this was done.

The miner peered up, eyes narrowing as he looked at Marran with renewed respect.

"I apologise Ranger Second," he grunted, "Didn't see the Hawkshleth," he nodded at Marran's throat where his insignia hung on its thong. "If you're looking for a new roost, there's not much to suit you hereabouts.

A pair of pale grey eyes swept down the track, presumably looking for another group following, but Marran laughed, putting the man at his ease immediately.

"We came only as new neighbours to introduce ourselves and bring you some trade." he said, asking almost immediately,

"What do you mine here Master? I must confess that I thought most of these mines worked out."

As the miner considered his reply, Marran shaded his eyes (conscious that the glare of noon would soon be upon them) and continued to scour the landscape looking for shelter, as the miner snorted indignantly.

"Topsiders can't read this land for looking!" he proclaimed in a strangely accented voice, and then he seemed to remember his manners.

"Well then Ranger...?" brightening as Marran supplied his name.

"Dorenard you say! Well, that's a proud name to live up to young man. I once knew an Anelm Dorenard..." he sighed nostalgically, "Used to hunt by here regularly, but he's long gone now... Oh, yes I remember Anelm may the One give him a blessing!"

Jalni gazed at her Ranger, watching the glow of pride lift his chest. Her heart ached for him, remembering how he had reacted when Daro (in magic) first revealed himself to the Children of Scartel, by bringing them messages from their families from beyond the grave. She watched Marran gulp to clear his throat then heard him say firmly,

"Now I walk in my Grandfather's footsteps, the One granting me grace to return to Scartel with my own Keld to elect."

In that statement was the revelation that Scartel would once again be home to Rangers. That already, eleven families were prepared to follow a leader and establish an independent settlement, at which the tough old miner paused, head on one side as he observed Marran's face. Shrewd eyes studied him, and then the miner clapped him on the back saying cheerfully.

"Well said Ranger Dorenard. If Scartel's free of plague now, that's great news, and a Tawn? Sheer wolves and all?" the miner was bubbling over with enthusiasm, then he invited,

"Don't suppose you've ever visited a mine have you? I'd be proud to welcome my old friend's grandson. We can even offer shelter for yon daft Zeglur, so come you in, never let it be said that Ayloth and Agar turned visitors away.", he turned back to his dog, altering the length of its chain, encouraging it to lie in the shade, then patting it fondly, he headed off at a trot towards a bulge in the ground, roughly forty paces away.

Torvin followed, leading the Zeglur, as Marran glanced at Chrysim.

"I should think that Echo will be happier out here." he suggested, aware that he hadn't seen the Mystcat for some time. Jalni, Terris and Nona caught up as the cat's minder said cheerfully,

"He's gone to find his Clan. He remembers this place and knows his way. He'll come back when he's ready."

Jalni looked at Duvell's disabled son remembering Daro's intervention. It had given this simple soul a voice and independent living. The easy tears of fatigue dimmed her eyes as she watched Chrysim gather up a shovel, collecting the Zeglur dung and spreading it to dry for fertiliser. Doubting seriously that anything could grow in this inhospitable wasteland, she followed the others round to the back of the low mound that she now realised was a working mine. Coming up behind Terris and Nona, she stopped short in surprise, because she found herself facing a growing ground. Terris was waxing lyrical over a tall fernlike plant, cupping her hand under the fronds to catch the seeds that Ayloth was offering her. She listened to his gravelly voice explaining.

"I had business further north from here, where the fire river never passed." he said cautiously watching the Rangers as he spoke.

They have earth, mean stuff, very gritty in places, thick and slimy in others. It doesn't seem to grow anything much except these Meddle plants without help. Because we don't see many Zeglurs, I trade ash, and other minerals for seed. North of here, the Fire Rivers carried stone with it, burned everything to a crisp, then set solid. No-one noticed, they were all dead." he sniffed, then said contemplatively,

"Well, not all of them I suppose, the next lot had to come from somewhere! Now, where was I?" he paused, then answered himself slowly.

"When we started looking for minerals, we found out that where there had been fire mountains, they often leaked great deposits onto the ground around them. Sulphur, carried along in the fire river, with all manner of mineral deposits spread over the Ashgenar, and where there's anything worth mining, there's always a miner!!", he touched his nose indicating some special secrets still existed, as Jalni warmed to this odd quirky man. He looked proudly at his growing plot, saying lightly to Terris,

"I'm all but retired now, but I like growing things, and can see a trade here Mistress Apothecary. Perhaps you could find something in your scrip to ease the pain from my Aygar's sore knees, while I look for new additions to your range of medicinery. By the way," he looked sheepishly up at Chrysim, "I hope you will leave me some of your Zeglurs leavings for my plants? I only wish we still saw the old apothecary through Scartel again. He used to leave his herd with Solana from time to time, and her youngsters used to gather droppings to dry, for which I traded seeds and herbs."

He looked slyly at Orto as he came back towards them smiling, the Zeglur tethered and sheltered.

"Seems to me that looks like her deaf mute!", he muttered, "but I'm getting old, forgetting faces.", he lifted aside a sacking curtain hung across a rough doorway into the mound, beckoning as he walked down a solid stairway, which led into a large tunnel under the surface.

The others followed, curiosity filling their faces as they descended through what appeared to be part solid concrete, part rock. They progressed into a large room where an elderly woman sat, apparently working on accounts. She made a note on the wax tablet she was using, and then politely closed the cover before looking up at the increasing crowd in her room. Her eyes widened in amazement as she took in the Rangers, and their companions, then, without a pause she smiled at Orto, and began to sign swiftly.

"Look whose back." she signed, "I thought you'd gone to the Sands in the plague. I'm so pleased to see you, but what of the children? Did they all die? Someone told me that strangers stole them away."

Shocked, Jalni glanced at her Uncle whose hands were flashing in response.

"Yes it's me!" he signed smiling, "but we don't have to sign now, I'm cured and I brought my Healer with me!" he grinned at Jalni

"This is my niece Aygar. We found each other, and then I found out that she and her Lord were the ones who rescued the children. They are all well, most of them resettled in Holmgarth, but I'm stupid!" he slapped the side of his head, laughing as he said,

"Ranger Dorenard, come and remake acquaintance with Aygar the Seer."

Jalni's heart thudded painfully as Marran came forward, followed by Torvin, then it was her turn.

The woman, huddled in a soft brown blanket looked into her face, into her eyes then said dreamily,

"Your child will be healthy Healer. He will be like his father, powerful, loving. You will be blessed, but there is a long dark path to that blessing. A sword will come between you, but neither of you will die by that sword. It is a Sword of truth, a trail-blazer.", she stopped abruptly, her hands shaking as she reached out, pointing directly at Marran.

"The Trail-blazer!" she croaked…"The Trail-blazer!"

As she sagged back in her seat Ayloth took hold of her hand, and as he did so, Jalni became aware of a tiny emblem tattooed onto the web between thumb and forefinger.

'A Sword!' she identified it fearfully, 'A Seer unaffected by this dampening field which separates me from the Source, from Daro!'

The old woman roused, reached out a hand saying softly, privately.

"You will never be without the Source Lady; you just can't hear it sometimes. Keep the faith Jalani del Orto…it will return after your child is born."

Her last whisper was all that Jalni clung to as they followed the map provided by Ayloth, which took them north-east to mines where they could trade for the gemstones required by Duvell.

They also took samples (both root and seed) of the 'Meddle' plant. Terris listened to Ayloth outlining its properties. Listing relief from poor digestion, he claimed that the seed, while being infused produced medicinal oils which treated the effects of bloating. They all tried the tea, finding it light and invigorating.

Eventually, they left Aygar (sleeping whatever vision had visited her away), and Ayloth (mixing soil and dung enthusiastically) wistful for a Zeglur of his own.

They forced their way north-east, crossing from foothills to plain without a sighting of Echo, although Torvin seemed to think that a solitary Mystcat was keeping pace with their progress some distance away. They travelled light, the Zeglur carrying the tent in which the women slept. Jalni's pregnancy progressed as they travelled, until they began to approach the eastern boundary of the Ashgenar where their final trades could be completed.

They occasionally heard noises in the night. Low grumbling snores from Chrysim, a flurry of movement as a Ranger rose to change the Watch, the odd faint crunch and squeak as life (and death) went on. Then, just before they parted company with Orto, the Zeglur and his Ranger escort, there came the night of the Mystcats.

For about a day, Jalni had been faintly 'aware' again. She examined the Sand, but there was no hint of the deep azure of her birth and calling. It shone faintly crystalline, apparently infused with some sand, but there was nothing to give her a clue as to its origin. They pitched camp together for the last time, making good use of their combined rations, watching as the Rangers conferred, nodding over the lightweight tent they would now carry, and preparing for the morning.

Jalni knew that this would be the last time she would be able to talk to her uncle before he left, so they walked aside finding a low rock where Jalni could rest as he asked anxiously,

"Are you sure about this Jalni? Really sure? I'd hate to go off and leave you without making certain that you have arrangements in hand."

His faint air of masculine embarrassment made her chuckle, then as he blushed she roared with laughter, (inwardly wincing as she realised some of that might very well be her own nervousness).

"Yes, you are a Healer, yes Terris is an Apothecary, but whose going for help if you get into trouble?" he growled.

She reached up, stroking his cheek in affectionate farewell watching him stomp away, his question unanswered, for how could she tell him that all her decisions were based on a recurring dream. She returned to the timy single camp their smaller party had made, intending to rest until she saw the expression on the faces of "her" Rangers. She wandered over to the fire and sat down, waiting.

Marran said quietly,

"Look Jalni, the land rises abruptly to the right of us. That is the beginning of the Ranger trail to Scartel; we have nearly reached the end of the Ashgenar proper. Whatever happens, Terris and I remain with you, while we press on into the Unexplored Territories, but do I understand that you want to cross the barrier Jalni?"

His brown eyes were fierce, seeming to question the sanity of this extremely pregnant woman.

She pitched her voice low, emphasising with her expressive features how important this was, then, as she did so, she saw Marran's eyes glaze (as though he was in thrall). Jalni's skin crawled, leaving her wondering what was influencing her, (but she pressed on regardless, suddenly driven to complete this journey).

"I know nothing of any barrier Marran, but I saw Nishanawa coming and going from this part of the so called Unknown Territories. I know that they served at Sanctuary, as did my mother, and that there is a route to Sanctuary from the Temple of the Winds. I watched Jashell take Indeera's ashes into those lands, and she returned safely to the Temple. I have always felt that there might be a way into that region from here and if so, that is where I will bear my child."

She was unaware of the brilliant light that shone from her, nor the ring of command in her voice, but she was relieved when the Rangers nodded acceptance, feeling herself close to the edge of collapse.

Unusually exhausted, she allowed Terris to recommend she retire to the single tent they had erected, and slept like the dead.

Then, just before midnight the wailing started. It began with a low growl, and then slid up an unnerving scale to reach the dizzying heights of utter discord interspersed with soft yowling yips of pleasure. It was eerie, bringing the last night watchman to his feet in a single bound, every hair on his body erect in fright. Then it multiplied, not one voice but four or more, until the unearthly descant had travellers (and escort alike) clapping their hands over their ears and huddling together, wild-eyed and fearful. Eventually even the Zeglur joined in, at which point Orto stomped off to stand apart, legs braced and arms akimbo. He jammed his hukvah onto his head and yelled.

"For the love of the One! Silence!"

Whether it was just the shock of a human voice where few humans strayed, or whether the One heard his prayer, silence fell, and then Jalni heard a voice she knew.

"S'all right Lady Blue..." it slurred drunkenly. "Can't my friends sing every now and then?"

She came out of her tent into Jenta's gentle glow, pausing in the doorway as her baby kicked hard, turned and dropped. She gasped, caught in a ridiculous choice between the need to reassure the party that the Mystcats were not gathering for the kill, but were simply enjoying the fermenting fruit, and the pressing need to empty her bladder!

Terris followed her patient at a discreet distance, waiting until she was sure that nothing was wrong. Then, giggling at Jalni's interpretation of the occurrence she went back to bed. However, as the woebegone Mystcat re-joined the party at dawn, the young Apothecary found him a strip of hide, impregnated with Hollis juice for pain. Grinning at the animal's discomfort, she lifted a pack, following Jalni as she neared the completion of her task.

Chapter 37 -The Calling

Days after the Gathering dispersed, Beneva looked up to see Daro entering the Djellim. She watched silently as the distracted mage stood looking down at Shiarjha's growing map of Pelshar (apparently deep in thought). Continuing to list ingredients for one of Medrana's herbalists from an ancient scroll; she waited for the Sandsinger to speak, as he leant over the map, tracing a line with one forefinger, then, after tapping the scroll (as though making a decision), he said wretchedly,

"It's no good Aunt Beneva! This place is stifling me. I have to get out! Go! Preferably before I burst with frustration…and yet…", his voice tailed off miserably as he flung out a hand pleading, fingers tracing the carved inscription that had started this whole story as he spoke.

As she saw the tracks of despair lining his face, Beneva thrust back her chair and went to him, only too aware that after the funeral rites, grief might overcome him. Gathering herself to withstand the tumult of his emotions, she watched (aghast) as his carefully schooled features crumpled and the dam burst.

He spoke unsteadily,

"I'm sorry…I mean no disrespect dear Beneva, but if you touch me…I'll fold. I hear her everywhere I turn. She touched every surface, permeated every room with her presence, her beliefs, her perfume. Even though we clashed head-on, I loved her, I just didn't tell her enough…"

His voice broke, tears glistening as he grimaced, repudiating the grief that was tearing him apart. Abruptly, he turned his back, shoulders heaving, one hand rising to cover blind eyes as he wept, completely unaware of Suraya's approach.

With a swift slap of sandals, (empowered hands dispersing the field around the hidden Council Chamber) the new Sorceress gathered her foster-brother up, and swept him away. Beneva watched the chamber seal after them, used 'power of sight' to see how tenderly Suraya helped the blind mage into a chair, bending over him (discreetly influencing energy points with talented fingers while she comforted him), and relaxed. The tears would flow, their mutual grief for the only mother either of them had ever known would be expressed and just possibly the antipathy of their youth would dissolve, binding Sorceress to Sandsinger in the affection of sister to brother.

Gathering up her lists, the Guardian left the Djellim discreetly, quietly posting a guard to ensure that Ikella's orphans were not disturbed, going forth into the sunshine as mid-afternoon reached the Gathering square.

The doors to the Underground pastures stood ajar and as she reached the bench outside, she heard Carolus saying shortly,

"I heard it directly from Olneth, Sennia will not be returning."

There was a low mutter from inside, and then Beneva heard the Apothecary say sharply,

"Then it seems that both of them had a narrow escape. Whatever her skills were in embroidery, she seems also to have had a fatal attraction for men! Drenis appears to have poisoned himself on a sqrellwood skewer. Nobody seems to know what happened to her previous husband, but there were rumours that one cannot entirely ignore. The manner of her death was highly significant…"

Someone shut the heavy doors from inside and unable to hear more, Beneva rose. Catching up her finished list, she went in search of a herbalist, deciding that if she was free, Davina (their new Infirmarian) would know if they had stock of some of the rarer ingredients. Her mind went over the odd snatch of conversation she'd overheard as she passed through the stone archway leading to the Infirmary, arriving just in time to hear the tail end of another. She stood in the doorway of Hanna's old workroom, while Davina mixed some medication for Tobin.

Daro's body servant looked wretched. Hunched and frowning, rubbing his eyes and the nape of his neck as he said wearily,

"Glory, but he's tough going when he's moody! I love the man to death, would do anything for him, but three restoratives a day is too much to ask of anyone!"

Beneva choked back a chuckle, tapping firmly on the door to announce her presence, before taking a step inside. She looked at Tobin critically, noticing the fine lines round his eyes and the silvering of his hair as she reached out a hand and took his wrist.

"By your leave Davina?" she said formally, checking pulses, sensing the tension in the man.

"How old are you Tobin?", she asked, concerned at his rapidly fluttering temporal pulse, noting from the corner of her eye the slender man's flush.

"O don't," he begged, looking at his feet, the roof, anywhere but into Beneva's knowledgeable face, he continued, rattling on in his usual practiced diversionary tactic,

"I was Rotations old at birth or so I'm told!" he lisped, "I'd be younger if it wasn't for the like of Sandsingers!" The Guardian smiled grimly, and then faced him, eyebrows raised.

She spoke softly but severely,

"Tobin, for truth you must be on the northern slope of forty Rotations. Andrau (may the One give him peace), told me that you plighted your hearts when you already had thirty Rotations. Your life has never been easy, working long hours, then looking after your love. I think you probably performed all the care of a trained Healer from the time he was paralysed until he passed the Great Divide. Lifting, turning, washing, dressing, feeding…?"

She saw the glow reach his eyes as she recalled the name of his lover, saw the quick moistening of gathering tears, and said lightly,

185

"I know how sorrow for another reminds us of personal loss, but now you must listen to your body. You are how old? Tell me as your Healer, believe me, I shan't tell another man!"

He grinned suddenly shy, then muttering,

"O my! I get a Guardian to heal me?" he confessed,

"I am fifty five Rotations plus…nearly as old as Carolus, and only a might older than Daro!"

Completely nonplussed Davina patted Tobin's bent head gently.

"No wonder you are exhausted!" she commented, returning to her blending adding considerably more agrafuban seed to the grinding bowl to increase Tobin's stamina.

Beneva smiled approvingly,

"Tobin, you are far from being 'just Daro's body servant'. Here you have become Master of Ceremonial garments, finding, mending, cleaning for the Healer Hall's vestments. You serve Daro as the ears and eyes of the household, keeping a finger on the pulse of what ordinary people need and I'm sure you are in some ways, a lonely man's confidante. However, you have needs too and you can be no service to anyone (least of all Daro) if you make yourself ill by overworking."

She thought back to the earlier conversation about Sennia, wondering how Tobin would manage without a skilled stitcher to work for him, and decided to say nothing until she knew more.

Tobin said gravely,

"I can't retire Seris Beneva. For one point, I'd die of boredom, for another Ichspeller Selunsanni needs me, more now Seris Ikella has gone and things must change. I'm determined to see him through the next phase, train someone I trust to care for him, only then can I sit in the sun teasing the Guard and remembering my Andrau."

Davina pressed his medication into his hand as he smiled up mistily.

"He will leave us soon you know Seris?" he predicted. "This was never the Hall of those ancient Singers. Listening to my Lord, I think this may have been the place that one mage lived, but he has to think of the others. They need room and privacy in which to develop. They will go back to rule their own Sands, but they need the space which we can't offer. They need a Hall of their own, so he will leave us and me behind."

He bent his head, swiftly swallowing a draft of the tincture Davina had prepared for depression and exhaustion, while Beneva wished bleakly that there was some effective cure for sorrow and unrequited love. She took her leave, going out to underground pastures, seeking Olneth and an explanation of Sennia's story.

When she finally cornered her spy, he was in a savage mood. The tent he inhabited in the far pasture had been tidied, all portable surfaces scrubbed or polished within an inch of perfection, soft furnishings piled neatly as though he intended to leave.

She studied the swiftly efficient movements of Olneth's long body, (interpreting his barely contained fury) while remaining at the doorway (reluctant to leave yet uncertain of staying).

When he unseeingly stalked right past her to take his temper out on a rug, she waited with the unnerving stillness of a trained observer, remaining in the background until he was calm enough to approach.

She stood aside as he returned from his hanging line, smiling as he stopped dead, looking at her in confusion, muttering apologies as his surroundings came back into focus again.

Embarrassed by his own loss of control, Olneth found a pile of cushions on which she could sit, folding clothing silently while she studied him dispassionately, trying (by her own stillness) to enforce calm upon her companion before asking quietly,

"Sennia?"

He started, then turned towards her bright knowing eyes, groaning as he found his voice, saying piteously,

"Seris Beneva, I have failed you! Failed the Clan, failed myself. How will anyone trust another Sybillsce after this? She worked her way into the heart of Selesh, married a clansman, served the Sisterhood, yet she spied for the Gattarene! Worse still, she got by me!"

He felt his offense so acutely, that Beneva clucked, asking her questions using 'power of voice' in unyielding tones that blanched the anger from him as they spoke. Steadily, she calmed the fury in his eyes, impressing upon him her own high regard, intervening before shame overrode his native intelligence.

"Olneth, I need to know how Sennia operated. How would she pass word back through the barrier? Could she have accessed Lady Soloria's back door?"

His shock was so palpable that for a moment she wondered if he would remain to be questioned, so stiff was his spine when he turned an anguished face to hers, whispering painfully

"Seris, forgive me. I was attracted to her, but I am Telandra's mate! Sennia might have plied her wiles, but she was never in my arms, in my bed, nor even under my roof!"

His cheeks had flamed, his head was bowed as he continued, voice no more than a tortured growl.

"I knew nothing of Adruna's intentions when we left the sands for her Accession. Believe me Tellandra would have accompanied me into exile had I known, and Selesh would have been forewarned long before the events of that night! I never entrusted Tellandra with the means to work my Deshun's plan, perhaps something in me refused to let her become the potential victim of torture. No matter, that only caused my loss, and the Sands of the Union remain safe from the Gattarene."

The pain in his voice had grown exquisite in intensity as he cried out in anguish.

"I left her alone to bear our child! I left her alone Seris Beneva, to perform my duty to my Sands, to serve one I should have recognised as a threat to the Union! I left her alone to die at the hands of a heretic!"

His voice broke, and he turned his face away muttering indistinctly,

"Since you apparently know that I have passed the barrier, I have searched for my family in vain. It is all I live for, to find my child, for she is all I have left in life to love."

His agony and shame was imprinted on his mobile features, but he faced the Guardian head erect, eyes unwavering. Beneva nodded to herself,

"As you have searched, have you found any sign that others can come and go through that barrier Olneth?" she asked, trusting him with her eyes.

The spy considered his words, sighing as he said quietly,

"I have taken Carolus through a couple of times. He too is searching for something. I know not what, but I assumed it would be a scroll, or record to return to the Djellim. I have never seen any sign that he could cross the barrier without me and I know of no other who could pass from inside!"

He paused, then added soberly,

"I may be wrong, but I have the impression that the barrier is weakening. I don't think it has anything to do with my rare visits, but I no longer feel safe. There's something in the air I don't understand, yet it's my homesand."

Beneva frowned, saying shortly,

"Thank you for telling me that Olneth, I'll discuss it with my Sister Guardians. It is almost certainly time to review the barrier and its efficacy, as well as your impressions. If we can do so without preventing your access we will, but no-one other than a Guardian is to be entrusted with knowledge of your expeditions."

This last statement was accompanied by a subtle movement of Beneva's hands, describing a circle in the air. She stared at him unblinking, fingers flickering as she commanded,

"You will also forget this conversation as soon as I leave this pasture!"

Beneva tapped a foot on the ground as she pondered her actions, and then returned smoothly to her interrogation.

"So tell me about Sennia, I need to know her movements prior to her death if possible, and then I'd like to try and find out how she died. Was it by poison? Revenge by her husband's people, as I understand that you believe she murdered Drenis? Tell me Olneth, tell me everything you know or suspect. Remember that I am the Guardian of Knowledge, all knowledge!"

Her seldom used powers of influence poured from her suddenly and Olneth, caught in the flood, literally buckled at the knees, sinking to the roughly carpeted floor at her feet, where he remained, head bowed, as he told all he knew. From time to time she nodded but at the end of his recital, she summed up succinctly.

"So, based on what you have found out since her death, you and that old reprobate think Sennia was planted here long ago. She came not long after Daro, settling in when Deshun Ikella took the Way."

She ticked off points on her fingers as they spoke.

"She arrived with other refugees, purporting to be a young widow. She then courted Drenis; jumping the trave with him about the time Suraya left for the Tourmaline to study with Kerisima. however, although her cousin didn't come to her wedding, Sennia seems to have developed an affection for her now she's alone. I wondered if she is looking for an escape route after Drenis died, conveniently close to Ikella's Rites. "She paused, eyes narrowing as she homed in on another point.

"…or was that after the revelations that Daro sprang on us at the ceremony? Did she leave in panic suspecting that she was in danger of discovery?" she continued voice and manner growing grave.

"Now, her elaborately dressed body is found in an alley, throat cut; but what is very odd, no sign of blood on the wound, on her clothing, or on the Sand!" she continued (as if musing to herself).

"Which seems somewhat symbolic, as though someone wanted to send a message without staining our Sands?"

Her eyes met his steadily as he nodded.

"Traditionally it is the way spies are silenced!" he spoke uncomfortably, and then Beneva said softly,

"How ironic. All the 'usual suspects' half a Sand away, yet one of Adruna's most successful spies is murdered! By whom I wonder? Furthermore, she was clutching a wax tablet with an unusual sigil impressed on it, like some dire warning!"

She leant forward, flipping back a rug to reveal levelled sand beneath. Slowly she drew (in detail), the outline of an eye and Olneth gasped aloud.

"Are you sure Seris Beneva?" he questioned her, prevaricating when she wondered what he knew. She left him, staring abstractedly into the sand, remembering a voice as a thumb impressed a mark on his forehead.

"Here I place my mark, lifting you from mere existence to my Sandsworn. Remember this sigil and know I watch over you and yours, that in life I might call you to my service, knowing that I expect loyalty from those I honour. While you live, I too am bound to your service. Call on me, you who have taken my sign. Know your enemies and mine by my mark, so as they enter the darkened Halls of Hadda, they shall even be known by this mark as mine! Thus is the calling, with me to ultimate life, against me to ultimate death."

Beneva glanced back at her spy as she left the pasture; he sat as though carved from stone, the terrible warning in his mind as he shivered. Had Sennia heard that voice as she died? How dread was his Lord's calling; how far was his reach?

Chapter 38 -Waking the Sands

Drawn and cold, Olneth eventually roused, frowning in bewilderment as he tried (unsuccessfully) to work out what he'd been doing, leaving Half his tent hangings in disarray and floor coverings lifted. He stared at his Lord's sigil inscribed into the packed sand beneath his tent, then shrugged and began putting the tent to rights.

Having finished this task, he was about to draw water for a sweetdrink, when he heard visitors approaching and paused to watch as a number of light riding animals (ridden by Jedrun Clansmen) appeared.

"Ho ancient Olneth!" a lithe man in his prime dismounted, greeting him warmly.

"Where can we graze Deshun Serafina's animals? She's gone directly to the Guardians, leaving me to this fine lot!"

He indicated his escort ruefully, as a prickle of alarm warned Olneth that this was not a conventional visitation. The young man's teeth flashed in a huge grin as Olneth gaped at the sight of Serafina's Court Guard.

The four other men dismounted and bowed, all hugely built, bearded and turbaned, clad in the brilliant hued silks of their sand and armed to the teeth, jewelled dagger hilts thrust through wide sash belts.

"Is that Timmin?" the aging spy asked uncertainly, and then grasping the hand held out to him laughing.

"By all that's holy, you're full grown little worm! Let me look at you..."

Noting the fine strong figure, Olneth looked up into brilliantly sparkling eyes enquiringly,

"Your mother and father?" at which Timmin, child of Derun and Sanra replied cheerfully,

"Mother's still mixing concoctions for all and sundry. Father's still wearing out scribes constructing a book about teaching the blind." pausing awkwardly as the spy's knowledgeable eyes fell on the guards.

"...and you?" Olneth prompted, but was interrupted by the restless beasts jerking and plunging in an attempt to attract attention.

"Later perhaps." Timmin whispered, and then went to assist his escort settling the beasts.

Never one to miss the opportunity to pick up gossip, Olneth took the small escort through to the Hall of Welcome (seeing them settled as honoured guests), before suggesting that Timmin eat at his table. They eyed each other uncertainly as Olneth questioned the possibility of Timmin staying in his tent to catch up on old times. Watching shadows darken the smooth unbearded face as he reminded him of his childhood (spent in Selesh), Olneth couldn't help wondering what brought the son of the Carnelian Desert's Senior Healer back in disgrace, but he kept his counsel and did not have to wait long to find out.

Permitted to return to the care of their animals (under Olneth's supervision), he talked as they returned to the pastures, voices lowering as one of the escort positioned himself at the door of the hostelry (where he could see anyone entering or leaving the underground pastures).

"I don't know how long I can stay." Timmin confessed awkwardly, "I'm in serious trouble…that's why I'm here. Deshun Serafina wouldn't include me in her retinue for Seris Ikella's Rite of Passage, I was in lockup, and I'm not sure that won't continue once she talks to the Guardians."

They were passing back through the doors of the underground pastures as he spoke and Olneth, sensing the wistfulness in the younger man's voice, took the opportunity to duck inside the stabling that provided the offices of the free traders to leave a message.

"If anyone comes looking for Timmin, he's with me. We'll feed Deshun Serafina's fine mounts some extra hay, and then get ourselves fed and watered. We're within shouting distance if anybody wants us."

Ivinish looked up from his own supper.

"Reckon the lad that wants you could make you hear wherever he called you from, but I'd make haste getting there, he's been waiting awhile!", the old beast handler warned.

Deciding to leave his companion in blissful ignorance of what awaited him, Olneth trailed through the pasture, slinging up a couple of hay nets and chatting companiably, before turning into the tent, ushering Timmin ahead of him.

They entered a luxuriously transformed interior. Gone were the worn old hides that had carpeted the packed sand floor. Now, new hides, new hangings adorned the walls, softly shaded cushions were piled in one corner, and interior sections disguised sleeping chambers, while a low table was set along the front of Olneth's couch. Seated in a separate chair, his other visitor waited patiently, hands busily folding and refolding something that glittered once, and then seem to disappear into his sleeve.

Timmin's steps slowed as soon as he'd ducked through the entrance flap of the tent, a gasp audible to the spy who brought up his rear.

Olneth paused in the entrance uncertain of protocol as the blind man rose smoothly and turned to face them, eyes open and glowing with magic.

"Come…" Daro invited, as Timmin was drawn under the sphere of his influence. Using neither power of voice (nor any other discernible gesture) he drew the Jedrun to his side as though magnetised, then when they stood only a span apart, Daro's aura enfolded both of them.

Peculiarly sensitive to the atmosphere that the mage had created, Olneth knelt where he stood, aware that for the first time he was to witness something both private and yet ceremonial, as a hush fell.

Daro spoke softly,

"Do you know your truename?" he asked. There was an intake of breath, and then came the reply, tremulous with anticipation.

"I am Timmisandro Lord. I did as you asked and came as soon as I could." Placing a pouch in Daro's hand. the Jedrun knelt, watching as Daro moved the pouch beneath curious fingers, exploring its contents dextrously. The expression on Daro's face caught at Olneth's heart as he placed a hand on Timmin's forehead. There was wry amusement, tolerant affection, yet a stern resolve that no man could withstand as the mage continued. Olneth 'felt' Daro's voice surround him. It was inside his head, speaking directly to him as much as he spoke to Timmin.

"If the One wills…" he began, and then the pouch he held flashed Carnelian red, streaming the light directly down on Timmin's face.

Quivering Olneth leant forward, unaware of the Opal thumbprint on his own forehead glowing brightly, as Daro questioned Sanra's son. Lightly touching on subjects far beyond the spy's comprehension, the Sandsinger asked when Timmin had felt 'different', a chuckle at his lips as the answers came readily.

"I thought it sprang from boredom." he explained sincerely. "I was always happy with my own company, didn't enjoy games of chance, because I could win too easily. As a child I gave up eating meat, it made me sick, and as an adult I never quite got the hang of hunting, can't enjoy what others call 'the thrill of the kill'. My mind was always asking 'What of their young?', when the hunters brought home a fine beast.", he gurgled with suppressed amusement, "I must have been very difficult to live up to, even in childhood, but mother tinkered with my diet, made sure it didn't make life a misery for them or me. She thought I might become religious, an Adept or Seer. There are plenty of cults that support those ideals! It was the other things I did that caused trouble!"

His voice lowered as he told Daro about his unhappy habit of predicting disaster, of 'knowing' when someone was lying and lastly of his desperate need to share what he had learnt by himself.

"Which was?" asked Daro, lips twitching as Timmin lowered his head in shame.

"I could 'be' where I wanted to be as soon as I'd fixed the place in my mind", the Jedrun admitted. "It was very useful as a boy." he explained ingenuously. "Mother often left a list or a book behind when she needed it and I found 'being helpful' earned me credit at home. Only I got careless, made one or two 'hops' that weren't reasonable and got noticed. Olneth watched Daro struggle to suppress a grin, and wondered how often poor Jashell had been confused by this unnerving capacity in his own Lord, as Daro prompted,

"This episode with the stone mason?" and a wave of dark blood mounted the Jedrun's cheeks.

His manner grew sheepish, but his words were stubbornly defiant.

"Daro Ichspeller I couldn't let Kahdesh die could I?" he demanded hotly. "He has been my second father, he has held me to my education, taught me skills I would never have learned from another, besides how would I ever have faced his family, my family, myself, if I had saved myself from notice by permitting that stone to crush him where he sat? That is not the Way; certainly it cannot be my Way even if my life is forfeit as Deshun Serafina fears."

When Olneth peered at him, he could see the angry flush ebbing. Even in protest, his voice kept level, but his eyes were lit with a curious intensity as he said deliberately,

"Ichspeller, you could no more allow Harmeister Patris to die unnecessarily than I could permit the death of a decent old man who has shared his skills, his hearth and his food with me. If Deshun Serafina had not been present, nobody would have known that I intervened. As it is, Kahdesh lives and I die in chains for using what I could to save him."

There was no anger in Timmin's face, only weary frustration and intolerable regret as he lowered his head and said quietly,

"So be it! I only ask that you tell my mother and father that I didn't mean to shame them, but I couldn't let my Second Father die!"

Daro nodded, face serious, and then said slowly,

"I understand completely now, but it wasn't very adroit to pull off your first major use of power in front of your Sorceress." Olneth could see Daro's smile now as he added ruefully, "Although the circumstances differed, you are not alone in shocking our Sister's in Sorcery! Seris Ikella seemed to take my emergence as a personal affront, but then she was my mother in everything but flesh and didn't feel the need for a Sandsinger about the place!"

Olneth nearly laughed at the expression on Timmin's face as realisation dawned.

"I, my Lord?" the whisper came as Daro bent, touching the centre of the Jedrun's forehead, seemingly igniting a soft ruby aura around his companion. He extended his hands over Timmin's head, steadying him, as he said softly,

"You, my brother! You are called to the service of your Sands Timmisandro, to form a guard against the evil that threatens to overwhelm us. Once more the Union of the Sands calls us to defend Pelshar and its people. I have summoned the Appointed to meet their responsibilities, to fulfil their potential. So, Timmin, child of Sanra and Derun, present at my birth, step forward as Timmisandro Derunta, Sandsinger Designate, and the Appointed for the Carnelian Sands in this Second Age of Mystery."

His voice rose in command,

"Now my brother, Ichta Derunta of the Carnelian, waken your sands."

At Daro's words the pouch he held one handed opened, Carnelian Sand pouring to the floor at his feet. Timmin sighed, plunging his hands down into the forming pile, as it flashed into life. Glowing jewel bright, it flowed like a living entity around his hands, then returned to the soft hide container of the pouch in a fiery stream.

Impossibly, Olneth felt the echo of those words deep in his own blood, looking up to see that without his knowledge others had joined them. Shiarjha, Beneva, Serafina and Suraya encircled the mage as Timmin glowed, radiating all the shades of Carnelian. Olneth listened carefully, certain that Daro heard another voice, and then the mage raised his head and spoke.

"I summon all present to witness the waking of the Sands.", and in his hands there was ruby fire building, increasing in brilliance until with a slight sigh, it was possible to see that he held a chain on which spun a glowing pendant. He slipped the chain over his hand, then, placing that hand on Timmisandro's head, the blind mage slid the pendant down to rest, glowing against his acolyte's throat, the Seguidor of the Carnelian Sands.

The Lord of the Opal straightened, and then facing Seraphina said gently,

"Come Sister Sorceress, welcome your 'brother in magic', may you work together towards the complete restitution of Pelshar."

Obediently Serafina placed her hands between Timmisandro's, giving (and receiving) the kiss familiar from the engaging scapegrace turned Appointed, managing to mask her shock as they knelt at Daro's feet.

Reclaiming his Staff, Daro raised his voice as though he spoke to all sands and with a shock, Olneth realised that he probably did, filing away his impressions for Carolus, whose curiosity was legendary. When he returned from escorting Deschima back to the Malachite, Olneth planned on reporting all of this, at length. He hunched, concentrating on Daro's words.

"I hope to repeat this reception over the next few ninenights as we prepare to leave Selesh for Tirjhinar. I have no idea who will answer my call, or when, but those that do will be welcomed, accommodated, accompanied or not by our Sisters in Sorcery. When we have assembled enough to remove, we will leave Selesh to find our own training ground, then to prepare ourselves for whatever threatens our way of life, our world?"

***For Olneth, this privileged introduction to Higher Magic was a revelation. Over the following moons he watched visitors coming and going from the Underground Pastures as he always had, one eye on the security of Selesh, the other on the growing group that were housed separately in the old barracks tent that appeared late one afternoon. He kept his counsel, grinning when Carolus grumbled around the pastures on his return, remaining unsurprised when the old man retreated to the herders hut in the far pastures above Selesh. He seemed undiminished by age, but Olneth suspected that a deep weariness pervaded the Apothecary's soul and left him strictly alone. He maintained his distance as everyday Daro grew in stature, finally coming into his own, no longer hiding who or what he was, blazing Seguidor and Anduigor proclaiming his status as he roamed Selesh, cheerfully robbing the Djellim of small artefacts, perusing scrolls and (as Beneva protested) making a shameless nuisance of himself.

Gradually, the tented dormitory filled with a mixture of highly charged members of the Appointed and their entourage.

Then the Czerezin rode in.

For days something ominous had hung over Selesh. There was no change in the light, but it seemed darker and people were growing fretful.

"Storm brewing?" Olneth thought, but when Lallee ran in calling for Healers, his heart sank. Shortly thereafter, he saw the Apothecary hurrying towards him with Rann, Timmisandro and Daro at his heels.

The Sandsinger gave no greeting but commanded abruptly,

"Olneth, tell Diras to get the villagers back to Selesh Minoria, call the reserve guard to duty and find handlers, wherever they're hiding, we have visitors and they're in a hurry!"

By the time the Gate in the Rock opened to admit Medrana's escort, Davina and other senior Healers were waiting in the gathering gloom, prepared to isolate whatever dread illness had provoked the Sandsingers alarm. Ivinish and his men ran forward to hold exhausted clohzen or assist their reeling riders, while Daro went to Medrana's side, holding out his arms for the pathetic bundle she carried. Immediately his aura sprang into life, almost before he'd taken the child from the Sorceress, who was speaking rapidly to Davina, as she dismounted.

"This is no ordinary fever. Shula was well when we left Kilashen, she turned towards the Sandsinger, "We did everything we could as soon as she complained, but we've not been able to get her to drink, let alone eat. All she does is ramble in delirium, but what she says makes no sense."

Gently Davina persuaded Medrana to follow Daro, who was headed for the Underground Pastures, his Staff keening a note that he could follow at a brisk walk. Swiftly, Olneth met the Sandsinger saying urgently,

"Ichspeller, my tent, the furthest sleeping area."

Then a strange thing happened. The blind mage put the child into Olneth's arms, throwing a protective weave around both of them as the spy ran, knowing he could get to the designated emergency bed before Daro. He was not surprised to find Beneva and Carolus there, but blinked as he saw the other Appointed crowding into the main tent as well. Suraya appeared, serene but pale as she held out her Staff, wings hovering over the desperately sick child.

There was no hesitation. With one lift of.an empowered hand, the curtained area expanded silently, as Olneth relinquished the child into the Healers hands.

Medrana slipped in behind Daro, who positioned his Staff at the head of the bed, lighting the area as the Healers stripped the shivering girl to examine her. Clad only in a thin shift, her normally bronzed skin seemed sallow and waxy then, as Carolus appeared, they donned shantana's before rolling the small body from side to side, in an attempt to see what ailed this small, but very precious candidate to the Cynabarr Sands.

Sweat poured off her, pooling in her eye sockets, soaking her midnight black hair and while they worked, the deadly fever grew. They wiped her dry, fanning a cooling breeze on to her face, and then wordlessly the Apothecary pointed to a small raised mark on the back of her leg, turning aside to catch Medrana's muttered comment.

"Deo mi!" the Sorceress swore angrily, "She said she'd been bitten by a 'landrigal', but she was in bed and sleeping! We thought she was dreaming." she added hesitantly, "With two candidates, we thought it better that I came ahead with Shula because she is so young." her dark eyes glistened as she reported rapidly,

"We don't have 'landrigals' in the Cynabarr, but assuming they are venomous, I checked the child myself. She was unmarked, seemed drowsy, wanting to go back to sleep. My bodyguard turned out the tent, stripped the beds, searched high and low while I took care of the child. They found nothing, and neither did I, but the child still complained, so I gave her a sleeping draught and kept watch. Towards dawn she became restive, hot and cold sweats, delirium and fever. Six of my Honish rode with me, leaving Shyl Nighthawk (our other candidate) with Anyay Littlebear (my Elect) and the rest of my Honish."

She saw the Apothecary grimace, his hands hovering over the hot flushed face of the whimpering child, as he bent over, listening to the muttering as the girl sank further into delirium.

"I hear Drum Sands!", she struggled upright, glazed eyes rolling, "They come, Sister Mother, they come!", the Sandsinger listened in horror as the child wept, "The snarling ones, the slithering ones, the dark ones I can't see, sandrigals, landrigals, the ones that eat your brains! Sister Mother…they bite me, eat me, strip the sand from my soul!"

This last was accompanied by a cry so desolate that the hair on the heads of the Appointed rose, as did the child's voice, rising from a whimper to a shriek so agonised that every magic user or Designate's aura flared. The Apothecary stepped back, allowing the Healers to advance, cool rubs and wet cloths at the ready.

Withdrawing to the main gathering area, the Sandsinger faced his entourage gravely and spoke, his voice (little more than a whisper),yet reaching the ears of all as they stared at him, stupid with grief for an unknown child who was obviously dying in the next room.

"Come closer all of you." he instructed, then his voice changed as he repeated the lesson he had learned through bitter experience himself.

"We are not gods my children," he said steadily, aware of his Songfather's approving gaze. "We are not gods, although once, long ago, we thought we were."

The light in the tent grew pouring down on the Sandsinger from the multifaceted roof of the Underground Pastures as the mage recalled his own devastation at a time very similar to this. His voice shook as he remembered Brus, but true to his mentors, he carried on with conviction enough for all of them.

"Death is the way of all men, and we (while we live long in the power) are only men, not gods. We cannot predict it, prevent it, or stay it from its course, but we can transform it, from the meaningless waste of a young life, to something positive, something meaningful. Shula is beyond our help, beyond any or all of us combined, but we can change her fate, for the betterment of our world and the solace of her family and Clan."

He turned his head, seeking someone, and then called Olneth by name.

"I will provide a mount Olneth," he said gravely, "One you can ride like the wind, one that will keep you safe, never fear. The time is short and you should sleep until you are needed. I will call you myself, so go now."

Olneth obeyed instantly, aware that in his Lord's mind every order was part of a pattern, and the One only knew that he recognised death as just another thread in the warp of time.

He followed his Lords commands, preparing the almost silver mare that Daro described as the fleetest of foot, wondering as he brushed and plaited her mane, why he didn't remember seeing her before, then, swiftly curling himself into a rug in the stable besides the chosen one, he slept.

In his sleep, (or so it seemed to Olneth), his Lord came to him, holding out a tablet containing Medrana's orders.

"Go swiftly my Olneth," he said gravely, placing a pulsing amulet around the spy's upper arm. "Stop for nothing, stop for no-one until you reach this point." He reached forward, placing his thumb on the bemused man's forehead and a clear map sprang into Olneth's mind.

Daro's finger was on his lips cautioning him to silence.

"Say nothing!" urged the mage, "Diras will lead you out, and while you wear that amulet, no-one will see you. Be warned Olneth, do not dismount, do not pause, ride like the wind my trusted friend. I send you into danger I fear, keep your dagger handy. Once you sight the Czerezin, bring them back as fast as you can. Stop for nothing, just make sure Shyl Nighthawk is with them!"

He leant forward as Diras appeared with a night lantern gleaming fitfully from its shaded cowl. He spoke softly, as though to himself, but Olneth heard the words that started the oddest journey he'd ever make.

"Tok Mirayen eddish", said the mage, and the sands shifted as Araneus flew!

Long after that night, the spy's only memory of the events that followed was a jumble of impressions. Perhaps it was the rolling thunder that fragmented his normally acute memory; perhaps it was only severe exhaustion that conveyed the impression that he rode a path of no man's making, that at every rock, the sparks that flew from his mount's heels flashed a corona of lightening behind them. Whatever it was, he was convinced that he descended from a great height to the plain below the Low Pass, a glowing current fizzing along his hair and skin, casting an eerie glow ahead of him, which made it all the easier to sense shifting shapes slithering away as his mount careered through the Azure Sands to find his stray travellers.

He crouched over the mare's neck, one hand gripping her mane, feeling the surge and soar of her body as she made for the Traven Gap, where they were to be found, and saw them, a small party, dust billowing in their wake as they fled a veritable tide of horror.

Never stopping to consider dismounting, Olneth obeyed the instinct to remove his amulet and was relieved to see the riders swerve towards him. He remembered peering into the darkened writhing mass of reptilian pursuers, and then his mount reared up, wheeling in her tracks to follow the Czerezin riders, lightening hissing to form an impenetrable barrier as he circled behind them protectively.

In the midst of the group, two figures glowed every shade of cinnamon; those he decided must be Medrana's other candidate and her Elect. Then the speed and adrenalin coursing through his veins muddled his memory, removing all impressions of a whirling screaming storm horse as both the wind and the magic drove back the denizens of the dark reaches, before they could once more threaten the sands.

He remembered nothing of the concussion of thunder, the sizzling death of lightening, the sheet of sand, nor the howling of the wind. He focussed only on the strong limbs lifting him forward, pounding hooves, and the ululation of the warriors that saluted him, surrounding him, as though he were one of their own. They took the trade route under the high rock where Caranchar crouched, keeping west of the Great Divide, and spilling across the sands until they slowed to a canter, climbing the rise up to the Gate in the Rock, then silently (single file), trotting down the passageway to meet their red-eyed Sorceress at the door of the Underground Pastures. He saw Carolus, and made his way toward the Apothecary, who said gruffly,

"Daro said I should collect you, and take Araneus into the stable. Ivinish will feed her and rub her down. Have you got that amulet?"

Olneth hesitated, uncertain that he should part with the magical thing until Daro asked for it, then Carolus smiled.

"You are a good man in a crisis my friend. Here's its pouch, our Lord and Master suggests that you keep it in this and wear it round your neck!"

They were interrupted by a low keening from the Czerezin warriors grouped around the doors, plainly grieving for Shula as their Sorceress broke the news. Feeling like a rank outsider, Olneth would have slipped past them, but a beaded and feathered Clansmen stopped him.

Tears glittered on the tall man's face as he studied Olneth, gazing into his eyes, long and hard.

"You saved us Rides like the Wind." he said brokenly, "I salute you and your Thunder Horse. I welcome you also to attend my daughter's death…" he continued devastatingly, "As the father of a girl child you will understand our loss!", then with a swirl of his magnificent camp-fire cloak, he was gone and the spy stared silently after him, wondering how the man knew of his missing daughter.

Time passed slowly. In the main tent, the Appointed huddled round Daro, who supported by Suraya spoke quietly of their responsibilities. Carolus nodded quietly to himself, wrapped in a blanket Olneth slept restlessly, while Healers came and went and the Guardians stood watch. When the first light started to appear over the horizon there was a stir, then Medrana and her Clansmen appeared, Shula's father leading Shyl Nighthawk by the hand, the teenager carrying an elaborately embroidered blanket. One of the other tribesmen was beating softly on a drum, the insistent rhythm simply the background of life in the red brown dunes of the Cynabarr Sands. They processed into the dying child's sickroom, where once more, the tent simply resized itself to accommodate them.

All eyes went to the piteous little body (barely breathing now) on the bed, then, with infinite pity, the Sandsinger stood aside, indicating that Shula's father should sit on the chair which had silently materialised as a dais formed behind Medrana.

Taking no notice of the Sandsinger's own sigil on the chair back, the father simply sat and held out his arms for his dying child, as Medrana herself lifted Shulahh and placed her in his arms.

Now Daro placed the Appointed around the room, dematerialising objects, furnishings and hangings where he needed to create more room. Carolus touched Olneth's arm, producing two cushions and the two sat together, mindful of strange harmonics as the Appointed began to hum, low-voiced as Shulahh began to whimper.

"Beware Drum Sands," the throaty whisper came from no child, and for a moment, Olneth lost focus as he searched Czerezin faces for some sign of the speaker.

In Daro's hands, the embroidered blanket glowed, and then as he wrapped it around the child, the quiet beat of the drum became a harsh staccato.

"Beware Drum Sands, their beat beneath you warns the predator." a long sigh of foreboding rose from the Czerezin, a rattle sounded, for all the world like the ringed Sandrigal it imitated. Then with her Clansmen continuing their own funeral rites, Daro called Shyl Nighthawk to him.

Olneth watched closely, hearing the beat of the dying child's heart in the drum, the rhythm of her breath accentuated by the slow shuffling dance of the Clan as they bid her farewell, interspersed by the Sandsinger's own ritual.

"Do you know your truename?", "When did you know you were different?" then the drum began a low roll, the rattle sounded, and the same questions were being put to Shula's astonished father. Eventually, with the girl panting in extremis, the sand pouch opened, and the tawny red sand poured into Shula's hands and flared. She raised her head gasping,

"Father? Am I Sandsinger?", then the drum rolled, the child sighed and the sand flamed. When Olneth could see again, Shula had gone and the fiery sand had returned to the pouch, which remained glowing.

Daro stepped forward, a sad smile on his face as he held the sand pouch out to Shyl Nighthawk. She opened her hands under the pouch, crying out as the flare enveloped her, sand spiralling around her in a glorious burst of colour and light.

A bright determined voice, much younger than Shyl's declaimed,

"My truename was SaShulahh Wild Owl, and now I am Sandsinger, and so are you my sister in magic. Keep the faith, believe in the One…and listen for the Drum Sands…they are beating!"

Slowly, the pulsing heartbeat of the drum stopped, the sand returned to the pouch, as the bereaved father wept with pride. Olneth and Carolus crept away, out into the pasture as silent groups passed them on their way to bed. The two spies slipped past the tents, making for the old hay barn where Rotations ago, they had fought for the life of another child and won. They said very little, there was nothing much to say, but as he sank into dreamless sleep, Olneth touched his amulet, wishing fervently that there was a potential Sandsinger ready to do battle with the heretic who'd seen him exiled from his own child.

Chapter 40 -A Distant Song

Daro reviewed his guest list mentally, listening to them chatter, as he made graceful obeisance to Suraya (in whose Audience Chamber they gathered).

Deep in the heart of Selesh, he had secretly garnered every Sorceress alongside his group of Appointed candidates, as he sought to strengthen the barrier against the heresy of Adruna and protect the Union of Sands.

He had not baulked from using power to collect them, for time was of the essence as his mother's weave around the Amethyst Sands weakened dangerously. Now, with his plans about to come to fruition, he sat, visitors on all sides cheerfully wiping away centuries of exaggerated rumour, (replacing what many held as common belief) with the truth as he knew it. He was talking quietly to Nahamida as Olneth arrived with Carolus, who glanced at the assembly astutely, turning his head to whisper,

"Good lad, he's mixed them up properly. That way, they'll be forced to exchange news, share information and even boast about their Clans. Communication is the key to confidence, both at home and away."

Olneth nodded, he knew the truth of that statement all too well. Noting Shula's father talking to Hanna, their retired Infirmarian, he moved nearer, interested despite his fatigue.

The Elder of the Clan Czerezin was describing a rare plant, one that needed certain minerals not present in the Cynabarr and Hanna (with lips pursed), was running through the healing qualities he was describing.

"Helps digestion, prevents bloating... let me think a moment Two Moons.", she broke off frowning, and then asked doubtfully,

"How tall does it grow? What part of the plant can be digested and in what form?"

Olneth found himself considering the description Two Moons gave as the Healer went to consult her fellows, nearly jumping out of his wits as the bereaved father grasped his arm and said hoarsely,

"Rides like the Wind; you have accrued much credit in the tents of the Czerezin my friend. Though you wear the skin of a Sybillsce refugee, your Lord says you have the heart of a Shalhanhi, the intellect of a Sorceress, the strength of ten Kora-Mai, the sensitivity of a Seer, and the soul of a cut-throat pirate...whatever that might be!", he held up a hand to still the spy's protestations. "Know this. In our lands there will ever be a tent, a living, a woman to warm your bed on a cold night. You have lived with and served the Shalhanhi since you came amongst them, but know this...I, whose sons have joined their ancestors welcome you to my hearth and home as a son. I have many Rotations now (and with no wife to warm my blankets); I hear voices in the night. One of those spoke to me when my Shula lay dying, which I think you'll remember!"

The wise brown eyes met Olneth's, holding his gaze steadily.

"When you come to visit us, I will drink again of the seed wine that helps me hear my voices, and then I will speak to you of your lost and parted ones. Now I am tired, but I will remain while your Lord honours you." he turned Olneth gently, as Daro beckoned him.

He went reluctantly, wondering a little at his Lord's recklessness in recognizing his spy openly (even in such exalted company), but there would be no denying the Lord of the Opal.

He heard Daro explain (with embarrassing embellishments) his part in the extraordinary events of the previous night, and didn't flinch when the Sandsinger surrounded him in the embrace of his aura, standing perfectly still, feeling the strange sparkle holding him firmly in his Lord's magical grip. He had no fear of Daro's power, this (he thought) was but the hug of a brother, and then the Appointed joined in!

He struggled briefly (to no avail) unprepared for the corona of colour that blazed around him, then as he stood pinioned by their combined power, the Czerezin sneaked up on him. He only saw Rann Godway grinning, Daro smiling secretively, as Lallee tried (unsuccessfully) to look reassuring. When Timmisandro chuckled wickedly, Olneth looked to Shyl Nighthawk, but only silence greeted his unspoken plea for mercy

Then the Sisters of Sorcery stood. For a moment there was silence, then every Staff was lifted as a gentle drumming began, then Shyl Nighthawk stepped forward, holding a campfire cloak, pressing the wonderfully embroidered thing into his arms.

As he grasped it, two Czerezin Clansmen appeared, one to each side of the bemused man, who gasped as they gleefully pulled his own clothes from his back, stripping him to stand naked shielded only by the blanket he'd been given.

From somewhere he heard Carolus say quietly,

"The Czerezin honour you friend, stand still, let them have their way, it might provide additional links we could all use."

Then chaos descended as the Clansmen claimed him for their own. He was taken captive, dragged to the hot spring baths, where he was scrubbed, oiled, and every body hair plucked by an astonishingly beautiful woman. His breathless pleas ignored, she washed his hair, murmuring over the unusual length of it as she massaged his scalp with an oil that smelt of flowers. She smiled into his eyes as she braided it Czerezin style, gathering heavy bunches to each side of his head. Perfumed and oiled he was then subjected to the most sensuous massage he'd ever experienced, before they dressed him in the Irix hide trousers and tunic of a warrior brave. After submitting to having his hair decorated with feathers, (held in place by a beaded browband) He gazed at his own reflection in a copper panel suddenly sure that his life was about to change again, as his Czerezin trail-brothers gathered him into their midst.

They returned to the Audience chamber where a sombre faced Carolus greeted him.

"Welcome Rides like the Wind!" the Apothecary said softly, poker-faced. "Come and join us, we would be grateful to hear your impressions of what occurred last night."

Solemnly, aware that his words were to instigate further action against his homesands, Olneth decided to take the lead from the Sandsinger, who'd greeted his arrival with a simple nod.

He described his impressions of a carpet of reptiles, answering Medrana's horrified aside regarding insects with caution. He'd only seen sandrigals, lizards and something small and vicious that moved too quickly to identify, but in his mind he heard a child's cries, as did they all.

He surveyed the collective thoughtfully. Only magic-users present now, he quickly took stock. Daro and four Appointed, nine Sisters of Sorcery, including all three Guardians. Each Sand was currently guarded by a Sorceress-Elect, but as his mind went over the members of this elite gathering, only one was most palpable by her very absence! Adruna the Heretic…and in his own mind he knew he was a condemned man.

His eyes flickered nervously over the Audience room, envisaging spies huddled listening in every corner, then, aware of Daro's voice, he tried to concentrate.

"My brother." the Sandsinger was saying privately, his inner voice calm and authoritative.

"You are no longer safe with us here in Selesh! We have considered your past, and provided a future, one in which you can continue to work for us, or retire into obscurity once more. Medrana and Two Moons will adopt you formally as a full-blood Czerezin Clansman. You look the part and the life will suit you. I, in return for your service will provide the means by which you can continue to search for your child, but it will be necessary for you to surrender Soloria's backdoor key."

Stunned, Olneth looked up to see Daro's eyes open, glistening fire opal orbs trained on him, as though in magic, the blind Sandsinger could see.

Their private conversation continued, as a chuckle sounded in Olneth's mind.

"Perhaps I can?" Daro suggested slyly, "I'm told that you look very pretty under all that finery and there's at least one woman ready to warm your blankets at night!"

As Olneth's whole body blushed, Daro grew serious.

"There's a breach in Ikella's shield!" he said shortly. "We have to be certain it stays sealed and that whatever came through is destroyed. The shield (created by a Guardian Sorceress must be reinforced by a Guardian Sorceress and thankfully, Kerisima was present when it happened. The Sisters will support the original weave, while we…" he indicated his pupils, "…deal with anything living that has passed through that shield to the outer Sands."

As Daro spoke the Guardians stood to leave, followed by their Sisters in Sorcery. Olneth was touched to see Suraya looking at her foster-brother uncertainly, then watch Daro catch her hands in his, squeezing them between his own in support.

He heard him say huskily,

"I know, it's the last thing we want to do, but it's necessary. None of us is ready for battle yet!", then the women were gone, and Daro was holding out his hand for the spy's only way to get back to the Amethyst. His heart lurched as he took Telandra's locket welded to the chain that held the vial from his pouch, but the Sandsinger's fingers closed over his own, thrilling ice cold shivers ran fizzing down the chain, then the vial dropped into Daro's grasp.

"Hold on Olneth. She's still alive, I know it, and I hear her name in a distant song!" he said enigmatically, then he was gone and Two Moons gripped his arm, refusing to let him falter.

"Courage my son!" said the wise man of the Czerezin, "We must prepare our defences.", and so it was that Olneth, proud Captain of Soloria's Household Guard, became Rides like the Wind, Czerezin brave, oldest son of Two Moons, Tribal Elder of the Cynabarr Sands.

In the Hall of the Healers, the Guardians quietly entered the Sacred Circle, taking up position around the Book of Rule on its lectern. Carefully spaced around them, the Sisters of Sorcery took up their posts, leaving only the ninth point untenanted, as they positioned the ritual Staffs of every Sand into the slots that held them in place.

Daro listened until Beneva nodded and a peal of chimes rang out as her wristlets flared silver in the near dark of the immense Hall. Then, he stepped forward aura engaged, as he slid his own Staff into the ninth position, actively preventing any power inside the Amethyst Sands escaping to frustrate the purpose of this Gathering. Thunder rolled in the background as each Staff's powerstone sprang to life following the hierarchy of the Sands. Everyone's head lifted, listening, as Daro suggested slyly,

"Footsteps in the dark?", then the silence grew as the Appointed stepped in behind Daro, symbolic of the blockade they formed to the desires of the Heretic.

Again, silence grew, and then the chant began, the soaring fluidity of Kerisima's *othervoice* proclaiming Adruna's fate once more, against the background of an intense rhythmic chant from the chorus of Sorcery. The tension rose as strange shadows leapt and danced against walls veined with natural Opalstone. The wind howled as magic stirred to life, crackling and flaring Sister to Sister, Staff to Staff as the chant wove the combined *othervoice* of Sorcery, thus sealing the Sands against contamination, condemning friends and enemies inside the Amethyst desert alike.

Then Rann's head lifted in astonishment, another voice was singing and he could hear it clearly, sealing the Sands from within! He stole a look at the Sandsinger, but there was nothing to show that Daro heard it too, so he stilled, refocused, aware that he must guard Daro if necessary.

A lifetime later, on a sobbing ululation of grief for the innocents thus trapped, it was over and the sobered magic users dispersed Kerisima lifting Ikella's glass easily, sending her Sisters in Sorcery through Jocasta's door as Medrana and her entourage withdrew for one more night in the Underground Pasture.

It was there, that Olneth remembered the Sybillsce he'd buried in his own cloak, accosting a weary Sandsinger as he left Medrana's camp-fire.

"Lord…" he hesitated, something of the new distance he must maintain in his mind, but Daro smiled.

"There you are Olneth," he said cheerfully. "I have just consulted with Medrana, who says every brave brings two mares with him, so I'm lending you that wrinkled face brown you usually ride, along with Araneus."

He smiled to himself, remembering the night he'd first danced in the storm over Scartel, Araneus just a stripy faced foal at the time. He cleared his throat, thinking of Jalni suddenly, and instructed firmly.

"No-one else is to ride, clean, feed, or groom her. She's not for human handling. If she disappears, don't panic it's one of her traits. Just put on the amulet I gave you, and she'll reappear. Everything is arranged my friend, I will see you again, never fear! Now, you wanted me for something?"

Olneth explained, describing the unknown Sybillsce clansman's injuries, and how he'd reburied him near the cave on Aramand's Peak then while the mage considered this, he made a suggestion.

"Lord, you've done your best to protect me, why not complete the task? I am very sure that the Heretic has spies deeply embedded in the Union. I can't think that the spate of killings we had happened through chance, I already worked out that there was an assassin at work, and perhaps that was Sennia? Who knows? However, this last incursion was different. This involved magic so far beyond the basics that I'm afraid. Why don't we use the opportunity to let them think they've succeeded? I can disappear if you don't like the idea, but that has its drawbacks. Why not give them a body that they can't identify for sure?" he offered, grimacing distastefully at the idea of disinterring his Clansman.

Carolus spoke gently from the back of the room (where Olneth hadn't noticed him).

"It goes against every grain Ichspeller, but it would give the unknown man's death some meaning. I don't doubt that he might have been caught by one of Adruna's pets, but someone out on our side of the barrier, contrived to make him an example for any of us to find and I (for one) would like to make his death an honourable one! You could sufficiently disguise any features to stop them realising what we've done."

Daro frowned, questioned his spy more fully about the site of the burial, then said shortly,

"You are still leaving in the morning Olneth! We'll deal with the matter in hand, partly because I'd like to use that body as bait to identify whoever it is that reports to the Heretic. He'll find it harder to do so from now on, although I'm minded to let this message through. We can and will retrieve your Clansman and provide a suitable funeral, but his resting place will be marked with your name my friend, for after you have gone, Olneth the survivor will officially die. I hate every bit of our parting brother. I remember so clearly what you went through to get here, but I think we both know that until the Heretic is brought down, your name must pass from memory."

He paused, sighing, then said his farewells abruptly, lit the powerstone on his Staff, and left them, walking in its wake stiff necked and unyielding, leaving Olneth behind with Carolus for his last night in what had been his home for Rotations.

At dawn the following morning, as the Czerezin trotted out ahead of their Sorceress, one amongst them could feel watchers crowding the rampart from which Jashell, Carolus and Indeera had watched Daro banished from Selesh. A voice in his mind said softly,

"I have grown to realise your courage and tenacity my loyal friend. Tonight we will do you much honour and the grief amongst your friends will be real, for I dare not reveal what we have undertaken. Already your Clansman is on his way to us, our first Watch being alerted to the presence of a dead man near to the three border crossing."

The reference to the peculiar junction of the Cynabarr, Amethyst and Azure Sands caused the silent brave in the midst of his Clansmen to purse his lips in a whistle, which died at birth.

Daro continued softly,

"Your life belongs to me remember? I will always be there for you Olneth, not just as a fumbling child uncertain of his actions, but as your Lord, your Clansman, your brother..."

The Czerezin rode into the Azure, heading south for their own Sands and it was not only Two Moons that faced the future with tears in his eyes.

Chapter 41 - Other Barriers

Within his Eyrie Daro could relax. Lights (and voices) were kept low, personal assistance was provided by Tobin and since Jalni's departure, the Watch posted in his anteroom had learned to go about their duties discreetly.

On the night following Olneth's 'funeral', Daro reached his sanctum with relief; sickened by the charade he had put his whole Clan through, desperate to find peace, tranquillity and the privacy of his own thoughts.

After an exceptional day in which he had seen the opportunity to fool Adruna's spies, he had parted from Olneth, connived with his Songfather's assistance to retrieve the body of Olneth's Clansman, effortlessly wielding the powers in which he'd been invested, but now (exhausted), he needed solitude in which to recover. Perhaps the day's emotionality had roused a sensitivity that the Sandsinger would rather not admit to, but he was suddenly convinced that Jalni had returned and threw open the door to their bedroom to investigate. Two heads bent over a pile of clothing rose, as Tobin said gently,

"Did we disturb you Lord? I'm sorry. I'm just going through the list of repairs with the village tailor!"

Disappointed, Daro wordlessly retreated, his Staff emitting an encouraging hum as he turned towards the door of his great-room and entered slowly, feeling (rather oddly) like some stranger who no longer belonged here.

Wearily passing a hand over his face, he swung out a chair, sending his Staff to its stand in the corner as he slumped, elbows on the ancient table, chin cupped by the heels of his hands, as he unwillingly contemplated life at Selesh without Olneth.

His mind drifted back through his last two days. From the arrival of the Czerezin with their sad burden, he had tirelessly worked his weaves.

Primarily supporting his Sisters in Sorcery to understand that the new order of magic meant breaking down cultural barriers a thousand Rotations old; he'd then forced himself to draw on his power to sustain a dying child long enough for her successor to arrive. He smiled grimly as he tried (in vain) to work out what he'd done without using magic during that period. The tally multiplied exponentially as he remembered retrieving the Sybillsce body to the tent in the far pasture.

Here, a quick inspection by his Songfather convinced him that Olneth's suggestion had merit. He remembered warding the entrance to indicate a need for privacy (a common event whenever Daro was in conference with his spy) and then, Carolus had taken over, skilled eyes and hands examining the sad remains.

"It's astonishing. The level of preservation would deceive anyone without training in mortuary skills!" the old man reported, "The only real problem is his tattoos."

Daro thought for a moment, and then bowed his head, concentrating. A light glow touched the nape on the neck of the corpse as slowly, the existing tattoos reformed, colours unchanged, the two men conferring, sharing their memories of a close friend as the Sandsinger magically sculpted the body until Carolus gasped,

"Enough!"

Moving closer, Daro held an empowered hand over the body, only then lowering his eyelids on an exhalation of breath that began as a sigh and ended as a moan.

"Deo mi…" he whispered, shaken to the core by his own accuracy, and then the impact of his actual loss lent him the tears that their silent companion deserved. Carolus patted his Songchild's shoulder, saying gruffly,

"I know the depth of your loss Selunsanni. Friends like Olneth come once in a lifetime, but your sacrifice may yet save his life! Now this poor lad can be buried with dignity and honour, his "other self" will be able to live as a normal man again and the Heretic's spies will be confounded!"

Daro smiled guardedly, as the unnerving double of Olneth disappeared, to reappear near the crossing in the Azure Sands, while he and Carolus would emerge from the spy's deserted tent, looking for all Pelshar as though they had been searching for clues to his disappearance.

At Daro's insistence, the First Watch recovered the body shortly after dawn, bringing it home in solemn torch-lit procession as Olneth himself. From the stately progress of the Inesh, to the Apothecary's grim face as he 'identified' the body at the Gate in the Rock, nobody could have told that this sad relic was not their friend. Daro had 'removed' all memory of Olneth's true destination, using an infusion created originally to prevent patients remembering their experience at the cost of their recovery, inwardly grinning as friends and magic-users alike fell prey to his manipulation, while ostensibly drinking to Olneth's memory. As word filtered through Selesh, the Sandsinger took note of the reaction to the news and waited for someone to make a mistake.

From the slow drumbeat of the funeral procession, the sad faces of the free traders (who'd lost a neighbour and drinking companion), to the cooks and drudges, healers and students and lastly the inhabitants of Selesh Minoria, all were filtered through the enhanced mind of their Sandsinger. However, his own sorrow at losing his trusted spy must have affected his talent, for he still had no idea how word filtered back to Adruna and her henchmen as he thought back over Olneth's 'committal' to the Sands.

With his own empowered hands, Daro had blazoned his spy's name on an Amethyst tinted sandstone marker on the memorial wall, unaware that such an act might precipitate his too recently abraded emotions. He felt a fool standing there weeping as Olneth's name, rank and 'death' dates appeared on the stone, for after all he knew the truth, but as a light patter of applause rang out, he felt the kindred spirits of his Clan enfold him, and was comforted. Now, he sat in state in his lonely apartment, wondering what to do next, and missing Jalni dreadfully.

From his bedroom, he heard the gentle instruction of Samass, the village tailor who had come to assist Tobin.

"That's right", said Tobin encouragingly. "Lord Daro needs to know exactly where things are. Move that chair so that he can get out of bed without falling over it, then place a drink beside his bed on that low table. He never calls for help if he can manage by himself, so it's in your own interest to be very exact. No clutter, clothes hung away at night, a warm sweetdrink before retiring…result - one happy Sandsinger! Prepare his washroom as I showed you, clean and tidy all waste between uses, and never, never, never fail to respond if he calls you."

Daro winced inwardly. He was leaving, and yet Tobin was instructing a potential replacement ahead of his retirement. This young, promising tailor would have little work from him, and despite the loyal service and discretion of Tobin, he still hadn't given a thought to rewarding him. He frowned, finally raising his voice to bellow,

"Tobin? Samass?" Where in Hadda's Hall are you?"

There was a discreet tap at his door, and then they arrived, Tobin calm and ordered, Samass goggle-eyed and pale with fright (or excitement). Daro gestured invitingly, at which his faithful servant fetched cushions, the pair sitting cross-legged almost at his feet as he began quietly.

"Tobin, I am sadly remiss in my duty of care for you, for which I sincerely apologise. Please forgive me and introduce me to your new assistant!"

Samass nervously lowered his eyes as the ritual handshake was performed, Daro, 'reading' the slightly built, softly spoken man as their hands connected. Evading the natural barrier of privacy with consummate ease, the Sandsinger obtained a picture of a shy man, treading on eggshells, in case he offended one who was the object of adoration. Daro blinked, releasing Samass to focus on Tobin.

The realisation that he was not the only one with long term plans thwarted by insurmountable barriers dismayed him, for it proved that not only was he physically blind, but he hadn't even noticed the distinct tremor of utter weariness or the wistful tone in Tobin's voice either.

His servant was saying sadly,

"Of course I understood that your destiny would take you away from Selesh my Lord. That's why I worked hard to retain my skill as a tailor, in which I practiced as a Master until I met Andrau. I always planned to return to tailoring, but the One only knows of a place situated near Selesh Minoria from where I could afford to set up shop."

Daro looked at Tobin incredulously, then realising his own sensitivity might be lacking, he said hesitantly,

"Perhaps you wouldn't consider remaining in Selesh? The apartments where you lived with Andrau used to be a weavers loft. That wouldn't take much to convert to a new use and if you wanted to live there too, nobody will object!"

Tobin's reaction to this proposal was a stillness that Daro could feel clear across the great-room. Eventually he spoke, voice neutral, but if the vibrato in his breathing could be believed, Daro was convinced he'd made Tobin feel that his particular Heaven was in reach.

"Can I think about it Lord?" he said cautiously, but Daro shook his head.

"I leave as soon as you two are gone." he said, surprising himself with this instantaneous decision. He could contact the Guardians from Tirjhinar, he thought as he walked to his ante room with Tobin and Samass waxing lyrical over some materials he had given them. As he stood in the doorway, listening to the Watch change going on outside, he held out his hands to both of them.

"If time, knowledge and desire are present, then actions can only be weighed by the amount of time, knowledge and desire it takes to make them work!", he knew the words, felt them on his lips as though he'd said them many times, but deep in his heart he also knew them for the ancient things they were. Yet, as he said them, knowing that when they returned he would be gone, he also knew that he was right. He needed to take his own advice. He had the desire, the time was now and the knowledge awaited him at Tirjhinar.

"Good luck Tobin," he murmured thoughtfully. "Good luck with the apprenticeship Samass." he watched them leaving, then as his body servant turned anxious eyes on him, he whispered (entirely privately),

"Good luck with Tobin, Samass. Take care of him for me.", and knew from the sudden stay of the young man's steps that his silent instructions had been heard.

Quickly he retreated back into his great-room, hand extended for his Staff, which flew to him humming happily. He paused, hands running over the Torrenwood shelving that held his treasures, pausing as his fingers brushed against the oddly shaped piece of pottery that he'd thrown at his late mother, feeling the flush of power at the flowering of 'truesight'. Looking down, he mentally 'touched' the fine spidery lines asserting themselves on the corner of the oddly shaped shard, counting. He nodded then with a wave of his hand, dematerialised the entire collection, certain that it would re-materialise wherever he wanted it. That thought, stemming from the memories he had absorbed from the cloak he had worn all too briefly, made him think of Jalni again. Unbidden, desire rose in him, the feel of her skin, the touch of her hand, all the things he had lost with her departure returned to haunt him as he stood grim-faced, battling his human frailty and wondering why, if he truly loved her, had he sent her away?

The stillness, the emptiness, his feeling of disengagement with Selesh grew, and as they did so, he felt himself begin to fade and was not surprised to find himself rematerializing in the barracks tent occupied by his company of would-be Sandsingers, who were gathered with their possessions, talking to Carolus. The Apothecary nodded as Daro silently appeared in their midst, then held out his arms to embrace his Songchild.

"Go well my son," he murmured, "Take your unruly tribe and make them work for their livings."

The old Apothecary saw the determined set of Daro's shoulders, felt the warm arms close around him, (eyes closing as Daro returned his hug), and then he stepped back as they disappeared leaving only a slight sparkle in the atmosphere of the empty tent. He grumbled softly to himself as he went back across the pasture, housed beneath a roof of scintillating crystals, to the wooden barns, now occupied by his trader friends. They knew better than asking questions, but after a discreet reconnaissance by Ivinish (excusing himself to tend a weak foal), they clustered around the old man and if he drank a little too much, what of it? They too knew the meaning of the empty tents in the pasture. Olneth was dead…and the Sandsingers had gone…Selesh might now return to normal, but there was no-one who would miss them more!

Four days hard travel away, Jalni also faced what seemed like a barrier. Two pairs of angry eyes blazed into hers as she told the Rangers what she intended. Terris spoke first.

"Jalni! You can't entertain the idea of crossing the barrier. It's impossible! Do you even know what you plan to put your unborn child through?"

Hot angry tears flooded her eyes, as she vigorously pushed hair to the back of her ears, leaning forward, her hands earnestly twisting into the semblance of a plea.

She spoke through gritted teeth.

"There is a myst rolling in the gully that used to be the river that divided the Forbidden Territory from this end of the Ashgenar. For many Rotations, men talked of fabulous fortunes lying beyond in those lands. Many fools thought they could cross the Myst River and take possession of whatever lay beyond, but we Rangers have come to recognise that death is too high a price to pay for the chance of making that crossing, and believe me…those deaths were not easy ones!"

Her face, pale with suppressed horror crumpled as she began to cry in earnest, leaning on Marran who had preserved his silence until this point. Now the nut brown eyes locked with Jalni's, no apology visible in a hard furious glare.

"Dommichspeller!" he said quietly, in a voice that brooked no argument. "While I recognise your rank and right to command my attention, you do not have the right to insist on killing both yourself and the child of my sworn Lord. If you speak of your intentions again, or make it clear by your actions that you intend to fulfil this mad idea of yours, I reserve the right to bind you hand and foot, taking you to the Temple of the Winds, where you can be confined until this madness leaves you, or you birth your child, whichever comes sooner!"

Jalni, who was seated (rather uncomfortably) on a large backpack looked into the face of a potentially implacable foe and decided not to respond, testing the resolve of the Ranger. He stood, towering over her, a study in patch dyed blues against a pearlised sky as day sank below the rugged horizon. Still Marran's eyes kept her prisoner, his voice low, even and full of bitter contempt.

"Is this the way you repay our care Jalni? Turn and enraged Sandsinger loose on all my people when he discovers his child was murdered by its crazed mother while we stood by and allowed it to happen? Oh no woman! I'll call him myself, right now rather than let you entertain any thought of physically crossing the barrier! Do you want your skin pierced by crystalline needles? Do you want those pretty blue eyes of yours burst the same way? You might get the chance to scream a few times, you might not, but believe me there can be no more terrible death, and your baby would die with you, pierced to the bone."

As Jalni drew breath to argue, to tell him of her dream, he raised a hand pointing directly at her mouth, ordering curtly.

"Don't even begin to speak. I'll hear no more from you tonight Jalni! Consider yourself lucky that I haven't bound your mouth already. If you didn't know it, Terris is again with child and I won't have you distress her, whatever debt I stand in."

His free arm was round his mate's shoulder as he stalked away from the tent where Jalni and Terris often giggled and chatted before sleeping, but tonight she thought sadly, as she prepared for sleep, she would be alone, having found not just one barrier to her ambition, but three.

Chapter 42 - The Waiting Game

There was to be no remission for Jalni. After a sleepless night during which she became aware of mild gripping pains across her lower belly and back, she woke to discover Chrysim had already left her breakday meal at the flap of the tent. He was stationed nearby, crouched in a fair imitation of the Ranger's traditional 'rest' posture, scowling in her direction.

Deciding to ignore all of them, Jalni collected the flat bread and withdrew, deliberately closing the ties that secured the opening to indicate that she wanted to be alone. She sat, awkward in her late pregnancy, eating her breakday meal slowly, as she contemplated this revolt in her companions. For the first time in a long while, she considered a solitary existence. She dared not dwell on it further, for even the thought of Daro set her heart thumping when she needed calm. She cradled her belly, realising she was carrying low, the baby engaged, birth imminent.

No sooner had she started to wonder how long she dared wait, when a discreet 'cough' interrupted her thoughts.

Scowling ferociously, she called out,

"Can I help you Ranger Dorenard?"

He cleared his throat, "Harrumph!" (sounding so like Carolus about to deliver some stinging rebuke) that her lips curved involuntarily.

"Are you well this morning Dommichspeller?" he asked (tone carefully neutral); "We were concerned for your comfort. Will you allow Terris to check on your health?"

The slumbering flames of Jalni's anger stirred as she mentally sharpened her claws, saying nastily,

"I don't need an Apothecary, I needed friends, but you've all deserted me. I'd sooner manage alone than with folk who don't trust me! You and your Tawn are dismissed. Take yourselves (including that boy and his cat) away whenever you like!"

However, picturing the hurt and dismay on Marran's face gave her little satisfaction, for on the other side of the canvas there was utter silence. She listened carefully, but there was no sound, not even the sound of breathing to tell her where he was, so ignoring the ache in her bladder, she curled on the bed (vainly struggling to sleep again).

Outside, the silence lengthened, only broken by the sounds of natural things. Somewhere (close by) she could hear the call of a hawk, and supposing that Marran was hunting Kreel, she shifted restlessly, trying to ignore physical symptoms that refused to diminish. She turned over, wondering if she could 'escape' from the rear of her tent, turning onto her other side to lie uncomfortably, listening to busybugs humming about the bushes.

Finally, deciding to brave their displeasure, she got up, opening the ties on the flap with clumsy fingers, only to walk into a totally deserted camp. She gulped, and then took herself off to the latrine area, nature having given her no choice.

Returning (somewhat shaken), she began to search the camp; trying (and failing) to work out which direction the Rangers had taken. Quartering the immediate area, moving outward from the empty fire-pit, she looked for signs or footprints, disturbed earth or trampled vegetation, only returning to the tent when fatigue and thirst drove her back. Collapsing rather unsteadily on the bedroll, Jalni leant against her pack, easing her lower back as she stared into space, before focussing on a pile of three other backpacks.

She had been there some minutes, slow tears trickling down her cheeks when the light dawned. They hadn't left her! They couldn't have done, for their packs were under cover in her tent! She felt so stupid, she started to laugh, hiccupped, then couldn't get her breath as a spasm of pain shot across her belly, gripping her in its intensity, squeezing her pelvic floor until she was forced onto hands and knees, panting and praying for relief

Gradually, the pain wore off, but Jalni remained where she was, counting grimly. Only after she had counted to ten twenty times (and her knees threatened to kill her) did the Healer move, deciding that her own retention of urine might be to blame. She eased herself down, and then shuffled awkwardly onto her bed, to lie gasping with relief, eyes firmly closed.

An interested voice came from the entrance to the tent.

"Puhrr aow", it said, at which Jalni's eyes flew open, registering Echo's presence gratefully. Awkwardly, she forced herself to a semi-recumbent position, concentrating fiercely on communicating with the Mystcat, who had advanced into the tent, sniffing warily.

She tried (unsuccessfully) to re-engage Healer mode, becoming panicky when the pain she'd recently experienced returned, leaving her gasping and helpless. Echo nudged her gently, his huge shaggy head pressing firmly into her back and the pain miraculously eased. She rolled, linking her arms about his neck and he lifted her enough to shunt back against her pack once more, grimacing as the pain ebbed away gradually.

"Kitt pains!" pronounced her companion thoughtfully. "Lady want help?"

Jalni nearly laughed out loud, but an image of herself rolling in agony leant her control as she considered the Mystcats suggestion. She knew very well that he'd fetch the Rangers himself, but that didn't begin to address her current problem. She frowned, remembering the dream that troubled her night after night, refusing to ignore it, certain that this was to guide her.

Sighing, she shut the door firmly on self-indulgence, leaning forward to touch Echo lightly on the top of his head. He never wavered, admitting her once more to that strange style of communicating they'd discovered between them.

"How get help?" she thought at him, as one ear twitched forward, tickling the palm of her hand.

"Echo fetch Rangers?" he'd suggested, followed by a litany of those he could summon. "Chrysim? Carolus? Beneva? Orto?" this somewhat incoherent chain of thought produced a near hysterical response as Jalni fought back tears of laughter, thinking that her child stood no chance of surviving with such a medley of midwives on call. She sobered, sensing the Mystcat's reluctance to list anymore of her known confidantes.

"No men!" she signalled urgently, which the cat seemed to understand, for abruptly, Jalni 'saw' only thoughts of Sushanna, Hanna, in company with a range of women she hardly knew, none of which matched the images she held over from her recurring dream. The tent grew warm and (with a shock), the Healer realised Height of Sun was upon them, and she hadn't begun to think her plans through. She settled, back against Echo's flank, dozing as tensions ebbed away, then the dream started again.

She was in a procession of death. Every face, a well-loved face. Her mother, her father, Jashell, Indeera, a full Watch of the Inesh who had served in her lifetime. Dora (her first Novice Mistress), Ahnell, Healers past from every Sand and (of course) the students lost at Selesh in the plague. Shivering with this knowledge, she looked for enemies, but none registered, so leaning on Echo, pausing every now and then to let a birthing pang pass, she walked along what was clearly a processional colonnade (in the same style as the buildings at the Temple of the Winds.

She could hear the marching feet of the parade, but no voices interfered with her progress, so on she walked, more alone in this great company than she'd ever been before…

She was climbing now, lifted in some strange manner that she could not comprehend. It seemed that she stood on the edge of a precipice. To the right death boiled inches away, a rolling Myst, sparkling white, sometimes thick, sometimes ephemeral, always deadly. To the left, a river of Myst flowed towards her, beguiling in its beauty, fascinating in its movement, sinister in intent. She looked back, gasping at her elevation. She looked down, straight into the swirling death below. Then she looked forward as a shaft of sunlight poured down on great stone pillars and saw friends and mentors waiting for her, waving encouragement, singing a strange harmonic scale.

A voice said gently,

"Remember this Jalni? You never could get it right, but now is the time, now is the place. Now is forever, for you, your child and all Pelshar!"

Once more she could see her, Ikella te Syrene. Mentor, tormentor, enemy, guide and friend. Silver hair sparkled as though bedewed by the myst swirling between them, green eyes flashing her perpetual challenge as she leaned on a great curving Staff and sang a series of distinct notes. As she did so, the most amazing vista opened up behind her. The land fell into a long narrow valley with something sparkling in the distance, which curved out of sight behind an amazing mountain range. Jalni was transported, mentally filing away the notes of Ikella's pure soprano voice, completely awed as she saw the size of the massif beyond.

"It hasn't got a peak!" she exclaimed astonished by this giant's table as it soared skyward, a day's walk away. She looked at it carefully her vision untroubled by the usual mists that seemed to gather about the summit of high ranges.

"Perhaps it's another caldera?" she questioned, unconvinced by that assumption, then realisation dawned.

"That must be the Star-Weaver's Table! It isn't a joke! It's the name of that mountain!" and her heart thumped as she recognised where her child's destiny lay.

"Remember…" said a whispering voice in her ear. "Remember, this is forever, for you, for your son and the future existence of Pelshar, our beloved world!"

She didn't doubt the truth of that prophecy for one moment, waking to find she was stiff and cold, pillowed on her backpack. There was no sign of Echo, but the Rangers were back, so she rose and went stiff-limbed to join them, hearing a dissonant scale she'd heard somewhere in a dream, as a small breeze stirred the wind chimes that Terris was hanging from the ridge of her tent.

Intrigued by the Wind Chimes, Jalni roused, apologising for her lethargy, but Terris frowned, saying kindly,

"You stay there resting if that's what suits you. Marran is gathering things we'll need later, but I want you to rest a mite longer. Will you let me look at you now?"

Jalni, however, wasn't listening. Her attention had been diverted to the contraction that was tightening its hold on her body. The walls of the tent seemed to have drawn in on the breath she was holding, her ears were only attuned to the odd harmonics she had dreamed, and then, it was over. The pain faded from body and mind, her momentary confusion eased as she released that pent up breath, hissing with relief as the pang died away.

Terris stared in dawning comprehension, and then giving Jalni what Mina might have described as 'an old fashioned look', she muttered crossly.

"I might have known it! Just a short walk to a far better camp and you go into labour!"

Jalni protested vigorously.

"I'm not in labour yet Terris Amstellern", she said vehemently, "I shan't stop you from moving camp, and in fact a gentle walk might do me some good. Ikella and Mina used to insist on women walking the pastures if they were in labour so that they eased the babe down naturally."

She accepted Terris's instruction to "Lie still for a moment!", then the Ranger Apothecary left her, calling to Marran in a serious (but unhurried) tone.

"Keep the fire my love; I need to boil some water to make Jalni a hot drink with some medication."

Jalni scowled; disgusted at her own weakness, annoyed that she seemed to have lost the best opportunity to look for a crossing point into the Forbidden Territory. She moved cautiously, afraid to provoke further contractions, although she knew that (theoretically) position had little influence on when true labour started.

She wished with all her heart that she was back in Selesh, where Mina could assist with the birthing process, biting her lip to fight back tears as she remembered how badly she had behaved to the only woman who'd wanted to mother her, when she so badly needed mothering. She refused to entertain the image of Daro pacing in agitation, replacing the mental parade of those she would have wanted present, with the images from her dream.

There was a light breeze lifting the skirts of the tent as she turned on her side, so she closed her eyes, breathing in the scent of something sweet and honeyed, drifting gently as (above her head), the wind chimes tinkled softly.

She couldn't have been resting for more than ten sectors of the sand-glass when Terris and Marran reappeared, (Marran carrying a makeshift tray for his wife). On this, Terris had placed a linen tool roll, (rather like the one Jalni had stowed in her backpack), alongside the more familiar pots and bowls used by Healers and Apothecary's alike.

Struggling up as Marran placed the tray on a level surface, she watched in disbelief as the Ranger stood waiting to hand his wife anything she required. Completely unmoved by her patient's agitation, Terris placed a water carrier nearby, then proceeded to roll up the sleeves of her tunic preparatory to scrubbing her arms with the solution that Marran was mixing into the hot water.

Accepting (very reluctantly) that Terris needed to examiner her, Jalni rolled over onto her back, while Terris washed her hands and arms in the sterilizing liquid she had seen the Rangers ritual tattooist use.

Lifting her head, she scowled at Marran's continuing presence but the Ranger only said apologetically,

"I will stand outside while Terris makes sure you can walk without endangering your child. I'm sorry we sent Nona back to Scartel, she would have helped Terris, but you'll have to put up with me I'm afraid." he grinned engagingly as he added,

"Trailfinder Grobold says I'm a good midwife, so don't worry. In Ranger circles we tend to use whatever skills we have without worrying about gender or formal training. Better a live child and mother than not!"

Caught between a giggle and outrage, Jalni managed to protest,

"But I'm not a birthing Sheer wolf!" to which Marran said equably,

"Neither was Grobold's wife and she had twins!"

As she had absolutely nothing she could add to that comment, Jalni fell silent, grimacing to Terris, who said steadily,

"By your leave Dommichspeller?" commencing her examination.

It was rather more uncomfortable than painful and Terris seemed pleased when she stood to wash her hands again. She thought for a moment, then said cheerfully,

"That's fine! I can see no reason why we couldn't stay in our new camp until we see how you progress tomorrow. It's getting warmer, so there's no reason to rush. We can send word to the Temple if we need help, that's part of the reason for bringing Kreel. She's used to flying message and knows the Temple well. I'd like you to take this medication, which contains various plant extracts for pain relief, then rest for a while before we walk onward."

She handed Jalni a mug containing a pale green liquid, which smelt pleasant but tasted horrid. Wincing as she swallowed the bitter stuff, Jalni didn't argue, she was too tired, her head was heavy, her eyelids closed, as unable to fight the impulse to sleep, she dozed while the Rangers struck camp around her.

It was the smell of roasted biroots that wakened her and across the flickering flames Terris smiled at her gently.

"Hello sleepyhead." the Ranger girl greeted her warmly. "I'm glad that Carolus hasn't lost his touch!" she exclaimed thankfully. "He gave me some instructions and a whole package of slips to prepare for every different eventuality under Seleus the last time we saw him. I spotted some brennish plants a day or two back, they're bitter, but they loosen your muscles, reduce cramp and seem to improve the pangs of early labour, so I picked a head of flower, cut a few stems and set the lot to dry. There's a good breeze around at the moment, so I took the Wind Chimes down so that you could nap!"

Jalni sat up and stretched, only then realising that she was out in the open, gazing about her open mouthed as she realised that Marran and Terris had taken down her tent while she slept completely unaware.

Terris chuckled.

"Marran has rolled the tent and taken it ahead of us. By the time I've fed you, he'll be back for his supper. It's still warm and quite light, so we thought it better to let you rest and get over your sleepless night before walking to the new camp."

Her eyes twinkled as she said poker-faced, "You are going to be very impressed by what we've found!"

She would add no more to this mysterious comment, but when later, after a comparatively short walk, the two Rangers led Jalni into a broken colonnade; she stopped dumbfounded, for she was walking on the ashes of her dream.

As soon as her back had stopped aching, and she could sit on an ancient set of steps, she took another careful look, saying nothing to the Rangers, who were too pleased with themselves to notice Jalni's abstraction. Here were the columns she had passed in her procession. Here were the shattered pediments of others besides steps that led nowhere. The base of walls appeared to poke through the pumice resulting from some cataclysmic overflow of molten rock, but she stared in vain for the view she'd expected, shivering as she realised a low mist was gathering on the opposite side of an enormous trench.

She stood, following Terris to see their new camp, which formed in the angle of two walls edging a level piece of ground, gave a measure of shelter for the tent, as well as providing a splendid arena for Marran to excavate a large fire-pit, around which he'd built up a stock of cut turves (to cover the fire at night) and an impressive stock of burnable material.

Jalni stared at this, until Marran diagnosed her unspoken question. He spoke gruffly, in the manner of a man with concerns he doesn't want to share.

"I thought I'd prepare ahead, in case I can't go foraging. The weather along here can change quickly, there are female Mystcats about, they have to feed their young and I don't want to be lunch for any hungry feline!"

"Who'd want to eat a thing all skin, bones and sinew?" questioned a mildly aggrieved voice from the gathering shadows, as (with amusement) Jalni saw Echo leave to join the others of his Clan hunting.

She visited the latrine that Marran had made, feeling as if she could sleep the next ninenight away, yet unsettled, as though she should be working at something. Terris caught her mood and swung into step with her as she returned to the camp.

"We ought to string that baby sling." The Ranger Apothecary said diffidently, so Jalni, unrolled the small sheet that protected her baby's clothes and handed the strong woven pouch to Terris. Together, using some leather thongs they worked, gathering the pouch ready for the new-born. In addition, Jalni extracted some ready prepared straps that needed threading through channels (cunningly fashioned from folds) in the strong material that would support the baby against her body, and began to pierce the straps with holes to support the two new buckles that she'd brought from Selesh. The women sat, by the firelight, night drawing in as they threaded thongs, stretched leather and fastened buckles. Marran paced the perimeter of the camp, dragged in some more dry tinder from the bushes, and then began banking up the fire, ready to take first Watch. Terris touched Jalni's arm gently,

"I will stay here with Marran." she said firmly,

"You've had a bad night followed by a tiring day and yes, I know you've rested, but the last days of pregnancy can be very wearing. Take it from one who knows! If I were you, I'd rest while you can."

She didn't need to add that there would be little rest once Jalni's babe was born! As a Healer, she had seen this phenomena many times, yet this was different. Even though she didn't resist the suggestion, Jalni felt energised and knew that if she had a house of her own, she would (no matter what the time or place), have been cleaning it from cellars to roof. She nevertheless nodded, wished them both a peaceful night, and then returned to her tent, where she stared at the contraption rigged by her bed in astonishment.

Wedged firmly between two large stones (presumably from a broken pillar), was her wind-chime. Tied to one of the unusual metal appendages was a thread. No thicker than the thread women used to stitch saddle blankets, it ran down the pillar, through a metal loop (which to Jalni's untutored eye) looked like a broken trace ring, hammered into a convenient crack. Here, above her bed there was indeed a driver's trace, supported by the tent poles, on which Terris had hung the thread, weighting it with a large bead. Jalni frowned, then realising that they had rigged up a means with which she could summon them quickly, she smiled, pulling the little cord to test her friend's ingenuity.

The jangling of the wind-chime rang out, startling Jalni with their volume. From outside there was a chorus of concern, then a voice asked tentatively,

"Jalni, do you need Terris?"

Smiling at Marran's attempt at dignity, Jalni chose not to notice the edginess of his alarm, replying confidently,

"I am perfectly well Marran, I just wanted you to know that I noticed the chimes as soon as I came to bed, and wanted to thank you both. I feel much safer knowing I can call you easily."

Their chorused replies were full of friendly concern, but Jalni had already noticed the additional thread that would ring the bell should she decide to leave her tent unnoticed. For a moment, her eyes blazed a true Azure fire, and then she gave in to fatigue, crawling into her bed with weary gratitude, unaware that the day of the wind chimes would turn so quickly into the morning of the rolling Mysts.

Chapter 44- The Morning of the Mystcats

Jalni woke several times during the night. Once, she managed to make it to the latrine unaided, but received such a scolding from her friends that she gave in, permitting Terris to accompany her when necessary.

The night had been warm and windless, so much so, that having agreed to the suggestion of a strip wash when it became light enough, she immediately fell into a deep sleep, waking grumpy and disorientated, convinced that she needed to do something of significance.

Once she had woken fully, she sat, staring around her, trying to see a good reason for making this homely tent her child's birthplace, eventually deciding that in all charity, she could not.

She shifted impatiently as Terris came for her, but when she saw the beauty of the little ruin in which Terris had found a spring, she became impatient to be rid of her clothing, stripping herself naked as a small breeze touched her body and laughing as she heard her Wind Chimes tinkling in the distance.

She stood in the niche where the spring flowed into a small pool, no bigger than a span outside her own dimensions, feeling the welcome chill of the cool water washing the trail grime from her head, neck and shoulders, feeling lighter and more womanly than she had done for many passes of the moons.

It was surprisingly warm for early morning and it took some time for Jalni to feel the chill of the water fully, but gradually as Goosebumps formed on her arms, she allowed Terris (who had willingly helped her to wash), assist her out of the small shelter, wrapping her in the warmth of a long Rella robe which her friend produced smiling.

"There, you are ready for the most important journey of a woman's life." Terris exclaimed, "If I am right, you will begin to labour today. It is nothing to fear, but you may feel better for your shower and I can't see any reason why you'd want to give birth while feeling grubby!"

She laughed at Jalni's frown, then said wisely,

"I had such a robe for my birthings. The soft weave is very absorbent and believe me, we may not yet have reached Spring Rites, but you'll sweat!"

Faced with this information, Jalni grew silent and introspective while Terris bunched up her hair, and then showered herself.

Returning to camp, assailed by ravenous hunger, Jalni wolfed down three flat breads with fruit and honey, then after sinking two mugs of stemmis, she began to yawn. The Rangers seemed unsurprised when she retired to rest shortly thereafter, closing the flap of the tent loosely before curling up on her bed to sleep. She was warm, clean, well fed, and mentally content as she lay down, listening to her wind chimes being caressed by a stray breeze.

She drowsed, feeling the breeze stroke her face and learning the cadences of the wind chimes, which in her mind seemed to call a word.

"A name?" her dreaming mind questioned, as her inner voice sang it once, then the small wind was back, tugging her, pulling her out of her somnolence as her waters broke.

"Deo mi!" she swore, thankful that she had managed to slide out of her bed, out of the tent as they spilled, feeling her 'Healer-self'. coming to the rescue. Her hand flicked open, a low note sounded in her mind as she chimed in with her *othervoice*.

"*Arishu anverse*", she sang, not recognizing the words of one of Solana's lingering Songspells, taking a hesitant step backwards as she realised that there was no evidence of the latest turn of events, no water, and no stain on clothes or bedding.

"Which," she reasoned silently, "only buys me time, but time for what I wonder?"

Cloaking herself in the shadows thrown by ruined walls, she returned towards the privacy of her tent, convinced she was being watched. Reluctant to let any man, let alone a Ranger get the better of her, she sat on the stone steps fronting her tent, staring into middle distance absently, trying to pick out where Marran was hiding. Slipping into a light reverie, she thought of her own mother, idly wondering if she had marched this way to Sanctuary, coming to her senses when she realised that she was staring straight at her watcher and it was not Marran, but a beautiful female Mystcat, lying quietly in the bushes not twenty spans from her.

She took a long breath, refocused her gaze and found another and yet another. She was encircled by lithe tawny felines, all apparently waiting for something...or someone!

Abruptly she heard Echo saying encouragingly,

"They wait to show you where they birth our young. They will guide you, they will take care of you, and after, I will fetch you myself. They have given me leave to pass on your service."

Jalni's head reeled, but she dared not question this turn of events. For now her Ranger companions were both sleeping, she only needed her baby's sling and her backpack. Rising slowly to her feet, anxious not to scare the Mystcats or wake the Rangers, she went to gather her possessions.

As she stood beneath the silent wind chimes she looked up, thinking that she ought to be hearing their clear notes sounding, and discovered that Terris must have silenced them so that she could rest. Each piece was wound in the thread that suspended them, forcing them to stay still and silent despite the powerful gust that howled around her, filling her tent with a yearning moan, like some dying man seeing salvation slip away. For a moment, Jalni felt like asking this stranger wind to accompany her, wild thoughts turning to one of the many private lectures she had attended in Ikella's rooms. She remembered the Sorceress pausing in mid-conversation and turning towards her, saying (apropos of nothing in particular),

"If it is ever your privilege to deal with magic, you will recognise it by its very synchronicity! Always keep a finger on the pulse of the Source then, when you encounter that moment, you will know how to take advantage of it!"

A bright shaft of sunlight fell on the Wind Chimes, then moved as if searching, out into the light of a rapidly changing future, as Jalni 'reached' for the truth of that moment.

"Sorish moi", she said, opening her backpack to hide the chimes, before (heart beating painfully); she slid back out into the morning again, but what a change in atmosphere!

Outside her tent she stared across the camp in dismay. While she had hastily thrown a cloak round her shoulders and collected her belongings, a Myst of monumental proportions had invaded the ruins, blurring the outlines of walls and pathways, hiding the fire-pit, and obscuring even her enhanced vision. Moisture clung to vegetation, slid off buildings and cloaked her silent progress towards the huge trench in which (Marran believed) a river of water once flowed. As she thought of that river, the memories of a long ago birth and her first experience of Ranger craft touched her mind, bringing with it the memory of her trance in which she discovered the river of life sings. She was humming that song, hearing in it the cadence of the wind chimes when she came to the edge of the trench, and looked across the wide canyon to see the faint shadows of figures gathering on the opposite side.

She felt the gentle pressure of forms gathering behind her, the soft furry flanks of the Mystcats brushing her bare legs as she recoiled from the edge, then began the calls.

"That's right Myarni...one paw in front of the other...don't listen to the pains, it's not far now. Jump!"

The Healer stared into the miasma of sparkling fog, ducking as a dark shape leapt past her, hurtling above the void to safety on the bank opposite. More and more of them streamed down what she now perceived to be an ancient route, which seemed to terminate to the north of where she presently stood wavering. As they passed her, more voices clamoured for her to stop dithering on the brink and join the stream of feline females in the traditional birthing grounds, but still she hung on, fearful for herself and her child.

The last female approached her boldly, staring up into her face with lambent golden eyes; she rubbed her head on the back of Jalni's hand, purring throatily.

"Ruhr owah?" The she-cat enquired softly, as if chiding a reluctant student. Almost immediately, into Jalni's entranced mind an autocratic old voice interrupted sarcastically.

"Scared?" Ikella taunted, eyes challenging Jalni to try her *othervoice* (if she dared!). She quivered, then her head came up, scowling and defiant, she stepped out into the Way of Passage and felt a mighty wind thrust her forward and up.

She gasped as her bare feet touched stone and caught in an impossible maelstrom of howling wind and swirling mist, didn't pause to look down, but took another step up, and another, until her legs trembled. She would have fallen at that point had it not been for the Mystcat, but somehow, she pulled herself together and continued to where she could see clearly the wilderness open up below her, steps descending now, as she pressed onward.

As she reached the other side however, she 'felt' the ground shudder as Tekrun's Bell rang out, followed by the anguished shouts of two thwarted Rangers.

She dared not linger, nor look back as Terris wept helplessly.

"Jalni! How did you do that? How can I help you if you run off into the forbidden Territories?" The pleas rang across the divide in vain, Marran's voice tried to calm his distraught wife, but Jalni; part propelled by her retinue of Mystcats, part by her own needs was already entering the head of the valley. Overlooked by the mountain they called Star Weavers Table, she pursued her dream, marching firmly towards an unknown destination accompanied only by the lonely wind and her new feline friends.

With Jalni's internal clock suspended, her contractions were to drive away all remaining sense of time or place. She didn't doubt her involvement in another significant event, but for now, she was physically unable to concentrate as she normally would. Every sense was directed to the next footstep, the next contraction, the next turn of the trail, then the next contraction…and the press of the Mystcats surrounding her.

From time to time she picked up the thread of feline conversation, but as soon as she concentrated on the soft growls and rumbles, the meaning slipped away behind the wall of pain that enveloped her.

Her surroundings, companions, everything was surrendered to the pressing need to move ever deeper into the strange lands before her. The older female that had encouraged her to continue, stayed beside her, brushing the back of her hand when she faltered, pausing with her when a severe pain left her sweating.

Thinking of her last conversation with Terris as she shook lank hair out of her eyes, she gritted her teeth, struggling on, wondering why she hadn't stopped to pick up her walking Staff as the trail became more difficult to navigate.

The light was fading fast as she rounded a narrow defile into a steep downward slope. Nearing exhaustion, she bit her lip, wondering how in Hadda's Hall she would climb out of such an inhospitable place clutching a new-born, when the path jinked to the right, passed under an enormous (and clearly man-made archway), then opened up into a large cavern, where the Mystcats came to a halt.

She stopped dead in pitch darkness and blinked, trying to adjust her eyes to this new environment. From just the echoes she judged that this cave must have stretched back forty spans. In the one brief glimpse she'd had of the entrance, she thought it was high, but now she could see nothing, a twist of the fault line that had created it plus the descent into night leaving her at a total disadvantage.

Her uncertainty brought the feline that had befriended her to her side and gradually, Jalni was persuaded to rest on a convenient slab of rock that lay to the immediate right of the arching entrance. She was cold, too tired to think and she had no covers, no blankets, and the pains were really gripping her now.

She collapsed sobbing as the cat pressed her down onto the slab and it was all she could do not to scream when the next contraction began. She took no notice of the pride as they settled around her, had no time to watch the older female tugging at an ancient wall-hanging, and less time to realise that this place had once been a human home for she was deep in the throes of labour.

Later, she felt hot, (throwing off her cloak despite the cold night air) then she was shivering, clutching the warm fur clad body that supported her as she came to her knees panting, certain that she was about to deliver. Then the pains died away…completely.

She woke, curled into a ball, legs throbbing, outraged muscles protesting as she moved on the stone slab to find no comforting fur blanket, no gentle body warmth, then worst of all, no companions either. Her feline escort was gone, but as she sat up cold and confused, a ray of sunlight told her that Seleus stood high in the sky, for an even, faint light penetrated the gloom of these ancient habitations.

Recalling her contractions, she set about applying gentle self-examination to establish that her pregnancy was proceeding normally, and then relaxed, looking about her as she dressed. The cavern was long and narrow, all light penetrating from the narrow fault through which they had entered. There was evidence of previous occupation, but it seemed ancient, threadbare hangings like the one she was lying on, it's only decoration. She could see nothing recent, nothing Nishanawa, but decided to explore anyway. Rolling herself off the slab, she padded thoughtfully around the walls, peering into corners, looking hopefully for anything she could use as a Staff, but as she returned to sit glumly on the slab once more, she had gained the impression that this ancient hold had reverted to the wild, only offering shelter to Nightlingbys, Mystcats and the occasional misplaced Healer. Grinning with wry humour, Jalni picked up her small pack, retrieved her cloak and set off to locate the pride.

Thirsty, she carefully negotiated the odd turn that had hidden the cave from the trail and went looking for a spring. Reasoning that nobody settled where there was no water, she went slowly back to the turn in the trail and found the young Mystcat they'd called Myarni lying on her side in a pool of sunlight, nursing two kittens. She blinked at Jalni, watching as the Healer found the small spring running down a nearby crack in a rockface, then when Jalni had slaked her thirst and filled her flask, the cat padded down the narrowing trail, kittens dangling awkwardly from her jaws.

Jalni followed Myarni's lead, turning to the left where the pathway branched, gasping as the enormity of Star Weaver's Table opened up before her. The entire horizon was dwarfed into insignificance as clad in shades of gold capped by the dazzling white of snow; it soared into a wreath of low-lying cloud that curled protectively around its unusual flat summit. Jalni shaded her eyes, leaning against the wall of the short ravine, beyond which the trail widened out, passing down a shallow valley which lay below her.

Feeling her baby stirring restively, she found herself regretting the loss of her plain old walking staff, realising she might be in for a long haul as they wended their way onto the trail towards the mountain. She briefly considered returning the way she'd come as the first contraction started, wondering why she had given in to some stupid sense of destiny, however, if she'd known of the panic she'd left behind at the Ranger camp she might have reconsidered her eagerness to rejoin the outside world.

As the Myst descended on the camp, Marran woke. The deathly pale miasma was acutely bewildering, rendering him unable to determine whether they were in immediate danger. His nostrils quivered as he tried to distinguish local scents, certain he smelt something uncommon, and not too far away, and then he saw the Mystcats. Crouching silently by his sleeping wife, he leant forward, rousing her with silencing fingers against her lips. Rotating stealthily (still at the crouch), he peered into the swirling depths as light started to filter in between the shadowy walls of the ruins, then he saw them!

He hissed,

"Sssh Terris… company!"

He allowed her to slide out of her bedding, pointing to the pride as they padded into the Myst, then a curse left his lips as he saw the woman wandering amongst them.

"Hadda's balls…! Terris, Jalni's out there with them! She's out of whatever mind Daro's left her!" he rose to his feet hastily, followed by a determined Terris, who whispered urgently,

"Marran! For the love of the one, she may know something we don't. She's a Healer; she knows how to take care of herself. The Mystcats might be part of Echo's family, what if he needs help?"

As Marran peered into the fog, Terris knew she was just clinging on to hope. They had both witnessed events that belonged firmly to the world of magic, neither of them discounted such things easily, besides what could two Rangers do to prevent the big cats crossing the Ashgenar if they wanted to do so?

She spoke quietly,

"Just follow them dearling. We can see whatever draws them to the barrier for ourselves. They don't appear to be dangerous or Jalni would have stayed in her tent. Perhaps she's just following them too."

Marran didn't wait to talk. He held up two fingers, then pointed to a wall just a few spans away, vanishing silently into the fog, leaving Terris to follow after counting two long breaths (as he'd instructed). She slipped after him, thankful that he hadn't moved too far away as the Myst suddenly thickened.

She stretched her neck, peering around for any sight of Jalni, but the Healer had faded into the dawn, disappearing beyond their encampment so swiftly that Terris wondered if indeed magic was afoot. She touched Marran's arm doubtfully, signing the symbol that the Rangers had ascribed to the Sandsinger as she tipped her head questioningly, but Marran just shrugged, pointing to his next place of reference, holding up three fingers spread widely, following that instruction by placing a finger to his lips, admonishing silence.

Terris stared at him, aggrieved by his constant cautions, but nodded acceptance as he moved away like some wraith in the foggy light that was dawning beyond him. She waited (not bothering to count her breaths), then swiftly followed her mate, pausing just long enough to realise that they had come almost too close to the Healer for comfort, as she saw not only the broken parapet of an ancient bridge but the shadow of the yawning trench beyond that. She rubbed her eyes, convinced that she'd seen figures poised on the brink, then realisation dawned…it was Jalni, surrounded by Mystcats and she was staring out across the rift as though she could see beyond the Myst, into another world.

Marran was listening, head cocked on one side, eyes quizzical as she joined him. For a moment Terris thought she heard voices, and then Jalni turned apparently conversing with her companions as she strode towards the broken edge of what must have been a bridge of inspiring proportions.

Amazed both Rangers stood up, staring as the Myst retreated into the space between the banks, still a good thirty spans high, it was thickening, roiling like cloud as a young Mystcat leapt forward, bounding up invisible steps above the trench, hind-quarters disappearing into the wavering fog as though trotting across a bridge, to arrive fit and well on the opposite bank.

As soon as Terris divined Jalni's intentions, she would have screamed, but for her husband's silencing hand. He held her tightly as they watched the Mystcats flow like some unstoppable tide, over an invisible bridge to their traditional birthing grounds, then watched appalled as Jalni moved like one entranced.

Before Terris could protest, their friend stepped straight into the Myst seeming to ascend before their disbelieving eyes. Only then did they see the movement below Jalni's feet, stepping-stones appearing as she walked forward, each one higher than the last. Terris frozen by the fear that Jalni would fall to her death finally found her voice, croaking as she grabbed her husband firmly,

"Marran! Remember the rifts in Scartel and Daro crossing them? This is more of the same power. We can't follow her. We can't even call her back until we know she's safe!", then she clung to him, first sobbing in frustration, then sighing in relief as Jalni passed to the other side of the Opaz trench. However, when the Healer didn't stop, she called out sharply.

"Jalni? How can I help you if you go into the Forbidden Territory? How will you manage alone?"

Realising the futility of protest when Jalni didn't respond, Marran held her as Jalni passed beyond their recall. Then the Myst descended again, blotting out all sight of the land beyond the trench like some arcane wall, leaving the Ranger party alone on the Ashgenar bank staring into a barrier that separated them from the most precious of their current responsibilities.

Chapter 46 - Harmony in Crystal

As he stood (cursing himself) on the Ashgenar side of the Opaz trench, Marran caught Terris by the sleeve, as another of his responsibilities crossed his mind. Almost dragging her away, the worried Ranger returned to find Chrysim and Echo placidly minding the fire. He hadn't thought about them since dawn, anything could have happened in his absence and he mentally berated himself as Terris (half-heartedly) began to make a breakday meal. Echo lay peacefully washing his paws as Marran questioned his minder helplessly.

"Didn't you see anything at all? Didn't you smell the Mystcats; they were here, walking through the camp as if they owned it. Jalni has gone where we can't help her and you say you just slept and didn't see anything! Well, if harm comes to her, Daro won't be amused!"

They both sighed, but soon, Chrysim (incapable of feeling deeply troubled) lightened the mood as he began to play pounce and pull with Echo. For a moment Marran glowered, then, realising they could do no more, settled close to the fire-pit where he squatted to make a sweetdrink for all of them. He spoke thoughtfully,

"We'll send Kreel to the Temple of the Winds. Jalni needs us here to return to afterwards!" he said with a small grin.

"I'm beginning to think that magic rubs off these Sandsingers you know! First Daro, now Jalni. I can't help wondering what their babe will become!"

Virtually the same thoughts ran through Jalni's mind as she rounded a corner on the rising trail, to see great gateless pillars rising out of the ground to her left. She was distinctly uncomfortable now, having been forced to stop halfway up the trail that curled around the great mountain, doubled over with pain, knowing real labour would begin soon. She paused, easing her back, braced straddle-legged and arching as she looked up, watching the cloud wreath swirling high above her. She felt oddly light-headed, not dizzy, just different, knowing she had to rest for tonight her baby would be born. Myarni came wearily towards her, only carrying one of her kittens which she carefully deposited at the Healers feet as she ran back to pick up the other. Jalni crouched protectively over the kitt, not daring to touch it despite its heartbreaking cries, (for she had heard that wild things abandon their young if humans intervene). She stayed there, watching as Myarni struggled back to her, and then, to Jalni's amazement, the Mystcat dropped the kitt she was carrying, straight into Jalni's hands. She watched as Myarni lay down trustingly, offering swollen teats to her kitts. At first hesitant, Jalni watched the slow blink of the Mystcat's eyes, and decided that she was asking for help.

"Oh, you poor thing, you're tired and thirsty!" Jalni said out loud before she found herself thinking, "You are mad del Orto, utterly insane. You're about to birth your firstborn sands away from any help yet here you are herdsman to a Mystcat!"

She carefully looked at the kitten she held. It was searching, little tongue working as she touched Myarni's swollen nipple and expressed a little milk to tempt the kitt. It wriggled, waving paws as it struggled to get purchase on Jalni's finger, and then (with relief) she saw the little mouth latch on. As she lifted the second kitt into place, the Healer glanced at Myarni. There was a glaze over the mother cat's eyes that told the Healer that all was not well. She struggled up, feeling ungainly, feet swollen, legs tired, back excruciating and knew she had to take another break to help herself and her companion or there would be no going on.

She glanced around, looking for somewhere to sit, but having found nowhere, knelt on the ground to rummage in her backpack. Her scrip lay on top of everything else, so she reached into it, feeling for the longer slips that Carolus had left with her.

She could hear his voice in her head as she examined her haul.

"These long slips are for Echo. The cats need various elements for full health. We no longer have huge amounts of vegetation that they can browse on, and yes, animals also need plants to thrive. I make a concoction that seems to stimulate skin, muscle and bone, assists in clearing up all manner of infection, besides preventing hopping ticks!"

She concentrated, knowing that cats lap liquid, wondering what in the Nine Sands she could use as a bowl, when she caught sight of her Wind Chimes. Each of the metal pieces was hung from a decorative dome shape, which, if tipped upside down, would create a bowl.

She dragged it out, lifting each piece out of the way, then setting the dome between two large stones to anchor it. She opened her flask; half-filled the bowl, and then poured in two of the slips, stirring rapidly with one finger, watching as the powder dispersed.

She held her finger up to Myarni and as the big cat sniffed, then licked, Jalni felt the same 'thrum' in her veins that she felt when healing.

She found a note in her mind and humming gently lifted the makeshift bowl, eyes widening as the Mystcat lapped at it delicately. She thought she was hearing things when she realised that the note she was humming had been taken up by the Wind Chimes, feeling the vibration under her hand as she wiped the inside of the dome. Laughing, she sang the cadences she had taught herself, shrieking as the mountain boomed the notes back to her.

Even the cat had jumped to her feet and was retrieving her kitts as something groaned, then the rest of the pride surrounded her. She chuckled as they greeted her, pressing her into their midst as they headed between the pillars and into a shallow cavern complex under the mountain, seeming to enjoy her amazement when she found herself gazing at a Healer warding not unlike the one she'd opened at Fronish, on the very journey where she'd met Echo.

As she stared at the fizzing barrier, Jalni reviewed something Ikella had told her just before she'd died.

"Of course, our population is so sparse, most Healers from the same sands will use the same keynotes to unlock and lock their warding. While we share our knowledge with our own Clan, keeping strictly to our own sands, that might work. However, ask yourself what happens when we share sands with other people? We might want to ward something to protect it, or protect others from it. If everyone can work out the keynotes, that won't work. It is for that reason I warded the Amethyst, to protect outsiders from significant danger."

Jalni was tired, but the memory spurred her into action. She dropped her backpack, took out her wind chimes and held them by the dome shaped cap, looking for somewhere to clip the centrally mounted hook.

In a dream, she saw the chain dangling above her, reaching for it as lightening seared the evening skies outside. In a dream she felt the lightest of touches as a gentle breeze stirred the ancient mountain hallways, stirring her chimes into life as it passed.

Jalni concentrated, willing her recalcitrant *othervoice* into life, and then she began to sing softly.

She mirrored the mantra of the Wind Chimes, watching the ancient barrier flicker as she counted firmly, entering each number she remembered from the skipping rhyme they'd all learned as children.

She went through the sequences one after the other, using the Order of the Sands to refresh her memory, but still the stubborn barrier persisted. She was nearing collapse when the merest whisper of memory made her think, running through all Nine Sands again. Finally, feeling almost sacrilegious, she made one more choice.

None of the Nine Keynotes she knew would work, there must be an alternative, and an ancient voice came flooding into her mind.

"Never you mind all this schooling children," Carolus had grinned impishly as Jalni and her friends escaped classes, twirling their skipping ropes around the Apothecary and despite his age, he'd joined in, twirling a long rope with practiced ease so that all the girls could skip. He'd taught them the old skipping rhyme too, and then teased them outrageously.

"What if there are more than Nine Sands?" he'd chortled, "Which colours shall we add?"

She eased her neck, feeling a familiar tightening in her belly as a light contraction began, then fear lent wings to her mind.

"If that madman was right, the next number would be ten, even though we don't know the colour, I bet that's the number. "

She felt her lonely wind caress her hands as she sang the first note of the chimes, entering the number one as she did so, now she sang each following tone, until, at the last note she realised she'd entered ten notes, and pressed the central symbol for zero.

At first, it seemed that nothing had happened. Then the wind rushed past her, deep into the heart of the mountain and the barrier had dissipated. She walked forward slowly, seeing all around her the comforts of a Healer station that in all likelihood hadn't been opened in millennia. As she took her first steps inside, the mountain chimed in response, welcoming her with a harmony composed in the crystals it harboured.

Overcome with fatigue and emotion, Jalni found the first cot, crawled into soft pillows and warm blankets, sliding into oblivion gratefully and dreamed.

Chapter 47 - Prophecy Fulfilled

Conceding that her experience was very peculiar, Jalni dreamt that lying on the cot in the Healer hold that she still walked amongst those of whom she dreamed. She giggled, imagining how difficult that would have been to explain to Ikella, then blushed in horrified comprehension as the Sorceress in the midst of another group turned, fastening green eyes disdainfully upon the giddy Healer who dared to chuckle in her presence.

She gulped, believing she was indeed skirting the whirlpool of insanity, and then Ikella spoke. Calmly she said,

"Jalani bin Selesh, did you not wish for those you love to be present at your child's birth? Have you so little faith in the One, in magic, or in yourself that you didn't consider yourself worthy to fulfil Prophecy? Shame on you child!"

She remembered staring at her, wondering if she was a wandering shade herself, then she caught sight of the statuesque form guarding the door.

"Jashell!" she thought hysterically, then, another hovering in the background caught her attention,

"Oh…Indeera!", and found a lump in her throat forming, tears misting her eyes with gratitude. She was not alone in a strange land, she was amongst friends.

Eyes closing (despite her best efforts), she drifted away, re-inhabiting her 'other self' in a comfortable cot, where someone she didn't know was ruthlessly stripping off the bedclothes as they prepared her for labour. She shivered, thinking she should recognise the features beneath the shantana, then, as a clean sheet was laid over her, she felt a strange sensation of warmth and looked up, straight into the most brilliant eyes she'd ever seen.

He nodded, listening apparently to someone Jalni couldn't see, as her gaze clung to his features, noting every detail, hungry for recognition. He was definitely Shalhanhi, his Clan braid elaborately decorated with Opalescent threads tied back behind one finely moulded ear. Set into its lobe was a delicate silver ring, which sparkled as though set with stones she didn't recognise. He was probably in his forties, slender, tall and elegant in his movements, but it was his eyes that drew her, Sandsinger eyes, Opal eyes.

She struggled up on one elbow; trying to get closer then he placed his hand firmly on her shoulder, smiling down at her as he spoke.

"Brave girl…" he said consolingly, "I expect you're very confused, but I want you to remember one thing. After the storm, Seleus always shines, and what you do today will ensure the safety of the sands you've left behind. We understand your intent, but you must change the thought, or you'll only punish yourself. Your child is already loved and longed for by many who follow the Prophecy. He will be safe, cared for and if prophecy is to be fulfilled, will return to you at the time of Pelshar's greatest need."

His remarkable eyes (filled with Opal fire) found hers, and then as she lost consciousness, she heard him say,

"She will feel no pain for now, but call me once she starts to deliver.", then all awareness fled as the darkness claimed her again.

Sometime later she roused again, this time feeling wet and uncomfortable as a female someone wiped her forehead with a cool cloth. She was lifted to a semi-recumbent position as a drink was pressed to her lips. Then he was there again, the Sandsinger, who seemed in some way to also be a Healer, or apothecary. He was sorting through a capacious box of medications. She saw slips containing powders, jars containing ointments, bottles holding liquid and she watched his long fingers swiftly sorting slips, hearing a gentle thread of song as he hummed over his choices. As though aware of her interest he turned, an engaging smile on his lips, saying softly,

"Hello…you're with us again. I'm told you're a fine Healer, what would you dispense to make sure a patient in labour can cooperate without unnecessary suffering? She seems to be bearing a fine healthy child, is young and fit herself, but is tired and too weak to push for too long."

She thought carefully, then suggested,

"Serenngrass is a hypnotic, which will keep her calm and cooperative. Bladeroot for severe pain, because it acts quickly and leaves the mother's system quickly too, but caution is advised over doses."

He smiled down at her, as the first major contractions began, saying lightly,

"One who speaks well of your talent was not mistaken," before he bowed gracefully and moved beyond her field of vision. Jalni groaned, as someone held another vial to her lips, then she knew nothing but the urge to bear down, to deliver her child, to be free of pain.

She remembered someone screaming, someone else rolling her, holding her shoulders down as she struggled. Piercing green eyes held hers until her mind twisted away. She was sweating, tormented, and then she felt her body surge into action as the contractions took over her life. During her labour she called helplessly,

"Daro, help me, take away the pain!" obeying mindlessly as a man's voice said soothingly,

"Hold on. I'm not Daro, but this will help.", then she smelt the sweet spicy aroma of burning Serenngrass. She remembered insisting that they let her kneel on all fours as the pains began to exhaust her, then it seemed as though time itself had collapsed, forcing her to only pay attention to 'the Voice'.

"That's right, push gently. Now push for all you're worth followed by sympathetic murmurs "Not long now, we can see his head."

"Pant for me Jalni, now push…' then it was done, and the babe slithered out, wailing before he was lifted into exultant hands.

She collapsed onto her stomach then rolled to look at the results of her labour. He was a fine child, a little red, a lot crumpled, nothing like his father, and unlike her, she decided. However, he was healthy, and she had survived his arrival!

Someone placed him in her arms, as (without thinking) Jalni uncovered her right breast and placed the hungry little mouth to her nipple.

"Yes", a voice in her mind reminded her, "Let every babe drink his mother's milk for its protective ingredients. Any wet-nurse will do later, but his mother's own milk is essential to give any child a good start.

She seemed to be alone with the baby, everyone had disappeared and as she gave her child the other breast to be sure of his well-being, she wondered if they'd all been part of some hallucination. Her own scrip was open on a nearby bench, while she was lying on a birthing couch, yet she couldn't remember getting there. In fact, the only thing she did remember was the man with the wonderful eyes. She wrapped her child in the cloth she had woven for him and stared down, engraving his features on her memory. Then, she placed him in his sling, drew him close and kissed his nuzzling little head, tears running down her face as she stood, facing the door she'd noticed 'the others' coming and going through.

She knocked on the door, shaking as she stood for the first time, and then stood back as it slid noiselessly open. He was there, a soft glow surrounding him as he stepped through the doorway. She was nearly as tall as he was, but his presence was overwhelming. She trembled violently as he said gently

"You have to name your child little one, and then you must seek a place of safety for him. I could tell you much, but it is written that you must seek the answers yourself. Only then may I help you."

He waited, as Jalni glanced down at her child remembering the notes she had sung with the Wind Chimes. She sang the fragment now, seeing in her mind's eye letters appearing on a book. She gasped in delight, bending to kiss the sleeping child's head as she whispered,

"I heard his name in the wind when I sang the chimes. He is Darayen and I believe the wind is the Tenth Wind!"

The Sandsinger nodded gravely saying,

"I believe you have something else to ask me?", as Jalni's eyes filled with helpless tears.

"I need a place of safety for him", she begged, suddenly uncomfortable with her reasons for concealing his birth from Daro.

"Yes", the Sandsinger conceded, "but not for any reason of spite!" he looked at her seriously,

"Name your reasons for seeking my protection." he challenged, as words tumbled off Jalni's lips.

"Look," she said (in tones of deep exasperation), "About now, a very young, blind Sandsinger is going to become responsible for a large number of those who will become Sandsingers themselves. I don't know how to tell you this, but Sandsingers died out about a thousand Rotations ago during some great Cataclysm. The one we've got is Opal like you, but he's blind! I think I'm intended to be his Azure, I've had quite a few odd things happen when I'm in my homesand, but I can't help him tied down by a child! I'd have to foster him;

then again, Darayen could be used against him as a weapon, particularly if Adruna's spies got hold of him! I must put his safety ahead of my happiness…don't you see?"

She was sobbing, fat tears falling onto the child's face as she stared up into impenetrable eyes that shifted from turquoise through fiery rose to deep purple as she watched him think. At last he spoke,

"Walk with me to the entrance, while I consider what you've told me. ", he moved gracefully, opening doors into a corridor with a wave of his hand. She drooped, desperately hoping that her baby could be safe in this strange nameless place, then at the fizzing barrier he turned, eyes bright with power.

Weakly, Jalni slid to the floor, holding out her child imploringly, as the Sandsinger spoke.

"You can leave Darayen with me safely Dommichspeller Selunsanni.", he said calmly, "I will set my seal upon him, and he will be under my protection. We haven't the time for longer explanations; even as we speak I feel the pull of the Sands upon me. Your son will return to the outside world when Ichspeller Selunsanni fulfils his part of the prophecy, but know this, tonight your courage, determination and honesty has taken a great leap forward, for which you will be rewarded in time."

His eyes blazed into hers as he took the child and kissed the top of his head gently.

"Know this O Mother of the Tenth Wind…your trust will not be betrayed.", his tone gentled as Jalni, legs quivering, rose and picked up her carrisack, feeling how light it was without the chimes, the baby clothes and food, then resolutely turning her back, she walked through the barrier as though it didn't exist and seconds later it didn't.

In her mind she heard only a soft voice saying quietly,

"I, Darius Selunsa give you my word!"

There was a long sigh, and then he said even more quietly,

"Forget this place little mother, forget all I have told you…forget!"

She stood, staring at the smooth wall where seconds ago she thought she'd been talking to someone. She looked around at the featureless corridor shrugging, as she hefted her backpack into place. She fastened her scrip back to the belt that hung loosely around her waist, making a mental note to get Duvell or one of his sons to put an extra hole or two in the leather so she could cinch it tighter. Then she swung back out of the corridor, through a natural opening into a dusty clearing, hoping to find the Mystcats and longing for sleep.

She remembered little of her journey back from the Forbidden Territories, other than the feeling of astonishment when, on climbing the gulley to the ridge where they had made their first stop, she could see no sign of either the small hold, or of Star-Weaver's Table! Whether she'd dreamt the whole thing or not, she remembered meeting someone who looked shockingly like Daro, in the shadow of a mysterious mountain.

Whereas she could believe an exhausted dream of a person who didn't exist, she could not believe that an entire mountain (larger and more unusual than any she'd ever seen) could just disappear at will. She grew silent and introspective; sitting apart from the Mystcats as their journey progressed, spending long periods scanning the horizon for a glimpse of the mountain.

Eventually, Myarni brought her twin cubs to her, growling softly to attract the Healer's attention.

"Oho!" said the Healer (feeling absurdly honoured, "Getting too heavy for you are they?", as she picked up the increasingly heavy kitt she'd been offered. The kitten nuzzled her hand, sleepily curling into the crook of her arm as they resumed the climb, this time taking a route that led directly towards a small Temple, hidden in the fold of the land that rose towards a cliff like barrier, two days march ahead of them. When the Nishanawa patrol greeted her, she was somehow not surprised and nor it seemed were the Mystcats.

They were travelling slowly, due to the large number of kittens being carried, the need to feed, the need to shelter from the sun and find water. In the early hours Jalni had attended the birth of a single large male kitt and was still wearily toting Myarni's girl kitt, when a voice said conversationally,

"Ho Healer! We have been looking for your company of Mystcats this last week or more. Are you well?"

She was walking below a rise that must lead to the small Temple, and when she peered up at the ridge, she was not too surprised to see a young priestess descending towards them. She rounded a corner, her arm aching from the weight of the kitten she carried, and then as if she herded them, she was surrounded by her feline companions, all happy to arrive in the shadows of a small courtyard that opened directly ahead of them, straight off the path.

She stared around her, noting the open shelter containing ledges at differing heights for the cats, hearing odd snatches of conversation as they settled down to rest, then turning to look for Myarni.

She found her swiftly, repatriating her daughter to her as she settled, and then turning at the young Priestess's voice.

"Please be our guest Healer," she invited. "Tomorrow your sisters will attend you and take you back to the Temple of the Winds, where you are welcome to stay and rest for as long as you like. Your onward journey can be planned from there, but tonight we have food, a bathing pool, and everything you might need before you rest. The Temple of the Tenth Wind welcomes you now, and whenever you want shelter from the outside world."

Jalni gulped, uncertain of why she suddenly felt so emotional, but the girl simply dipped her head respectfully, as the start of another journey began.

Chapter 48 - Broken Vows and Promises

The Appointed entered Tirjhinar during the moon before Spring Rites, and as they gathered eagerly around the Opal Sandsinger, he was amazed (and touched) by their concern for him. Far from home, without favourite servants, friends or relatives, they would be truly alone with their powers and once in the ancient city of magic, they would have to study their craft, to the exclusion of all other activities.

Wondering if he was equal to the task, Daro stood in the immense Hall of Welcome half afraid he might succumb to the influence of the cloak that his old friend Olneth had unearthed. However, rejecting that notion violently, he left his followers to their own devices, after insisting they explored as a group, never touching articles they didn't understand, in addition to reporting to him three times daily.

Within days they had all learned that running, whooping, or hanging upside down from various impedimenta wasn't tolerated. They had found strange courtyards, with roofs set with crystals in which such activity could take place; they had even found stores of rope, posts for creating their own games and rooms which filled with music if desired. Gradually, he had been both relieved and delighted with their progress through the silent halls, but today the routine would change, today his Appointed would become serious students, and it was for this purpose, that Daro convened a gathering.

As he entered the room, his students stood, watching as he walked to his chair and sat. He smiled at them, feeling huge affection and pride in each one. Rann, who with his Ranger graduation guaranteeing him a long, fulfilling life uncomplicated by magic, had chosen to follow his Calling; Lallee, who had known she was special from childhood and had merely waited for the summons, Timmisandro who had been with him at the beginning, now making his own journey into life, no longer the troubled would-be stonemason, and lastly Shyl Nighthawk, whose predecessor had fallen before she could be Appointed. He frowned slightly, counting himself and four others, then he realised that Jalni was missing from the complement he'd always imagined, there were also many other potentials too young to respond to the summons.

Anxious not to bore them, or put them off studying, he spoke casually, having already made the decision not to throw rank or precedence into this arena until he had to. Tailoring his words to resonate with each culture, age group and gender, he started simply.

"Well my dears, it's time to begin the serious business of turning young hooligans into mages worthy of consultation. The only thing is, I don't have any idea of where to begin. Shall we discuss what you want to know most, rather than confuse ourselves with things of little import outside our own Sands? When we get to issues I cannot help you with, I propose to ask a Sentinel to assist us."

Lallee regarded him steadily.

"Is 'Sentinel' a real name or a rank of being?" she asked softly, as from the well of memories Daro dredged up an answer that clearly pleased all of them.

"A Sentinel watches for Sandsingers emerging without support. He (and it's always a male position Lallee) can choose whether to guide in form, guide remotely (by dream or revelation) or by influencing another Sandsinger to take on a student."

Four pairs of eyes surveyed him with interest.

"Spirit of the Sand!" Shyl gasped… "Some poor Sentinel must have had his work cut out with you then!" she declared, subsiding as Daro's right eyebrow rose quizzically.

"Thank you Shyl" he said agreeably, "I aim to please! I didn't have a Sentinel; I had the shade of a Sandsinger to myself! Now if you'll all settle down, you'd learn faster."

They listen breathlessly as he continued,

"I don't believe that the number of Sentinels is finite, given that before Cataclysm our forefathers in magic were plentiful. I also believe the Pelshar we know, is only a small part of a world far greater than we can imagine. There are vast wastelands outside the Sands that lie unexplored. That doesn't mean they are unoccupied. Since Cataclysm, there have been no Sandsingers, no knowledge of those earlier times, and precious little guidance until our Sisters in Sorcery emerged. Despite a thousand Rotations of study every Clan had to survive on its merits, each member, footstep by footstep. No enhanced skills, no guidance and precious little magic. Now, it is for us to rebuild what Pelshar has lost, with our higher Calling, it is up to us to make sure that Pelshar survives a threat that I believe could be imminent."

He drew breath, then rose to his feet, glowing Staff in hand as he paced to a table stacked high with scrolls. At a gesture, the air quivered busily, scrolls, books and tablets sorting themselves onto nearby shelves, leaving the table covered by a drape.

The Sandsinger's hands strayed towards it, unconsciously encouraging the group to cluster around the table, then he twitched the material away, as all Pelshar was revealed in the Stillglass surface.

There was a concerted gasp, then four pairs of eyes bent over the portrayed terrain and the blind mage held out a hand glowing palely, following a track leading from the high plateau above the Azure sands towards Scartel.

Gradually, the focus of the map shifted. One moment they were watching the Azure, and then they were seeing their own corner of the Opal glowing brightly. Directly south was a dulled area that the four youngsters shunned, averting their eyes as the map spun towards the Amber Sands and a bright dot set within. Sliding down to show the Onyx, Rann said abruptly,

"That's odd Daro. Give me your hand so that I can show you something."

Daro grinned,

"Right! Let me show you all something." He shook his hair off his forehead, pinched his nose, and then appeared to be entering a light trance. Beneath their gaze the map spun again, back towards the dulled Amethyst, where in the far south west the merest spark glowed for an instant. Fire bright and fearless it flicked on and off as incredulous eyes fixed on the Sandsinger's face.

"My oath…" Timmisandro spluttered, "We've got someone behind the barrier Ichspeller?" then as Daro nodded silently, the others chorused.

"Whew…", "Bless the One!", "Shades and Shadows!" before a very small voice said questioningly.

"How are we going to get him out Lord? How can we protect him against the Gattarene?"

At once Daro saw his mistake. These might become powerful mages, but at the moment they were still children in the craft. He had with him two young girls with loving hearts; then again, he had two young men anxious to try their mettle, now he'd given them a cause to fixate on, before they had learned to control stray thoughts. He gave himself a little shake, then said swiftly,

"For the moment, we can't be sure if that refers to another depository of knowledge, or a person. See, the light isn't moving, it's blinking rapidly. Let's see if there are other lights like that."

They collectively moved the map, finding several instances of similar lights, totally different to those given off by potentials, and in the end the class ended with a decision to make further investigation when time permitted, but veering towards consensus over a library of some kind.

Closing the session, Daro repeated his intention to seek the advice of a Sentinel, sending out a heartfelt plea as he gathered the group for evening prayers.

"Guide us in the light of the One, towards understanding and forgiveness so that slights and disappointments neither trouble our days nor make restless our nights." he prayed in all sincerity, the others responding. He found his mind touching on the conversations they had held regarding their vows only that evening, then continued slowly, hesitantly.

"Help us to understand our own faults and limitations so that we learn not to expect more from another than we are willing to give. Make us aware when others are troubled so that we do not trouble them further. Help us respond to another's needs without judgment. Prepare us to take our vows with an untroubled heart, keeping us from breaking promises to those who trust in us."

There was silence as the others absorbed the meaning of this prayer, then they quietly crept away, leaving Daro kneeling where he had once sung his vows knowing nothing of the terrible price he would pay to become a Sandsinger.

The days passed slowly as they listened and learned together. Every night, when his students left him, Daro sat alone, eyes stinging with remembered grief as he listed his losses. Sight; followed by Sararrh and Ahnell, Brus and Ikella in death then amongst the living, Olneth and Jalni. He weighed them in the palm of his thoughts, daily invoking the pain of loss, of separation, allowing the agony of unfinished business to wash over him. He knew what he was doing, simply didn't bother to stop, plunging into instructing the Appointed by day, tormenting himself by night, then he hit on the idea of trying to pinpoint the ancient sites of magic, searching for answers, for artefacts, for Jalni.

The summer moons waxed and waned over Tirjhinar as Daro's school for Sandsingers began to take shape. In the cavern outside, the dry bowl where Arriera had borne him glistened, as the waters fell from above constantly reminding Daro that the search for fertile land (and water to nourish it) dominated his search for the truth.

Using immensely increased power, he spent most of his days poring over ancient maps. He had learned how to extend the time he could use 'true-sight', turning their Council Chamber into a research tool, using the Stillglass table to scry, tracing the undersand water courses known as dinajh, then the old man arrived.

Lallee came to tell him the news. She had been practising the craft of 'far viewing' with Rann and had got into trouble when she reported that all she could see, was a very old man filling his flask in the outer cavern. At first, Rann had been uninterested, then disbelieving, finally giving in and demonstrating himself.

"First we settle. Let the blood in your veins still, calm your thoughts and clear your mind. Concentrate on the area you want to view, then form (with your right hand only), the 'circlet of sight'. Place it to your closed right eye, and then open your mind and view."

He had sat on the floor bare footed (as Daro had done), demonstrating each action with great deliberation, watched breathlessly by both Shyl and Timmisandro. To Lallee's satisfaction however, after a long considering pause (and without altering his position), he had exclaimed,

"Sandrigals! You're right Lallee. There is indeed an old man sitting in the shade of the cavern. He looks about six hundred Rotations old mind you. I wonder what or who he wants?"

Shyl said sarcastically,

"He's probably sitting in the shade thinking he's lucky to find it before Height of Sun, not wanting anything or anyone, but water and shade!"

However, Lallee having taken a second viewing, was leaping to her feet, had crossed the room running, then was calling anxiously,

"Daro, where are you? I think it's Grandfather, in the cavern, by the waterfall! Daro, Ichspeller Selunsanni…where are you?"

A disembodied voice remarked shortly,

"I'm glad you reviewed your mode of address Lallee, however, you should all be resting as I am, it being Height of Sun. What's all the excitement about?"

Lallee explained, hiccuping with excitement as she did so. Daro's response was muffled, as though he was hastily dressing, then he said sharply,

"Colours everyone.", and to their astonishment, brilliantly hued ceremonials replaced the clothing they wore. They observed each other critically, then formed up on the Sandsinger who had just materialised in their midst. He wore the flowing robes that he favoured, face glowing, hair braided and caught back behind one ear, which sported the nine chained loop set with Opals that he had found in his late mother's effects.

He glided towards the cavern, signalling the girls to remain with him, as both Timmisandro and Rann revealed the entrance. Both boys closed their eyes momentarily, as they silently communicated the presence of another, then Daro stepped forward, allowing his Staff to guide him, with his entourage falling back to either side of the revealed entranceway.

He was immediately reconnected with the one he had summoned. Reconnected at a level that the Sandsinger had not expected as he clasped the dry, papery hand in his, facing the mentor he had brought from Scartel.

He lowered his own head submissively, whispering a title that had not been heard for millennia,

"Lord Voechshpeller, Sentinel..." he fumbled for words, then the gentle mellifluous voice, so dear to his memory carried clearly to his companions. "We welcome your return to Tirjhinar." he finished simply, as the old man straightened saying softly, privately.

"Grandfather will do young man! I hope to make friends of this new young crop of potentials, not scare them to death with pomp and ceremony!", then he was walking slowly into the great echoing depths ahead of them. Daro clicked his fingers once and four young heads swung round as he laid his fingers to his lips, silencing the questions that had risen in the throats of the youngsters, then, flanked by the girls and followed by the boys he walked quietly in through the entrance, making two curious gestures with his free hand as he did so. Behind him, a soft sighing wind blew all the tracks in the sands outside the cavern away as the waterfall trickled to a stop and the basin beneath it began to dry.

Silently Sentinel padded around the Hall of Welcome, gently guiding the blind man as he told his own story. They paused outside the remarkable chamber that held the bodies of Ahnell and Sararrh, before moving to the study where Daro had encountered his first mentor, which he had now made his own. The old man ran his fingers over the curious building blocks that had so fascinated Daro during his studies, an odd guarded expression on his face. Then he sat at Daro's desk, and the chair adjusted to his form as he spoke firmly.

"I will stay with your Appointed until your Azure responds." he said calmly, "After that I will return to Scartel, to oversee the rebuilding of Scharatel."

He leant forward, flexing long finger joints until they cracked, whereupon he sighed with relief before continuing.

After a while, you will come to realise that you cannot put all your faith in the continuance of one settlement. This was true in the far past, it is true now. The reason behind that is quite simple really. People are attracted to anything outside their own experience. It is all very well to have Sandsingers return, but they must study and train, as do our Sisters in Sorcery. Study and practice cannot take place at the same time or in the same place. In addition, there is a hierarchy to preserve, which neither you nor I can do anything about. Therefore, young

Sandsingers train at Scartel, candidates more advanced in years or practice train or rest in Tirjhinar."

He raised a silencing hand as footsteps sounded in the corridor,

"I know, you are Opal to this clique...but even parents need a break, particularly if you have differences to make up!"

He stood at a muffled tap on the door, smiling as the students entered, Lallee to the fore, clearing her throat hopefully.

"Ichspeller? May I introduce our group to Sentinel before we go to bed? They are dying to meet him and I have so much to tell him."

Reluctantly, Daro stood, inclined his head to Sentinel deferentially saying gruffly,

"Of course Lallee. What was I thinking about, keeping him from you so long. Let him introduce himself, then you can kidnap him, find him something to eat and drink while you bore his ears off. I must continue with one small project for another sector or so, but one of you can bring some soup to my rooms before you turn in. First light tomorrow, we'll all exercise under Timmisandro's guidance, and then you'll begin classes in earnest."

With this threat ringing in their ears, the students swept Sentinel away chattering happily, as Daro dragged his footsteps back to their Council Chamber, uncovered the Stillglass table and leant heavily against it, staring down with sightless eyes.

"Jalni..." he breathed, "How can I tell you how much I regret our last words if you won't respond to my call?"

He held a hand out over the table, desperately trying to summon some power, but emotion just got in the way. He whispered painfully,

"I miss you. Miss hearing you, miss our arguments. Nothing can be worse than this terrible silence! Not even unfulfilled promises, nor broken vows! I miss holding you, loving you, hating you and it's not over, not until I say it's over...not until I beg you to jump the trave with me, belong to me, one against all odds forever. Jalni, come home, come back my love...my love!"

There, he had finally admitted it, he loved her, couldn't bear to be without her, yet there was silence in his heart, in his head, in this accursed room, until he collapsed against the table and wept inconsolably.

During that first Rotation, as the students matured from being merely appointed to being wholly Elect, they discovered the many disadvantages of rank. Despite Daro's famously professed antipathy to all things formal, Sentinel groomed them tirelessly. From dawn to dusk he drilled them in conduct, what to wear (and when), processing them through silent corridors rehearsing, until he was satisfied.

Together they learnt Sentinel's 'Rules of Engagement'. This mixture of diplomacy and mystery was designed to provide the essential 'distance' they would need in order to function effectively. So Daro watched as Lallee grew tall and mysterious, realising that his personal approachability had become a two edged sword. As Rann returned to his customary silence and Shyl became aloof, the Opal Sandsinger absorbed the knowledge he had missed, vowing that if they could learn the lesson, so could he. As Timmisandro learned to glide with an air of inapproachability, Daro realised if he was to get the privacy he craved, or the respect his position demanded things would have to change.

The Elect learnt that while they ruled, they would also train those who would succeed them. Confused, Lallee looked sternly at the Sentinel, tossing her great mane of silver blonde hair back as she said scathingly,

"I thought Sandsingers were immortal!", at which, Shyl slid into the next chair, turning entreating brown eyes on Sentinel, as Daro (registering the importance of the question), surreptitiously 'prodded' Timmisandro and Rann, who paused a game of Nine Winds to listen.

They had just celebrated Jentaroth quietly. No loud Inesh drums, no small children squealing, only a succession of reminiscences' from Sentinel to liven an atmosphere of calm serenity. However, the question had dispelled that, creating a frisson of expectation as Daro and the boys joined in, moving to sit around the Library with the others, as Sentinel sighed, adjusted his position and prepared to answer.

"Oh Sandsingers have a kind of immortality..." he said dubiously, "... (apocalyptic events notwithstanding!). I also think it's rather early in your training to discuss these matters. However, I'll try to clarify some issues now, if you promise not to pester me for more information than I can give."

He pursed his lips, and then began carefully.

"The ordinary mortal can never understand a life radically extended by use of magic. For us, time stops when we engage our powers. You know for a fact that Shiarjha was a young woman when she came to Selesh; you also know that she is still a young woman, but in reality she is exactly the same age she was when her powers engaged, plus the odd Rotation or two when she wasn't empowered. She has already lived far beyond the lifetimes of the rest of her family or friends, as must we. Magic is a lonely business, so it's better that we keep to ourselves, there is just so much pain to get through if we get close to humans. However, there's always someone watching us to see if they can breach our security. Therefore, we play dead from time to time, but only when our work is done, and it's time to hand over to another. Then, we enter transition. While we undergo a period of Retreat, Pelshar undergoes a period of refreshment; this is where you learn that change is inevitable and often beneficial"

He seemed disinclined to explain further but Lallee persisted.

"Where do 'dead' Sandsingers go then?" she demanded curiously, and Daro (sensing something worrying the gawky teen) spoke up.

"Yes…what happens to us Sentinel? After all, if we are truly immortal, it would be possible for the ancients to return wouldn't it. That is, if I'm right, and re-transition is possible?"

The old man scowled, then leaned back in his chair and began to tell a story.

"You're not mistaken Selunsanni." he sighed, "Re-integration was rare, bound up in holy vows of secrecy, but possible. However, the process was difficult; few applicants were suitable, as evidenced in the litany of despair that lies around us."

He turned searching eyes on Daro, asking curiously, "I thought perhaps you'd know the answer to that particular puzzle my boy, but I must have misread the threads I held."

He continued thoughtfully,

"The case in question is also a love story…", he grinned, laughing at the rapt expression on the girls faces (and the groans from the boys), then quite suddenly, Daro felt a cold shudder run through him and *knew* beyond a shadow of a doubt that he might regret listening, as his mentor began

"Long ago, the Lord of the Opal fell deeply in love with his Azure, who was a remarkable woman, a greatly skilled weaver who held court at Scartel. They were inseparable, travelling backwards and forwards between their Sands on a wonderful sailing craft that floated on the great waters that once shaped our world.

Sometimes they spent so much time on the water that their people began to worry. They had held no audiences, the sick would have died but for the intervention of Aramand's Elect. He was fascinated by the concept of Healing by *othervoice* and (as I'm sure you'll find out) had to pay a very heavy price for his dedication to duty. To him fell the work of providing for the Clan Shalhanhi; to him fell the responsibility of plotting the course of a moon, which had attracted attention. Aramand and his mistress were too wrapped up in themselves to spare anytime for their Sands or for our beloved world. No, their responsibilities were ceded to younger less experienced mages, who were struggling to meet the commitments of their seniors."

Daro shifted uncomfortably, perfectly aware that this story was somehow aimed at him and his unsettled relationship with Jalni. The old man quaffed the last of his redberry wine and pinched the bridge of his nose, familiar gestures that irritated Daro (who chided testily),

"Well Grandfather? What happened?"

Sentinel's face stilled for a heartbeat, and then he said gravely,

"Cataclysm! That's what happened Selunsanni, and then every one of us was lost." He leant forward, hands clasping his drinking vessel, as though unaware that it was empty.

"For Rotations the Greeeyn had been tracking the stars, creating sailing maps for the masters of the vessels that provided our transport. Then they started to notice that one of the bodies that circle stars (like our moon Jenta) had broken free. They met, conversed, then decided that a watch should be placed on the body they eventually called Gatta. During this time, Sandsingers were supposed to provide great underground fortresses to protect their people. They had to be less than a day's travel from all centres of habitation, well stocked with food and inhabited by a trained team."

Five pairs of eyes searched the old man's face, but there was no trace of subterfuge, what they listened to was truth. They sighed and shifted, pulling their evening clothes around themselves seeking comfort in cloaking their tangled emotions. Sentinel said quietly,

"One of the mages of that time firmly believed that Gatta was part of some religious destiny. He somehow got the idea that Gatta would replace Jenta in our skies. As this idea was fed by some arcane influence, we put it down to the fact that Loran was himself re-integrated. He was inclined to have rather wild ideas anyway and had built a great Library, where most of his disturbing thoughts were consigned to the care of the priests serving the cult of Gatta, which he had founded."

Daro's focus abruptly disengaged, as across his memory swam the image of a hideous face. The immense bald pate, deeply scarred with ritual cicatrices, the moon shaped face horribly tattooed to resemble some reptilian creature, the weirdly pierced mouth that yawned open like a rictus, the black tongueless void dominating reality. The terror rose inside him like bile, robbing his naturally tanned features of colour. His mind raced fearfully as a voice dripping honeyed evil chanted fervently.

"Let the unnatural one, he who is called the son of the Opal Sorceress, be cast into Gatta's holy darkness and let the Curse of Night fall upon you all!"

In his mind he was surrounded by light, but still the face glared down on him, his eyes opened, seeing nothing but the night of his blindness…it was true, he was cursed…then, his hallucination returned, closer and more threatening, as the terrible mouth smiled and the eyes opened, staring straight at him!

Sentinel applauded his group of students as they caught the fainting Sandsinger. Bending over Daro, he briskly demanded,

"One of you make a sweetdrink, one of you warm his bed and the others stand by to help me. This is nothing but exhaustion, there's no need to worry".

However, his face was grave as he set about distracting the young mages long enough to impose a silencing hand on the Sandsinger's shoulder, standing over him as he sat up looking vulnerable. He scowled after him as Timmisandro guided Daro to his bed, ever the Sentinel who insisted on the last word.

His unmistakeable tones sounded in Daro's ear.

"Later young man, after you've slept, I want to know what that was all about." he said as Daro shakily departed, turning to the rest smiling a reassurance that privately he didn't feel.

"in the meantime my dears, it's far too late to continue, so remember where we were and I'll tell you the rest tomorrow!"

However, in the morning when they reconvened, Daro was gone. Sentinel (declining to breach the Sandsinger's privacy), only remarked cryptically,

"Perhaps the threat of a love story reminded Daro of his own." he smiled mysteriously, forbearing from telling them about Daro's messenger.

Long after everyone had retired, a single Inesh warrior had appeared in the outer cavern. Troubled by dreams, Daro had sought the solace of Cathedral Cavern kneeling in prayer, convinced that his 'vision' was a suppressed memory. Vainly trying to pinpoint the occasion, he was entertaining the wild thought that, the other' entity had been recalling the same event simultaneously.

He shuddered, recalling cruel reptilian eyes meeting his in an unblinking stare of hatred. Considering the nature of synchronicity and magic, he prayed devoutly never to meet the owner of that terrible visage, then rose and went silently to his study to think.

Before returning to bed, the Sandsinger sought the answers in his precious Book of Rule. Having just opened it, he started when something triggered a series of chimes set around the hidden entrance.

Summoning his Staff, he became aware that a light metallic clatter might indicate a rider, so swiftly pocketing the Book of Rule, he rose to investigate.

In the outer cavern Diras filled a leather bottle with water before leading her Zeglur to drink. She was uncapping the flask as Daro stepped out of the shadows disguising the entrance, saying quietly,

"Ho the Guard! On what business do you travel Diras?" cursing himself as his bodyguard jumped and paled, he listened as she explained.

"I travel to find you Lord, charged with bringing you a message from Seris Beneva.", she managed to say, undoing the traditional messenger's bag (that he hadn't even noticed), retrieving a scroll bearing the seal and sigil of the Guardians.

It glowed warmly, warded he thought, as an item in Diras's hand sang to him. Carefully retrieving a small Azure emblem set in silver, she swung it on a chain she had wrapped round one hand. His head turned, tracking the source of the sound. His hands reached out trembling, grasping the Seguidor of the Azure Sands, with fingers closing convulsively. A movement that was not lost on Diras's observant mind.

"Jalni?" he croaked, "Jalni? what's happened to Jalni?"

Diras put a steadying hand towards her liege lord.

"I know nothing that should distress you, Ichspeller," she said, "I took this pendant from her own hand while I waited for a mount."

She concentrated on repeating Jalni's message verbatim, no flicker of interest on her smooth olive face.

"She commanded me to tell you this. 'I await my Lord at Selesh. I know you are occupied with matters of great import, however, I beg you to reconsider my position, and I only want to be of service. I return your gift in case you feel that I am no longer worthy to wear it, although, perhaps you should also know "This is not over until I say it's over!"

Diras's eyes were affectionate as she said quietly,

"I think you'll know what that means my Lord!" but the blind mage was concentrating on stowing the Seguidor away safely, face averted from her knowing gaze."

He said grimly (to himself as much as anyone else),

"She'll put that on again if I have to weld it to her throat!" a curiously tender smile hidden as he turned back towards his bodyguard.

Then a dry voice rustled in the background.

"Humph!" it said as Sentinel appeared from the shadows.

"We wait Rotations for you to get out of Selesh to a place where a mentor can be appointed, and then you rush away at the first crook of a woman's finger. Girls…" he growled, "will only get you into trouble!"

To add to Diras's consternation, Sentinel yawned, then started to fade away before her eyes, while commenting,

"Oh well, I suppose you'd better open the Guardians' message before you go, don't worry about the novitiate, I've got them in hand! We'll look forward to welcoming your Azure on your return."

Then he was gone, as Diras crossed her fingers to ward off evil. Daro caught the movement, laughing as he said briskly,

"Don't mind him, I can top any of his tricks!", then with a click of his fingers, he bowed towards the cavern entrance as Araneus materialised.

"Shall we go?" he suggested with dry appreciation of his companions gasp, and then they were away, thunder rolling and lightening flashing at their heels.

In the Library (much later that morning), Sentinel took up the story again. His face was grave, and none of the Appointed felt like asking too many questions, they were all worrying about Daro's absence, but after a judicious 'sweep' of his students, the Sentinel said calmly,

"To return to my tale…" and four pairs of eyes swivelled in his direction.

"By now, everyone was aware of impending disaster, but deflecting another moon from hitting Pelshar was beyond our capabilities. We invited the scientists to help us, and we believe that a great conference was held at Sanctuary, unfortunately, no records of that time still exist. It appears that Aramand and Feydora decided that as we were doomed once the Source was disrupted, they might as well set sail to spend their last hours together."

Timmisandro looked up horrified,

"They abandoned responsibility?" he asked quietly, but Sentinel shook his head,

"We don't know." He replied flatly, "They seem to have left Selesh for a conference with many of the others, but we only have fleeting glimpses of what happened next. Daro has had very disturbing visions of a great battle, and we believe the lovers were separated as Cataclysm began, but nothing makes sense during events such as they encountered."

He listened to the flood of outrage expressed by his young altruistic audience, then said gently,

"As you can see, all was not lost. Somehow, although the plans of that time never came together, and immense damage was done to our world, part of the spell weaving protected the people so that eventually another race of Sandsingers could emerge once the Source recovered sufficiently. However, it is necessary for me to caution you before you take your vows. With great power comes greater responsibility. Your pleasure, your interests must be subjugated to the service of the people. You are not here to perform magic to impress, curry favour or even provide luxuries for your homesand. You are here to serve, often not knowing what we are expected to do. I will help you prepare, after which you must follow Selunsanni no matter where he leads. Unlike Aramand, he will not shirk his duty, nor will his Azure when she is in place. Just in case you wonder what happened to them, Aramand was lost and in her despair, Lady Feydora decided to become a messenger for the future as Cataclysm began. She had studied re-integration, and created a sub-spell, which would be triggered as soon as the Source recovered enough to support a Sandsinger. From the time of Daro's arrival the Source has been getting stronger Rotation by Rotation. As soon as he was old enough to understand, her sub spell re-integrated her shade." there was a concerted hiss of pity from all present as they envisioned the grief that would have preceded such a decision. Sentinel lingered a moment, then finished quietly,

She condemned herself to the constant repetition of our history, in order to protect you, the next generation of Sandsingers. In a way, you are all Feydora's children, the children she could never bear as a Sandsinger."

In the Library there was a thoughtful silence. Outside in the Sands a lone wind blew away the tracks of two mounted animals heading for Selesh, as two brilliant stars gleamed down from the night sky. Once they had been known as Star Weaver's eyes, but that time was long gone, and the only Star Weaver standing, mourned his losses as he set about repairing the damage his generation had done.

Chapter 50 - Divided by the Sands

When the door opened on the familiar surroundings of the Eyrie, it was as though he had merely stepped out of the apartment a sector ago. Torrenwood shelving reassembled itself in his great room, treasures tumbled into their allotted spaces and the lamps glowed. He slipped inside, allowing his Staff to guide him through his bedroom to the bathing room, sighing with relief as the warm spring fed pool filled at his presence. He mourned the missing unguents that his body servant had always provided, and then blinked as the door opened to admit Tobin.

"My Lord," the cheerful voice greeted him deferentially, "Would you prefer the gerumtree oil or the latherroot?" he asked innocently, and Daro fought down the impulse to hug the man who had made his life so easy. He consulted his inner clock,

"Hmmm! Let me think about that," he prevaricated, saying mildly,

"The latherroot," he said decisively, "I think my hair could do with it after riding through the Sands."

Tobin was obviously looking him over critically, and then he said softly,

"If I didn't know better, I would think you had another man serving you Lord. You have a glow about you, your robes are immaculate and your physique needs no comment. You only need a wash and a brush up really, was your journey a good one?"

Taking the hint, Daro allowed Tobin to assist him to bathe and refresh himself, keeping that margin of distance he had promised himself, but before they parted, the mage asked him softly,

"Are you well Tobin...and happy?"

He felt the warmth of his servant's smile in his voice as he said carelessly,

"Well, except for my creaking knees. I must use a bucket of joint ill salve every moon. Happy, yes at last, thank you my Lord. Our business thrives, we are rich in friends and customers, and I even have a new embroideress working for me, so that my duties to the Hall can continue."

Daro smiled putting out a hand to clasp Tobin's.

"Thank you for everything Tobin," he said, "Now, I must go about my business, but you may find another on your doorstep seeking refuge before this day is over. Make her very welcome for me; I'll be with the Guardians."

He sped away thinking how grateful he was that Jalni hadn't already been installed in their old apartments, concentrating on the next part of his task.

He had slid into Selesh with no fanfare of welcome, so now, speeding through the secret corridors to the Djellim, he hardly expected a welcoming committee. He stilled his rambling mind, considering the few lines of text that had been entrusted to Diras, Familiarising himself with the reason for his recall before consulting the Guardians. However, when he materialised in front of an inexperienced guard, he was dismayed to find his way barred.

Esural blinked at him doubtfully, rigidly maintaining the pose she'd adopted, feet braced, eyes steady behind the half-veil of her uniform, as she tilted her head defiantly.

"I can't consult my senior, who is not present Clansman," she said stoically, as Daro protested, "My partner has already gone to the Guardroom to report as usual, so I may not leave the doors to go anywhere. I'm afraid you'll just have to wait, whoever you say you are!"

She stretched to her full height, re-braced her spine, grasping her spear in such a way that Daro doubted he could have gone more than ten paces before it passed through him. He grinned, mildly amused by her implacability and stood, pretending to wait patiently while he wondered if he could pass through the wall into the Djellim before she acted. However, he didn't have long to wait before Diras came striding down the corridor. She paused, thoughtfully looking over her latest recruit, as the Sandsinger straightened expectantly.

She read the situation perfectly. Wheeling, she dropped at Daro's feet in an upright kneeling position, hands graceful in ritual obeisance, but as she touched her forehead, she completed the ancient form of the salute, prostrating herself as she said commandingly,

"All Hail the Opal!"

To her everlasting credit, after a widening of the eyes, Esural followed her senior swiftly and Daro smiled at both of them as he waved a hand in dismissal, and then walked straight through the heavy Torrenwood doors that had been closed to him, (shoulders shaking with suppressed laughter).

Beneva rose, her own hands flickering in the ritual greeting as she said softly,

"Bad boy Daro! Esural is only standing her second duty and you shouldn't play such tricks when we summoned you in all seriousness.

He grinned, threw her a combative glance, then said softly,

"You said Master Doloran had found something of interest to us?" swinging a long leg over his chair, which had slid out from the table where she worked. Beneva peered at him, rolling the parchment she was scanning onto a long rod to secure it, her place marked.

She nodded, forgetting that he couldn't see the ordinary everyday gestures that sighted people use without thinking. She bit her lip, continuing brightly,

"Yes! He thinks what he found is a magical artefact Rotations old, but he can neither bring it from Omnel, nor could he expect his lawgivers to allow a Sandsinger into the city. He hears gossip in their marketplace which shows how fragile our society is, how suspicious of everything the Greeeyn have become already. I suggested that you might take a look at this artefact covertly and he has agreed, however it is up to you to work that particular weave. The Guardians cannot openly support anything that could inflame one caste against another."

He heard her out impassively, then said quietly,

"The Greeeyn live in the Opal as well, If they want to benefit from having more to eat, better modes of transport, or healers willing to treat them, or even teach them, they must make terms with their Sandsinger. I will not have one caste put against another either aunt Beneva, nor will I tolerate the Felmin being caught between warring factions. We are all equal under Seleus, all children before the One, so this stupidity must stop!"

Beneva eyed him doubtfully, but nodded, smiling as Shiarjha joined them. As the second Guardian sat at the centre of the Djellim under the great four branched lamp that provided the light for her work, she paused, aware of a light frisson that whispered over the long table. Wordlessly she 'reached' for the other minds in the room, as a long sigh echoed in the depths of the repository. She frowned, saying mechanically,

"All hail the Opal!", but Daro (while acknowledging their use of his rightful title, was convinced they ought to remove to the Council Chamber which (as usual) lay hidden, cloaked by a magical screen. He stood abruptly, the others following him, and then the screen dissolved as he walked toward it. He entered, resting both hands on the second Stillglass table, as something in its depths shifted and changed.

They both saw the Sandsinger gasp, as a face appeared shadowed, mysterious. It was a young face, thought the Sandsinger peering into the clouded distance, struggling with his "truesight" firmly engaged.

"Who are you?" Daro demanded and the image wavered (as though some barrier prevented the boy from full materialisation). Then the voice came. Liquid in entreaty, masked by distance, it nevertheless prickled the skin, making the hair stand up on the back of Daro's arms. He stilled, listening to the quality of it, sharp with terror yet poised on the edge of remarkable. He pinched the bridge of his nose, concentrating every inch of his mind on this manifestation. With power emanating from every syllable, he accepted without question that he was listening to another of his kin!

"I am Tanneus," said the voice calmly. "Who are you?"

The Guardians by now had joined Daro, one on each side, and as he reached blindly, Beneva caught his left hand, and then reached with her left for Shiarjha's right. The younger Guardian reached for Daro's right hand, and thus joined, all three placed their hands down into the Stillglass concentrating their efforts, boosting Daro's power infinitely.

The boy gasped, Are you Opal?" he asked incredulously, then tremulous he spoke sotto voce.

"I cannot have contacted the Opal with my first attempt it's impossible!"

The image surged as though hope fed more power to the connection, then hurriedly the young man began to explain.

"I am resident in the Black Tower, built by Loran an ancient, whose writings I am studying."

In Selesh there was stunned silence, and then the voice began again,

"I seek a man, born in the depths of a Storm, who may be found at Selesh!" His obvious plight was desperate, but Daro admired the manner in which Tanneus was trying to protect him, whether or not he knew about Sandsingers, he very obviously wasn't going to endanger a man he'd never met. One of Daro's eyebrows rose a fraction as he spoke levelly, voice neutral.

"What is this man to you Tanneus?" he asked gently, keeping his eyes closed in his normal manner, knowing that all the boy could see would be a blind man flanked by two women.

Tanneus spoke up bravely,

"He is the Head of a Guild to which I would belong," he said humbly,

"I believe I might have some of the qualities he is looking for, but I don't know his name."

Slowly the Lord of the Opal revealed himself; his eyes opened fire Opal bright. About him, his aura crackled into life, shimmering colours fizzing along his body, making his hair writhe like some living entity. Awed, Tanneus dropped to one knee, head bowed solemnly, and then Daro said gently,

"Tanneus, I am the one you seek. My name is Daro."

He watched the young man rehearse his name soundlessly, as though the very possession of that name was the most important thing in his life. The boy's eyes lifted proudly, Amethyst glints gleaming as the Sandsinger said (in the voice of command).

"Wherever you are Tanneus, never reveal it by as much as a nuance or inflection of speech. You are indeed what I am looking for, but you are trapped. Do not however, think for one instant that you are alone. When the auspices allow, I will contact you, but you must stay where I can rescue you. Your brothers and sisters in magic will welcome you with open hearts when we can release you, but in the meantime…" he bowed his head, intoning solemnly,

"May the One preserve you and those who you'll rule under the light of Jenta, moon of forgiveness and peace."

The image of Tanneus flickered and faded, as Shiarjha turned to face Daro.

"He must be very powerful to get through that barrier (even in image form)", she said thoughtfully.

"Do you think he'll survive until we have an answer for Adruna?"

She rubbed her wrist ruefully as the man who had bruised it stood summoning his Staff. He smiled in her direction as he walked towards the doors,

"I have every hope Seris Shiarjha, but first, I've to talk to a Healer, impressing on said Healer that she cannot, positively must not desert a patient in mid recovery. When I've convinced her of the sad neglect of her duties, I'll give our new problem some careful consideration.", he waved a hand of dismissal as Beneva gazed after him indulgently.

"Jalni?", she asked cheerfully, and her companion nodded.

"Jalni!", she sighed, but this time there was no amusement in her eyes, only the sad reflection of the pain that was to come.

Daro went silently to the Infirmary, where a healer sat under a dimmed glowstone lamp making notes on a wax tablet. He listened to the scratch of the enscrasure, knowing better than to interrupt her. He sensed that she was aware of his arrival, but she turned over another wax tablet to finish her notation before saying comfortably,

"How can I help you Clansman? Are you seeking someone in particular?"

He heard the scrape of her chair as she rose, then a hiss of breath as she became aware of the light aura he was projecting. Not knowing her voice he said gently,

"Infirmarian, I don't mean to disturb you or your patients, but I seek one of your Healers. Can you call her for me, or tell me where Jalni bin Selesh is at the moment? Obviously, if she is on duty I will call again."

The woman's voice faltered momentarily, then she said huskily,

"I believe that I am addressing Lord Daro, am I not?', and something in her tone gave rise to a query in his mind.

"You are indeed, yet you have the better of me, you know my name, but I am more than usually in the dark. What have you done with dear old Hannah?" his voice was light, but he still maintained a distance.

She swallowed then said softly,

"We have met before Lord, but you were very, very small. Only a newborn babe in fact. I am Davina, late of Caranchar where I was privileged to see Seris Ikella summon the winds with you strapped to her body."

Daro grinned,

"Well then Davina, I know of you, as well. My mother always said you would make a remarkable Healer, and it seems her predictions were fulfilled. What of Hannah?", he sensed the change in her before she spoke.

"Sadly, she went to the Sands almost two moons ago. She was well until the end, passing within two days of getting a chill. Privately I think that while she had the Infirmary to live for, she could have beaten anything, but while she was very happy, relaxing in retirement, her work was done, and she was tired."

Daro thought back, recalling Hannah at minor and major turns in his life, grimacing in sympathy with the new Infirmarian.

"I am sorry to learn of her death.", he said, "but she had a good life, a happy life, and I thank the One for her time with us."

Davina stared at him. He was no religious she knew, but his total sincerity, his obvious love and care for an elderly Healer touched her deeply and all at once she believed what she had seen as the Winds hailed him shortly after his birth. She whispered confidentially,

"You will find Jalni with Mina bin Attwa ", she said. "They were going to mend some sheets, then take a bath."

She was about to offer to get her Healer, when she became aware that he wasn't there anymore, right in front of her eyes he had simply dematerialised to go where? She asked herself numbly, smiling as she realised what a stupid question that was.

The door to the Eyrie closed some ten sectors later as the mage and his love returned hand in hand, with more than the healing of a misunderstanding to talk about, but if the evidence of that night's weather was anything to go by, little talking was done, and in the comfort of their bed, Jalni's tears of fulfilment were mirrored in the dawn dew as she slept against Daro's chest.

When she woke, he was kissing her again. His lips were tender, pliant and she melted against him, stirring his desire to new heights. He stroked her hair, tenderly lifting strands off her face, letting them run through his delicate discerning fingers, breathing in the scent of her, nuzzling at the nape of her neck. She gasped, made an inarticulate little murmur, then he leant over her as all thought fled and he fell into her arms.

At last they lay spent, side by side hands clasped. He raised his own, feeling her delicate fingertips wondering at the smoothness of her skin.

"Pumice-stone", she offered as he blinked in surprise.

"Did you hear me?" he asked tentatively, wondering silently how much had she heard of his longings, how much had she known of his distress, his agony of depression?

She rolled over, leaning on an elbow as she walked her fingers up his chest, to his throat, his lips…silencing his inner thoughts with a kiss, her eyes blazing Azure fire, flickering lights of turquoise, midnight, gold in their depths.

"I know everything Selunsanni.", she whispered provocatively, "everything you think you've hidden from me. We may have been divided by the Sands but I have my own methods. Surrender, I know where the keys to the Eyrie are, where you lost your virginity, even where you've buried the bodies! Now, submit to me, or pay the penalty!"

She giggled at his alarmed expression, then she sighed,

"I'll bet it's me that'll pay the penalties though…", groaning as he captured a breast with his lips. He teased her dutifully, then swung his legs out of bed.

"Most of Selesh is up and about and although we Sandsingers can have an extra sector or so, I should hate to advise one thing and do another. Ikella always said that double standards were the road to Hadda's Hall."

He grinned at her invitingly,

"Last one in the pool is a Dolcan!", then turned with his new self-assurance and fled towards the bathing room. She scrambled up on her knees terrified that he might fall, but Daro had practised the same movements daily. His apartments at Tirjhinar were laid identically. He knew that six long paces from his beds foot, there was a door to the bathing room. Inside that room was a large rectangular pool, deep end nearest to the door, which opened as he moved towards it. Jalni sat upright, bare-breasted as Daro (counting paces) performed quite a credible somersault on the edge of the pool, then disappeared into it with only a gentle splash. She giggled as he rose to the surface, resting his elbows on the side as he blew water off his face laughing.

"The One defend you from broken limbs, you fool…" said the Healer equably, as she moved to join him, then, as though taking courage from an inner voice, she added,

"That extra sector of sleep sounds interesting, but I'm only a Healer. How can I become Sandsinger? I might need to in order to recover from mornings like this!"

She slipped decorously into the warm water, straight into his arms, which enfolded her tenderly as his lips found hers again, When he had roused her to fever pitch, clutching her trembling body against him, the Lord of the Opal bent his mouth to her throat, murmuring softly,

"When we are really sure of each other dearling, I will show you how, then we will be together always."

The days he had planned for lengthened into ninenights, the Rotation moved steadily onward as preparations began both at Selesh and Tirjhinar. Mina fluttered in and out of the Eyrie, generally scolding, or exhorting the drudges to do better by her nursling before she left for the ceremonies at Tirjhinar. She would accompany Jalni, along with her Uncle, foster parent and nearest male relatives being acceptable in the eyes of the Guardians.

In the meantime, Jalni and Daro worked tirelessly towards giving her confidence in her other voice, he having explained patiently to her that a Healer amongst their group would follow tradition, having gleaned that much from Beneva and Shiarjha's research. They had opened the Hall of the Singers with reluctance on Jalni's part, as she recalled the shameful episode in her past.

Daro had listened sympathetically to her story. The child orphaned by stealth and evil, yet remaining true to a purpose that further alienated her from her homesands. He had comforted her, hearing the piteous sobs as she confirmed what he had suspected, that she had (by some inner sense) realised that she needed to be supported by one who could recognise a power before it matured. He heard Mina explain how at less than fourteen she had suspended her Grandfather over the table in Ikella's Inner Sanctum, had seen her horrified realisation that she had used a medicantric long before conventional wisdom had admitted the presence of Sandsingers in their midst. He had held her while she wept inconsolably, then stiffened her resolve by saying lightly,

"I'm just glad that my mother never learnt that trick or my *othervoice* might never have developed!"

She chuckled, then said softly,

"Well Selunsanni, don't forget that I know that secret. It gives me a hold over you when you get too high and mighty!"

He didn't fear her at all, she noted wondering just how much he could read of her 'hidden pockets of sadness', which he put down to her Zurian heritage. They were well known for swinging between the heights of joy and the depths of misery, much drink and music intervening to embroider the picture of a robust, intelligent and valiant Clan, for which he was grooming a leader.

He reviewed all they had learnt together, thought long and hard about his choices, then made a momentous decision.

"Dearling, you must come to realise that although we love each other, we will spend much of our time apart, divided by our Sands and our pledges of trust. We will always be able to travel to each other, but once you make the decision and take your vows, there is no turning back. You will, by virtue of your Sand, also stand as second to me. I welcome that, but you must take responsibility for your own Sand, I cannot do anything other than advise you. When you are ready for that, then you are ready to take your vows."

They were in Daro's great-room as they spoke, Daro seated at the table, Jalni roaming free as they talked. She had noted amongst his trophies the Heart of

Darkness, inert now, sitting harmlessly amongst a group of other spoils, gathered on his foraging trips around the Lower Caverns below the fortress where he had grown up.

The reminder of her own Sands brought a lump to Jalni's throat. She could smell the air off the desert, feel the pull of familiar sounds, the click clack of the weaving sheds as looms worked intricate patterns, the cry of a Sheer Wolf as Rangers came and went in the night... She paused in mid reflection, leaping to her feet in fright as a silver snout appeared (shoulder high) around the door.

"Grey!" exploded the mage leaping to his feet as a Ranger was towed in her wake apologising.

"Your forgiveness Lord Daro," Garald begged as Daro held out a hand to his Sheer Wolf, "We have trouble at Holmgarth!", and he said cryptically, only then registering Jalni's presence.

"Healer Jalni", he said, too deeply disturbed to note her panicked expression. He carried on, "Ranger Dorenard will explain further, but as I was on my way here, and Trailfinder Grobold is tending a sick animal, I brought her straight to you. She might tell you something that we can't follow!"

Garald sagged against the wall as Grey whined piteously to Daro, who leant forward until she could put her great forehead against his own. He felt the warmth of her fur pressing against his sightless eyes, the soft thrum of her breath as they pressed together, then he felt the cold.

She was showing him something, showing him a place so bitter cold that just listening, struggling to follow the images she was projecting in truesight his skin pricked with goose bumps. He checked her paws, feeling the pads so that he could tell where she'd been, then he realised what he should have known instinctively. Appalled, he caught Grey's snout, placing his head where she could lean against him once more. She shuffled closer, whining as she fought to communicate, then his stupid prejudices slipped away as he looked into the face of Draille Skellin. The man was lying on his back, arms relaxed against his chest as though he slept, but Daro knew different. He forced himself to examine every inch of the Ranger's body, but could find no evidence of injury, and very little to tell him exactly where Draille lay.

There was a voice, wheedling at him for attention and at first Daro thought it must be Jalni, then he registered the paw being draped over his wrist as the wolf pleaded with him,

"Daro...fetch Draille home to Holmgarth. Don't leave him in the Sheer. He found what he was looking for, but he was so very tired. He could not reach the ledge, and he fell, I could not catch him, he was too far away. I will take you safely, Blue could bring Ranger Dorenard, and Sobix could bring Rann if Dream Walker Garald will permit. Ranger Skellin is hunting in different lands now, he cannot be hurt or tired anymore. His loneliness is over and yet he has fulfilled the greatest purpose ever, and if you will it, I can help another complete his task."

She was panting softly, little grumbles accompanying the words he heard, but his mind, his eyes were locked on the features of a man he had both admired, and jealously ignored.

He spoke bitterly,

"Garald, I would speak to you alone."

The joy of the day was lost, frozen to death in the Sheer, along with the Ranger that might have comforted and loved Jalni. He turned to her,

"Dearling, we have very grave news, and it is only right that I tell Garald Dream Walker first, do you understand me?"

He saw her face still, her eyelids closed for a long moment, then, when she lifted them slowly, they were swimming with tears. Inwardly all she could see was a silhouette against a summer dawn, lure whirling round his head as he trained his hawks, his beloved hawks…

Her pale lips moved, trying to form words but she remained silent as she rose and quietly left the room, the Sandsinger and the terrible news behind.

Daro looked across at Garald, who said in a desperate whisper,

"Draille?" bowing his head as Daro nodded.

"I wondered.", the Ranger admitted. "He was like a man in a dream, from the time that Jalni went to the Ashgenar with her Uncle he was like a man condemned. He seemed older than his years, then I think his duties took a hold on him. He has tasks that no other living Ranger can share, which I admit must be onerous. Did Grey tell you how?"

Daro moistened suddenly dry lips, then said softly,

"Are these tasks known to other Rangers? Who will take them over?", his concern must have communicated itself to grey who whimpered in the light doze she had fallen into, as Garald fought with himself over trusting the Sandsinger. Eventually, Grey's agitation and Daro's sensitivity won out, and the Dream Walker said quietly,

"Rangers have an allotted task Lord. I may not speak of it, but I can give you a dream if you like?"

Daro thought about this, he had undergone 'dream-walking' with Garald before, but his curiosity was roused and he had to know what task was too secret for a Sandsinger to know about. He raised himself from the Ranger squat he had adopted to talk with his wolf, as Garald, miserable with the fatigue of a journey taken in vain, came behind him and flexed long fingers.

Daro leant back trustingly. He nestled the back of his head into Garald's chest and allowed those trained fingers to settle (light as a feather's touch) on the points of his face, along the planes of his cheeks, and just below his eyes, welcoming the vision he anticipated.

His eyes flickered open in absolute darkness. Then there was a shimmer, something pale glowing in rows, long rows stretching far away into the distance. There was a soft rhythmic thudding that he took for the beat of a distant drum, or possibly the beat of Garald's heart, then the scene shifted and he saw the Rangers. They stood about a brazier, alight and glowing sorrons fruit bright. He watched the older man carefully, as he took down what Daro presumed to be an orb of some kind, rotating it over the warmth of the brazier. The orb was heavy, Daro conceded as the man struggled to put it back on the next shelf down to the one he'd taken it from, but the young Ranger laughed, coming to his father's rescue cheerfully. He spoke,

"You're tired Keeper," he said provocatively, "You need an assistant or one day you'll drop an egg, then there'll be no rescue for you!"

Suddenly Daro could feel Garald's fingers although the hypnotic chant of the Dream Weaver kept him passive. He felt the threads of millennia knitting in his own hands, felt the explosion of pain on his back, in his heart where a voice had imprinted itself indelibly. He struggled up from the deep well of inertia that Garald was weaving, crying out.

"Yaydoran!" he croaked as Garald put his hands on his shoulders to wake him, and the Ranger blinked in surprise.

"Or the clutch that we carried away after Cataclysm before she was found in stasis. She's healing, ready to fly any day soon Draille said, and now she won't have her Keeper to protect her. Oh my world afire!"

The muffled curse was not lost on Daro as Marran entered the room silently with Jalni at his heels. The young ranger took in the scene, saw Grey blinking in exhaustion at Daro's feet, and said roughly,

"It would seem so Garald. Have you come to tell Daro the worst of it?", he didn't wait for an answer, but plunged straight on bitterly,

"As Ranger Second, I now take over Draille's place. I've just settled my first families back at Scartel, we have a full Tawn that know the heights inside and out, a Trailfinder and a wolving hold, yet now I must return to Holmgarth to become Ranger Leader. On top of which, I inherit the care of other duties, about which I know nothing, the knowledge having died with Draille. How can I keep faith with my Grandfather's wishes when I am torn this way and that?", he cried out in sudden exasperation.

They stared at each other, then Daro said mildly,

"Why don't you enlist the help of your Sandsinger Marran?", and behind the Rangers Jalni gasped.

"If we had our own, I would", the Ranger shot back angrily, as Daro beckoned Jalni to him,

"Dearling…" he said softly, "All those things we talked about have risen up to thwart all our best intentions!", he exclaimed, suddenly very sure that this was right, that this was the Way.

He consulted his inner clock, saying softly.

"We'll go straight to Tirjhinar tomorrow. You are as ready as you'll ever be, so take one night to be sure, then if your Sands still call you home, you shall take your vows. Our friends need our help, and I am always with you wherever you are, all you have to do is to remember what I've taught you, or think of me, and I'll be there for you."

Marran stepped back as Jalni turned radiant blue eyes towards her Lord, wondering how he could keep her secret, but certain in his loyalty. He felt Daro's hand on his shoulder, the Opal eyes burning into his, then a strange sensation filled his veins, a voice said slowly,

"You have a mountain to climb my brother, take my strength, take my goodwill, and go with this woman who will be your Sandsinger by nightfall tomorrow. Whatever you guard, guard it well for her, whatever your duties in the Tawn, wear that coat lightly. Defend your Clan, defend your loved ones by the kindness of a kiss or the threat of the lash, knowing that I am ever your blood brother but no longer your Lord."

He sagged as the Sandsinger said smiling, "I own your trust as a man Ranger Dorenard, now, let us go and get Ranger Skellin from wherever he has fallen. If a Ranger can serve my cause through friendship alone, then I can at least return him to those he loved."

Marran was to remember all his life that moment. That was the time when he felt more able to face his duties than he could have believed possible. The Three Rangers and the Sandsinger went into the Sheer to collect Draille's body without delay, and so it was that the greatest Leader of their times was carried home to his ritual pyre, and burial in the funerary cliffs of Holmgarth. As his successor sadly accepted the symbols of Ranger Leader from his mentor, he turned to Lladro, appointing him Ranger Second in his stead, wishing him success at Scartel, where even as the exchange was made, another Sentinel was waiting to greet the woman who would be returning there within days.

Daro walked alone unguided by anything other than his Staff to a room where Decrian Kilda Pagthorn and her assistant waited. He spoke only once,

"If you remember my symbol Kilda, now is the time to place it on my back!"

Garald Lightfoot, dressed in the guise of the Dream Walker placed the stool for him, bracing him lightly by the shoulders, as Kilda soaked her arms in preparation. Only then did she notice the outline of a wing traced across his spine. She hissed bending to her work, following the lines that seemed to spring as living things from the end of a curious coloured bone she was using as a point.

When it was over, the Sandsinger stood tall as she committed a design she had never drawn or seen to memory. There had been virtually no blood, he seemed strangely pain free, but as he walked out of her rooms, she turned and hurried to a hidden wall painting, lifting the curtains aside to look at the back of a man who had never seen this fresco.

Garald accompanied the Sandsinger back to the Keld who were gathered on the walkway in the depths of the summer night, waiting for him. He walked proudly, his singing Staff leading him to where they could all see his back, then with a single movement he shrugged the light cloak aside to a roar of approval. The drums spoke from the dark, the fire glowed, and gathered in with the people he loved, the Sandsinger had a sudden glimpse of a man in patch dyed blues, who watched with deep set brown eyes smiling wryly as his successor put up his hand to collect the hawks who flew the valley, jesses streaming to honour the memory of Ranger Draille Skellin.

After that it was all rush and ceremony. Daro's head reeled with it. The swift ride back to Selesh. The quick conference with the Guardians, then collecting Jalni and the ride to Tirjhinar. With all the finery to transport, Daro paused, clutching his aching head.

"What are you doing?" he demanded, as folk fussed over who was carrying what to the ceremony.

"Look", he said grimly, "Wear what you like, Jalni will be the only one in the Hall. No-one will notice what you wear, they only have eyes for her.", he corrected himself immediately,

"Of course, Timmisandro and Rann may have family or friends present as well.", he assured them, delighted that the older members of the Elect had decided to take their oaths at the same time.

"All of you, put everything you need together, then stand in the Audience Chamber. There is no need for all this fuss!"

He watched Jalni longingly as she assisted Mina, and she turned catching his gaze and blushing furiously. He made a signal with his hands, pleading with her to gather everyone closely, then he joined them, took a long breath and said simply,

"Mahanesh!"

There was no sound as the group and all their belongings vanished, and only a few squeaks of amazement as they re-emerged in Daro's Inner Sanctum at Tirjhinar. Jalni raised her eyebrows, then turned smiling as Lallee walked in, beautifully robed and looking every inch prepared for this invasion. Timmisandro bore down on his aged parents and a little old man that Daro had almost overlooked, then Rann Godway took hold of Marran's outstretched hands.

"I heard about Draille brother.", was all Daro heard as the Rangers departed to support their friend, then he was alone, feeling very strange as he remembered his own solitary induction to the status of mage. For a moment self-pity threatened, then recalling the fact that once Jalni took her vows he could offer to jump the trave with her, he went off jauntily to seek Sentinel and find the most elaborate robes with which to honour his beloved.

He pointedly ignored the rooms set aside for Jalni to bathe and robe in, thinking of his own solitary walk to Cathedral Cavern, and made himself go down to his study, taking out the Book of Rule left at Selesh in the depths as the apocalyptic events of Cataclysm wiped out his predecessors. He settled, opening the book, hands suspended lightly above the pages as true-sight revealed their contents to him, then he heard the distinct tinkle of bells, running footsteps and a gentle laugh.

The voice was husky as she whispered,

"Remember Selunsanni…this world is more at threat than you know, and only the Azure can help you. Many and many are the secrets of the Sands, but all you have to do to uncover them is to remember…", then she was gone.

He was suddenly deeply exhausted, freezing cold, and the One help him, there was music coming from somewhere! He leapt to his feet, pocketing Jalni's Book of Rule as he did so, then his Staff was singing a high urgent note as he swept down the corridor toward Cathedral Cavern.

He could feel power emanating from the cavern and paused long enough to sense Rann (in his Ranger blues) and Marran kneeling to each side of the entrance forming a guard of honour for their Sandsinger. He went to stand near them, ready to greet his Azure as she emerged. He wondered how she would feel then, (apprehensively), what she had surrendered to obtain her power. Filled with a longing he had always suppressed, in case she rejected him for another more able man, he heard a small patter of applause, then her footsteps approaching. The love poured from him in undeniable waves, as adopting his own powers, he engaged true-sight and turned to face her.

Then, he looked into those impossibly complex eyes, awash with the Azure fire of power, and knew what she had surrendered.

She stared past him, noting her Rangers kneeling to do her honour, and winced as she came level with him. She merely glanced at him, noticing the Opalwear as she dipped a courteous acknowledgement of rank, but in her eyes there was no love. Her body was cold to his, the blaze quenched, and he was alone within a hands breadth of his heart's desire, yet she knew him not.

The howl of despair was wrenched from his very depths as his soul withered and died. He felt his world break up around him, everything he had suffered for sliding away, he was nauseous with sleep deprivation, giddy with anguish, and the skies outside the cavern were darkening, just as they had on the terrible day he lost his sight. He felt the difference, the heat vanishing as the chill of a sudden storm washed over him. He stumbled towards the entrance, reaching for Marran's shoulder to lean on. Searing pain brushed his hand, which closed around the hilt of a sword, as he thought numbly,

"If this is all power gives me, let me go. Take it back and let me die for this is nothing without her!"

He was unaware that Jalni had come to a sudden stop, her dream coming to life in front of her.

She screamed as Daro flinging out a hand for balance encountered the hilt of Marran's sword, sleeping in its scabbard, suspended down his spine.

Her cry hung in the air, as a flash of lightening seemed to join the roiling sky with the hilt, but that was not quite true, she thought later, replaying the events and their dreadful consequences through her memory.

She thought she heard the Opal Sandsinger say something in low broken tones. Something about not wanting his power anymore, but that she kept to herself. Her most lasting impression was that the sword had leapt into Daro's hand, as though he'd summoned it from Rotations of sleep. The next instant, both her Ranger and Rann Godway were lying on the floor bewildered, and the Opal Sandsinger had vanished.

She remembered very little else. Rangers gathering around a howling Sheer Wolf, guest's spilling out into the Sands, then Mina gathering her up, insisting that she go straight with the Rangers to Scartel, where she was needed. She had gone, though it felt like a desertion. Rann and Timmisandro had taken their vows, but remained at Tirjhinar with Lallee and Shyl Nighthawk and their Sentinel. She promised to come back once she had settled in her own Sands, but what of the Opal? No-one seemed to know where he was, or even if he lived. She had no personal memory of the man, but he was her Lord and it seemed that he had departed in possession of her Book of Rule which was entirely inconvenient.

Brooding, she took possession of the Lookout Cave at Scartel then, sat overlooking Gateway…waiting.

THE END?

Now read on …

From "Shadow Lord" Part 1 of "The Shadow of the Singer" (© Julia Cæsar 2014)

He woke slowly, certain he was dead. There seemed no other explanation, for a grey light penetrated the blindness that he had accepted as his penalty for power. Moving experimentally; he shivered, painfully cold and stiff, one hip agonised with the pressure of something digging into his back. Miserably aware that his mouth was dry as dust, he lay quietly unwilling to open his eyes, the sweat of some unnamed fear bedewing his brow, where all too recently Ikella had placed an Opal redic, proclaiming his status before the Clan.

The tear shaped stone seemed to evade the touch of his sensitive fingers as he felt for the reassuring 'hum' of power that linked him to his Sands. He froze; seeking the Source; his entire being focussed on that familiar thread of joy that ran through his being…in vain.

His eyes flew open clouded in dismay, as he sought the tingling awareness of power; desperately he tried to focus on the thread of song that played in his mind endlessly, in shock scrambling to his knees, eyes wide open and seeing!

He was in a small room, kneeling on the bare floor and he could see, he could see! For a wild moment he thought he must be in the Infirmary at Selesh; all that had gone before merely a dream, but even as the thought crossed his mind, he knew he was wrong. There, he had always been aware of others, here he could detect no-one.

Worse was to come as he moved. Cramp seized him, doubling him over and reducing him to tears of pain. He stared at his hands as the liquid he'd wiped from his face dripped from his fingers; thinking that it was so long since he'd imagined hands or tears, let alone looked at either, and bent his head to examined them curiously.

Stupid with fatigue he stared blankly at long tapering fingers, taut tanned skin, pale sensitive palms, with a ring of glowing Opal (deeply engraved with his sigil) on his index finger. He fingered it lightly, feeling the eye shape carved into the stone, knowing that his Sands depended on his return to survive whatever cataclysmic event he had been born to prevent.

His head reeled under the pressure of so many responsibilities, and then (despite his best intentions) he allowed himself to drift towards that well of sleep that would protect him from this state of conflict.

He yawned, astonished at how tired he felt, then his memory began to stir and his throat contracted painfully as he remembered what had brought him here. Lurching upward, he looked around, noting that the small cell only had a bed, a tiny table, a rug, but no window, unlike the room he had occupied in the Infirmary, where patients were situated in rooms overlooking the Gathering Square so that as they progressed back to health, outside stimulus could be provided.

Shifting to kneel upright, he continued to assess the room, until he was reminded of the earlier pain in his back; at which he grimaced, reaching behind and delving into the pouch that he wore tucked under his ceremonials. A familiar shape revealed itself to exploring fingers, and he paused, tracing it lovingly before withdrawing his Book of Rule!

Relieved, he bent his head, thanking the One he hadn't lost it, head bowed over to open the flimsy pages eagerly, for the first time actually seeing the fine spidery script that scrawled across each page.

He traced the cover, hearing in his own memory Feydora's trembling voice as she'd read the ancient script aloud,

"For the Singer of the Song..

His voice murmured the words, tailing off with a howl of despair as he realised that he could no longer understand the page! His true-sight would not engage, his powers had deserted him! For a long moment all his mind would do was to moan piteously, then his resolve clamped down hard, forcing him to stay sane enough to examine this incredibly altered reality.

A sound from the doorway broke into the stream of desperate prayers he was engaged upon, and he looked up frowning as a man clad in glowing robes appeared there looking at him wryly.

"Yes Selunsanni," he said reprovingly.

"You've provided yourself with a pretty set of problems haven't you? Only half your Sands appointed, only your Azure confirmed and now it seems that although you have certainly proved that there's no limit to your power, it's not precisely matched with intelligence!"

Too shocked for anger; Daro's eyes narrowed as he looked at his visitor critically. There was nothing overtly proclaiming a direct relationship to Ikella, but the scorn in his voice matched hers 'tone for tone'. He shook his head miserably, and the voice continued.

"As usual, I expect you're asking yourself "What have I done?" Well boy, let me tell you precisely what your impetuosity has achieved this time! You've left a world unprepared for Sandsingers without the one that matters. On top of that, you've brought the key Book of Rule with you as well! Where do you think you are? You're in the one place where there is no power, where magic can't exist, where I have been trapped since Cataclysm!"

He waved an elegant hand.

"Welcome to my Sands, where colour, life, magic vanished long ago. Welcome to the Sand that is no more, the tenth Sand of Pelshar. Welcome to The ancient Crystal Desert; from which even you cannot escape!

"The Tapestry of Tten", what is it? Where is it? and why must they find it? The story begins at the

"Dawn of Darkness"

They were all doomed until the Sorceress remembered an ancient incantation, but as she chanted the forbidden words, what has Ikella unleashed on her unsuspecting world?

Hidden in the brilliantly hued deserts of Pelshar are the clues to its secret past. Strict obedience to the "Way", has prevented their discovery until, engulfed in an apocalyptic storm, a party of Healers accidently fulfils ancient prophecy. Now launched on a perilous journey of self-discovery and emotional awakening, Ikella reaches far beyond her previously circumscribed existence, as she adopts a foundling of the Storm. Facing a choice between the child she loves, and the security of a world teetering on the brink of ecological disaster, she must discover why the word "Sandsinger" haunts her dreams, and how their very existence depends on finding a mysterious "Tapestry of Tten".

The reader will agonize with her over baby Daro's future, relax in the reassuring company of an aged Apothecary, and be on the edge of their seats, waiting for the sequel, "Curse of Night."

"The Tapestry of Tten", a gripping series of Fantasy Fiction novels by Julia Caesar is published by Arima Publishing. To order, please visit our website, http://www.arimapublishing.co.uk, or write to us at,

Arima publishing
ASK House
Northgate Avenue
Bury St Edmunds
Suffolk
IP32 6BB
UK

If you have enjoyed this book, follow the unfolding mystery in

"Curse of Night"

Following the Storm, Jentaroth (the annual Rite of Passage), takes on new significance. Amidst mourning rituals, Ikella must protect the Union of the Sands from treachery within, whilst resisting her growing emotional attachment to the frail orphan she longs to adopt. Beset by premonitions as she gathers her Sisters in Sorcery at Selesh, Ikella is forced to defend the Gathering as one of three new Candidates reveals herself as a practising heretic, with command of Dark Magic. As she confines Adruna and her followers to her own Sands, Ikella cannot prevent her cursing baby Daro, but did her curse have any effect?

As Daro grows up, how many Rotations must Ikella endure his relentless obsession with the ancient mages of the past? Is this something to do with "The Curse of Night? As his obsession leads him into perilous places, can he survive to find "Another Shade of Mystery?"

"The Tapestry of Tten", a gripping series of Fantasy Fiction novels by Julia Caesar is published by Arima Publishing. To order, please visit our website, http://www.arimapublishing.co.uk, or write to us at,

Arima publishing
ASK House
Northgate Avenue
Bury St Edmunds
Suffolk
IP32 6BB
UK

"Another Shade of Mystery"

Having exiled Daro for his obsession with the ancient mages of their secret past, life is still far from peaceful in Selesh. The aging Sorceress has found no relief from troublesome children, for she has given refuge to Jalni. The girl, hotly pursued into the heart of the community, has an intriguing (though erratic) command of power. Admitted as a novice, Jalni commits a catalogue of crimes, and is on probation when Daro returns empowered, to challenge his foster-mother's long held beliefs.

Determined to ignore the personal price he has paid for his power, the Opal Sandsinger takes Jalni as his guide, and sets out to save the children of Scartel. Encountering Myst-cats, Wanderers, Storm horses and a mysterious mentor, Daro must also find his feet in a strange new world, looking for "Another Shade of Mystery", to help him understand, "The Song of Sorcery".

"The Tapestry of Tten", a gripping series of Fantasy Fiction novels by Julia Caesar is published by Arima Publishing. To order, please visit our website, http://www.arimapublishing.co.uk, or write to us at,

Arima publishing
ASK House
Northgate Avenue
Bury St Edmunds
Suffolk
IP32 6BB
UK

"Song of Sorcery"

Returning from Scartel to safety, Daro and Jalni are shaken by the death of a child. As Daro questions his faith in magic, Jalni decides that if he can face the past of a world, she can face her own, and slips away unseen.

En route to Jerritol, followed by an old friend, she encounters Orto and decides to help him find the Tapestry of Tten. At the Temple of the Winds there's no trace of the relic, but the Oracle predicts, Jalni will become, "Mother to the Tenth Wind."

Jalni goes into retreat, but when the Sorceress Tirjella is poisoned, she usurps Sandsinger powers and saves her. Returning to Selesh, Jalni can predict Ikella's reaction, but Daro's she couldn't have foreseen in a thousand Rotations!

Empathise with Jalni's struggle to control her own destiny. Watch Daro confront the limitations of his power, and smile as Jalni finds love. Does it last? Read the sequel, "Sword of Sanctuary" to find out.

"The Tapestry of Tten", a gripping series of Fantasy Fiction novels by Julia Caesar is published by Arima Publishing. To order, please visit our website, http://www.arimapublishing.co.uk, or write to us at,

Arima publishing
ASK House
Northgate Avenue
Bury St Edmunds
Suffolk
IP32 6BB
UK

Coming soon...

"The Shadow of the Singer"

Relinquishing all memory of her love affair to protect her child, the Azure Sandsinger returns to Scartel to take up the burden of leadership. However, her history at Selesh, and the need to consult her fellow Sandsingers keep her constantly travelling between Sands, while the leaders of the Clans puzzle over the whereabouts of the Opal Sandsinger. As Rotations speed past, the rumours start.

"He's been seen in the Tourmaline"; "He's studying in the Onyx Sands"; and now the younger Sandsingers are emerging, and the Star Watchers have become uneasy again. When the Greeeyn demand assistance from the Sandsworn, the Lord of the Opal is needed, but will he return in time to save his Azure from an almost Terminal depression?

Will Marran regain his precious Sword without which Pelshar is doomed, or must they rely on the mysterious "Lord of Night" to save them all?

"The Tapestry of Tten", a gripping series of Fantasy Fiction novels by Julia Caesar is published by Arima Publishing. To order, please visit our website, http://www.arimapublishing.co.uk, or write to us at,

Arima publishing
ASK House
Northgate Avenue
Bury St Edmunds
Suffolk
IP32 6BB
UK

RNIB Talking Books - A message from the Author.

A proportion of the purchase price of this book, is being donated by the author to RNIB, The Royal National Institute for Blind and Partially Sighted People, and will be directed to their National Library Service which runs the Talking Book Service and the Learning and Skills Library. These provide visually Impaired people with an accessible source of entertainment and education, through the conversion of books into an audio format, known as DAISY (Digitally Accessible Information System). This is a unique system that allows navigation of audio books.

The resulting CD's dropping through the letterbox are a powerful tool in the battle for equality, giving blind and partially sighted people access to thousands of books which were previously not available. This lifeline service is invaluable to some tens of thousands of people across the UK.

"You have already supported this significant service simply by buying my book, but if you want to help further the aim of making it possible for all books to become accessible to Visually Impaired Readers, or need information about the RNIB Please call their helpline on
0303 123 9999 or visit www.rnib.org.uk

Thank you for your support,

Julia Cæsar